"With three races, licit and illicit loves, prophecy, fraternal hatred, and enough battles for several campaigns, Douglass has whipped up enough raw material to avoid shortchanging readers throughout her vast undertaking. Moreover, who has plenty of talent . . . No one who liked its predecessor is likely to complain about Enchanter."
—*Booklist*

Starman,
Book 3 of The Wayfarer Redemption series

"[*Starman*] should satisfy a fantasy readership hungry for strong female characters."
—*Publishers Weekly*

"A superior adventure fantasy right to the last."
—*Booklist*

Hades' Daughter,
Book 1 of The Troy Game series

"A dazzling start to a new trilogy, Douglass once again combines mythology, fantasy, magic and romance to produce a consistent, well-rounded story full of seriously flawed characters both abhorrently evil and enthrallingly empathetic. Douglass continually surprises, and readers will eagerly await the next two books."
—*Publishers Weekly* (starred review)

"Combining history, myth and fantasy, Sara Douglass introduces her new Troy Game series with the first book *Hades' Daughter* . . . Ms. Douglass recreates the Aegean world and a Pre-Celtic England in a sweeping epic that grabs your attention at the first page."
—*Romantic Times Book Club* (4 1/2 stars)

"A soap opera for the ancient world."
—*Kirkus Reviews*

THRESHOLD

THRESHOLD

SARA DOUGLASS

A TOM DOHERTY ASSOCIATES BOOK
NEW YORK

This is a work of fiction. All the characters and events portrayed in this book are fictitious or are used fictitiously.

THRESHOLD

A Tor Book
Published by Tom Doherty Associates, LLC
175 Fifth Avenue
New York, NY 10010

www.tor.com

Tor® is a registered trademark of Tom Doherty Associates, LLC.

ISBN 0-765-34277-4
EAN 978-0765-34277-5

First U.S. edition: September 2003
First mass market edition: July 2004

Printed in the United States of America

0 9 8 7 6 5 4 3 2 1

Threshold is for Karen Brooks as part thanks for being such a dear friend during one of the very best and very worst years of my life.

Thanks and acknowledgments also go to Rodney Blackhirst for his enthusiastic exposition of the One (and for those fascinating bodily fractions), Terry Mills for his interesting association of infinity with a Big Mac, Cliff Carrington for his knowledge of the pyramids, and Roger Sworder for an illuminating (and refreshingly frank) discussion of the nuptial number. It was fun guys, but I bet you wish now you'd never let me in the front door.

And with deepest apologies to Pythagorus, Plato, Euclid . . .

Two are better than one; because they will have better reward for their labor. For if they fall, the one will lift up his fellow; but woe to him that is alone when he falleth, and hath not another to lift him up. Again, if two lieth together, then they have warmth; but how can one be warm alone?

Ecclesiastes 4: 9–11

ONE

Viland is a cold, brutal place, yet I grew there and loved it as much as it would allow. Cruel seas batter rocky harbors through winters that last a good nine months of the year, months when all crowd about fires amid the cheerful belchings of onion and ale fumes, and tell endless stories of adventure at the end of the harpoon. In the brief flowering of summer, the Vilanders hurriedly eke out their living from the whales that throng the icy coastal waters, selling the great fish's meat, oil, hide, and bones to any who care to pay for it. Not many, some years. Yet in those years when the whale sold well, my father gained enough in commissions to keep us through the leaner seasons.

But there wasn't much to spare, as we came to discover to our sorrow.

Despite the ice and the ever-threatening poverty, my father and I were happy, content. Until the day my father's thoughtlessness and poorly buried heartache matured into the sour fruit that destroyed us both.

Mam had died young, before I was two. Rather than hire a nursemaid, my father took me into his workshop, and my earliest memories are of the fascinating world encompassed by the shadowed spaces beneath my father's worktable. Here I played blithely all day amid the shavings of glass and globs of discarded enamel, scraping the bright shards into piles and sifting them through hands too small and fat to be of practical use to my father. The table protected me from the worst of the furnace heat and from most of the problems of the outside world, and when the workday was over my father lifted me into his strong arms and carried me back to our cold, motherless home.

Always I yearned for the morning, and the warmth of the workshop.

When I was five, and too curious to fit comfortably beneath the table, my father decided to teach me his craft. Along with the techniques of mixing, firing, and working the glass, I had to learn the common trading tongue of nations, as well as several other languages. All craft workers needed to converse with those merchants who might bring them the one commission to keep starvation at bay for another month or two.

I was young and quick-witted, and I learned the languages and the craft easily. By the age of ten, my hands were slim and capable enough to take on some of the fine work my father increasingly found too difficult, and my tongue was sufficiently agile to chatter to the occasional merchant from Geshardi or Alaric who passed by the workshop. I did not mind spending my days at the worktable, learning a trade, when I could have been imbibing the raucous street games of my contemporaries. My father and the glass formed the boundaries of the only world I needed, and if my father was more often silent than talkative, then I found all the conversation and company I desired in the shifting colors of the glass.

The glass told me many things.

When I was eighteen my father often left me working on the final engraving of a goblet or, more and more frequently, the finishing work for cage lace, while he wandered the streets in search of old friends with whom to pass an hour or two. At least, that's what I thought until the bailiffs came. I did not know that my father's long festering grief for my mother had found outlet in the quest for luck at fate. But luck deserted him as completely as my mother had. My thoughtless, loving father lost our freedom on the spin of a coin and the sorry futility of a fighting cock with a broken wing.

I was at the table in the workshop when they came.

The vase I had in my hands was the result of four weeks' tireless work and it was at last approaching its final beauty. My father had fashioned the mold, mixed the glass, and added the deft flurries of base metals and gold that produced the exquisite marbled walls that were the mark of the master craftsman. Then he had sat over the kiln as the fires patiently birthed his creation. It was his finest effort for six months, and he could hardly bear to pass it over to me to cage.

But caging would produce a work guaranteed to feed us for

the next year, and his hands could no longer be trusted with the delicate touch.

It was one of our best works. I had caged to create one of the Vilanders' favorite myths—Gorenfer escaping the maddened jungles of Bustian-Halle.

The workroom door burst in and I spun around on my stool, the vase in my hands.

My father stumbled in, followed by five men I knew by sight and reputation. Instantly, intuitively, I understood the reason for this ungracious entrance.

One of the debt collectors shouted my name, his face red and sweaty, his hand outstretched and demanding.

Shocked, and frightened beyond any fear I'd experienced before, I dropped the vase—its death cry adding to the terror about me.

That vase could have saved us, it could have paid my father's debts, but I let it shatter on the floor.

After that I could blame my father for nothing. If he had temporarily impoverished us, then he had also created the beauty that would have saved us.

But I dropped it . . . and condemned us to slavery.

Neither my father's entreaties, nor my tears, could move these five hard-souled men. There were debts, and they must be paid. Now. Nothing in our poor house (save the once beautiful vase scattered in useless shards at my feet) could be sold to pay recompense—except us.

We were handed directly to the local slaver who dusted us down, inspected us from head to toe, and stood back, considering.

I had learned my father's craft well. For that reason the slaver kept us together, even though, at nineteen and fair enough, I would have fetched a reasonable price hawked to some tired bureaucrat or lordling bored with his wife. So I was saved from the bed of some paunch-bellied magnate, and my father kept his tools and the last living reminder of his wife. After our initial tears and protests, we resigned ourselves to our fate. It was regrettable but not unknown; over past years I had seen three other craftsmen sell themselves and their families to escape starvation. We would still practice our craft, if to the dictates of a master rather than to the satisfactions of free choice.

And we would still be together.

We did not stay in Viland long. The slaver, Skarp-Hedin, decided we'd fetch the best price in the strange, hot realms to the south.

"They have fine sand a-plenty for you to melt," he said, "and the nobility to buy what you craft of it. You'll fetch five times what you will here in this sorry land."

My father bowed his head, but I stared indignantly at the slaver. "But Viland is our—"

"You *have* no home!" the man shouted. "And no country, save that of the marketplace!"

Within the day we were bundled into the belly of a whaler for cheap transport south. For six weeks we rolled and pitched in that loathsome cavern, my father clutching his tools, I retching over whatever stale food the crew provided us. We were chained, he and I, although where anyone thought we would escape to in the glassy gray waters of the northern seas I do not know, and the chains ate at our ankles until they festered and screamed. The pain drowned out the soft whisperings of the metal links.

Finally, gratefully, the whaler docked. My father and I sat in the hold, trying to ignore the bright pain of our ankles, listening to the muted sounds of a bustling port. Over the past ten days the weather had warmed until the interior of the hold sweltered day and night. The whale meat stank with putrefaction, and I wondered to what possible use it could now be put. After an hour the crew swarmed into the hold to begin the disagreeable task of forking the meat into cargo nets to be offloaded. On the fourth load one of them remembered we were confined somewhere in the dim hold as well; he soon caused us to be netted along with the rotting meat, and we were unceremoniously swung ashore.

Outside, the intense sunlight seared my eyes. I cried out in pain, and my father tried to comfort me, but his mumblings did nothing to ease my terror. I felt the net swing high in the air, and I almost vomited, clutching at the rough rope, trying to gain any handhold that might help save me should the net break. Beside me I heard the bag of tools rattle as my father clutched it closer to his chest.

The next instant there was a sickening jolt as the net landed on the wharf. I lost my grip, and my father and I slid down the pile of sweating whale meat to land in a tangle of chains and rope and greasy, rotting fish flesh on the splintery boards of the pier.

"*Kus!* Is this what you have brought me, you god-cursed whale-man? *Look* at them!" The man spoke in the common trading tongue of nations.

He was bending down, a robe of shimmering green weave drifting free and cool about him. His hand grasped the net and shook it free as men hurried to unhook the loading chains. Then he caught my upper arm and hauled me to my feet.

I stumbled, my ankle chains snagging amid the rope and fish.

The man breathed in sharply, then he helped my father to his feet.

"Strike these chains from their ankles. Now!" And men hurried to do his bidding.

I wept as those hateful metal bars and links fell free.

Our rescuer was a man of middle age, dark-haired and ebony-eyed, with swarthy skin stretched tight over a strong-boned face. His robe was of good linen, loose-fitting and hanging unbelted to his sandaled feet. He looked clean and cool and very sure of himself. I had been none of those things for a long time.

He inspected my hands carefully, then those of my father.

"Well, at least your hands are undamaged, and that is all that counts." He caught my chin with his fingers. "And you have a pleasing face under that grime and stinking oil." Now his fingers lifted one of the lank strands of my hair. "Blond, I'll wager, to go with your blue eyes."

His voice was softer now, thoughtful, and I could see him sifting the possibilities in his mind. "Skarp-Hedin sent word that you work glass. Is that true?"

"I have been a master craftsman for over twenty years," my father said, "and my daughter has more talent than I." He hesitated. "None can mix the colors as I, nor carve the molds or blow the glass. And my daughter cages as though blessed by the gods."

The man's eyes were very sharp now, and they swung back my way. "You are too young," he said.

"I have been working at my father's side since I was five," I replied. How much longer would he keep us standing in this frightful sun? "And caging since I was ten."

"Well," he said, "you have come from Skarp-Hedin, and I have never received anything but the best from him previously. I will trust him on this as well. See that cart?" He inclined his head to the side. "Then get in."

He turned and left us to clamber in.

As his driver slapped the mules into action, the man told us his name was Hadone, and he worked in occasional partnership with the Vilander slaver who'd sent us south. They would share the proceeds of our sale, but Hadone had no intention of presenting us to the market in our current state. From the wharf, we drove to quarters deep in the town—Adab, Hadone informed me as I peered over the rim of the cart, too unnerved to sit upright.

"And this is the realm of En-Dor." Again he ran his eyes over my face and hair as he twisted about on the seat next to the driver. "Although glassworkers sell well here, I wonder if I might get yet a better price for you in Ashdod."

My father noticed Hadone's tone and the direction of his eyes. "Skarp-Hedin said we'd be sold together. That's how we work. A team."

"Of course," Hadone said, swinging back to face the street before him. "That's how I intend to sell you. As a team."

My father and I exchanged a glance, then turned our eyes back to the strange sights around us.

The dirt-packed streets were crowded with men and women dressed much as Hadone was—in brightly colored robes that swung loose to their feet. Many had lengths of fine white cloth wrapped about their heads, the tasseled ends drifting lazily about their shoulders.

We were surrounded by blocks of mud-brick shops and houses, plastered either in white or pale pink, with flat roofs and canvas awnings that hung out into the street and shaded those passing by.

Among all the people wound donkeys bearing loads on their backs or pulling carts like ours. An occasional rider on a finely boned horse, always gray, pushed through the crowds; both horse and rider were invariably richly draped with silks and ropes of jewels.

About all hung the dust of thousands of scuffling feet, and a rich, heady odor of spices and fragrance that did nothing to soothe my stomach.

It was so strange, so unlike what I'd known in Viland, and every minute the sun beat down with increasing fierceness. I crept as close to the walls of the cart as I could, trying to escape both the sun and the strangeness. Opposite me, my father huddled miserably about his sack of tools.

"We'll be there soon," Hadone said, and I closed my eyes and hid my face in my arms, almost undone by the kindness in his voice.

Within minutes we'd turned into a shaded side alley, and then into a cool courtyard. I heard Hadone jump down from the cart, and I sat up, looking about. The spacious courtyard was bounded on two sides by what looked like Hadone's residence, and on the other two sides by stables, storehouses, and a slavery large enough for several dozen inmates. The buildings were all clean and in good repair, and the courtyard itself was paved and swept clean of any dung or dust.

Hadone's man—I never knew his name—helped us down from the cart, then Hadone handed us over to a man and a woman who escorted myself and my father to the separate men's and women's slave quarters.

I watched my father being led away with some nervousness, for I was loath to be parted from him, but I let the woman, Omarni, guide me to a cool room. There she bathed me, tended the festering sores about my ankles, and persuaded me to eat some fruits and drink some milk.

Despite my fears, I slept better that night than I had in weeks, and my sleep was dreamless.

For eight days we were left in peace while our sores closed

over, our ankles thickened with scar tissue, and our faces plumped out from their gauntness. But on the evening of the ninth day Hadone sent for me.

His man escorted me to Hadone's residence, where he stood looking me up and down, and fingering my now clean and shining hair. "In a week or so I will take you and your father to market," he said, "and for the remaining nights you will spend an hour or two in my quarters. You will be sold for your talents at glassmaking, not for your virginity."

And so he proceeded to divest me of it.

He was vigorous and painful but not intentionally unkind and, to be frank, I had known that sooner or later rape would be an inevitability of my enslavement. Well, I should not have dropped that vase. For all pain, there comes pain repaid.

When it was done he sent me back to the slavery, and Omarni gave me a cup of a steaming thick herbal to drink.

"It will save your belly from swelling with child," she said practically, and I realized she must have served this brew to a score of slaves before me.

It was bitter, and it made my stomach churn, but I drank it gratefully. The last thing I wanted was to walk into a lifetime of servitude encumbered with the squalling brat of a slaver.

A week later we were taken to market—I with a little more experience and a few more skills than I'd had when I landed amid the pile of stinking whale meat on the wharf.

Who would buy us? Would he be a kind man, or a harsh taskmaster? And, I wondered further, would he be a satisfied husband, or a man seeking diversion amid the trapped delights of his slavery?

Neither, as it turned out.

The market was crowded with vendors selling fruits, cloths, plate, and lives. One corner was devoted exclusively to the trade in human flesh, and there Hadone directed us and three other men he intended to sell this day. We were guarded, but only lightly. None of us had anywhere to run.

The guards took the three men directly to the open slave

lines, where prospective buyers could prod the merchandise and inspect their teeth, but Hadone took my father and me to a stall at the back of the lines.

There a tall and painfully thin man, as dark as Hadone, unraveled himself from a stool and bowed slightly. His eyes were as sharp as his face was thin, and I decided instantly that I did not like him.

Hadone returned the bow with far greater obeisance than he had been afforded. When he spoke, he kept his hands clasped over his heart and his eyes fixed on the dirt. "Kamish. May your sons win renown and your daughters rich husbands."

Kamish's thin mouth twisted cynically. "I have no children, Hadone. You know that."

"I was merely trying to be polite," Hadone said, finally rising, and I realized he did not like Kamish very much either.

"These are the two you wrote me about?"

"Indeed," Hadone said. "The man has won renown over many nations with his skill at mixing and molding, and his daughter"—he paused slightly—"has been trained well. Among her many skills, she can also cage."

"She cages?" The gleam in Kamish's eyes increased. "My masters—"

"Would surely pay well for the skills these two carry. I believe your masters are scouring all living lands for such as these."

"And she cages," Kamish repeated. I waited for the inevitable "She's too young," but it never came.

"Cages," he said yet again.

Hadone's mouth drooped in imitation woe. "And with such skills, Kamish, I regret that I must ask a price to match."

Kamish had given too much of his eagerness away, and his bargaining power was severely curtailed. Within minutes, as my father and I stood by while our lives were haggled away, Hadone had won a price for himself and Skarp-Hedin that would not only pay our debts but leave the two slavers rich men.

As Kamish bustled about, shouting for his men, Hadone

turned to my father and myself. "I wish you well," he said, and his eyes met mine.

I was astounded to see a trace of regret there.

But then he jingled the coins in his purse, and the regret faded and he turned away.

I never saw him again.

TWO

Kamish had us chained again, but only lightly, and not to each other. These bonds did not rub too much on our previous chafes, nor weigh down our limbs as had the others.

He bade us walk to a cart he had waiting. It was larger than the conveyance Hadone had owned, and was pulled by a quartet of stout mules. Five other slaves were waiting in it: two stonemasons, a carpenter, a metalworker, and one other glassworker.

My father cheered as we gleaned their occupations.

"A building site, then," he said as the cart moved off. "And a rich one," he added, remembering the amount Kamish had paid for us.

His fingers tightened about his tool sack, and he dropped his voice. "Are you well?" he asked me. "Did he hurt you?"

I jumped, for I thought my father did not know, and then I reddened. "He was good enough," I said, and hoped it would do.

"You have paid a high price for my foolishness, daughter," he said, and turned his head away.

And if I had not killed that vase, I thought bleakly, I would still be home dreaming foolish romanticisms about the manner of husband I would win myself. I could not blame my father for anything, not the loss of my freedom or of my maidenhood, and I rested my hand on his arm and hoped he understood.

From the back alleys of Adab we traveled into open countryside—a low range of rolling hills that descended into a flat, featureless plain. I looked at the position of the sun—we traveled yet farther south.

"We go to Ashdod," one of the metalworkers said, noting the direction of my gaze. "Kamish's masters come from Ashdod, and there we go now."

We passed an hour exchanging information in the common trading tongue. Of the five, three had been forced into slavery by debt, while the other two had known nothing but that life, being born to mothers already enslaved.

No one had any intimate knowledge of the southern realm of Ashdod, save that its people kept well to themselves, and that over the past fifteen years an increasing number of factors such as Kamish had appeared in marketplaces, spending freely to buy workers for a construction site.

And the highest prices of all they paid for glassworkers. Again my father fingered his tool sack.

Soon the sun glared overhead in its full noonday heat, and Kamish called a halt.

"We will wait out the next few hours in the shade of these palms," he said, and waved the six men who rode guard to help us from the cart. "Each day we will rise at dawn, travel until noon, rest through the heat of the day, then resume our journey until starlight."

"And how long is our journey?" I dared to ask.

"Long enough," Kamish said, "long enough." He turned away, and would say no more.

And long enough it was. After two days we joined with a trading caravan, a line of heavily laden camels and mules and some twenty men. The traders sent us to the rear of the column, their mouths thinning with disgust at the idea of joining with a convoy of slaves. But Kamish had six guards, and in open territory where bandits lurked, the extra guards were worth the indignity of seven slaves.

The climate grew ever hotter the farther south we traveled. My father and I wore the light robes that Hadone had clothed us in, but soon even they grew too confining, and on one noon stop we tore out the sleeves, and ripped the garments off at midthigh, using part of the now spare cloth to wrap about our waists and between our legs for decency. Decency only, for modesty had long been left behind on a journey where I was the only female among several dozen men. But amid slaves there is a shared respect, and none of them ever tried to touch me, while Kamish, the guards, and the traders completely ignored me.

After a week of traveling through arid plains, relieved only by the occasional stand of date palms grouped about a spring or well, we entered a rugged range of rose- and sand-colored mountains. I had never seen anything so wild or so beautiful, and although the peaks and cliffs were barren, the ravines were filled with springs and ferns. Everyone took advantage of the plentiful water to wash themselves and their clothes, and Kamish even ordered our chains removed, reasoning we were far enough from any civilization to try to escape.

The absence of those chains enslaved us more than their presence. With his order to have them removed, Kamish had shown without words that he believed there was no hope left for us.

We traveled slowly through the mountains for some twelve days, and then passed into stony desert that ate at the strength of human and animal alike. We traveled at night; the day hours we spent lying motionless beneath tarpaulins that kept the sun from us, but which trapped thick heat and countless flies to torture us and keep us from sleep. Water was rationed, and we sucked what extra moisture we could from the dates and figs fed to us at dawn and sunset.

My father grew ever closer to his sack of tools and drew farther from me, as if his guilt over our plight had created a chasm between us. Even though we traveled hip to hip in the cart at night, and lay sprawled side by side during the day, it sometimes felt as though the vastness of the desert lay between us, and I mourned that growing distance as I had not mourned the loss of my freedom.

After countless days we left the desert behind us, and the weather cooled slightly. We passed through lands made fertile by regular irrigation channels. Perfectly square fields appeared—flat expanses of grain, grass, and legumes—worked by swarthy dark-haired men and women, their naked children playing about their legs.

"We are in Ashdod," Kamish remarked, "the land of the One," and he spurred his horse away.

I looked at my fellow slaves, but they only shrugged. Curiosity had been dulled by the weeks of harsh traveling.

Eventually the caravan reached a wide river, its waters languid and green and bordered by thick reed banks. Here Kamish parted our company from that of the traders with brief farewells.

The river was called the Lhyl, one of the guards told me as we waited on the wharf, and it was the lifeblood of Ashdod.

"Rises far to the northwest, in mountains so cold it's said even the air freezes."

The guard paused, as if trying to picture this implausibility in his mind, but eventually he continued. "The Lhyl flows south for many weeks until it empties into a great lake called the Juit."

He spoke in his native Ashdod tongue, but I had no trouble understanding it. I was used to learning languages, and I had listened carefully to the guards' conversation whenever I could on our journey.

" 'Tis said that the lake is surrounded by flames and ghosts. Now *that* I won't credit." He spat in the river, and the gracious Lhyl absorbed his phlegm without a murmur.

Kamish wasted no time in hiring river transport, and soon herded us aboard a craft of bound river reed with sun-yellowed sails.

We sailed for two weeks—weeks when I savored the gentle rocking of the boat, the cool air, and melodious chorus of frogs at dawn and dusk—until we approached a massive sprawling city. Kamish's manner picked up the instant he caught sight of it, and he pointed before us.

"See? There lies Setkoth, greatest city in the world. It is home to hundreds of thousands, and in its heart spreads the magnificent palace of the great Chad-Nezzar, Chad over all Ashdod."

"Is it there we will be set to work?" asked one of the stonemasons.

"No," Kamish said. "Nor will such as you ever lay sight on his royal face, or even his regal abode. You are destined for mightier, holier labor."

Infuriatingly, he shut up after that, and we were left to gaze silent and openmouthed in wonder as Setkoth swept into full view. The city was crowded with the same mud-brick, white-and pink-washed houses, flat-roofed and canvas-awned as they were at Adab, but dotted among the houses, and clustered near what must be the heart of the city, were great domed buildings, some with minarets and spires that reached for the sky. There were towers, too, so spindly I could not conceive how they managed to stay upright, and graceful bridges that arced over the river and the myriad canals that branched off into the city itself.

The crew docked our boat at a stone pier, behind which reared a featureless brick wall with a heavy wooden gate in its center. Into the central panel of the gate was burned a single, strange symbol.

Kamish was now openly nervous as well as excited, and he clutched at his robes. His mood was catching, and I smoothed the cloths wrapped about my body as best I could, wishing I had not so mutilated my robe and that I'd had the opportunity to wash off some of the grime of travel.

The guards hustled us onto the pier, the stone hot on our bare feet. Kamish gave us a cursory inspection as we shifted from foot to foot, frowning as if noticing for the first time how we'd cut down our robes to the briefest of garments, then spoke to the riverboat captain.

"We'll probably be back in an hour or less. Wait for us, for we still have some way to travel."

The man eyed the wall, then dropped his eyes to us. "To Gesholme, no doubt."

Kamish nodded curtly. "No doubt."

Then he knocked at the gate. It opened instantly, as if the servant within had been waiting for us. Kamish waved us forward, and in single file and more than a little apprehensive, we stepped through.

An extraordinary garden stretched ahead of us for some one hundred paces, and was almost thirty wide. There were manicured trees, brightly flowered and darkly leaved, and neatly raked paths between carefully laid-out flowerbeds where plants bloomed in orderly rows and concise geometric designs. They reminded me of the perfectly square fields of the countryside. Everything here had its assigned place, and nothing was allowed to extend beyond that place.

Everything, I realized in my next breath, was ordered with the utmost precision.

"This way," Kamish said, and marched down one of the paths, the guards motioning us to follow.

He led us to a tiled verandah, and bade us stop just beneath its shade. "Do not speak," he said, then disappeared inside the dark well of a door.

He was gone for some minutes, reappearing with a subservient smile on his face and wringing his hands humbly.

"Your Excellencies," he murmured, and then waved whoever followed to inspect the line of slaves.

Two men stepped through the door, their very bearing sent chills down my spine. One was middle-aged, the other ten or fifteen years his younger. Both had the dark hair and swarthy complexion of all southerners, although the younger had gray eyes rather than the usual black of his race.

Their coloring was the only feature they shared in common with anyone else I had seen since docking in Adab. Their robes were of the finest linen, the under robes white and belted with a sash of shimmering cobalt, the outer a radiant blue, and left to float free about their forms. Their hands, fine but strong, were folded before them. Both had their hair swept back and clubbed into queues in the napes of their necks. Their entire bearing screamed of enveloping confidence and authority.

But it was their faces that caught and held my attention. Both were striking, but their expressions were predatory, and they possessed barbed and cruel eyes that radiated supernatural power—as if from a virulent sickness within, rather than with the power that understanding and knowledge gives.

"Sorcerers!" my father whispered.

"Magi!" Kamish growled. "Fall to your knees, filth!"

We fell.

The Magi were unperturbed by my father's thoughtless whisper, if they'd even heard it, and proceeded to stalk about us with measured paces. Power drifted after them like a cloying scent. I hastily averted my face as they passed by.

"And what have you bought us this time, Kamish?" the

older Magus inquired, his voice a lazy, dangerous drawl. He spoke in the common trading tongue.

"Two stonemasons," Kamish replied, his voice oily and subservient again. "A carpenter, a metalworker, and three glassworkers."

The Magi exchanged glances.

"And how much of our wealth have you spent on them?" the younger asked.

"One hundred and seventy-five sequents, Your Excellency."

Both Magi took great, shocked breaths, but before either could speak, Kamish continued.

"It was these two who so raised the price, Excellencies," he explained, gesturing toward my father and myself. "They are glassworkers of high renown. The man mixes and molds like no other—and you know how much need you have of such talent—and the woman . . ."

He paused, then flared his hands dramatically. "The woman can cage!"

The Magi stared at him, then at me, then back to Kamish.

"*Fool!*" the younger Magus cried. "The maggots that infest the corpses of dung beetles enjoy greater intelligence than you!" And he stepped forward and struck Kamish a great blow across his face. The factor fell to the tiled walkway, his face impacting with a sickening crunch. I cringed, expecting to be the next struck.

But the Magus's attention was on Kamish. He leaned down and seized the man by the front of his robe—its fine weave was now stained by the blood that trickled from his nose.

"Boaz," the older Magus muttered. "There is surely no need to so dirty your hands."

Boaz ignored his companion. He hauled Kamish to his feet and shook him until the man whimpered in pain.

"How dare you even draw breath in my presence," Boaz said, his voice flat and deadly. "*See* her! No one that young, that inexperienced—"

"I *can* cage, master," I said as deferentially as I could.

Boaz dropped Kamish, who surreptitiously scrubbed at his nose with a spare fold of his robe. "So she has a voice to lie with," Boaz said. "Stand up."

"She is of the northern races," the older Magus observed as

I stumbled to my feet, wishing I'd never spoken. "As is her father. See their hair, and the fairness of their skin."

"And she still smells of the whale oil, Gayomar," Boaz said. "Her race has barely learned the art of fire-making, let alone the finer skills of craft work. Girl, why do you lie?"

I could not bear the intensity of his eyes, and I dropped my gaze. "I *can* cage," I whispered with the last of my courage.

"Look at me."

I could not, and I felt my hands tremble.

"Look at me!"

Not only his voice but his power reached out, and my head was flung back so that my eyes stared into his.

"Did you learn to lie from your father, girl? Should I have him put to death alongside Kamish and you?"

I was saved from replying by Kamish himself. "Excellency!" He was back on hands and knees now, his face pressed so close to the tiles his voice was only just audible. "Excellency, they came with the best assurances. And I trust the slaver who sold them to me. Over the years he has provided us with some of the best—"

"Shetzah!" Gayomar exclaimed. "You have not *seen* them work? You waste our money on word alone?"

Kamish could only shake, and Boaz ignored him. "Caging is the provenance of master craftsmen alone," he said. His eyes had not left mine for a moment. "It takes a lifetime of skill to perfect. You are . . . what? Eighteen? Nineteen?"

"She is nineteen, my Lord." Now my father spoke. I jumped, for I had forgotten his presence. "And she was born with the skills that usually only a lifetime of experience grants. Her delicacy of touch can free lacework from the inner walls of glass with only minimal struts. Her ear for the drill bit is phenomenal—I have never seen a piece of her work crack as she excavates."

Gayomar stepped up behind Boaz and put a hand on the Magus's shoulder. "The old man speaks as one who knows glass, Boaz. Perhaps . . ."

Boaz shifted his gray eyes to my father. "You have your tools with you?"

My father nodded.

Boaz smiled, thin and cold. "Then, Gayomar, we shall have

ourselves an amusing afternoon. Kamish!" he called.

Kamish leaped to his feet.

"Kamish, there is a small table and a stool inside. Bring them out."

Kamish stumbled as he hurried to do the Magus's bidding. When he returned, Boaz wheeled away and disappeared momentarily. He reappeared carrying a lump of murky glass, roughly rectangular, the height of a forearm and the width of two palms. It was thick, thick enough to be caged, but to my dismay I heard it groan as Boaz set it roughly down on the table, and I saw that scores of tiny fracture lines ran through it.

It would prefer to die than be worked.

I looked frantically at my father, but the next moment Boaz seized my arm in tight fingers and dragged me to the table. I almost overbalanced, but managed to sit down on the stool.

"Cage!" he said and, grabbing my father's tool sack, threw it on the table.

I halted its slide in the instant before it shattered the glass. An unwelcome memory of the vase I had dropped surfaced, and I managed to quell it with only the most strenuous effort.

"It . . . it is bad glass, my Lord," I murmured.

"Bad glass or not, it is the only thing you have to work with. *Cage it!*"

I took a deep breath, clenched my fingers to stop their trembling, then stared at the glass, trying to see what I could do with it. But all I could feel was the weight of the Magus's eyes behind me.

I cleared my throat. "I will need oil. Something fine."

Silence, then Gayomar spoke. "Kamish. There is a jug of linofer oil standing on the shelf by the inner door. And bring the cloth that is folded beside it. We do not want her to ruin the tabletop as well as the glass."

There was rough amusement in that voice, and deep within me, anger stirred.

I raised my head and twisted on the stool, staring Boaz in the eye. "What would you like me to cage?"

"Something that will save your life, your father's life, and that of the foolish Kamish," he replied, then stood back a pace, arms folded, waiting.

And so, with the slaves—now forgotten by all—the two Magi, the ashen-faced Kamish, and my father watching on, I did what I could.

For some minutes I ran my hands over the glass, feeling it, feeling for its soft voice, wondering what it would permit and what it would not. It was rough, discarded glass, a grayish and cloudy blue. Thrown away because of the myriad tiny fractures and air bubbles it contained. To try and cage it . . .

I wondered what design would please the Magi, what design would save my life. I knew nothing of their culture, or of the patterns that they considered pleasant. Would one of the myths of Viland please them? No, I thought not.

I turned the glass over and over in my hands, listening as it finally spoke to me, and I made up my mind.

I set the glass to one side and opened the tool sack. I took out several pliers of differing sizes, a slender hammer, an even more slender chisel, a drill, two glass cutters, a wax marker, and a small, pliable ball with a slender nozzle—this I half filled with linofer oil. It was not the best oil for glass-working, but it would do.

I took the wax marker and quickly sketched a design on the face of the rectangular glass, and then on its two narrower sides.

Boaz breathed deeply behind me, and I let myself relax slightly, relieved. This was an arid country, and the Lhyl River was the source of all life. Its culture, as Setkoth itself, was undoubtedly river-oriented, and thus I had sketched the outline of river reeds, two frogs clinging to them. It was a simple design, but pure and delightful because of it.

Using one of the glass cutters, I scored over the wax markings, cutting thin tracings into the glass. I was careful to only barely score the surface of this delicate and fractured glass, and when I was finished, and the wax wiped away, the score marks were visible only as lines of light running over the surface.

I breathed more easily now, and smiled, understanding the glass, knowing it would do its best for me.

"There is no vise here," I said, and looked at my father. "I need someone to hold the glass as I drill it. Father, will you—"

"I will serve," Boaz said, and Kamish scrambled to fetch another stool.

He sat down opposite me, taking the glass between his hands. My confidence faltering again, I hesitated, then moved his hands slightly so that the glass tilted away from me.

He made no comment at my hesitant touch, his eyes remained unblinking on my face.

With the drill I made two score of tiny holes across the surface of the glass, avoiding the fracture lines, and praying to the glass that it would tolerate my intrusion and not shatter. When this was done I drilled more deeply, using the linofer oil to soothe the shock of the drill's penetration, listening to the song of the glass as the drill bit ever deeper, adding more oil whenever its song swerved toward harshness.

Then I took the hammer and chisel and tapped out the sections of glass that had been weakened by the drill holes. I held my breath as the glass closest to the most dangerous of the fault lines fell safely out, then I reached for the finest of the pliers, using them to chip and nibble at the outline of the reeds and frogs until the design stood out from the supporting glass.

I raised my eyes to Boaz.

By this stage he must have realized that I could work glass with the best craftsman, but it was still not enough. If the design now stood out from the glass, then I had to free it—create the cage.

Caging was traditionally reserved for round vessels. An outer design, called the lacework, was carved from a thick wall of glass, and then all but freed from the remaining smooth inner wall. Only a few, almost invisible struts would support the outer design—which then became, in effect, a cage of lace about the inner, plain wall of the vessel.

This was a freestanding block of flat glass, and faulted and sad. It would not cage well, if it would tolerate it at all. But I could do my best. I turned the glass in Boaz's hands, so that it faced me almost sideways, then I picked up the drill again.

Use of the drill now was more than dangerous. Normally I would have worked at the glass patiently with chisel and pliers, forceps and soft words, but that process would take days if not weeks, and those I did not have.

Closing my eyes briefly I winged a prayer to the gods and a gentle lullaby to the glass, then I set to work.

The glass cried almost instantly, and I winced, but I soothed as best I could, and murmured to it, and pleaded with it, and finally it acquiesced. It was a brave glass, and tears came to my eyes at its courage.

These drill holes moved horizontally behind the outline of the reeds and the frogs, and despite my best efforts, one or two cut directly through fault lines.

Laying the drill and oil bag to one side, I again picked up a pair of pliers, using one of the handles to tap at the glass.

Sections cracked, crumbled, and then slid to the table.

I took the glass completely into my hands now, cradling it against my breast, tapping, tapping, tapping, using both drill holes and fault lines to my advantage, murmuring wordlessly, soothing, reassuring.

There was utter silence about me, and I could feel the eyes of slaves and Magi alike riveted to my face or to my hands, but I did not care. There was only me and my glass and the growing mound of fragments and dust in my lap and on the table.

The cage was emerging now, and with it emerged the true hidden color of the glass. Once gray and cloudy as an unwanted and discarded lump, the glass now shone a deep, vivid blue. Most of the air bubbles and the fracture lines had been chiseled out, and despite what I'd originally thought, the cage had been almost entirely freed from the inner wall.

"Let me see," Boaz said, his voice peculiarly tight, but I shook my head, my eyes still on the glass wrapped in my arms and hands.

"No. Wait. Let me just . . ." Using the inner teeth of the finest of the pliers, I smoothed the rough edges as best I could. The glass should have been patiently sanded over many hours to hone it to its best, but in less than an afternoon I knew I had created something wonderful from a glass that had thought itself fit only for grinding into spare chips.

Finally I took a deep breath, and inspected it. The intertwining reeds stood completely free from the inner wall of the glass. Two frogs leaped playfully among them, their back legs serving as struts to anchor the cage lacework to the supporting inner wall.

It was beautiful.

My hands shaking, I held it up for all to see.

The failing sunlight—how many hours had I been working?—caught and twinkled in the blue glass, and the reeds and frogs danced back and forth in the shimmering light.

Boaz stood up slowly, his stool scraping behind him, and lifted the glass from my hands.

"She has astounding talent," Gayomar said in the language of Ashdod. "Astounding."

Boaz's face hardened. "Perhaps the glass . . . speaks . . . to her, Gayomar. Perhaps she is . . . Elemental." His eyes slid over me, their power seeking, searching, and I dropped my gaze quickly, guiltily. Elemental? What was this?

"Well," Boaz continued to Gayomar, "I can warn Ta'uz about her, but he will never listen to me. He thinks all Elementals were gone generations ago. Bah! *All* glassworkers should be watched. Ta'uz has ever been lax in that regard. If I were Master of Site . . ."

His fingers tightened about the glass. "What is your name, girl?" he asked, again using the common tongue.

I told him, and then said my father's name.

Boaz regarded me steadily. "Your names are as heavy and cumbersome as your language. You belong to Ashdod and to the Magi now, and from henceforth will wear names that please us. Your name"—he indicated my father—"is Druse, a good worker's name. And you"—he swung his eyes back to me—"shall be called Tirzah."

Gayomar jerked with surprise, but did not speak.

I was not so reticent. I stood up, my eyes angry. "No! My name is—"

"Your name is Tirzah!" Boaz shouted. "Do you understand?"

I closed my mouth with a snap, but my eyes were no less angry and resentful.

"This glass is very beautiful," he said, his eyes harder than I'd seen them yet, "and its beauty catches at the hearts of all who gaze upon it. But I own it as tightly as I own your soul, and it will do my bidding as will you. Do you understand?"

I was still silent, my entire body stiff and resentful.

His eyes dropped to the glass, and I thought I had bested

him. His hands ran over it, and I could see how gentle their touch, how caressing their passing.

I relaxed. He thought it beautiful, and for its beauty, he would not deny me my name.

Then he hefted the glass in one hand, raised his eyes to mine, and opened his fingers.

The glass smashed into a thousand pieces on the tiles, and as I heard its death cry so I remembered the death scream of the vase I had dropped.

I hated Boaz at that moment, and knew I would take that hatred and stoke it and feed it until I could repay him a thousand times over for the humiliation of my slavery and my rape and the death agony of that brave glass.

"And so I will dispose of you, Tirzah, should the whim take me. *Do you understand?*"

"Yes, I understand, Excellency."

THREE

Kamish bundled us back through the garden. His relief in being left his life found outlet in his anger at us—particularly me, and by the time I clambered back into the riverboat my arms were already darkening with livid bruises.

"Gesholme!" Kamish shouted at the riverboat captain.

We huddled in the belly of the boat, out of the way of the oarsmen, my father's arms wrapped protectively about me. He realized a little of what I felt, although not all, for he'd never heard the glass in the same manner I had. The other slaves regarded us silently, then Mayim, the other glass-worker, reached out and gently touched my arm.

"That was wondrous," he said. "I thought that glass was fractured beyond help, yet you still worked it into beauty. You must have magic in your fingers, Tirzah."

I eyed him carefully, wondering at his choice of words, but then decided it was simple praise. Nothing else. I nodded, grateful, then cuddled a little closer to my father. Druse.

I thought of my new name—Tirzah. It was pretty, and rolled off the tongue with its own special music. But I would ever associate it with Boaz, and with my slavery.

One day I would cast it off.

But not now. Tonight all I wanted to do was cling as tightly as I could to my father, and close my eyes and pretend that none of this was happening.

Time passed, and I dozed.

I dimly realized we had left the confines of Setkoth, for the sounds of the city grew dim, and the smell of the river changed from rotting vegetable matter and human filth to that of the sweet cleanliness of open countryside and thick reed banks. The breeze grew cold, but my father was warm and there was a tarpaulin beneath our feet that our small group managed to wrap about us to keep out the worst of the night chills.

I wondered vaguely where this Gesholme was, and what it was, but the river was soothing, and I slipped deeper into sleep.

Hours later a shout woke me. The night was dark and still, and the boat's crew had shipped their oars. There were shouts from the crew, and answering shouts from the bank as ropes were thrown and tied. The boat shuddered, then jerked as it bumped against its mooring. It was cold now, and I shivered in my thin cloths and wrapped my arms about myself.

"Get up!" Kamish shouted, and we struggled to our feet, straining our eyes in the darkness.

A settlement sprawled from the western riverbank far to the west and south. It was tightly walled and closely gated, and guards watched atop towers and walkways.

A slave encampment, then.

To the northwest there appeared to be another compound, also walled, but with buildings too low to be seen from here.

Beyond that loomed a massive structure that ate at the darkness and the stars. I could not make out its exact shape or dimensions, but the cold deepened about me, and the bruises on my arms throbbed anew.

One of the crew leaned down to offer me his hand in alighting. He noticed the direction of my eyes, but kept his own carefully averted.

"Threshold," he said.

A contingent of guards arrived from the compound to escort us inside the gates. Kamish gave them a small scroll, inscribed with our names and our abilities, then stepped back into the riverboat.

"I wish you the best," he cried as the crew pushed out into the current and slowly turned the boat about, yet I knew he wished us anything but, and I thought I saw a gleam of teeth as the oarsmen finally made way for Setkoth.

The walls of the compound were of sandstone and at least five paces wide and fifteen high, the gates of wood reinforced with metal bars and covered over with sun-hardened mortar.

One of the guards atop the wall leaned down as we passed. "Welcome to Gesholme," he called, and ghostly laughter followed us along the narrow street.

Regular blocks of tightly packed tenement buildings, some four or five stories high, loomed to either side of us. An occasional light glinted behind their tightly shuttered doors and windows. Streets intersected the main way at regular intervals, and I realized that the encampment—Gesholme—was much larger than it had appeared from the river. Many thousands must live here.

The walls and close buildings let no breeze through, and the air was thick and humid. Where minutes previously I had pulled my wraps closer, now I loosened them about my neck, and slapped at the hundreds of small, biting insects that hovered about our group.

The lead guard called a halt. Another wall loomed before us, but with a smaller gate this time, and the two guards who stood by it were better uniformed than those who escorted us.

"New arrivals," said our lead guard, and one of the men by the gate grunted, inspected us, then waved us through. Into a different world.

Here were no streets, but spacious avenues. The buildings were low, and sprawled comfortably. Pastel lights glinted, not only in windows but strung through date palms and across cool pools of water.

There were no biting insects here—none had come through the gate with us.

"The compound of the Magi," said one of our guards. Then he smiled at the apprehension in all of our eyes. "It seems you've run up against them before. Well, here you'll have to get used to their presence."

We stopped while he went into a particularly fine building, surrounded by columned verandahs festooned with hanging, crimson- and purple-flowered vines. The sound of murmured voices came from within a dimly lit room, then the guard reappeared accompanied by two Magi.

Without prompting, the seven of us fell to our knees, while the guards bobbed their heads and saluted with their spears. "Excellencies!" they shouted.

"Excellencies!" we murmured in quick echo.

These two radiated the same power as Gayomar and Boaz had done, and were similarly dressed. Their black hair was also clubbed back into severe queues, and sharp eyes swept over us as vultures survey carrion for the most vulnerable flesh.

One dropped his eyes down to the scroll Kamish had given the guard. "From Boaz, no less," he muttered, then grimaced and rolled his eyes as he read what followed. "Elemental? The man has been reading legends. But he sends three glass-workers, and that is good." He raised his eyes. "Druse, Mayim, and Tirzah. You will accompany me. My name is Ta'uz, and I am Master of this site. Do you understand?"

"We understand, Excellency."

"Good. The other four," he read out their names, "will accompany Edohm. Come."

Rolling up the scroll with a snap he waved at my father, Mayim, and myself. We scrambled to our feet and hurried after him.

I only ever caught glimpses of the other four slaves again, rare flashes of friendly faces within the walls of Threshold, and what happened to them in the end I know not.

Ta'uz led us back through the gate of the Magi's compound, then turned sharp left, hurrying us toward a quarter in the northern part of Gesholme. Eventually he stopped outside one of the tenement buildings, and spoke to us. "Mayim, you will work in Izzali's workshop. Druse, you and Tirzah will work in Isphet's workshop. You may well see each other during the day, but at night men and women are quartered separately. Do you understand?"

"We understand, Excellency."

"Good. This is Yaqob's tenement, and this is where Druse and Mayim will live. You"—he waved at one of the guards—"wait here with the girl."

The door of the tenement opened at a sharp knock from a guard, then Ta'uz, my father, and Mayim, accompanied by five guards, disappeared inside. I wanted to wish my father good night—this was the first time we'd been separated in weeks—but I knew enough now to keep silent. I was content that we'd work together in the same workshop.

I glanced at the stars. By the gods! That would be in only a few short hours! I felt desperately tired, and wished more than anything else I could have a long night's sleep in a bed that was anywhere but here.

The guard stood wary and silent, his eyes not leaving me for a moment, and I stared at the ground, shuffling uncomfortably from foot to foot. I remembered Hadone, and shivered.

Ta'uz abruptly reappeared, guards in attendance, and the door and the tenement slammed shut behind him.

"Now you," he said, and marched off ahead.

Surrounded by guards, I felt more alone than I ever had in my life.

He led me to another tenement, almost identical to the one where he'd left my father and Mayim, and ordered the guard to knock at the door.

There was no answer, save a soft scuffling inside, and Ta'uz stepped to the door himself, and delivered it a hard blow and a shouted command.

Steps sounded and the door opened a crack, then was flung wide as the person saw who waited outside.

I gasped. Even in this flickering torchlight, the one who opened the door was the most exquisite woman I'd ever seen.

She was perhaps thirty or thirty-one, with shining black hair and almond-shaped dark eyes that were intelligent and all-knowing. Her face was as astounding in its strength as it was in its beauty.

"Yes?" she said.

Ta'uz held her stare, then cursed. "Did you think I would not know, Isphet?" he asked as he shouldered past her.

She turned to follow him, but at that moment one of the guards seized my arm, intending to drag me through as well. I cried out as his fingers bit into the bruises Kamish had given me, and Isphet turned back in my direction.

"Oh, gods," she whispered, "you have the most exquisitely bad timing, girl."

We hurried into a room filled with blood and screams, and with birth and death. A woman lay on a pallet against a wall, her face drawn and damp, her robe patched with sweat and the fluids of birth. A tiny baby sprawled across her belly, her stump of umbilical cord wobbling pathetically in the uncertain light.

Ta'uz leaned down and seized the baby; she squalled, and the mother screamed. Isphet stepped forward, her hand outstretched, but she halted as Ta'uz rounded on her, his face contorted with fury.

"Did you think to keep this hidden from me, Isphet? I knew she was breeding, and that she had not understood. *Nothing* here breeds save the One. *Nothing*. Is *that* understood?"

Isphet opened her mouth, her eyes fearful, but Ta'uz gave her no time to answer. In one shocking, vicious move, he swung the baby by her feet and smashed her skull against the wall.

Then he threw the broken body down on her mother's belly.

"I will expect to see you at your post by the furnaces in the morning, Raguel," he said to the mother, who was staring appalled at her dead infant. "And you can use this useless lump of flesh to stoke their fury." He looked up, stared at Isphet, then shifted his gaze to me.

"Her name is Tirzah, Isphet. She works glass. She and her

father, Druse, will join your workshop in the morning." Then he strode out the door.

It slammed shut, and for a moment there was utter silence in the room.

My heart was thudding painfully, my throat dry, and I thought I would faint. I wished I could close my eyes and forget what I had just seen, but it was seared so painfully into my mind I knew it would give me nightmares for weeks.

Gods knew what nightmares the poor mother would suffer. *Why?*

I felt a hard hand on my arm, and somewhere in my nightmare I wished people would stop punishing my bruises.

Isphet.

"Sit here in the corner, girl, and shut up." And she shoved me down and left me.

That was unfair, for I had not made a sound since my arrival. But I sat silently anyway, grateful to be off my feet, and watched as Isphet and her companions tried their best to modify the horror.

Isphet was as blunt with the mother as she had been with me. "You were a fool, Raguel, and well you knew it. Ta'uz would never have let the baby live, and you can only thank the Soulenai . . ."

Soulenai?

". . . he did not tear it from your womb while it yet grew. That would have killed *you*, as well."

"But he fathered her!"

Isphet struck Raguel across the face, and the sound hid my own shocked gasp.

"Enough, Raguel! If you had listened to me in the first instance none of this would have occurred, and Ta'uz would have no reason to keep such close watch on my workshop. Now, because of your stupidity, we will have no opportunity to—"

Abruptly she remembered my presence, and she slid a careful eye my way. She hesitated, then turned back to Raguel and plucked the still body of her daughter from her hands, handing it to a woman in her mid-twenties.

"Kiath, take this and wrap it. Ta'uz was right enough when he said it would feed the flames."

There was silence again, everyone staring at the body in Kiath's hands.

"But not yet, I think," Isphet finally finished. "We can make better use of this fuel on a day when the guards keep less close watch. Kiath, store the body in a tightly sealed jar. But wrap it tightly first so that its fluids will not seep through and reveal it to curious eyes. Saboa?" Isphet motioned to a girl about my own age. "Take these"—she roughly pulled several stained cloths from beneath Raguel's hips, causing the woman to cry out in pain—"and wrap them about a loaf of bread. We shall make much cry and sadness and toss it into the furnace in the morning, and no one shall be any the wiser. You!"

I jumped. I wanted nothing more than to huddle in my corner and remain unnoticed.

"You . . . Tirzah? Come here and help me make Raguel comfortable. Come on. If you're going to share my quarters and my workshop, then you might as well dirty your hands in this little disgrace as well. And bring that bowl of water with you."

I dared linger no longer; I had no doubts that Isphet would physically haul me over if she thought I'd not make it on my own.

A large bowl of water was warming by a small brazier in the center of the room. I took careful hold of it and walked over.

"Good," Isphet muttered, not looking at me, then began to wash Raguel down. As she did so she talked in a soft, gentle voice, surprising me. "You are not to blame for this disaster, Tirzah. Ta'uz would have dealt this babe death at some point, even had we managed to hide the fact of the birth from him. Perhaps it was kinder this way, before Raguel had a chance to form too close a bond with her."

Before she bonded with her? Did not carrying a babe in your womb for nine months form a bond? Without thinking I glanced at the stain on the wall.

Isphet thrust a wet cloth into my hands. "Wash it away, Tirzah, and then help me turn Raguel over and change her bed linen."

I did as she asked, and when Raguel was washed and lay on clean sheets, Isphet took my hand in hers. "A rough welcome for you, Tirzah." She gazed steadily at me. "You are not of our race, girl. Where do you come from?"

"Far to the north. A place called Viland."

Isphet shook her head dismissively. "I've not heard of it. But you speak our tongue well, if with a heavy accent. How is that?"

"My father and I traveled for many weeks with guards from this land, Isphet. I learned from them."

"And your name? You bear the name of a princess of our realm. Why is that?"

My hand jerked in hers. The Magus had named me after a princess? I told her something of my encounter with the Magi Gayomar and Boaz.

Isphet's eyes widened. Gayomar she'd only ever seen briefly about Gesholme and Boaz she did not know at all, and dismissed them as quickly as she had the land of my birth. She even forgot the mystery of my naming in her intrigue with my story of the caging of the glass. Her hands tightened about mine. They were very warm.

"You are a very interesting girl, Tirzah. You seem to become one with the glass." She smiled as if she had made a bitter joke to herself. "We shall talk some more of it, you and I, but not now. I have asked enough questions. You must have some of your own."

I glanced at Raguel. She had turned her head to the wall. "I don't understand," I said inadequately, and then wished I'd not used those exact words.

But Isphet did not mind, and knew what I meant. "Come," she said, leaving Raguel alone to cope with her misery as best she could. She led me to a pallet on the other side of the plainly furnished room and pulled me down beside her. "How much do you know of the Magi?"

"Nothing, save their cruelty."

"And of Threshold?"

"Even less."

"Save *its* cruelty, you should have said," Isphet remarked, but then patted my hand. "Well now, how shall I begin? With the Magi, I think, for you already have some understanding of them. The Magi are . . ."

"Sorcerers, my father called them. But priests, perhaps?"

"Sorcerers of a nature, certainly, but not priests, as perhaps you understand the word. The Magi are mathematicians, and once that was all they were. But they found power, cruel power, in the understanding of the properties of, and the relationships between, numbers and forms. They control the power of number and form."

I was beginning to understand. "I saw the regular forms of field and garden."

"Yes. If the Magi had their way, *everything* in Ashdod would be laid out according to the pure principles of mathematics and geometry. To some extent they have succeeded with the shape of fields and gardens, as streets and many buildings. They have a powerful influence over the monarch, Chad-Nezzar, and much of what they desire is enacted in royal edict." She sighed. "But Ashdod is large, and it cannot all be arranged according to the dictates of mathematics. The Magi have only succeeded completely here . . . with Threshold."

"I saw Threshold, although not well. It . . . it ate at the sky."

Again Isphet glanced at me sharply. "Threshold is—or will be—the physical manifestation of pure mathematical formula. The Magi have been overseeing its construction for many generations, and even yet it has over a year's work left before completion." She smiled grimly. "Threshold is a beast of consuming need. It has literally eaten the resources of Ashdod. *Everything* Ashdod produces is channeled into the effort to complete Threshold, and even that is not sufficient. You are proof enough that the Magi must now scour far-flung realms to find the workers Threshold needs."

There was a long pause. "Isphet," I said eventually, "what did Ta'uz mean when he said that nothing breeds here save the one?"

"Ah, the Magi are mathematician-magicians, and they worship the number One. They teach that the One is the number from which all numbers spring, and into which all numbers collapse. Creation and Doom, all in one." She shook her head at her poor joke. "All forms spring from and collapse into the One as well, for the Magi believe that geometric forms are composed only from the properties of numbers. Thus the One represents both birth and death—Infinity. Contemplation of the One and meditation upon the mysteries of number and form are how the Magi derive their power. They constantly seek complete union with the One . . . and that is where Raguel came undone."

She shivered, and now it was my hands that tightened about hers. "The Magi seek union with the One through many means, Tirzah—I believe Threshold will eventually provide the ultimate means of union, although the Magi never speak of it. Until Threshold is complete, the Magi must make use of lesser means of union. Occasionally a Magus will take a woman into his bed in order to touch the One."

Again she paused, and I realized she was recounting not only Raguel's experience, but also her own.

"In that moment of physical release during the sexual act the Magi claim they experience a hauntingly brief union with the One . . . with Infinity. The woman they use to achieve this moment of union matters not." Isphet forced a humorless grin to her face, but it faded almost as soon as it appeared. "I don't know why they do not use goats . . . goats would be far less trouble. Women are not allowed to breed from this act, for to do so would be to subdivide the One, to subdivide its power. I do not know how Raguel managed to become pregnant—usually the Magi are painstakingly careful to prevent pregnancy—but that is why Ta'uz reacted so violently, and why he instantly killed the baby. The baby had violated and subdivided the One. Her life was an abomination. And so that beautiful little girl died."

I put my arms about her, and Isphet wept.

FOUR

Eventually we all lay down for two or three hours of restless sleep—I shared Saboa's pallet—and rose to the dawn chorus of frogs in the reed banks lining the Lhyl River.

I helped Saboa fling wide the shuttered windows, and as the

others stirred the fire and set pots to warm, I surveyed my new home. Of roughly plastered mud-brick, the square apartment was roomy but featureless. Sleeping pallets lay against the walls, and clothes, pots, and urns were stacked on shelves. More urns lay embedded in the dirt floor to keep their contents cool. Besides the brazier in the center of the floor, there were three wooden stools with woven reed seats, a low table, several scattered reed mats, and oil lamps hanging from ceiling beams. Little else. Even our small home in Viland had more cheer than this.

The two windows looked out onto an abutting alleyway. The main door led to the street, another opened into a small storeroom, and a third to an ablutions block in a tiny internal courtyard shared by all apartments in this building. There were no internal stairs visible, but a set in the courtyard led to the higher levels.

Isphet had helped Raguel out to the ablutions block, and now the woman struggled back inside, her face gray and lined. She sat down at the fire and silently accepted a bowl of warm porridge, listlessly shifting her spoon to and fro.

Isphet took a long look at my travel-stained clothes, and sent me outside to wash. When I had done so, she gave me a length of pale cotton, thinly striped with green, and showed me how to wrap and knot it about myself to form a functional garment that left legs and arms bare. All the women wore similar wraps.

"You'll not need much more in this place, Tirzah. Graceful robes belong only in your lost past. And tie your hair back, loose hair has no place in my workshop."

No one else spoke, and everyone tried to ignore the fact that Raguel cried silently, uselessly, into her bowl. I ate some of the warm grain, but my stomach still hadn't recovered from the shock of the previous night's events, and after some minutes I set the bowl aside.

As Kiath dampened the coals, and Saboa straightened the sleeping pallets, Isphet took the loaf of bread wrapped in the stained cloths and gave it to Raguel. Her voice was harsh, but her eyes were gentle. "Take it, Raguel, and cast it into the furnace when the guards a-watch. Don't look so, 'tis only a lump of bread."

Maybe so, but in which of the urns was the body of the baby stuffed? And why did Isphet want to keep it? As hard as the death of her baby was, it surely would not help Raguel to know her child putrefied close to hand while she lay awake on her pallet at night.

I hoped Kiath had stoppered that urn tight.

"Work," Isphet said.

The workshop was close by, which was just as well, because I do not think Raguel could have managed a long walk. As it was, Kiath and Saboa had to support her the last lot of steps.

Walking along the alleyways, I could sense Threshold's presence, but I still could not see it above the close shadows of the tenement buildings.

Isphet saw me twisting and craning my neck. "You'll see more than you'll ever want of Threshold soon enough, Tirzah. Patience."

And then we were at the workshop.

I stepped inside, then halted in amazement. In Viland, my father and I had worked in a tiny workshop that suited our needs, and the workplaces of our neighbor craftsmen had been similarly small. But Isphet commanded a workshop of immense proportions that would easily hold more than a score of workers. In a far corner three furnaces glowed, ready to be stoked for the day's firing. Against one wall stood deep racks that held hundreds of sheets of glass. Another wall was shelved with scores of pots and urns that contained the powders and metals of our trade. Elsewhere neat racks held tools that made my father's sack look like the insignificant plaything of a child. Around the workshop were the tables and work areas necessary for the manufacture of glass. An internal staircase led up to a level where I guessed the finer work that needed good light and tight concentration would be done. Is that where I would work?

Kiath gave me a gentle push, and I closed my mouth and stepped into the central work space. Seven or eight men were here already, my father among them, and a younger man introduced him to Isphet.

His introduction was terse, for he had caught sight of Raguel and the sad bundle she had clutched to her breast.

"By the Place Be—"

"Careful!" Isphet hissed. "We have newcomers among us!"

He steadied himself. "What has happened?"

Isphet briefly told him, or at least she told him that Ta'uz had discovered the child when he delivered me to Isphet's door, and had killed her.

The man's mouth thinned and he looked me over consideringly. He was handsome, perhaps seven or eight years older than I, with black hair cut short and impatiently thrust back over his brow, intelligent brown eyes, and a wide, sensual mouth that, as it finally relaxed, revealed a warm and friendly smile.

"My name is Yaqob, and you are Tirzah. Druse has told me how well you cage." He took my hand briefly, and I smiled for him.

"That may be so," Isphet said. "But, like all newcomers, she begins at the grinding tables until she learns the ways of my workshop. Yaqob, you will take the girl and her father to Yassar's table and set them to work."

Grinding glass? That was a task for a first-year apprentice, but I said nothing, and walked with Yaqob as he introduced me about the workshop, and explained the manner in which all worked here.

As I sat at Yassar's table, my father on the other side, a look of utter disgust on his face at the grinding pestles before us, there was a step at the door, and the entire workshop stilled.

Ta'uz.

Several guards flanked him, and two moved to stand farther inside the workshop.

Ta'uz stared across to the furnaces, and all eyes shifted that way.

Raguel stood close by the open door of one of the furnaces, the wrapped bundle in her hands. She stared at Ta'uz, and I wondered briefly at the hatred she must bear him, then she noticeably shook herself and heaved the bundle into the flames before any could inspect it too closely.

Then, her shoulders shaking wretchedly, she turned aside and would look at Magus or furnace no longer.

Without a word Ta'uz left, but the two guards stayed.

I felt a hand on my shoulder, and Yaqob squatted close by my stool. "Was that the baby?" he asked quietly, his eyes still on Raguel.

I hesitated. "No."

Yaqob looked at me now. "But the baby *is* dead?"

"Yes."

He was silent a moment. "So Isphet has put it aside."

"Yes."

He nodded slightly. "Good." His hand tightened momentarily, then he stood and lifted it from my shoulder. "You will work today and tomorrow at this table, Tirzah, but then, I think, Isphet will allow me the privilege of showing you about our small world."

Then he walked away.

My father looked at Yaqob's retreating back, looked at me, and grinned.

I settled in quickly. For two days my father and I ground glass to use for the manufacture of enamels, and then, as promised, Yaqob rescued us, and set us to more demanding tasks.

This was Isphet's workshop, but she seemed content to let Yaqob keep an eye on us for the first week or two. I saw her often enough at night, anyway, when she always questioned me on my day's work, but I think that while the guards still kept a keen watch on us she did not want to be too closely involved with my work.

Besides, like my father, Isphet's own speciality was in the mixing and firing of glass, and she stayed by the furnaces. Not only to supervise the blending and firing, but also to make sure Raguel did not throw herself in after her sad, cloth-wrapped bundle. Raguel hardly spoke, and while she physically recovered from the birth of her daughter, her spirit sickened and died further each day.

Three days after I arrived, Yaqob took my father to the corner of the workshop where the glass was mixed and molded, leaving him in Isphet's hands, then he came over to me and smiled. "This way."

He led me up to the next floor where two men sat at a table in a shaft of sunlight that fell through glass panels in the ceiling. The area was clean and airy, and I took a deep breath, enchanted. Both men were caging.

They looked up from their work, and grinned at my delight.

"The guards rarely come here," Yaqob said. "You will enjoy the work, and I can hardly wait to see how good you are. The tale of what you did in Setkoth has spread about most of Gesholme."

He was surely lying, but he did it well and my smile widened. "Is it normal to have such close guard in the workshop?"

"No. Ta'uz is punishing us for trying to hide Raguel's pregnancy from him. He will soon tire of the sport and withdraw the guards. The Magi generally keep the guards around the perimeter of Gesholme, and in and about Threshold itself—where we must sometimes be 'encouraged' to work. The Magi occasionally visit us, but they too prefer to linger about Threshold."

"Yaqob . . ." I looked outside. An open doorway led to a balcony, and I could see a great shadow spreading over Gesholme.

I had not taken more than a glimpse at Threshold, but it dominated my dreams every night.

"Soon, Tirzah." Yaqob's voice had darkened with my mood. "But first, come see what Orteas and Zeldon work at."

Neither man seemed discomforted that he would be joined by such a young woman—perhaps the story of the cage work I had done for Gayomar and Boaz *had* spread. We chatted politely for some minutes as I ran curious eyes over their work.

The men were working on flat sections that were designed to fit into a large panel. The glass shone gold—it had been beautifully mixed and fired.

"Isphet's work," Yaqob murmured, running his fingers over Zeldon's glass. "No one can match her skill at mixing the molten glass. She has a sweetness that can cajole the most stubborn mixing."

There was silence as Orteas and Zeldon stared at Yaqob, then dropped their eyes hastily back to their work.

Although I noted their reaction, for the moment I preferred to ignore it, more fascinated by the design itself. I moved closer to Zeldon and pointed at his work. "Yaqob, what is this?"

His face hardened. "This is part of Threshold's wrongness, Tirzah. See? These curves form pieces of numbers, and this section here, is the lower segment of a portion of writing."

"Why wrongness?"

Yaqob took a deep, uneasy breath. "You know of the Magi and their fascination with mathematics?"

"Yes, Isphet has explained some of it."

"Some of it is too much of it, but you need to know. Tirzah, can you read or write?"

"I can figure a little, and write numbers. All glassworkers need to be able to do that, especially for measuring powders and metals. But alphabets and words are beyond me."

"Then be grateful. The Magi control the power of numbers and form, but in doing so they have subverted the alphabet. For them, each letter of the alphabet is mated with a number, so that when they write, when they form words and then sentences, the writing has a double and darker significance. Do you see my meaning?"

I noticed how he had avoided the phrase, "Do you understand?"

"Yes, I think so. Each time a Magus writes words, he also writes calculations and formulas. Sorceries."

"*Everything* about them is dangerous, Tirzah, and evil. Beware of them, and especially beware of their writing."

He was angry now, and I nodded quickly.

"Never let one try to teach you letters, girl, for he will seek to ensorcell your soul with each word you write. Run screaming, for if you don't run, then you will succumb to their sorceries." He managed a small smile, although it did not quite reach his eyes. "And then you will not be the same sweet girl who stands before me now."

"Yaqob, I *swear* that I have no intention of ever learning to write. I won't be entrapped, nor entrap you."

"Good."

The promise finally satisfied him, and Yaqob continued to explain the caging. "The Magi need workers skilled in caging for two areas of Threshold. The first is the central chamber, called the Infinity Chamber, where these pieces will eventually fit. All wall and floor spaces of this chamber are to be covered in caged glass work depicting the words and incantations that the Magi require for their formula."

"And the ceiling?"

"There is no ceiling, Tirzah. No, wait, you will see eventually. You will have to take your work in there to be fitted."

"And the second area that needs caged work?"

He paused, and looked outside. "The capstone."

"Capstone?"

Yaqob smiled, but it was sad, and he took my hand and pulled gently. "It is time to let Threshold see you, Tirzah. Then I can explain."

As I was to find out, the glassworkers held high positions within the slave encampment of Gesholme, and perhaps that is why Isphet's workshop was allowed such a roomy balcony.

Or perhaps it was so Threshold's presence could the more easily infiltrate one of the most important workshops of its existence.

Outside it was hot and humid, but I ignored the discomfort as I stepped onto the wooden planking and stared northward.

It was over one hundred and fifty paces away, but it reared so far into the sky I had to crick my neck back to take it all in. Its shadow cut neatly across the outside wall of the workshop.

Yaqob stood comfortingly close, his hand warm on my shoulder. "Threshold."

It was a massive stone pyramid, yet unlike any I'd heard tales of as a child. I frowned, then pointed.

"Yaqob, what are those? Why have they not been filled in? Is that what remains to be done?"

All over the two faces of the pyramid that I could see, gaps had been left in the stone. Several score on each face, placed at regular intervals, and I guessed the two faces I could not see had similar gaps. Men swarmed over the structure, and I saw that near the base of one wall was a yawning entrance. As I watched three Magi emerged, their heads bent over a large scroll.

Yaqob stared at Threshold a long time before he replied.

"What you see now is the stone core, which has eaten more years and lives than anyone cares to remember. Now the

Magi are increasing the glassworkers on the site, for our work is vital."

He paused, and shifted his hand. "Eventually the Magi want to plate Threshold entirely with blue-green glass."

I gasped, and stared at him, then back at Threshold. It would be beautiful!

"The capstone fits on the very peak, Tirzah, and that will be in the same caged gold glass you saw Orteas and Zeldon working on. And the gaps in the stonework? They will be filled, but not with stone. These are the openings of shafts that eventually lead into the Infinity Chamber; the capstone will sit atop the great central shaft. All save the central shaft will be covered with the blue-green plate glass. Along their lengths are gates that can control the amount of light allowed to flood into the Infinity Chamber; the Magi command the devices which control the lighting of the chamber. It will be possible, I suppose, to open every shaft and allow Infinity to be flooded with light."

We stood there a long time in silence, staring at Threshold, staring at the beast that still lay silent, waiting.

Waiting. Watching.

The shadow deepened.

FIVE

After two weeks, the guards disappeared, and the workshop relaxed, but not entirely. I think it was because of the strangers present—my father and myself. And while all were friendly toward us, they showed a reserve that hid a watching. A careful considering.

I wondered at their secrets, but for the first few weeks I was just relieved to be working in an environment that I understood, and with people I liked. Orteas and Zeldon were far more skilled than I, and they showed me many new techniques and tools useful to the art of caging.

We worked from the plans the Magi sent us, carefully drawn and measured. None of their designs made sense to me, not only because I could not read or write, but because each piece we caged was only a small fraction of a whole panel, and it contained only fragments of the numbers, words, or symbols it would eventually help to form. That cheered me, because I did not think fragments could harm me.

Orteas and Zeldon taught me, but they watched me, too, almost as closely as Isphet did. Once the guards left she spent long periods of each day in the high workroom where we caged. Sometimes she chatted, sometimes she questioned, sometimes she told me of the history of Gesholme and more of the Magi, but always she watched.

"You work well with the glass," she said abruptly one day in the fifth week after my arrival, interrupting her tale of the day the Lhyl flooded and threatened to breach the walls surrounding Gesholme. "Almost as if you can communicate with it."

I kept my head bowed, feeling the thrill of the glass beneath my fingers. Isphet made beautiful glass—extraordinary, in fact. I had never worked with the like before.

She was waiting for an answer, so finally I shrugged, pretending disinterest. If they would not yet tell me why *they* watched, then I would not tell them all *my* secrets, either. "I take pride in my work, Isphet. My father taught me that."

She remained silent, and finally I could bear no more, and I lifted my eyes. Isphet was staring at me, her beautiful eyes veiled. "I was at Izzali's workshop four or five days ago, Tirzah. I met Mayim, who came down the river with you. He was astounded by the skill you showed in caging that piece of glass before the Magi. He said he'd thought that no craftsman could have done what you did. He said it was almost as if you had magic within your fingers. 'Magic,' Tirzah?"

I was silent, caught by her eyes.

"No one can work such glass, persuade such glass to her will, unless she can—" Zeldon broke off at a sharp glance from Isphet.

"I have a good ear for the sounds of the tap of the chisel and the drill through the glass, Isphet," I said. "Nothing else. You must know that anyone who works with glass develops an ear for the pure 'singing' as the drill bites. Sweet singing means the glass is being ground well, but if the glass screeches, or cries, then one must add more oil to soothe the passage of the drill. I used no magic other than a good ear, a sure sense of when I drew too close to a fracture, and years of patience. Perhaps Mayim was overly impressed by my skill."

"Perhaps so," Isphet said quietly, "but I wonder if your talent for the glass goes deeper than pure mechanics. Now"—she stood up—"no doubt the workshop below has ground to a halt without my presence to guide and encourage. I will look forward to continuing our conversation tonight, Tirzah."

I was growing tired of the subterfuge, but I bit back a retort. I knew the workers in this shop were hiding something, yet I understood their need to make sure I could be trusted before they revealed it.

Just as Isphet left the room and I was bending my head back to my work, Yaqob entered.

Behind him came a Magus.

All three of us at the worktable froze, tools half buried in the glass or half raised to our work. I stared at the Magus. I had not seen him before; his bulbous nose would have given him a comical air save for the power of the One that radiated from his eyes.

Yaqob's manner was perfect. If I had not seen him display his hatred of the Magi on numerous occasions, I would have thought him their deepest admirer.

He bowed low as he spoke, his voice soft and respectful. "Excellency Kofte has requested that either Orteas or Zeldon accompany him and myself into the Infinity Chamber to oversee the laying of several more panels of caged glasswork."

"You know the stresses such glass can take more than any other," Kofte said lazily, wandering across to our table. "To break it now, as it is finally laid, would be such a pity."

He had stopped behind my chair, and I could feel the soft breeze of his movement lift some loose hairs along my neck. Or was it the fleeting touch of his fingers?

I stared frantically at Yaqob, but there was nothing he could say or do. His pleasant expression did not waver, and he merely waited, head slightly bowed, hands folded, for the Magus's will.

"You are new here," Kofte said abruptly.

"Yes, Excellency," I managed.

"Your name?"

I opened my mouth, but horror had so dried my throat and mouth I could say no more.

"Her name is Tirzah, Excellency," Yaqob said, and I flashed him a grateful look.

Kofte leaned over my shoulder, his arm brushing my skin, and tilted the glass I was holding so he could see it the more clearly.

I was sure he could feel the tremble of my fingers through the glass, and I was sure he smiled as he felt it.

"You cage with great skill, young Tirzah," he said. "Do you understand the stresses of such glass?"

Gratefully I discovered my voice had returned. "Yes, Excellency."

"Good." Kofte's tone was now brisk. "Have you seen Threshold's interior, Tirzah?"

"No, Excellency."

"Then you shall now. Orteas, Zeldon, you may stay with your work. Tirzah will accompany me into Threshold."

I was torn between apprehension and excitement. I had not yet even been near Threshold, let alone inside it . . . but the last person I wanted to escort me was one of the Magi.

Still, Yaqob would be there, and his presence would make everything all right.

We left the workshop and followed the alley farther north, Yaqob and I several steps behind Kofte's languid stride. Yaqob risked throwing me a small smile and a wink, and I relaxed, determined to enjoy his company.

The alley led into a narrow street, bounded by the noise and stink of metal workshops, and that in turn led to the main thoroughfare into Threshold's compound.

I glanced at the compound of the Magi as we passed its gates. Unlike the close humidity of Gesholme, the Magi's compound was spacious, its palm-shaded avenues cooled by pools and canals fed from the river.

I hoped I never had reason to go in there again.

Above Gesholme, and to the east of the compound of the

Magi, lay Threshold. Like the other two, Threshold's compound was walled, but only lightly, and mainly to protect the tools and materials left there overnight.

No one spent any more time than they had to in that compound after sunset.

Kofte led us along the avenue toward Threshold, then through the wide and open gates in the compound's wall. Scores of other workers hurried to and fro: stonemasons, carpenters, surveyors, engineers, a large number of porters carrying sheets of glass—for the interior, I thought, for Yaqob had told me that the outer layer of glass would be the last applied—and two or three glassworkers, to whom Yaqob nodded silently. Every one of the workers, as Yaqob and myself, was dressed as briefly as possible to counter the heat of the sun and the sweat of work: body wraps for the women, hip wraps for the men.

Among the workers moved the Magi. They seemed to be everywhere. Some checked plans and calculations under shaded awnings. Others stood at corners or on balconies, adjusting their robes slowly, carefully, as they studied those who passed by. Some sat in chairs under the shade of broad palm leaves, making notes on papyri as they watched who went where, and why.

And, as we drew closer to Threshold itself, I saw several Magi silhouetted against the skyline as they stood motionless on the walls of the pyramid, staring at I knew not what.

Kofte stopped suddenly as we neared the entrance, and Yaqob and I almost bumped into him. We hastily took several steps backward.

He spread his arms wide and tipped his head back as he took an exaggerated deep breath.

"Can you not *feel* it?" he asked, turning about, and I could see that his eyes glowed with fanaticism.

"It never ceases to amaze and inspire me, Excellency," Yaqob murmured, and I muttered something similar.

Then I felt its shadow. That was strange, for we had been in Threshold's shadow for some time. But at that precise moment I did indeed *feel* it. Yet it did not inspire me or amaze me; instead it terrified me, and I had a dreadful intuition of such loss I thought it would overwhelm me.

A whimper escaped my lips, and Yaqob grabbed at my arm as I swayed on my feet.

"It is her first time, Excellency," he said, and I felt his fingers tighten about my elbow. *"Courage, Tirzah!"* he whispered.

I managed to straighten and somehow forced a smile to my face. "It *is* a wonder, Excellency," I croaked.

Kofte stared at me, and I wondered if he knew exactly how I felt. But he turned, eventually, and continued . . . into Threshold.

Yaqob dropped his hand, but he whispered further encouragement, and my legs obeyed me and carried me forward.

The opening was cut into the southern face, about ten paces wide, five high, and some thirty paces from the base of the pyramid. A ramp led to its mouth (somehow I only ever thought of this opening as a mouth), and as we leaned into its incline, I bowed my head and tried not to let Threshold's shadow overwhelm me again. It had caught me by surprise once, and I had let it see how afraid I was, but I was determined never to do so again.

There was a leveling out of the incline, a chilling of the light, and we were inside.

I looked up.

"Come, come," Kofte said impatiently, standing waiting for us, and he led us down the main passageway of the pyramid. It was flat for some twenty paces, then it shifted up into a gentle incline that curved about like the spiral staircases I had seen on Viland's whaling boats. The incline became steeper, and the curves tighter, and the breath came faster in my throat as the ache grew sharper in my legs.

Faint echoes sounded around the curved walls, but I closed my ears and heart to them. I thought if I listened too closely I would panic and run out. So I steeled myself against them, and they faded.

Shafts and corridors opened off this main passageway, but they became fewer the higher we climbed, and the number of workers, and Magi, we met likewise declined until there was only Kofte, Yaqob, and I left to climb into the heart of Threshold.

The heart. I wondered if it beat, like a warm human heart?

The moment that thought crossed my mind I cursed myself

for a fool. What was I so scared of? This was a building like any other, was it not? Built to stand for eternity, it was hardly likely to come tumbling down the instant I stepped into its heart, was it?

Was it?

The echoes threatened to break my concentration, and I had to bite my lip to keep them at bay.

Yaqob had noted my increasing disquiet, and now he spoke again, giving me the comfort of a human voice to cling to.

"Excellency, Tirzah is curious about the light. Will you explain to her? I . . . I find it beyond my capacity."

I almost smiled, loving him at that moment for his thoughtfulness and for his amusing flattery of the Magus. Surely the man could see Yaqob's words for what they were?

Apparently not. Kofte took Yaqob's statement at its face value, and spoke over his shoulder as he continued to climb.

"I will try to make my words understandable for you," Kofte began, and Yaqob's eyes twinkled merrily at me. I had to fight to keep my face straight.

I listened, fascinated, despite my amusement, for until now I had not realized that the interior of Threshold was lit with the soft radiance of the sun at dawn.

"Threshold appears as if solid stone from the outside, but that is false. It is more space than solid, and more light than darkness. Scores, if not hundreds of shafts run through it, not only from outer wall to inner chamber, but shafts that interconnect passageways such as this, and smaller shafts yet that connect other shafts. Eventually all will be glassed and mirrored . . ."

I looked at the masonry to my left as we passed. Yes, there were tiny spaces left in the mortar to hold the supports for glass.

". . . as many of the smaller shafts are already. They transport the light from the outside to the interior. See?" His hand stabbed upward, and my gaze followed. A tiny opening above was visible not as the mouth of a shaft, but as a glow of light.

"And there." His hand indicated a similar glow in the upper wall to our right. Now that I knew what to look for, my eye caught several others. Their radiance was so soft that they were almost impossible to spot until pointed out.

"Then Threshold will throb with light when it is finished, Excellency," I said incautiously, but still intrigued by the system that provided such light.

Kofte jerked to a halt and whipped about. "What do you mean by that?"

"Nothing, Excellency," I said, my heart pounding. Why hadn't I kept silent? "I just thought . . . with all the space . . . and the glass . . ."

He stared a moment longer, then reluctantly decided I had meant no harm. "We are almost there," he said shortly. "Yaqob, I hope you remembered to bring your measuring tape with you."

Yaqob patted the tool kit hanging from a belt about his hips. "Yes, Excellency."

Kofte had already disappeared about the next curve, and Yaqob and I hurried after him. I kept my eyes low, not as scared as I had been earlier, but certainly more wary.

I had no time for further thought, for the Infinity Chamber opened before me, and my previous intuition of loss ripened into full-blown grief and despair.

Despite the intensity of the emotion, I was more controlled now, and refused to let it overwhelm me. I took several deep breaths, and concentrated on Yaqob's back as we stepped into the central chamber.

Then I mustered every last piece of courage I had, lifted my head, and looked about me.

The Infinity Chamber itself was shaped as a pyramid. Four walls angled from the floor to a central shaft that led, I realized, to the peak of Threshold where the capstone would eventually rest. So that is what Yaqob meant when he said the chamber had no ceiling. The floor was perhaps fifteen paces square, and from its center to the apex of the walls another fifteen. I studied the floor more closely. It was one sheet of massive, solid clear plate glass, and I could see that there was a space underneath it for the golden and caged glass to eventually slide under—for one could not walk directly on fragile, caged work.

I looked across the walls. About a fifth of the area had been covered with Orteas's and Zeldon's work, and now I could see how the small pieces they (and, more recently, we) had been working on fitted into an intricate pattern of calculations in numbers, words, and geometric symbols.

A sickness bloomed in my belly, and I think I must have paled, for Yaqob took a concerned step in my direction.

"Yaqob!" the Magus barked, and I waved Yaqob away.

"It was just the climb . . . breathless . . ."

He could see the lie in my face, but he turned back to Kofte, taking out his measuring tape. Yaqob was one of the most skilled glass cutters on the site, and I saw that Kofte needed him to measure for some fine connecting panels of uncaged golden glass that would form bridges between the main areas of caged work.

As they measured, I stepped closer to one of the completed panels. I raised my hand, then, my fingers trembling so badly I thought they might actually break the glass, I touched the panel.

Instantly I felt the wrongness of Threshold flood into my body in one crushing wave. The glass was screaming, pleading, weeping, trapped in an existence that was not life but that was worse than death.

Help us! Help us! Help us!

I took a shuddering, despairing breath, and gratefully fainted.

SIX

I came to with my head in Yaqob's lap, listening to his voice as he thought of every possible excuse to explain my faint to the Magus.

"She is young, and still recovering from a harsh journey to Gesholme, Excellency. The climb into the chamber taxes the fittest of men, and has proved too much for her. The excitement, perhaps. She has wanted to see the Infinity Chamber for many weeks, and has been overawed. Perhaps the time of her moon flux is upon her, and . . ."

The excuses were sounding increasingly thin, so I opened my eyes before he moved even further into the intimate details of womanly weakness.

"Ah, Tirzah. What happened?"

But his eyes pleaded into mine, and I knew he wanted me to say anything *but* what really happened.

I sat up slightly. Yaqob had dragged me into the passageway outside the Infinity Chamber, for which I was thankful. Nevertheless, the despair of the glass still reached me in palpable waves of grief. Kofte stood to one side, his face a mask of irritation that was rapidly darkening to anger.

"The climb," I stumbled, "and the excitement ... the beauty ..." I hoped it would do.

Kofte opened his mouth to say something, but Yaqob hurried to speak. "I have the measurements I need, Excellency, and if I hurry Tirzah outside now I can send Zeldon or Orteas up to oversee the placement of the glass."

Kofte's face twitched, and I could see the power rippling beneath his skin. Terrified he was about to unleash the fury of the One upon me, I groaned, and closed my eyes.

"Excellency!" Yaqob pleaded. "She is too valuable to lose, too skilled at the caging!"

Now I could hear the fear in his voice, and that terrified me even more. I screwed my eyes shut, and prepared to die.

But Yaqob had managed to deflect Kofte's anger. "Then take her!" the Magus snapped. "And send Zeldon. But *fast*! I have not the entire day to waste."

Muttering profuse thanks, Yaqob gathered me into his arms and hurried me away from those dreadful screams.

He held me close, trotting as fast as he dared down the incline, and with every step he took I could feel and hear the screams wane. I relaxed, my horror fading with that of the glass, and let Yaqob's closeness warm and comfort me.

He stopped eventually, and cradled me closer as he spoke. "Tirzah. We approach the busier sections of Threshold. It would be better if you walked by yourself now. Can you do it?"

I nodded, reluctantly, and he saw the reason for my reluctance and a grin tugged the corners of his mouth. "You *are* feeling better. Come now, stand." And his arms loosened about me.

I stood, straightened my wrap, and pushed my hair into some kind of order. Yaqob nodded, then walked forward, making sure I managed to follow.

We reached the mouth of Threshold without incident. Guards watched us curiously, but we hung our heads and shuffled past, and eventually their eyes wandered beyond us, looking for slaves more likely to be in the midst of subversive activities.

At its foot we met two of the craftsmen from our workshop. Yaqob took one of them aside, spoke quickly, and the man hurried back the way he'd come.

"I've sent him for Zeldon," Yaqob said quietly. "We dare not cross Kofte more than we have already."

"Yaqob, I'm sorry. I—"

"No. Don't speak now. Not here."

I knew he meant not only where so many guards huddled watchful, but also where Threshold's shadow lay at its thickest. I shivered.

"I know a place where we can have a few quiet minutes without suspicion. We need to talk, you and I."

We walked back through the gates of Threshold's enclosure, then down the main thoroughfare leading from Gesholme. As we walked past an overhang Yaqob took my elbow and pulled me into a dark, shaded alcove. Thick canvas hung above us and dropped to the dirt at our feet; Threshold's shadow was as trapped outside as was the sun.

We stood close, but not touching.

"Well?"

"I . . . the glass . . ."

"Tirzah, what happened when you touched the glass?"

I took a deep breath, sick of the secrets, and then the words came out in a flood. "It screamed to me, Yaqob. It was trapped, weeping, pleading. Its soul is sick, tarnished, but unable to die. It *wants* to die. It wants to escape."

He stared at me, his eyes unreadable in this dim light. "You hear glass speak? Is that what you're saying?"

"I . . ." I had mentioned this only once to my father, when I was about eight. He had smiled indulgently and dismissed my words as the imagination of a young girl. "The glass has spoken to me for a very long time, and I to it. This is the only way I know how to work it."

"And what else speaks to you, Tirzah?"

"Pottery, sometimes, but not like the glass. Not wood. Not cloth." I fingered the material of my own wrap, using it as an excuse to drop my eyes from his.

"And?"

"And metals, especially worked precious metals—a gold bracelet"—that had been Hadone's bracelet, and it had made my time with him bearable—"and the silver, copper, or jade rings on the hands of those I have held."

I paused again, but not through any wish to dissemble. I needed the moment to try to put what I had felt throughout my life into words. "And sometimes I hear echoes within and among buildings or while walking surfaced roadways, but they are very faint."

"Here?"

"No. Here there are no echoes. Gesholme is dead."

He was staring at me. "And Threshold?"

I shuddered, and wished he would put his arm about me. "I have told you how the glass in the Infinity Chamber screams, and there were echoes elsewhere within Threshold."

"Echoes of *what*?"

"Yaqob!" I pleaded, but he was relentless.

"Echoes of what?"

"Of pain and fear and entrapment." And of loss, I also wanted to say, but did not. I wondered if it was Yaqob I would lose.

"And Isphet's workshop?" Now his voice was very soft.

I began to cry. "Isphet's workshop is alive and warm, Yaqob. I love it there. I want to go back. Please."

He finally put his arm about me and held me close, soothing me. I never wanted him to let go.

"Please, Tirzah, let me ask just one or two more questions. I need to know these. What of Druse and Mayim?"

"Mayim? No. He is not even a particularly good craftsman, and he certainly does not listen for what the glass whispers to him. My father . . . no, also. He does not hear the glass, or anything else, I think."

I felt Yaqob nod slightly against the top of my head. "Yes," he said, almost as if to himself. "That is as we thought. Izzali says that Mayim has few skills, so I did not think he could be an . . ." He paused. "Druse is good, very good, but he does not feel the glass in the way"—one of his hands stroked my upper arm—"that you do."

I leaned back. "You hear it, too, don't you?"

A slow smile spread across his face, and his eyes were very gentle. "Yes. And Isphet, and Orteas and Zeldon and Raguel, poor, poor Raguel, do as well. As do numerous others within Isphet's workshop and scattered throughout this sorry encampment."

"But why can I? I come from a northern land."

"The ability to hear the glass is not confined to race. It is only that our people developed the ability to a greater extent than others have. I think that perhaps a number of the finest craftsmen in the north have the ability—even if they do not quite realize what it is themselves."

"Not my father."

"Tirzah, can we trust your father?"

I remembered how my father had laughed at me when I had tried to explain what I heard. I hesitated in my answer, and it was that hesitation, I think, that told Yaqob what he needed to know.

"My father is a good man, and would not willingly betray your trust."

"But he has weaknesses that might. He told me one night how his gambling enslaved you."

It was sad to hear that put into words. "Yes. Yaqob, who are the Soulenai?"

I felt him jump.

"Where have you heard that name?"

"The first night I arrived when Raguel . . . Well, Isphet was upset and unwary. She told Raguel she should thank the Soulenai Ta'uz did not kill her as well as her child."

Yaqob leaned his head back and laughed, but quietly, lest he attract attention. "Since you and your father arrived Isphet has been constantly warning us to be wary of you. Not to let slip any . . . well, to be wary. And now you tell me that Isphet herself revealed the name of the Soulenai to you. Well, well."

"Yaqob?"

He sobered. "Tirzah. The voices you hear, the echoes, are the voices of the elements. Some of the whispers might even be of the Soulenai themselves, reaching from the Place Beyond. No, wait. This is not the place. We need quiet and many hours. Tonight, I think, if Isphet is agreeable. And now"—he let go of me and stood back—"now I think we must hurry back to the workshop lest the guards discover us and wonder if we have, perhaps, been enjoying ourselves too greatly in this secretive overhang."

When we reached the workshop Isphet took one look at us, and came over.

"I head Tirzah fainted in the Infinity Chamber," she said, and stared hard at Yaqob. "Zeldon has gone to placate Kofte."

"She hears," Yaqob said simply, and Isphet shifted her eyes to me. Abruptly she thrust a small glass goblet into my hands.

"What does it tell you, Tirzah?"

This was as much a test as Yaqob's questioning had been, and I could feel many eyes within the workshop turned my way, although only Yaqob and I could have heard Isphet's question. I turned the goblet over in my hands. It was a plain vessel, used as a means to quench our thirst when the heat of the furnaces grew too hot.

"It tells me that it lives, but that it would prefer to live elsewhere. There is a darkness here it does not like."

Isphet stared, then jerked her head. "Very well. Yaqob, come to my quarters tonight. Will you be safe?"

"I am as nimble and invisible as a cat across those rooftops, Isphet. The guards will never see me."

"Well, be careful anyway, Yaqob. None of us can afford to lose you now."

Although the events of the daytime had twisted my world awry, the revelations of that night altered the very fabric of my life.

In the evening we dampened down the furnaces and I walked in companionable silence with the women of Isphet's household through the dusk to our quarters. We left the doors and windows open for the cool of the evening air while we ate, but once the meal was done and the dishes cleaned and set aside, Isphet ordered that the windows be shuttered, and all the doors save the one to the inner courtyard were locked.

Then we waited. Saboa and I played listlessly at a game of tebente, taking it in turns to throw the marked sticks and move our clay figurines about the wooden board. But our hearts were not in it, and we jumped every time an insect frizzled in one of the two lamps Isphet had allowed to be lit.

Yaqob came an hour after it was fully dark, and he brought with him a fellow glassworker from our workshop, Yassar. They had come across the rooftops of the tenement buildings, crawling slowly and silently, waiting as sporadic patrols of guards passed beneath them, then moving on again. Once they reached the roof of our building, they had come down the stairs of the courtyard.

"Druse and Mayim?" Isphet asked as Yaqob and Yassar sat down.

"They will sleep well tonight, Isphet. No, Tirzah, it is all right. A sleeping draft in their evening meal is all I have done. Your father will wake refreshed in the morning and not realize he has been drugged."

"We had to do it," Yassar said.

"Yes," I said, "I know it."

"Good," said Isphet. "Tirzah, I will now speak for some time. You will listen. If you have questions, you will wait until after I have spoken. First, I will speak a warning. If you betray us to the Magi, then you will eventually die, even if no one in this room is left alive to take the revenge. *Do you understand*?"

I rocked back on my stool at the threat in her voice and her eyes. I risked a glance at Yaqob, but his eyes were as implacable as Isphet's. "I understand, Isphet."

"Good. We place our lives in your hands with what we are about to reveal."

She breathed deep, relaxed, and spoke.

"Many generations ago, long before the building of

Threshold, Ashdod was a land where the people lived their lives surrounded by the voices of the elements—particularly the elements within metals and gems. The Elemental arts and magic flourished, as did reverence for the Soulenai. The Soulenai are deeply learned and magical spirits who live in a region we know only as the Place Beyond. They speak to us through the elements—they have ever had an affinity for metals and gems—and lend us the power for our work and our arts. So in the glass, or the metals and gems you handle, Tirzah, you may hear the voices not only of the particular element you hold, but sometimes also of the Soulenai, echoing from the Place Beyond."

I blinked. Very occasionally when I worked glass the voices were far stronger and more vivid than usual. Such was the case when I'd worked the glass for the two Magi in Setkoth. Had this then been the Soulenai speaking to me through the glass, rather than the glass itself?

Isphet watched my face, then continued. "Glassworkers— we in this room—are particularly attuned to the voices of the elements and Elemental magic because of the metals used in the making and coloring of glass. Any who hear the elements' voices or who practice the Elemental arts are known simply as Elementals. Once there were great magicians— Cantomancers—among us, many descended from the bloodlines of the Soulenai themselves. The Cantomancers attained a level of power that left ordinary Elementals gasping; Cantomancers were only one level below the Soulenai in understanding and skill. But they have vanished, and we lesser Elementals must make shift as we may."

Isphet looked to Yaqob, her eyes tender. "Yaqob has great talent, and I hope that eventually he may master the arts of the Cantomancers. I pray that he will, if one day we can find him the teachers . . ."

Her voice drifted into silence, then she shook herself and continued. "Among the other workers in Gesholme, the ranks of the metalworkers, as you would expect, and those few gemworkers in Gesholme have Elementals among them who still listen to the voices of the elements and the Soulenai as they craft. But of them Yaqob will speak later.

"Ashdod was a wondrous land when many could hear the elements, when the Soulenai were able to speak and laugh as they desired, and when we still had the great Cantomancers to work their wonders for us. The people of Ashdod would consult with the Cantomancers and the Soulenai for advice, or to beg their favor and intervention in our lives. We did not worship the Soulenai as gods, but we learned to respect them and to accept the advice and aid they were willing to offer. The crafts flourished, for it was among the crafts that Elemental magic was at its strongest.

"So Ashdod society existed for hundreds of years. But then came a change. The higher caste of Ashdod society has ever been inclined to the philosophical arts and less inclined to listen to the voices of the Soulenai." Isphet shrugged slightly. "In that sense, Elemental magic has always been strongest among the lower castes rather than the nobility. Anyway, over generations there grew among the nobility a taste for mathematics, and eventually this taste solidified into a caste. Men only, for they claimed that women did not have the agility of mind to embrace the myriad complexities of numbers and forms. As I told you on your first night, Tirzah, the Magi, as these mathematicians came to be known to distinguish them from the Elemental Cantomancers, command power through contemplation of the One, and of all numbers and forms that the One generates.

"Gradually their power and influence increased. The Magi loathed the magic of the Elementals, because they said it was unpredictable, reliant on chance and the whims of the Soulenai. *Their* magic, they claimed"—and Isphet's voice became hard and brittle—"was powerful because of its very predictableness and because, once its rules and parameters were understood, it could be manipulated to the Magi's needs. They work their magic according to set *rules*! Tables! Parameters! Can you imagine that?

"Their influence over the nobility and the monarchy increased, and eight or nine generations ago they moved against us, moved to destroy Elemental magic. Life became ordered—you have seen fields and gardens locked in to rigid geometric shapes, the length and angle of their borders carefully defined according to the Magi's dictates—and any Elementals caught practicing their arts were put to death.

"Tirzah, *never* let the Magi know you can hear the glass sing to you, for they would kill you on the spot."

I nodded.

"And so"—Isphet waved one hand about—"we practice in secret as best we can. Most Magi believe that all Elementals have been exterminated, but even so, we must be wary. If any really suspected . . ."

I thought of the Magus Boaz—*he* still believed the Elementals existed, and suspected me of the art. I closed my eyes briefly, thankful he was in Setkoth rather than here, then wondered if I should say something. But as I opened my eyes and prepared to speak, Isphet continued.

"Now, I want to tell you what I can about Threshold. Much of this is supposedly secret, confined to Magi circles, but we have gleaned it over many years, from indiscreet words and whispers and from what we have seen about us; the Magi are not always as inscrutable as they believe. Eight generations ago a cadre within the Magi conceived of a mathematical formula so perfect, yet so powerful in its perfection, that many among the Magi argued it should be allowed to fall into distant memory. Nevertheless, those in favor won out. The formula consisted—consists—in constructing a building that physically embodies the perfect mathematical-geometrical form."

"Threshold," I said.

"Yes, Threshold. For generations its construction has consumed Ashdod, and consumed us. Gesholme grew alongside Threshold to house the workers needed to build it. The encampment was once much larger, when tens of thousands were needed for the major construction work; what you see about you now is about a third of its previous size. Once the workers were free and paid for their labor. No more. All of us in this room, save you and I, Tirzah, were born into slavery.

"Threshold's purpose—the purpose of the formula—is not exactly clear to us, but some of it we can guess. The heart of Threshold is the Infinity Chamber." Now Isphet looked carefully at me. "The One."

I must have looked confused, for Isphet immediately explained. "The Magi believe that the One is birth and death within itself, for it is the number from which all other numbers and forms are born and into which they will eventually collapse and die."

"Thus it represents Infinity," Yaqob said very quietly to one side. "The Magi always strive for complete union with the One. With Infinity."

Isphet wriggled irritably at his interruption. "The fact that Threshold, as a building and as a mathematical formula, has as its heart a chamber named *Infinity* makes us believe that it is being built to enable the Magi to eventually achieve complete union with the One."

There was a very long silence.

"We believe," Isphet eventually said, very quietly now, "that when Threshold is complete, it will provide the Magi with the means to step into Infinity."

She let me think about this for a moment, then went on. "Frankly, if they want to step into Infinity and thus rid this land of their presence, then I for one care not. Indeed, there would be celebrations and laughing the night they stepped through. But there is something wrong with Threshold. All of us have felt it. Threshold's shadow stretches across us all, even at night we can feel its weight in our dreams. Day by day the sense of wrongness grows. Anyone who has been into the Infinity Chamber knows just how deep the wrongness has spread. Tirzah, you know."

I nodded again, not sure I could have spoken, even had I wanted to.

"Yes," Isphet said, "we all know about it but none of us can tell *exactly* what the wrongness is. The glass screams inside the Infinity Chamber . . . but *why*? Have the Magi miscalculated? Is the formula flawed? No one is sure and"—her mouth quirked—"no one dares question the Magi on the matter. Yaqob, I wish that you would now speak."

He stared at each of us in turn. "We are enslaved here, trapped unwilling in the wrongness that is Threshold by these loathsome dung lice who call themselves Magi."

My head snapped up at the bitterness in Yaqob's voice. I knew he resented his lot, but I had never realized the depth of it.

"It will kill us, eventually. And if Threshold does not do it, then once the building is finally complete, I believe the Magi will. We know too much about Threshold and its secrets."

Abruptly Yaqob leaped to his feet and started to pace restlessly about the room.

"But I want to live, as does everyone here. I want to be *free*. I want my children to be free and to grow in pure sunlight far from this foul shadow. I want us all to be able to practice our arts without constant fear. For months I, as Yassar and Isphet and scores of other Elementals in this damned calculus of a compound, have been planning. It has been slow, hard, and we've had to be careful, but it goes well. Within the year we hope to have built up a sufficient store of blades and to have enough support among the other slaves to overwhelm the guards and the Magi—and to *kill* every one of them!— and make our escape."

His anger frightened me, and I had to look away. Overthrow the guards? The Magi? How?

But escape . . . I had never dared hope. Free? Oh, to be free again!

"I will help," I said, my voice low but fierce.

"Yes," Yaqob said, "you will. You have no choice now that you have heard all you have this night."

He watched me carefully, then relaxed, reassured by what he saw in my face. "For a long time we would not trust you. We constantly fear that the Magi will plant spies among us. And your arrival on the night that Raguel gave birth seemed extraordinarily coincidental."

Raguel stared into her lap, her face hidden. She spent her days silent and still, her nights tossing in restless and noisy sleep. When she was with us. Over the past two weeks Ta'uz had occasionally required her presence for an hour or two at night.

"But no spy the Magi planted would be able to hear the glass as you can. Until we were sure you *were* Elemental yourself, well, we would not trust you."

"What do you plan to do, Yaqob?" I asked. "And where can we go once we escape? What is there for us?"

"There is no need for you to know the details of our plans

yet, and the less you know, the safer it will be for you. And as for where we go once we escape . . . well, Isphet?"

"I was born free," Isphet said, and her eyes were very distant. "Free. Far to the southeast of this place, across a great arid plain, stands a range of low hills that hide a lovely secret. Deep within this secret lives an isolated community devoted to the study and development of Elemental magic and service to the Soulenai. The elders among them are powerful beyond anything I could be; indeed, they live in such seclusion that few of us ever see them. We call them Graces, for the serenity their contemplation and power gives them. These hills are where I come from, and they are to where I hope the majority of us will be able to make our escape.

"Now, Tirzah, I know you must have questions, but I would like you to sleep on them, absorb what you have heard here tonight. I, or Yaqob, will be pleased to answer anything you ask—but *only* ask when you can be sure we will not be overheard."

"Yes, Isphet. Thank you." Underlying all the swirling thoughts and questions in my head was a sense of quiet gladness. They trusted me.

"Good," Isphet said. "Tirzah." She reached out and took my hand. "In the morning I will induct you and begin your instruction. Druse, and the three others in the workshop who are not among us, shall have to be sent on a long and involved errand to one of the other workshops, I think. Raguel?"

She looked up from her lap, her eyes dead.

"Raguel, I will need you in the morning, and Yaqob, too, I think."

Isphet's face saddened.

"It is time to farewell the spirit of Raguel's baby and to wish her well. Yaqob, your presence will infuse strength into the ceremony and into Tirzah, for already she hears the voices strongly and may well be afraid of what she will experience tomorrow."

SEVEN

I hardly slept that night. I had my own sleeping pallet by now, but I am sure that my tossing and turning must have disturbed everyone else in the room. For as far back as I could remember I'd heard the voices. As a tiny child, sitting under my father's worktable, I'd been mesmerized by the shards of glass sifting through my fingers. Not only by their colors, although they were glorious enough, but by their soft cries and their words. When I was old enough to work the glass I used what they said to make the working easier. Now I knew why I had mastered the art of caging so young: my voice shaped the glass as much as my tools did, and I listened to what the glass told me it could or could not bear.

Who were these Soulenai? Was it not so much the voice of the glass I'd heard, but the voices of these strange spirits who sometimes spoke through it?

I remembered how I'd sat before Boaz and shaped the glass, drawing on the voices to help me. He'd sat but a pace away, his hands about that glass, his fingers touching mine from time to time. Deaf to the beauty and music beneath his fingers.

Magus! I thought, and I put all the loathing Yaqob had taught me into that thought.

Thank the Soulenai the Magi here had shown no special interest in me. There had been Kofte's brief display, but that had been only a transient sexual interest that had faded the moment I'd fainted in the Infinity Chamber. Perhaps the Magi required their women to retain control of their consciousness while they communed with the One.

My mind drifted back to the glass. Why had Isphet said I'd be frightened? Surely she wasn't going to show me anything so horrifying as what had touched me in the Infinity Chamber?

Well, it would be good to have Yaqob there, anyway. I smiled into the darkness, and turned over, and spent the last remaining hours of the night drifting in and out of dreams of Yaqob.

My father was cheerful in the morning, and looked very bright of eye. He had slept extremely well, he said, and did not complain when Isphet sent him off with several others to help out in another workshop.

They would be gone for the rest of the day.

We continued working at our assigned tasks until almost noon, and then Yaqob came to fetch Orteas, Zeldon, and me.

"Will we be safe?" Orteas asked.

"Yes. Watch is being kept along the alley and down the main thoroughfare. There are no guards and no Magi close."

Later I would realize that when anyone in our workshop planned to practice the arts, an effective system of watch was kept by Elementals in the other workshops. But for now we followed Yaqob down the stairs.

Work had ceased. Most of the workers were silently lining the sides of the room, but in the very center of the room stood Isphet and Raguel in front of a small table.

In its center was a great bowl of molten glass.

"The others will watch," Yaqob said quietly, "but in this ceremony they will not participate."

Isphet nodded as I reached her, and I saw that she and Raguel had loosened their dark hair.

"Let yours out, too," Isphet said, and I hastened to comply, shaking it out over my shoulders. "If we were free we would come to the Soulenai garbed in our best raiment and garlanded with flowers. That is impossible here. The loosening of our hair from the chains that binds it is the best we can do. The Soulenai know of our difficulties, and appreciate the effort.

"Tirzah. You have heard the voices in the glass, and in many of the other elements about you. Some of the voices are those of the element itself, some of the voices of the Soulenai. But what we hear of their voices in our daily lives through elements like metal or glass is an echo only. Today we will touch them intimately, and let them touch us. It is a frightening experience the first time, and that is partly the reason I have asked Yaqob to stand with you. Already you trust him, and today you will learn to trust him further."

I wondered how much she realized of my growing feelings for Yaqob—how much did Yaqob know?—then decided it didn't matter very much.

"Tirzah, see." And Isphet passed her hand over the wide bowl of molten glass. I looked down. The glass glowed with heat, but was otherwise colorless. I wondered what she had done to it to keep it so molten, for glass normally cooled fairly quickly, and this was far from the furnace.

"Listen to my voice, Tirzah. Do what it tells you. And follow the movements of my hand."

Her hand passed over the bowl again, and I realized that the molten glass was spinning inside it. Around and around. I felt myself pulled into its thrall.

Again Isphet's hand passed over the bowl, and this time she cast powders in, metals, and color flared and swirled within the glass. Bright blue. Again her hand swept over the bowl, and now a vivid red swirled and intermixed with the blue, again, and then gold joined them.

"Watch the colors, Tirzah. *Feel* them. Listen to them . . . listen . . . can you feel us listening as well? Can you feel me? Can you feel Raguel? Can you feel Yaqob?"

I opened my mouth to say that, no, I could not, but my eyes were fixed on the swirling colors within the bowl of glass. Isphet's hand passed over again, and my head swam with its movement. Green swirled there now.

"Yes," I whispered, and indeed I could. I could feel them beside me, but I could also feel them *inside* me. Raguel was only a distant, pastel presence, but Isphet and Yaqob were strong and vivid, primary colors in themselves. I could feel them swirl with the rainbow in the glass. Were they in there? Was *I* in there?

"My friends." The tone of Isphet's voice was very warm, musical, like nothing I'd ever heard her use before. I sank deeper into the swirl of color, listening to her liquid voice sound through me as about me. I understood from Yaqob's presence that Isphet was no longer speaking to us.

"My friends. I speak to you with gladness and sadness. Gladness because today I bring to you one you have already whispered to, but who has yet to hear your full beauty. Her name is Tirzah."

Tirzah.

I reeled, uneasy, for a voice of unimaginable power had moved through me. Not sounded, for I had not heard it as such, but I had felt it.

Tirzah.

I think a sob escaped my lips. I had never conceived of such power in my meager existence, nor had I ever thought such beauty to exist.

Tirzah.

And I would have panicked save that I could feel Yaqob's presence, a strength that offered warmth and comfort and reassurance, and I took all it offered.

Listen to them Tirzah. Revel in their beauty.

He let me see how he had submerged himself in their voices, and then I felt Isphet, and she showed how she had submitted herself to their power. Neither Yaqob nor Isphet were diminished by such surrender, but enriched.

Surrender, they cried, and I did.

The Soulenai enveloped me, seared through me. The colors before me swirled at an impossible rate, and I was as trapped by their frantic motion as I was by the presence of the Soulenai.

They spoke to me of impossible things, of lives and experiences beyond my comprehension. But they were so gentle. I had not expected such gentleness, such tenderness. They touched me, and explored me, and encouraged me to touch and explore them. They laughed at my first tentative efforts and I cried out, and on some distant plane I felt Yaqob physically grasp me and hold me upright.

Tirzah, you are welcome among us. Nurture us, and we shall nurture you. Serve us, and we shall serve you.

Yes, I cried, and they accepted me.

My friends. Now Isphet spoke again. *Today we come to you with sadness amid our joy at Tirzah's awakening. Our friend and your servant, Raguel . . .*

Raguel, they whispered.

Raguel had her child snatched from her, many weeks ago. This is the first time we have dared join with you, and now we beg your assistance in seeing the child on her way into the Place Beyond.

Their sorrow pierced through me, but I was growing used to their intrusions through the spaces of my body and my mind, and I did not cry out. I felt Yaqob, as tender as the Soulenai, radiate pleasure at my acceptance of their touch.

There was a movement. Isphet's hands again, and as they passed over the swirling glass this time they threw not metals, but fragrant gum resin and as it hit the glass it began to smolder, and intoxicating smoke surrounded us. I breathed deeply, my hands acting of some accord not my own to waft the incense closer and closer to my face.

And through the smoke I caught glimpses of the Place Beyond.

What I saw I can hardly put into words. The Place Beyond was a land of sweeping distance, and yet enveloping warmth and security. It was infused with a peace so pervasive that anger, jealousy, and war were words and concepts not only unknown, but also unimaginable. I longed to be able to step into that wondrous land.

Give us the child.

Again movement, but this time Raguel—and Yaqob, who was tightening his hands about me.

I saw as if in a dream, caught by the incense and the continuing presence of the Soulenai.

Raguel bending, lifting something from the floor.

A sad, wrapped bundle. Stained here and there with the fluids of putrefaction. A movement, quick, but unutterable sadness swept through me.

The bundle hit the molten glass, and the colors splattered about us—only the presence and benefaction of the Soulenai stopped any of the droplets hitting us.

The bundle burst into flames. In the space of a breath it was gone, lost . . . but then I heard, *felt,* the baby girl.

She was among us now, touching us as the Soulenai did, exploring, her presence a soft sense of wonderment.

I cried, and I knew that Raguel did too, and the Soulenai comforted us both, and the child laughed, and all was well.

She did not stay long. The Soulenai took her with them

into the Place Beyond. As they sped away I felt a sense of loss
so palpable I moaned, and closed my eyes, and let Yaqob keep
me from falling to the floor.

There was a space of time in which no one moved or spoke.

Finally I felt Isphet place her hands about my face, and I
opened my eyes. She was smiling.

"Welcome among us, Tirzah. You are an Elemental born,
and now you have been accepted by the Soulenai. What we
did today was simple, a touching only. Over the next months
I will take you deeper and deeper into Elemental magic. You
will become great among us, I think, for your abilities are astounding, and if we are to right the wrong that is Threshold,
then I think that you will be greatly needed among us."

EIGHT

S ome eight or nine months passed. I moved from nineteen to twenty shortly after my induction into the arts
of the Elementals and I left what little remained of my
childhood and former life completely behind me. I grew further distant from my father. It was a distance I regretted, but
as Isphet increased her teaching, and as I accepted the presence of the Soulenai more, I found my need for my father
growing less. And he knew nothing of the Elemental among
us. He did not know that on some days when the glass glowed
bright the voices of the Soulenai reverberated about the workshop as our hands and hearts molded and shaped to the words
they spun.

I often wondered what it was like for the non-Elementals
who worked with us. Wondered if they ever realized there
was a depth and a joy to the workshop in which they did not,
could not, participate.

Now pottery and metal pots whispered and sang to me as

well, and sometimes echoed the words of the Soulenai, although never so much as the glass. Yet, with all the joy of the discovery of the Elemental arts came a tarnish. Nothing was right within Gesholme, not when the shadow of Threshold lay over us like a quiescent tumor awaiting its chance.

I continued my work beside Orteas and Zeldon, caging Isphet's wondrous golden glass. We took pride in our work, and lost ourselves amid the conversation of the glass, but it was sad also, for our work was destined for the Infinity Chamber.

I learned to go inside that abomination and neither faint nor let my horror disturb the tranquillity of my face. The Soulenai comforted me, even amid the screams of the glass nailed to the walls, and begged me to discover what it was that made the glass scream so . . .

What's wrong? What's wrong? What's wrong?

I tried, and the few of us with reason to go inside the Infinity Chamber tried, but we could not discern the "why" of the wrongness, only the fact and the horror of its existence.

Meanwhile, Threshold grew. Orteas, Zeldon, and I caged to the Magi's supervision and designs, and during these months our work spread over fully a third of the area of the Infinity Chamber. Whenever any of us went inside (and we tried to go in pairs, for that helped us cope) we would view the designs of the completed panels, fearing what sorceries the strange symbols, letters, and numbers constructed, yet yearning to understand what was wrong so we could aid the Soulenai. There was always a Magus with us—none of the slaves were allowed inside the chamber without at least one Magus to stand watch—and we dared not look too closely, let alone ask. But at night we would talk about what we'd seen, and try to understand. Try, and fail every time.

Elsewhere work progressed almost as rapidly as in the Infinity Chamber. Many of the shafts and corridors were fully glassed now, and on some days the interior of Threshold glittered with hard light. Sometimes, whether approaching the pyramid down the main thoroughfare, or standing on the balcony outside our workshop, we could see the openings of shafts on the exterior walls flare into light, and then die down.

Threshold not only took light into itself, but cast it out, too.

As the interior neared completion, the Magi gave orders that slaves should begin to plate the exterior.

Our workshop, as all others in Gesholme, worked eighteen hours of every day, mixing and firing the sheets of blue-green glass that would eventually cover Threshold. Even so, it would take a year before it could be done, if not longer.

I was lucky, for my workload did not appreciably increase, but Isphet worked hard, as did my father and Yaqob and many, many others.

I occasionally caught glimpses of Yaqob talking quickly, surreptitiously, with Yassar and other men not connected with our workshop but who I guessed to be part of the planned revolt. Yaqob rarely talked of it, only to say that, blade by blade, enough weaponry was being stored to stick every Magus twice over. Such talk, brief as it was, made me nervous. I was scared that slaves, even moderately well armed, could not overcome both guards and Magi. I also remembered the intuition of loss that I had the first day I'd approached Threshold, and I watched Yaqob, and wondered.

Yaqob. Yaqob and I fell inevitably into love. It was a courtship conducted for the most part under the benign eyes of the entire workshop, but the more meaningful and the sweeter for it. We had to be careful, for although relationships—even marriages—between slaves were not forbidden by the Magi, neither were they encouraged. Anything that distracted a slave from his or her duty to Threshold was discouraged, and it was safer to hide our love from the Magi than flaunt it.

Neither of us wanted to give the Magi, or Threshold, the knowledge whereby they might hurt us.

So we were circumspect, but within that circumspection, we indulged our love as much as we were able. But that was difficult in a world where privacy between lovers was more often a raging frustration than a reality. We each shared our quarters with four or five others, and neither of us could find the courage to ask our friends to wait outside while we luxuriated in a slow exploration of love.

There were the rooftops, out of view of most and only sporadically patrolled, but there was always the shadow of Threshold, even at night, and we were as compelled to hide from it as we were from the Magi.

So as lovers, I think Yaqob and I discovered every canvas overhang, every dim storeroom, every darkened space between or underneath or above cupboards and shelves in Gesholme.

Even if we found the privacy, however cramped and uncomfortable, then we had only moments to spare between tasks, or before we had to be somewhere else, or before a Magus passed by, or a patrol, or someone came to rummage through the storeroom or cupboard for supplies. We never had the time to sate anything but the most basic and animalistic hungers—a hard and brief thrusting, desperate attempts to stifle every gasp, a sudden, insufficient release, and then we would go our separate ways, furtively rearranging wraps and promising ourselves that next time . . . next time . . .

And we were tense because Yaqob feared each time he entered me that this would be the time he'd father a child, and that was something he refused to do until we were free, until we could choose the direction of our own lives, until we'd escaped Threshold.

He groaned, then tensed, and I hid his face in my shoulder and murmured, "It's all right, Yaqob, it's all right."

He took a deep breath, shuddered, then relaxed and withdrew from me, sliding his hands along my body.

"Are you sure?" He pulled my wrap down, then quickly rearranged his own more tidily about his hips.

"I have no intention of going through what Raguel did." Omarni had told me what herbs she'd given me when I'd been in Hadone's slavery, and most of them were available here, too. Isphet had contacts among the water-carriers, and they plucked the leaves from the riverbanks for me. Thus far they appeared to be working, and if not . . . well, there were other means to rid my body quickly and cleanly of any child that did manage to take hold. I was as determined as Yaqob not to breed more slaves for the Magi.

He kissed my cheek quickly. "Perhaps tomorrow . . ."

"Perhaps." But I was not overly enthusiastic. I enjoyed these interludes with Yaqob only for the emotional closeness they brought. Physically, our brief, anxious lovemaking was generally uncomfortable, and always left me with my body aching and my nerves screaming with frustration. I envied Yaqob that he managed to find some degree of physical fulfillment in our time together.

"Shush!" He pressed his fingers against my lips, and listened intently. Steps sounded in the alley outside, then faded.

"Come on," he said, "Ta'uz will be wondering where we have got to."

We had been summoned back to the Infinity Chamber: I to make sure that the caged glass had been placed with the least possible stress; Yaqob to measure for more bridging panels of glass.

We could have taken our time, for Ta'uz, rather than waiting impatiently, was actually hurrying to catch us up.

He threw a furious glance at us as he passed, and we lowered our eyes, muttering "Excellency!" and then he was in front and we matched our steps to his impatient stride. We tried not to look at each other, for to do so would be to smile; it was rare indeed that any of the Magi let themselves be caught in anything other than indolent splendor.

But Ta'uz was obviously distracted, and as we neared Threshold he actually stopped, and stared up at the peak of the pyramid.

Although the capstone was a year or more away from being placed, workmen were at the very peak of the pyramid preparing the masonry. There were five men, all tied to safety ropes, all moving slowly but surely. I did not envy them their task.

Ta'uz was fixated by the sight, and now Yaqob and I did glance at each other, all urge to smile gone.

"Ah," Ta'uz muttered, and we tried to follow the line of his eyes.

"There," Yaqob mouthed at me, and pointed surreptitiously. Ta'uz was staring at a small pile of stones to one side of the workmen; they were using them to build a ledge on which the capstone would rest.

The sunlight was bright, and the distance great, but what happened next I saw in such clear detail it was as if I was but three paces distant from the peak. None of the five workmen were close to the pile of stones at that moment, all absorbed by some problem in the mortaring farther around the peak.

But somehow . . . somehow the topmost rock lazily lifted it-self from the pile, seemingly hovered as if indecisive—as if *choosing*—then hurtled toward the ground, impossibly fast, *too fast,* a blur, and embedded itself in the head of a slave walking out of Threshold's mouth.

It hit with such impact that it burst the man's face and skull in a shower of blood and brain, and still had enough force to cleave his neck apart and completely embed itself between his shoulder blades.

Threshold's shadow winked.

For an instant, the entire site stilled, then Ta'uz gave a great cry and ran to the prone figure at the top of the ramp. Yaqob and I were only a step behind him.

Ta'uz dropped to his knees beside the headless corpse—everything within two paces had been splattered with blood and brain—and reached out a trembling hand. He stopped himself just before he touched the man's shoulder, the top of the rock clearly visible amid his smashed vertebrae.

I took a step backward, sickened, but not before Ta'uz had raised his face to Threshold and whispered, "Why?"

NINE

Ta'uz recovered within moments of the death. He ordered the body's disposal, then, beckoning impatiently to Yaqob and myself, he proceeded inside to inspect the Infinity Chamber.

It was bad, far more so than usual. Normally the glass screamed within the chamber, but this day it was subdued. Terrified. Whatever had possessed Threshold had also shocked the glass into almost complete silence, and when Ta'uz demanded of me why tears ran down my cheeks, I said it was because of the slave who'd died outside.

"Foolish girl," he snapped. "Lives are for us or Threshold to dispose of as we will. Does the glass fit well enough?"

"It fits well enough, Excellency. The stresses are minimal and it sits full square."

"Good." He paused. "You share quarters with Raguel, do you not?"

"Yes, Excellency."

"Then tell her to be at my quarters by star-rise. And tell her to wash first."

"As you will, Excellency."

With that he grunted and turned to Yaqob, telling him to hurry with his measurements.

The incident laid a pall over the entire site. Too many people had witnessed the death of the slave for any to discount the story of his lazy, deliberate execution at the will of Threshold.

No one within our workshop had known the slave, but we heard of him quickly enough. He was a simple laborer by the name of Gaio, and he was not an Elemental. There was no reason why Threshold should have chosen to kill him, save the fact of his existence. It could have been any of us.

The body had been removed quickly, but somehow the stain of Gaio's blood remained on the stones surrounding Threshold's entranceway for weeks, despite the most strenuous attempts to wash it off. It wore away only with the passage of feet, and then only slowly, for most took great care to avoid it.

If the Magi were perturbed, they hid it well. They stalked the precincts of all three compounds, their faces masked, eyes vivid with power, and they gave away none of their inner thoughts or worries—if, indeed, they had any.

But Ta'uz *was* disturbed. There were moments when his doubts showed through. After a week or two, Yaqob and Isphet thought to question Raguel closely about her time with him, and she reported that he was distracted, sometimes so distracted he sent her away without using her.

"The night of Gaio's death he told me to lie on the bed, and I did so. But then he paced to and fro, to and fro, staring out the window at Threshold. He muttered to himself, but I could not catch his words. After some time he turned and jumped, as if startled to see me. He used me, nevertheless, although I think that night he achieved no communion with the One. Since then he has called me back five times, but used me only once."

She looked considerably relieved about that, and I did not blame her. Since we had farewelled her daughter into the Place Beyond, Raguel had recovered much of her spirit, and I had discovered her to be an amusing companion. I wondered if the only reason Ta'uz constantly sought her presence was to commune with the One.

"Will he talk, if you prod him?" Yaqob asked.

Raguel looked frightened. "You know how it is with the Magi, Yaqob. You never speak to them unless spoken to first, and then only if they ask you a direct question. I cannot think what he would do if I tried to initiate a conversation."

"Nevertheless," Yaqob pressed, and I gave him an irritated glance. Surely he could see how reluctant Raguel was? And how dangerous it would be for her?

"Nevertheless, if you *could* ease him into conversation about what worries him about Threshold, we might find out what is so wrong with it. And Ta'uz is the Master of the Site. The information you could glean from him could be invaluable—"

"Yaqob!" I said. "Have a thought for Raguel's safety—"

He leaned across and seized my wrist in tight, angry fingers. "Tirzah, I have the responsibility to see that whatever uprising I lead *succeeds*. I will waste no opportunity to do so. If Raguel has access to information about patrols, weapons, stores, then *I want to know about it!*"

"I will do my best," Raguel said quietly.

"Good," Yaqob replied, still looking at me, then let my wrist go. I rubbed it, glaring at him, then I shifted my eyes back to Raguel.

Her face was rigid with dread.

Five weeks later I was walking back to our quarters in the cool evening air, chatting with Raguel; Isphet, Saboa, and Kiath followed some steps behind muttering over a firing that had gone wrong that morning. Raguel was reasonably cheerful even though Ta'uz had required her presence the evening before and might well do so again tonight.

"I really don't know why he keeps asking me back. Sometimes I think he just likes to have company."

"Does he talk to you?"

"Only rarely. I enter, he asks me to sit on a stool by the bed as if he can't make up his mind what to do with me, then he either paces back and forth, or just stands at the window and stares at Threshold. If he does that then he always puts the lamps out first."

I shivered. If Ta'uz was frightened of Threshold . . . "And he doesn't . . ."

"Use me?" Raguel laughed. "Only occasionally. I thank the Soulenai that it *is* only occasionally."

I didn't quite know how to phrase this next question. "It isn't enjoyable?"

Raguel pulled a face. "The Magi are brief and painful and utterly humiliating, Tirzah. Ask Isphet. She endured almost five years of use." Her mood lightened and she pinched my arm playfully. "I wish I had your Yaqob."

I grinned wanly. "Why the baby, Raguel?" I'd never dared ask this before, but she'd never been so open before, either.

"Because I was young and stupid," she replied, her tone harsh, "and because—"

But whatever she was going to say was cut off by a distant shout from the river and then, stunningly, a clarion of trumpets.

We stopped, and Isphet caught us up.

"Trouble," she muttered. "Where's Yaqob?"

"He's still back in the workshop," I said, "cutting glass for tomorrow's plating. Isphet? What is it?"

"I'm not sure—" she began, then another clarion sounded, much louder this time.

"Quick," she said, grabbing Raguel and me by the elbows. "Back to our quarters. *Quick!*"

She gave us no chance for further questions, hurrying us down the street, then into the alley that led to our tenement. Once inside she thrust empty grain jars into Raguel's and my hands, and grabbed one herself. Kiath and Saboa she sent to the roof to see what they could.

"Come on," she said. "We've run out of grain. A visit to the grain store is needed."

"But we've got plenty of—" Raguel began, then stopped at the expression in Isphet's eyes.

"Hurry!" Isphet hissed.

We left the building and walked down the street at a pace that was almost a trot. As soon as we turned onto the street that led to the grain store I realized what she was doing. The store lay close to the compound of the Magi, and the street we were on intersected with the main street close to the compound's gates. There we might have a chance of seeing who had arrived.

And, with a clarion of trumpets announcing their arrival, it surely wasn't a new complement of slaves. Or Magi, for that matter. Since I'd been in Gesholme Magi had come and gone, but never with this much fuss.

As we approached the intersection, guards thrust us to our knees, their eyes nervous but their hands hard.

"Where are you going?"

With our foreheads pressed to the dirt, we couldn't see a thing, but we could feel the tramp of approaching feet. Rhythmic, marching, frightening.

"We go to collect grain, master!" Isphet mumbled.

"It's the wrong time of day to—"

Trumpets sounded again, so close they drowned out the guard's voice, and he spun about on his heel.

I heard the other guards turn to look too, and I dared lift my head a fraction.

A contingent of armored guards had marched up the street, then arranged themselves in ranks on either side. My eyes widened at the sight of them. They wore loincloths of shimmering gold and their chests and backs were armored in bronze burnished to a mirrored finish. Metal-studded leather was wrapped about their arms and legs, and scarlet and emerald plumes crested bronze helmets, and hung in tassels from their spears.

Although they had arranged themselves in ranks down the sides of the road, forming an honor guard, I could still see between the legs of the two directly in front of me. The gate to the compound of the Magi had been thrown open, and now

Ta'uz emerged, his robes and face composed and tranquil, but his fingers tapping where his hands folded in front of him.

"He's furious," Raguel mouthed.

Unexpected and unwanted then, I thought. But who?

I was answered almost immediately. Another clarion sounded, now so close and so piercing I screwed my eyes shut and stuck my fingers into my ears.

When I finally opened my eyes it was to see Ta'uz abasing himself in the dust before a thin man in his seventies.

I took a deep breath; never in my life had I imagined to see such riches. The man would have been unremarkable, I think, save for the accoutrements of power appended to him. Although he was elderly, he was still vital, with a plain face dominated by a curved beak of a nose and a thin mouth. His graying black hair was plaited into hundreds of tiny braids, all bound with gold wire and studded with rubies and diamonds. But his hair was not the only part of him adorned with jewels. His entire body dripped obscenely with gems and precious metals—the three of us could hear them whisper and simper about him. He had a gem-studded golden collar so thick and wide it held his chin at an unnatural angle, while his earlobes had been pulled out of shape with the weight of the jewels that hung from them. Of clothes he wore only the briefest of loincloths (and even that, I think, of woven silver and gold wires). The rest of his body was banded, pierced, studded, wrapped, threaded, and looped about with gold and silver and gems of every imaginable hue and size. I wondered if what the loincloth hid had been similarly studded and pierced and banded.

He was obviously not an Elemental, for had he been, the whispering and chattering of those metals and gems would have driven him mad.

"Mighty One," Ta'uz said, and raised himself to his knees.

"Chad-Nezzar?" I mouthed to Isphet, and she nodded slightly.

Chad-Nezzar waved a bright hand about in the air, the sun's rays setting its gems afire.

"Ta'uz. I have grown bored in Setkoth, and I have decided to see how goes the construction. My nephew"—again the hand waved, and a Magus stepped out from behind Chad-Nezzar—"tells me that construction has slowed."

What Ta'uz said next I do not know, for my entire attention, my entire *life,* was riveted on the man who had stepped out.

It was Boaz.

I hid my face so deep in the dirt that I *breathed* dirt. I did not look up again. There were politenesses spoken, and formalities passed, and eventually the road cleared as Chad-Nezzar and his retinue passed into the compound. I dared move only when I heard the gates slam behind them.

A booted foot landed squarely in my ribs.

"Oof!" I collapsed briefly into the dirt again before struggling to my knees.

"Forget your grain tonight," one of the guards barked. "Get back to your quarters and stay there until morning!"

We hastily complied. No one spoke until we were safely back and the door shut behind us.

"Well," Isphet said, "*he* hasn't been here for over eight years. I wonder what brings him back now?"

"Boaz?" I asked, muddled.

Isphet looked sharply at me. "Chad-Nezzar. Who is this Boaz?"

"The Magus who stepped out from behind the Chad. Isphet, I spoke to you of him. He was one of the Magi I worked the glass for in Setkoth."

"Oh. Why are you so afraid of him?"

"I am afraid of all Magi." But that wasn't enough, and after a pause I reluctantly went on. "He suspected me of Elemental power."

Isphet's eyes narrowed. "You worked that glass too well. You should have been more careful."

"I was trying to save my life," I snapped, "and I had no idea of elements or Soulenai or even of Magi at that point."

Kiath and Saboa joined us from the roof.

"Chad-Nezzar," Isphet informed them briefly. "What did you see?"

"Riverboats," Kiath said. "Some forty or fifty. Packed with armored men, perhaps five thousand. Chad-Nezzar has come well escorted. The imperial soldiers are spreading throughout Gesholme."

"Is he expecting trouble?" Isphet murmured. "Does he know? *Can* he know?"

My stomach churned. Had Chad-Nezzar somehow found out about our planned revolt? Had an alert guard noticed Yaqob and Yassar talking? Had someone found the cache of blades?

Whatever, there was nothing anyone could do with five thousand soldiers come to visit.

Yaqob must be furious, I thought, and wished *he* would come to visit.

But there was no way he could. Not with five thousand men spreading throughout the encampment. Even the roofs would not be safe.

No one slept well that night.

The workshop was both subdued and alive with speculation in the morning. Word about Chad-Nezzar's presence had spread throughout Gesholme as fast as his soldiers had; everyone had a theory about why he might be here.

With several workers within the shop not Elementals and not yet involved in the plans to revolt, none of us could openly discuss the fear that we'd been discovered.

Yaqob, his face strained with sleeplessness, snapped at everyone, including me. The first piece of glass he tried to score shattered under his hands, and he cursed and threw the pieces into a corner.

I winced, shared a look with Isphet, then hurried to my upper room to cage. At least Orteas and Zeldon would be calmer.

Calmer, but also tense. I went to the balcony and looked about. Chad-Nezzar's imperial soldiers were everywhere. Most were arrayed in workmanlike armor rather than the golden finery of the Chad's personal guard, but they were all armed heavily, and were fit and alert.

I went back inside and sat down. Yaqob had been relying heavily on the fact that the usual guards within Gesholme had become complacent after years of compliance and subservience on the part of the slaves.

Now . . .

I took a piece of glass in my hand and drew an outline of the design on it with a wax stick. I had to rub my lines out several times before I got them right, and Zeldon glared at me.

I noticed he had been sanding the same piece of glass so long that it threatened to break under his fingers.

There was a noise downstairs, and movement. Shouts, then the sound of a large group moving about. Isphet's voice, calm but submissive. Orteas, Zeldon, and I gave up all pretense at work and stared at each other.

Motioning us to keep still, Zeldon put his glass carefully down and moved to the head of the stairs, peered carefully down for some minutes, then came back to our table.

"Well?" Orteas demanded.

Zeldon looked at us carefully. "Chad-Nezzar. And a substantial escort."

"What!" I cried, and Zeldon grabbed my arm.

"Quiet!" he hissed.

"What are they doing here?" Orteas said.

"Isphet is showing the Chad how the furnaces work." Zeldon's mouth threatened to smile. "And if Chad-Nezzar gets any closer, his golden finery will melt right into his skin."

Orteas was not to be amused. "Will they come up here?"

He was answered by voices and steps on the stairs.

"Get back to work!" Zeldon whispered.

My hands were shaking. Would Boaz be with them?

Isphet arrived first, gracious in her sweat-stained work wraps, waving her hand for Chad-Nezzar to inspect the room. Terrified, I looked back at my glass, gripping it as tightly as I dared, trying to stop my hands from shaking.

Chad-Nezzar stopped by Zeldon and idly looked over his shoulder.

"Fine work," he said, his voice lazy and bored. Even those two words sounded a great effort.

"I thank you, Mighty One," said Zeldon.

Others moved into the room. I dared not look up.

"This is where the caging is done for the Infinity Chamber, Mighty One," Isphet said.

Chad-Nezzar was by the open door to the balcony now, looking out. I heard him turn around. "Only three do this work?"

"Caging is master craftwork, Mighty One," I heard Ta'uz respond. "We scour markets for those skilled in the arts. If, perhaps, funding were improved . . ."

"But the girl?" Chad-Nezzar was closer now.

"The girl is unusually skilled for one so young," a different voice said. One I remembered.

And remembered hatred seared through me.

A hand appeared over my shoulder and plucked the glass from my hand. A younger hand than that of Chad-Nezzar, and un-ringed.

The tools clattered from my fingers as Boaz lifted the glass over my shoulder and turned to his uncle now standing beside him. "See how well she works it."

I looked up and stared ahead. Directly into Isphet's level gaze. Have courage, her eyes pleaded, and I took a deep breath, fighting to relax my shoulders. Was Yaqob in the room?

Yes, there, to the rear of several guards and one or two other workmen. His eyes were smoldering, their anger and frustration only barely veiled. I hoped he could keep his evenness of temper. If he lost control now . . . I forced my gaze away from his face, and realized Chad-Nezzar had spoken to me.

"Why so skilled?"

"My father trained me from the age of five, Mighty One. I loved the glass . . ."

Isphet's eyes flared in alarm, and I hurriedly tried to cover myself.

"I, ah, loved working the glass. It gave me satisfaction. I practiced many hours when I could have been playing."

"Ah," Chad-Nezzar's voice appeared cheered. "It is as I suspected, Boaz. The lower castes like nothing better than to be given some work to do." His metals and gems chattered brightly, intrigued by the caged glass they could sense in the room. I wondered how *anyone* here could fail to hear the Elemental conversations going on about them.

"Threshold is as a gift to them, Uncle."

Slowly I turned my head. Boaz was standing to my side now.

He held the glass I'd been working on loosely in his hands, his fingers lazily stroking it. His gray eyes were relentless, forcing me to remember.

He was playing with me. Would he drop it, kill it?

The glass thought it would be killed. It teetered between screaming and silence, and I thought I, too, would scream, if it did.

But Boaz put the glass on the table and looked to his uncle. "The best place to see this in its full glory is the Infinity Chamber, Uncle. Besides, it is time we saw how well, or not, the work progresses."

To one side Ta'uz opened his mouth to speak, his face beet red, but the Chad forestalled him.

"Yes, of course. I grow weary with this workshop. Will the lovely Isphet accompany us? I feel sure I shall need some of the technical details explained."

Isphet managed to hide her revulsion well. "Mighty One," she acquiesced, bowing.

"And the girl, Uncle. Best to have one intimate with the caging to answer your queries in the Infinity Chamber."

"As you wish." Chad-Nezzar waved his hand again, somehow I rose to my feet—Isphet's hand on my elbow—and we proceeded to Threshold.

The nightmare eased a little once outside. Isphet and I were the only ones from the workshop to accompany the party— and by now she must have been as sure as I about Boaz's suspicions. We were relegated to the back to be watched over by a contingent of guards as the Chad, the Magi, and several of the royal golden honor guard marched ahead.

The fresh air cleared my head, and Isphet's hand calmed me. I glanced up at Threshold as we approached. The Chad's visit had, perhaps, speeded up the work, and workmen were crawling over the outer structure of the pyramid. Its southern and western faces, those we could see on our approach, now had sections of blue-green glass attached to them. Mainly near the peak, for it was easiest to glass from the top down. As we watched, gangs of men painstakingly hauled sheets of glass skyward. Each one of those sheets had taken hours to mix and fire, and then further hours of scoring and breaking into the correct shape. Every time I saw one hauled skyward my heart leaped into my mouth, hoping that the work and craft of hours would not shatter with a loose step or knot in the rope.

There were still several piles of stones near the peak, awaiting the day when the capstone would be settled into place, and I looked away quickly, remembering the terrible death of the slave Gaio. None had died since then.

As we approached the ramp Ta'uz sent us to the top to wait with several of the guards as he, Chad-Nezzar, and Boaz wandered about the perimeter of Threshold. They craned their heads skyward as Ta'uz talked and occasionally gestured, and I found myself hoping that Threshold would decide one of them would make a more worthy sacrifice than a mere slave.

I glanced up again, wondering if one of the stones was lifting lazily from its pile to plummet earthward, then back at the Chad and the two Magi.

"No dog bites the hand that feeds it," Isphet remarked casually, understanding the direction of my eyes, and I nodded. Threshold would not take such as these. Only the expendable.

I wondered if I was expendable, and wished I was standing anywhere else than on the ramp.

Chad and Magi wandered back after some time, the Chad looking hot in his metaled finery, and tugging irritably at a heavy jewel-encrusted golden chain that ran from his left nipple to a ring in his belly. I wondered if he could unclip his chains, or if he had to sleep wrapped in them.

A guard rushed to offer goblets of water to all three, and they drank thirstily.

I prayed they were too discomposed to go farther, but after several minutes the Chad's irritation eased and his curiosity sparked anew.

"Infinity Chamber," Boaz said, then led the way.

Ta'uz, I noticed, was openly upset about something.

Glass now covered the walls and ceiling of the passageway; the floor had been left to last—until the Infinity Chamber had been completed. The glass was composed of a peculiar blending of metals, so that no one color could be assigned to it. As the eye roved and light shifted, so colors swirled and changed.

It should have been beautiful, and it should have spoken to Isphet and me—the Soulenai adored such ripples of color— but the glass was silent. Dead. Nothing lived in it.

In its own way that was as disturbing as the screams I knew I would hear in the Infinity Chamber.

We reached the chamber without incident. Isphet and I moved to stand in an unobtrusive corner as Boaz and Chad-Nezzar inspected the walls. Well over a third of the interior was now covered with the golden caged glass, a full wall and part of another, and Boaz, in particular, spent what I thought was an inordinate amount of time examining the symbols and writing in detail.

Finally he nodded slightly and stood back.

"It is good work," he said to Ta'uz. "Exact."

Ta'uz inclined his head slightly. "Of course. I have been careful."

"But not in any hurry," Boaz said. "This chamber should be almost completed by now."

Ta'uz took an angry breath. I think both Magi had forgotten there was anyone else in the chamber. "It has been your task to obtain the workers, Boaz. I need ten or twelve glassworkers who can cage. What we have done with three is extraordinary."

"We are behind schedule!" Boaz said. "And security is incredibly lax! What have you been thinking of?"

Isphet dared a glance at me, then, as one, we looked at Chad-Nezzar. He was watching the two Magi, a half smile playing about his lips.

"I have been doing my best," Ta'uz replied quietly but with the utmost dignity, "not strolling about arranging the gardens of Setkoth."

"I think," Chad-Nezzar interrupted before the tension got any worse, "that I would like to have this glass and this chamber explained to me. Ta'uz?"

"Mighty One. As you can see, eventually the entire chamber will be encased in caged glass, even the floor."

"It is very well done," and Chad-Nezzar turned and held out a hand for me. "Girl. It looks very delicate, how does it stay up there?"

Reluctantly I took his hand, concentrating on the murmuring of his jewelry rather than the despair of the glass, and explained as best I could. "And the panels are held in place by cunning hooks and bolts, Mighty One. I do not think even an earthquake would dislodge them."

Boaz's mouth twitched, but there was no humor there.

Chad-Nezzar saw and let my hand go; I quickly stepped back to join Isphet. "Boaz, I believe this glass is of your design?"

Boaz bowed. "Assuredly, Mighty One. I spent years perfecting the formula for the glass."

I felt Isphet stir in surprise. She was responsible for the mixing and firing of this golden glass, but she did it to a formula supplied by the Magi. *Boaz* was responsible for it? Surely it would have needed a master craftsman to produce the correct mixtures?

But no, apparently the glass was a product of a mind steeped in the power of the One.

"I had glassworkers supply me with the quantities of metals they used for glass," he continued, noting Isphet's surprise, "and mathematically refined them to produce this mixture. Perhaps, Uncle, a small demonstration."

"I hardly think—" Ta'uz began with a warning glance in our direction.

"No harm can come of it, Ta'uz," Boaz said, and stepped to the glass. "They will hardly understand. Now, tell me, the shafts running behind this wall are completed and glassed?"

Ta'uz nodded stiffly.

"And the gates in place?"

Again Ta'uz nodded.

"Well then," Boaz said, and he slowly ran his hand over a portion of the glass, and pressed.

I frowned—what was he doing? I had seen that portion of glass put in place myself and there was nothing behind it but solid stone. I . . .

The glass that Boaz was touching screamed with such horror that I physically rocked. Isphet, as badly affected as I, nevertheless retained her self-control, and her fingers pinched the soft flesh of my upper arm.

It was enough and I rebuilt my composure, although I felt sure Boaz had seen my reaction.

What's wrong? What's wrong? What's wrong? I heard the Soulenai cry through Chad-Nezzar's jewelry and metaled bands, trying to reach the glass.

What's wrong? What's wrong? What's wrong?

Light flooded behind the wall, and I realized Boaz had somehow activated a mechanism that controlled the gates that, in turn, controlled the amount and direction of light through the shafts running to the outer skin of Threshold.

But what was so appalling was not that light flooded behind and thus lit the glass, it was *how* the light lit the glass that made everyone in the room cry out, whether in excitement or horror.

Somehow, Boaz had developed a formula for the glass that, while the inner wall shone a deep gold, the caged lacework transmitted light as a vivid crimson.

Instantly, all the inscriptions, the symbols, the words, and the numbers that formed the lacework flared into life. They *seethed* across the wall as if alive, bloodlike, seeking, and they throbbed with the power of the One.

I had a sudden, too-vivid image of what this chamber would look like when it was completed and fully lit—blood-ied inscriptions crawling about the walls and floor with viru-lent life, the entire chamber throbbing with the power of the One that was called into being.

The chamber would not only *appear* alive, it would *be* alive!

What's wrong? What's wrong? What's wrong? the Soulenai cried and their voices rang about the chamber as the writing on the wall rippled and waved and the glass screamed, and I threw my hand across my eyes and stumbled out.

Isphet joined me immediately, and held me tight. I buried my face in her shoulder and sobbed.

"Sorcery," she said softly.

"Yes," I heard Boaz say behind her. "Sorcery. The power of the One." His voice was amused. "Which you and she have manufactured between you. Be glad."

TEN

Chad-Nezzar stayed a further three days, at which point he declared that he was utterly bored and pined for the pleasures of his court at Setkoth. At noon the next day, he embarked in a flurry of trumpets and regal waves of his hand. Leaving behind five hundred of his men—and Boaz.

Ta'uz and Yaqob, for different reasons, were equally furious. Whatever rift there was among the Magi, Ta'uz and Boaz represented different sides of it, perhaps even led the different sides. To have the two of them on site made life intolerable for everyone. Ta'uz remained Master of Site, nominally the senior Magus in a caste where there was, apparently, little in the way of ranking, but daily Boaz's presence undermined his authority.

We learned much from the careless gossip of guards that was overheard and spread about by slaves. Boaz was not only a forceful and powerful Magus, he was also favored nephew of Chad-Nezzar and younger brother of the heir to the throne, Prince Zabrze. Despite what many Magi may have wished, Chad-Nezzar still remained in ultimate control of the realm and Zabrze in ultimate control of the armed forces. Neither Magi nor guards wanted to alienate Boaz or, through him, Chad-Nezzar and Zabrze, and all sensed the shift in authority on site.

Yaqob was furious because he could see all of his carefully laid plans crumbling about him.

"We must move . . . *soon!*" he said, and stared about the room, daring any to contradict him.

Yaqob could no longer come across the rooftops at night—one of Boaz's first actions had been to instigate irregular but frequent patrols—so now, dangerously, we were grouped in the upper room of Isphet's workshop. Orteas, Zeldon, and me, simply because this was our work space and we refused to be dislodged; Yaqob, Isphet, Raguel, Yassar, two or three men from other workshops, and a big, brawny fellow called Ishkur, one of the prime gang leaders among the laborers.

"If we wait any longer then I am afraid this . . . this *Boaz*"—and the word was a curse the way Yaqob mouthed it—"will seize complete control from Ta'uz."

"The man would be an effective Master of the Site," Ishkur remarked.

"That's exactly what I'm afraid of," Yaqob said. "Ta'uz . . . well, Ta'uz is worse than the slime the river frogs feed on, but at least he is predictable and does not concern himself overmuch with security. *Damn! Everything* we've planned has been based on the presumption that Ta'uz would continue as Master of the Site. Raguel? What news?"

"Not much, Yaqob. Since Boaz has been here I have hardly been called to Ta'uz's quarters. When I do go, he is distracted, but not only by Boaz. He also worries about Threshold. I think . . ."

"Yes?" Yaqob asked impatiently as Raguel drifted into silence.

"I think that is partly the reason Boaz has stayed. He is concerned about progress, but he is also concerned about Ta'uz."

"Why do you say that, Raguel?" Isphet and I had told of the extraordinary scene within the Infinity Chamber, but any extra information Yaqob could get from Raguel might prove the key to understanding, and then destroying, Boaz.

"It was two nights ago. Ta'uz had finished with me, and I was standing behind the bed, dressing, when Boaz entered the apartment. There was only one lamp burning, I was deep in shade, and Boaz did not immediately see me. Ta'uz was furious at Boaz's entry; the Magus had not knocked, nor even wasted any time on polite pleasantries."

Raguel shivered as she remembered. "How they avoided striking each other I do not know, for the hatred lies deep between them. They began by arguing over some administrative detail that Boaz thought had been overlooked—I think Boaz had come straight from questioning one of the clerks. Then Ta'uz threw a pile of papyri to the floor, completely enraged, and shouted that administrative details were the last thing on his mind when Threshold . . . He stopped suddenly, and Boaz asked him what he meant. Ta'uz told him of the death of the slave, and then stood and looked at Boaz.

"Boaz was silent for some time, then said that the death of a slave was an inconsequential thing on a work site of this size. Ta'uz stared at him, saying that both of them knew better."

"What did he mean by that?" Isphet asked.

Raguel spread her hands helplessly. "I do not know, I'm sorry. By this time I had crept as far back into the shadows as I could. I was terrified that if Boaz saw me . . . even Ta'uz had forgotten me . . . and I thought . . ."

She shook herself and continued. "Boaz tried to change the

subject, intimating that Ta'uz was frightened of shadows, but then Ta'uz said, 'The next time it will be three, Boaz, and then five, seven, eleven. We both know what those numbers mean.' He said"—and Raguel's voice broke a little here—"he said that Threshold had fed. And, that having once fed, would have to continue to feed.

"Boaz was shocked into silence, but then opened his mouth as if to say something. Ta'uz stopped him, and said that Threshold should never have been built. He said that the formula was too dangerous and far too unpredictable. Then . . . then I think a breeze came in through the open window and shifted the drapery about the bed, and the next thing I knew Boaz was staring at me, then shouting for me to leave."

"And Ta'uz?" Isphet asked.

"Ta'uz hadn't even looked at me. He was staring out the window at Threshold. He said, as I fled the room, 'By the One, it's seen us!' "

There was silence for a while.

"We move, and soon," Yaqob eventually said.

Ishkur looked up from his hands; they were spadelike, and deeply callused. "We are not ready."

Yaqob took a deep breath, not liking to be contradicted. "We have thousands willing now. What if Boaz seizes control and asks his uncle to send a few more of his gilded spear holders? We have a chance at overwhelming the guards and soldiers here now, but *not* if any more reinforcements arrive."

"Weapons?" Isphet asked. "Without them . . ."

"Several of the metalworking shops have been making and secreting blades for months. But we need more—especially with the imperial soldiers that Chad-Nezzar left here. With luck we will be able to steal some from the guards—we know where they have several of their weapon caches."

"But if we steal from them, they'll know a revolt is planned," I said, worried for Yaqob.

He touched my cheek. "Don't worry. We won't go near the caches until we plan to move. Ishkur?"

"If we have men grouped near the caches when we give the signal for the uprising," Ishkur said, "then they can break in and seize the weapons before the guards realize what's happening. Then we might have a chance. *Might*."

It sounded like a chance that rested on hope more than surety. Might, might, might.

"Ishkur, we rely on the laborers for most of our fighters," Isphet said. "You command their loyalty and respect. *Will* they fight?"

"Yes," he said. "Yes. They trust me where they might not trust Yaqob."

Yaqob stirred, and Ishkur hurried on. "Yaqob, you live here as one of the elite glassworkers. You rarely have occasion to move among the laborers. But they will listen to me. Trust me."

"I understand, Ishkur," Yaqob said. "Look, I know that I've been pushing for an uprising, and I realize that some of you here feel it may be premature. We had thought to prepare for several more months yet. But"—he looked about the room—"we do have an alternative to launching a premature uprising before Boaz convinces the Chad or his brother to move more imperial soldiers here."

"Yes?" several people said at once.

"We can kill Boaz," Yaqob said.

Everyone stared at him, and my lips parted in a slow smile. Kill Boaz. Yes. There was nothing I would like more. My smile widened for Yaqob, and he saw it and grinned back.

"Boaz has disturbed all our plans. If he's gone, then we are left with Ta'uz. Nasty, but predictable, and a known quantity. And we have Raguel, who has some contact with him and, as we've all heard, can provide interesting information. Information"—he paused—"that will mean we can kill Boaz without fear of reprisal."

"What do you mean?" I asked.

"I think we should arrange for an accident on site," he said. "We know that Ta'uz, at least, is expecting one. Three will die, he thinks. Well, let's give him an accident. Boaz and two of the other Magi—not Ta'uz. Ta'uz will suspect Threshold, not us. Well?"

Ishkur's eyes gleamed, and I could see that he also liked the idea. "What do you have in mind, Yaqob?"

"Ishkur, is it your men who work atop Threshold, preparing the peak for the capstone?"

Ishkur nodded.

Yaqob's face and eyes were very cold. "I hear some of the glass up there is very unstable, Ishkur. It could cause a dreadful accident were it to fall."

ELEVEN

Boaz was unpredictable in many ways, but he never forwent his early afternoon stroll about Threshold. He would walk its perimeter once, then move to the ramp where he talked to various of the Magi supervising the site. Then he would just stand, looking, completely still, his eyes focused on Gesholme and then farther to the Lhyl River and the reed banks.

No one knew what he looked for, and no one cared. It was enough that we had this one moment of predictability, and it would be enough to kill him. He even stood in the same spot, day after day, the spot where Gaio had died, and that would be enough to ensure a neat, clean kill.

Which was more than he deserved.

I wondered if he would scream, as had screamed the glass he'd deliberately dropped. Well, today, glass would wreak its revenge.

We were all there. Yaqob, Isphet, and myself pretending concern about a delicate pane that was being transported into Threshold and that required our undivided attention lest the laborers trip and break it. Ishkur, standing to one side of the ramp, directing his gang of laborers. Raguel, taking some tools—unfortunately left behind—to glassworkers inside Threshold. Others, scattered about, pretending interests and problems where there was only one interest and only one problem.

Boaz.

He arrived as expected, Ta'uz with him today, and the

Magi hurried the inspection about the perimeter of Threshold. Neither wanted to spend too long in the other's company. Then Ta'uz stalked away, leaving Boaz to mount the ramp.

Boaz did not waste much time in conversation with the two Magi awaiting him, and within minutes had turned to stand motionless, gazing back across Gesholme toward the river. He was so focused on whatever it was he saw that I doubt he noticed anyone about him.

The two Magi stood slightly to one side of Boaz, discussing some calculation.

"Good," whispered Yaqob. "Three of them. Perfect."

I glanced about us. Guards were dotted through the crowd of laborers scurrying here and there around Threshold's skirts, but they saw nothing out of the normal. Ta'uz was still here, but deep in conversation with one of the captains of the guard, perhaps trying to find out whether the man was loyal to him or to Boaz.

Well, in a minute or two the captain wouldn't have a choice.

I frowned. Raguel was close by Ta'uz, and I wondered what she was doing there. Had he called her over?

Yaqob caught Ishkur's eye, and the man nodded slightly.

Then he dropped the hammer he was holding and bent down to pick it up.

It was the signal the men atop Threshold had been waiting for. I tensed, and felt Isphet do the same by my side. Yaqob muttered under his breath, his shoulders tight.

None of us dared look upward . . . until . . . until . . .

"The glass!" a guard screamed. "Excellencies, *the glass!*"

Our heads whipped skyward, relief that it was finally done rushing through our bodies.

"By the Soulenai," Isphet whispered, "let it fall true."

A great plate of blue-green glass, carefully chosen for its position, had been dislodged. The southern face, above the ramp where Boaz still stood utterly motionless, was protected from the wind, and the plate should fall straight and true.

Spearlike.

And so it did.

Slowly at first, twinkling cheerfully in the blazing sun, it slid free of its moorings, then picked up speed as it rushed down the center of the southern face. Its passage made a peculiar whistling noise, and I wondered that Boaz did not look up, or move, even though the two Magi with him had ducked for cover inside Threshold's mouth and several guards were rushing up the ramp to push Boaz to one side.

But the glass did its killing long before they reached Boaz. Some twenty paces above the ramp, as the plate glass was whistling down so fast it was only a blur, it screamed.

Every Elemental within two hundred paces heard that scream, for it tore through our souls, ripping and shredding. I cried out, as did Isphet and Yaqob, but our cries were lost among the screams of the crowd as the glass . . .

. . . as the glass jerked, then twisted and flipped, as if flicked by a gigantic hand. It somersaulted through the air, hit the lintel above Threshold's mouth . . .

Boaz smiled. I saw it, and I could not believe it.

. . . and broke into two murderous spears. One swept over Boaz, the wind of its passing ruffling his robes, and struck Ishkur directly on the top of his head, spearing down through his body. It clove him in two. The glass bisected his entire body, and the two sorry halves fell limply, bloodily, to either side of the now silent splinter protruding from the ground.

I had my eyes on Boaz and then Ishkur, and for a heartbeat I did not realize what had happened to the other spear of glass. I turned my head just in time to see the jagged piece impale both Ta'uz and Raguel.

She had been standing close to him, so close that she shared his fate—or perhaps Threshold had always meant them to die in that manner. Die together.

Utter, utter silence.

Then . . .

"Take those three slaves," Boaz said calmly to the captain Ta'uz had been talking to, "and kill them."

I thought he meant Yaqob, Isphet, and me, and my stomach curdled so violently I was sure I would vomit, but then I saw Boaz wave vaguely at Ishkur's three men at Threshold's peak.

The captain of the guard, his loyalties decided, hurried to do the Magus's bidding.

"Three," Yaqob said emotionlessly beside me. "Three. Dead. Threshold has fed. As Ta'uz said it would."

Isphet grabbed our arms. "Out of here, *now!* Before he sees us!"

I was unable to move, but Yaqob responded quickly to Isphet's urging and helped pull me down a side alley. Shocked and bewildered, we stumbled back to the workshop. As we waited for the others to return Yaqob held me tight, and tried to comfort me, but no comfort would help after what we'd witnessed.

It was that day we all realized just how malevolent Threshold truly was.

Boaz took over as Master of the Site quickly, efficiently, completely. Ta'uz was buried with the honors accorded to any Magus, but Raguel's and Ishkur's bodies were thrown to the great water lizards that lurked in the Lhyl.

I believe the three slaves taken from the peak were thrown in the water alive once the lizards had started their feeding frenzy on the corpses.

Ta'uz was dead. Ishkur was dead. Raguel was dead. Two of them mourned, one regretted.

And Yaqob's plans for a revolt lay as shattered across the dust of Gesholme as that glass had shattered three lives.

He needed the weight of numbers that the laborers would bring him, yet they had trusted only Ishkur completely. It would take Yaqob months, if months he had, to find someone of comparable standing and trustworthiness who could persuade the laborers to his side.

Raguel. Raguel had been loved by many of us, and had been badly treated by the Magi for years. To lose her like this . . . *and* her body. Isphet had raged for hours that night, striding about our apartment, tearing gouges in the mud walls with her nails, screaming her grief. Raguel could not be farewelled into the Place Beyond without the remains of a body. She and her daughter would be denied each other for eternity.

But Raguel had also been a source of information and, regrettably, Yaqob mourned her death for the loss it caused his plans.

In the end, ironically the greatest loss was Ta'uz. Now

Boaz had free rein, and within only hours we felt the touch of his power.

That night every tenement building in Gesholme was searched.

The guards came just as I had managed to get Isphet onto a sleeping pallet, my arms about her, rocking her, crooning wordlessly to her. I was appalled at the extent of her grief, yet my soft crooning was meant as much to comfort me as it was Isphet.

There was a pounding at the door. Saboa went to open it, but was thrown back as the door was kicked in. Five men shouldered their way past her, a mixture of imperial soldiers and old guards—but old guards with new resolve strengthening their eyes and hands.

They tore the room apart, breaking many of the urns, tearing others from the ground, ripping our sleeping pallets, tipping oil from lamps, thumping the walls to sound out hiding places. They searched us too, their hands rough and humiliating, then shoved us aside as thoughtlessly as they had the urns and lamps.

I sent a silent prayer of thanks to the Soulenai that at least we no longer had Raguel's baby stored in one of the floor-cooled urns; I wondered numbly what Boaz would have made of that had they thrown it triumphantly before him.

They were searching for weapons, and for other evidence of the plot to escape. The plot . . . I had no doubt that Boaz had somehow managed to scry out its existence; that he somehow knew a plot *must* exist.

Cold fear gripped me. Yaqob! But surely he would have the sense not to keep anything in his quarters that might incriminate him. Surely.

In the morning when we crept to work we saw guards posted on rooftops.

People nodded to each other as they arrived at the workshop, but few spoke. I looked frantically until I saw Yaqob's form in a darkened corner, lifting glass down from a rack. Unheedful of the eyes, I rushed across and wrapped my arms about him.

"Are you all right?"

"Yes." He managed to put the glass to one side. "And you?"

I nodded, unable to speak, and buried my face in his chest.

I felt his hands through my hair, and then one hand caught my chin and tipped my head back.

"They found the blades that we'd managed to make," he said, his voice dead. "And they're dismantling the guards' weapon caches, storing the weapons elsewhere. We've lost."

I buried my face in his chest again, fiercely glad that he was safe and that if his plans for an uprising were in tatters, then at least that meant he would continue to be safe for a while longer.

"We've lost," he said again. "For the moment." Then he put me to one side and went back to work.

Our lives continued to be disrupted by irregular patrols, unpredictable searches. Sometimes a guard was posted in the workshop, sometimes not. But if a guard was not there, then we never knew when one would be back.

Magi appeared in greater numbers, and a week after Ta'uz's death riverboats deposited another two thousand soldiers with which Boaz could work his will.

Yaqob's face grew lined and his manner abrupt, even with me. Life became even grayer in this the most dismal of places, and the shadow of Threshold stretched ever longer.

Sometimes it winked.

TWELVE

Three weeks after the disastrous attempt to assassinate Boaz, he came to visit.

I was in the main work area that morning, sitting with my father as he selected sifted metal powders for a mixing he would do in the afternoon.

Everyone, in fact, was in the workshop, no one at Threshold, no one out collecting supplies or helping in another workshop.

Boaz must have known this. How? There was no obvious guard or watch kept. How?

I was chatting to my father. He looked tired and drawn—all of us were, but Druse more than others—and I regretted that most of the time I'd spent with Yaqob had been stolen from time I would otherwise have spent with Druse. He was my father, and he loved me and had raised me. I did not want him to think I avoided him because I blamed him.

But Druse smiled, and said that he liked and respected Yaqob, and that he did not mind.

That day I loved my father very much.

There was a darkening in the doorway and, mildly curious, I looked up.

Boaz.

He looked no different from any other Magus, but there was something so infinitely dangerous, so cruel about him that I'm sure he would have intimidated a collection of Magi, let alone us.

Everyone stilled.

Some guards followed him, but Boaz waved them back into the street, and stepped down onto the workshop floor alone.

"Yes?" Isphet asked.

I envied her that single word. I remembered she had greeted Ta'uz thus, too, the night he had delivered me to her door.

Now she was just as cool and calm as she had been that night, even though here she had far more secrets to hide, and many more lives to protect. She stood in the very center of the workshop, her head slightly tilted back, her eyes challenging, questioning.

About us the glass chattered in an undertone, and the jars of metals hummed quietly in their racks.

I felt like screaming at them to shut up.

Boaz walked straight past Isphet, not acknowledging her presence. He walked to the furnaces, considered them a long moment, then strolled casually about the workshop. Every so often he would flick the hem of his blue robe to one side to avoid a patch of oil or a drift of dust.

"It seems fortuitous that I arrived here when I did," he said without preamble. "Threshold is of vital importance to Ashdod, to *all* its people, and yet when I arrived I found a site wallowing in inexactitude, its measurements imprecise, its practices unpredictable."

He stopped by Yassar's worktable, trailing a finger through some of the containers of glass that had been ground down for enamels.

"Such pretty colors," he remarked, then lifted his head and stared at Isphet.

"What do you want?" she asked, and now there was a brittleness to her that had not been there before.

"Respect, Isphet, is very important," Boaz said mildly, and Isphet suddenly whimpered with pain and doubled over, clutching at her belly.

To one side Yaqob shifted indecisively.

"What can I do for you, *Excellency*?" Isphet ground out, and then relaxed, slowly straightening up. But her eyes were frightened, as were mine, and every other pair I could see save Boaz's.

"I have come to restore order, predictability, preciseness."

"Nothing here is predictable anymore," Yaqob said, and stepped into the light. "Since you have taken over as Master of the Site, all is chaos. Excellency."

Boaz looked Yaqob up and down, measuring his potential for trouble. "You are but a glassworker, uneducated in the ways of the mind. I shall forgive your interruption."

Oh, Yaqob, I prayed, and screwed my eyes shut for a heartbeat, keep your temper!

"You do not know that in apparent randomness there is pattern and predictability," Boaz continued. "That in chaos there is law rigidly applied. You cannot see it, thus for you it does not exist. Now"—he dismissed Yaqob and turned away—"I have heard certain rumors during my time here. Rumors I first laughed at, but which now have come to irritate me."

He walked farther around the shop, inspecting some of the racks of glass. "That is why I am here. I wish to lay these rumors, if rumors they be, to rest."

He turned back to stare at us all, his eyes searching out each of ours, all bantering and lightness gone from his manner. I trembled as his gaze passed over me, hesitated, then passed on.

"Some say that there are those on this site who still practice the Elemental arts. I would call this silliness, except that, perhaps, it is true. I had thought that we had managed to educate the lower castes away from their Elemental foolishness generations ago. And yet . . ."

He moved closer to me. I tensed, but he casually perched on the edge of the table at which my father and I sat, his back to us.

"I remember," he said very softly into the complete silence, "that glassworkers were ever more susceptible to the lure of the Elemental arts than others. I remember hearing that they lost themselves in the swirling colors of the molten glass, and opened themselves to the evil voices of spirits that should have been long dead and forgotten. I remember hearing how some glassworkers claimed they could hear glass speak, and spoke back to it. Silliness, of course."

The glass continued to chat to and fro about us, and I was glad that Boaz could no longer see my face.

"But I will have *none* of this on my site!" His voice now cut into each and every one of us. "*None!* If I find anyone, *anyone,* practicing Elemental magic, I will have them killed as they stand. *Do you understand me?*"

"We understand, Excellency!" we muttered, almost as one.

"See that you do," Boaz said, then stood up. He walked across to the outer door and I dared let out my breath in relief.

"Oh," Boaz said as he reached the door. He turned about. "Tirzah, stand up, if you please."

My heart thudded so painfully I thought it would tear itself from my breast.

"Stand up!"

I stood.

"Tirzah. You will come to my quarters tonight. A guard will escort you from your tenement building. See that you wash first."

And he turned to go.

"No," I said.

I couldn't believe I'd said that.

"Did you understand me?" His voice was very soft, his face completely expressionless as he faced me again.

"I do not want to—"

I screamed, wrapped in such pain that I could not believe I could live through it.

There was a noise to one side—later I would find out it was Zeldon wrapping his arms about Yaqob to prevent him attacking Boaz.

"Do you understand me?"

"Yes!" I sobbed. *"Yes! I understand you!"*

The pain vanished, and I slumped into my father's arms.

I knew that night would be the worst of my life.

THIRTEEN

Yaqob seized me in his arms and carried me up the stairs. "Isphet, Zeldon, Orteas, Yassar. Upstairs."

I sat in his lap and sobbed, not caring what I'd just promised Boaz. "I can't go! Yaqob, I *won't!*"

"Shush, love, shush. I—"

"I *can't* go!"

I felt Isphet beside us on the bench, and her hand on my hair. "Tirzah—"

And suddenly I knew what they were all going to say. *"NO!"*

"Listen to me." Yaqob's voice was very firm. "*Listen* to me, Tirzah! This will be the best chance we'll ever have of getting inside that man's head. Tirzah, you *must* go. Don't you ever want to escape from here? Don't you ever want to be free?"

I couldn't say anything.

"Tirzah, you will give us the key to this man. Damn it, we *need* this chance."

"But I am afraid. I know he suspects me of being an Elemental. What if this is a trap? What—"

"Then you must be careful, Tirzah. Say nothing to him. He

won't expect conversation. Endure, listen, watch. We need your eyes and your ears close to that man."

"Yaqob!" I leaned back and stared at him with a tear-stained face. "Don't you *care*? Is your plot worth more to you than me?"

He took my face between his hands and I could see that yes, indeed, he did care, and he cared very much. "I will kill him for what he will do to you, Tirzah," he said softly. "Believe that."

And I believed it.

Isphet pushed the men from the room and talked to me for a very long time. She told me what to expect, and she gave me the courage to endure it. Later that evening I walked home with her, Kiath and Saboa silent behind us. I had been unable to look Yaqob in the eye as I said good-bye to him.

Hadone kept springing into my thoughts. He had also used me, but had tried to be thoughtful and not to hurt me too much. From what I had seen of Boaz and from what Isphet had told me, I could not expect the same from him.

Well, I had endured Hadone, I *would* endure Boaz. And perhaps I *would* learn the key to our freedom from a careless word.

That evening I pushed away the food Kiath offered me, then went outside to wash. When I returned a guard was waiting inside, a bundle of white cloth in his hands.

"For you. His Excellency does not want to receive you in your dirty wrap."

Isphet took it from him, then pulled me outside to change. It was a beautiful garment, a sheath dress made of pleated white linen hanging from a wide circular collar of blue beads that draped over my shoulders. It fitted perfectly, clinging to waist and hips, and hanging to the calves of my legs. A beautiful garment, but a whore's dress. And blue and white, the color of the Magus.

Thus marked, I would have to walk through the streets of Gesholme to his compound.

Isphet combed out my hair, leaving it loose about my shoulders. Then she gave me a quick kiss on the cheek. "Go," she said. "I'll wait for you."

I nodded, unable to speak, and followed the guard out the door.

The streets were almost deserted. Few walked out after dusk now, save those with good reason. There were some patrols, several pairs of curious eyes watching from high windows to mark my passing, and the evening chorus of frogs from the river reeds, but little else.

The guard did not speak. He walked slightly behind me, wary, expecting me to try to escape.

But I had no heart for that now. There was nowhere to run.

Finally, the compound of the Magi.

"Halt," the guard said, and he spoke briefly with the detail standing watch at the gate. In Ta'uz's time that had only been two. Now there were at least six heavily armed men to decide who passed in and out.

The guard—those at the gate had called him Kiamet—led me through the compound. I had not been in here since the night of my arrival, and I had forgotten how sweet and cool was the air, fragrant with flowers, how soft were the lights. I saw the carefully arranged gardens, but at night shadows hid most of their artfulness.

A few Magi passed me, but I averted my head and I do not know if they smiled, or lusted, or just did not care.

Kiamet led me past where I'd expected to go, the residence Ta'uz had used as Master of the Site. I'd remembered it from my own visit, and Raguel had described it to me often enough. Surprised, I lifted my head and paid more attention. Perhaps I could glean something of use.

He took me to a smaller, far less pretentious house than Ta'uz's; one that was almost hidden underneath the wall of the compound. It was long and low, widely verandahed, and plastered in a delicate cream traced with lemon. Soft lights swung from verandah posts, showing pink and blue flowering bushes bordering the tiled walkways.

It looked very beautiful and utterly gracious.

"There," Kiamet said, and he pointed to an open door. Light shone beyond. Then he took up his post under the verandah, no doubt to wait until I'd been used and dismissed.

I think I was beyond all feeling by this time. I hesitated, then walked through the door, blinking in the light.

The room was the width of the house, and ran deep into it. On either side, wide windows ran from ceiling to floor, all open. The room was spacious, not only because of its size, but because of the minimal amount of furniture in it. Several chairs, a small table, shelves for papyri books and rolls running the length of one wall, a desk, and two cabinets standing against the opposite wall from where I entered. On one of the cabinets stood a pitcher and a wide bowl, flanked by some cloths.

And there a bed, wide and accommodating.

I turned my eyes.

Boaz sat at the desk, watching me. Papyri rolls and sheets lay scattered before him. In one hand he held a reed stylus, sharpened at one end; his fingers were stained with ink. He was dressed in a loose-fitting white robe, and I realized he had but removed his outer garment of blue.

A lamp was burning at his elbow, and its light threw his face into shadows. He put down the stylus.

"You are here. Good."

He pointed to a chair pulled to one side of the desk. "Sit down."

I sat, wiping my hands nervously on my dress, then clenched my fists, worried I had marked the fine material.

"I must explain some things first. Do you understand?"

"Yes, Excellency." Just use me, and let me leave, I pleaded silently, but apparently he had to have his say.

"I will call you back, be assured of that."

"Yes, Excellency."

"Whenever you arrive, you will bring that bowl and pitcher, and wash my hands and feet. Do you understand?"

"Yes, Excellency."

"Good. Do it."

I did as he asked, fetching the bowl and the pitcher of water, and kneeling back by his side. I was grateful the pitcher did not shake in my hand as I poured out a measure of water, or that my hands did not tremble as I lifted the cloth.

He had nice hands, the hands of a craftsman, square-palmed and long-fingered, and paler-skinned than many of his race. They were very warm.

I dried them, then turned my attention to his feet.

As I folded the cloth he handed me a vial of oil, and I massaged the oil into his hands and feet. It was very fragrant, redolent with the tastes and sounds of a forest, and it caused me to remember the northern lands of my home. I was grateful when I had done and could stopper the vial and hand it back.

I returned the pitcher and bowl to their place, then, at his indication, sat down again.

"You will not speak unless I ask it of you."

"I understand, Excellency."

"You will not ask questions."

"No, Excellency."

He paused, and glanced at my ankles. "Why are your ankles so scarred?"

"I was chained in a whaler for six weeks, Excellency. My ankles festered and scarred."

"Well, they are distasteful. You will do your utmost to keep them from my sight while you are with me."

"Yes, Excellency." I crossed them and tucked my feet underneath my chair. It was the best I could do.

"In fact, you will do your utmost to look pleasing for me, Tirzah. You will ask Isphet how to apply kohl to your eyes."

"Yes, Excellency."

"You will do whatever I ask of you. Whatever. Whenever. However loathsome."

I took a breath. "Yes, Excellency."

"Good. Tirzah"—he leaned forward—"you will tell *no one* of what goes on in this room. Do you understand?"

"Yes, Excellency."

"If you *do* tell anyone," he said, very quietly now, "I will know and I will exact retribution. Not only you, but every person you tell shall be fed alive and bleeding to the great water lizards. Do you understand me?"

The power of the One rippled across his face, and I could see my death in his eyes. My voice trembled as I replied. "I understand you, Excellency."

He stared at me, then relaxed. "Good. Now, why are you here?"

"To provide satisfaction, Excellency."

"Good, very good. In what way?"

I could not help it; I blushed. "You wish to use me, Excellency."

He was silent, a finger tapping upon the desk. "Yes, but not in the way you think. I have no time for the type of weakness Ta'uz displayed."

My eyes widened.

"I *am* one with the One, Tirzah," he said. "I do not need to 'use' a woman to achieve that end. One will always be better than two; and two is but a sorry coupling seeking to imitate the perfection of the One. Ta'uz, as all Magi who seek to achieve union with the One through use of a woman, was a fool. No. I am going to teach you to write."

Now my shock was complete. I remembered what Yaqob had told me about the sorceries that would bind me if I learned how to write and I shook my head from side to side, very slowly, responding without thinking. "No!"

I'd angered him again. *"Yes!"*

"Yes, Excellency!" I'd learned my lesson well that morning.

"Why are you afraid?"

Yaqob's angry face swam before me—he would prefer that Boaz bed me than teach me to write. "I . . . I'm needed to cage, Excellency. It takes so much time. To learn to write as well . . ."

"You will continue to work in Isphet's workshop, but you will come here three evenings a week. Four, if I request it. Do you understand?"

"Yes, Excellency."

"Why else are you afraid?"

I hesitated, thinking past Yaqob's hatred of writing to the blood inscriptions writhing across the Infinity Chamber. "Writing is sorcery, Excellency. You pair characters and symbols with numbers, and so produce calculations and sorceries with your words."

He raised an eyebrow at my knowledge. "Do you think I am about to pass across my sorceries for your edification, girl? For you to take back to your friends in the glass workshop?"

"I—"

His mouth curled in contempt. "I will give you nothing that you can use to destroy me, Tirzah. Is *that* understood?"

I hung my head. "Yes, Excellency."

"You have a question, Tirzah. Speak it."

"Why teach me to write, Excellency?"

"You are young and quick-witted—your ability to grasp Ashdod's native tongue is proof enough of that—and I have need of quick wits about me. As importantly, you probably know at least two of the northern tongues, and the common trading language. Am I right?"

"Yes, Excellency." I hesitated. "I speak my native Vilander, as well as the neighboring tongue of Geshardian. Less well, but competently, I speak Alaric and Befardi. And, as you said, the common trading tongue."

"Then you *will* do well," he said. "Now listen to me." His tone hardened, and hate thinned his mouth. "You will tell your lover, Yaqob, that I teach you the arts of the whore, not the scholar. Do you understand?"

He knew about Yaqob? I looked stunned, and he leaned back in his chair, satisfied. "I know it all, Tirzah. In the end it will be safer for you to lie to Yaqob, because he will never believe the truth. And will *he* trust *you,* once he knows you can write? He will think, 'She betrayed me the moment she first picked up the stylus.'"

He reached out a hand and seized one of mine. I tensed, but did not resist as he pulled my hand across the desk. He slowly opened my fingers, one by one.

I squeezed my eyes shut, and a tear rolled out.

"Open your eyes, Tirzah."

I forced them open.

"Take the stylus from the desk."

I hesitated, and his fingers tightened about my wrist. "Did you understand me, Tirzah?"

My fingers shaking even through his grip, I took the stylus.

"Good."

I loathed him and I abhorred what he tried to teach me. I loathed that he'd so deliberately forced me to betray Yaqob. And my fear was even greater than my loathing because he'd known *exactly* how to make me betray my lover. Why hadn't I fought him? Kicked and screamed? But here I sat, struggling to grip the stylus in the way he wanted, struggling to understand what he told me, and the repulsion writhed and kicked about my belly.

The Magus kept me until the dawn light filtered through the windows. He taught me how to draw the basic characters of numbers and of words, and he made me draw them again and again until I had them approaching the precision he demanded.

I grew frustrated and increasingly angry, both emotions sharpened by weariness and self-disgust, but I dared show neither. So I bit my lip and did my best, and tried to understand the concepts he showed me.

It was easier for me than it might have been for Isphet or Yaqob. I was used to drawing on the glass, and to sketching the designs the Magi sent to the workshop. I discovered I had a familiarity with the figures, and that frightened me, and deepened my already raging resentment and hatred for this man.

I wondered what he really wanted from me. It was not only to learn to write, of that I was sure. There was no reason to teach *me* to write and to figure, for the Magi had clerks and scribes a-plenty. I tried to find some clue in his manner or words, but found nothing save coldness and impatience.

Possibly he was just one who found pleasure in forcing a woman against her will.

Finally he snatched the stylus from my hand in frustration at a particularly misformed character I had made, and scrawled a word—scrawled, but his characters were flawless.

"What does it say?" he demanded.

I looked at the word. "It is my name. Tirzah."

His mouth curled, the movement insulting, and I dropped my eyes. "And do you wonder, Tirzah," he said very softly, "what sorceries your written name hides?"

He stared at me, then put the stylus to one side and stoppered the vial of ink.

"I will remind you this once," he said, "that if you tell any of what occurs while you are with me then I will know. I do not think I need remind you of the consequences." He paused. "You may go."

"I thank you, Excellency."

His eyes sharpened at my tone, and he searched my face carefully for any sign of mockery, but I kept my expression bland, and he waved me away.

Kiamet, still standing as straight and tall as the verandah post, escorted me back to the tenement house, where Isphet flung wide the door with anxious eyes.

"Tirzah!"

She closed the door in the guard's face. "Well?"

"I have survived, Isphet." But she was not satisfied.

"You have been gone so long."

"He made me sit a long time, Isphet." I ached to tell her that he had not touched me, that he had not wanted to bed me, but then she would have demanded to know *why* he wanted me there. How could I explain that I had broken my vow to Yaqob, that I had possibly created Magi sorceries with my stylus? And I was afraid that if I did tell her all this, then Boaz would know, and we would all die. It was safer if I kept my silence, and surely no harm would come of it. "He . . . I . . ."

"It's all right, Tirzah, you do not have to go into details. I have endured it myself." She pulled the gown from my shoulders, and folded it neatly away. "At least he has not bruised you. Now, clothe yourself in your wrap. Good. Sit down here and drink this as fast as you can. We shall have to go to the workshop soon."

I sat, relieved that I had not actually lied to Isphet, and took the steaming herbal from her. I drank the bitter brew, not yet realizing that to take the herbal and drink it was as blatant a lie as having spoken an untruth.

"Do you have any kohl sticks, Isphet?"

At the workshop Yaqob smiled at me awkwardly, and turned away. I stood, unsure what to say, wondering at the images that must be filling his mind. Yet better those than the truth. I did not have the chance to speak to him, for Isphet hurried me up the stairs, told Zeldon and Orteas only that I had not been allowed to sleep, and laid me down on a pile of sacking.

"We'll keep watch," she said, and the two men nodded. "Sleep. There's no point in trying to cage in your state."

I let myself drift gratefully into oblivion, soothed by the whisper of the glass about me.

Zeldon shook me anxiously awake about midmorning. "Tirzah! Boaz is downstairs. Wake up!"

I struggled to my feet, rubbing the sleep out of my eyes, although the surge of fright at Zeldon's words woke me completely.

"Quick! He has asked for you."

I pulled my wrap into order, blinked rapidly to try to look as if I'd been awake, then walked down into the main workshop.

The Magus was inspecting the glass plates that Yaqob had been scoring and breaking ready to be placed on the western face of Threshold. He had pulled out a measuring tape, and was engaged in careful measurement.

Yaqob stood to one side, his face expressionless—but his eyes flickered uncertainly as I walked up to them.

Boaz eventually straightened. "Yes. Good. They will do, Yaqob. Ah, Tirzah."

He walked over to me, hesitated, then trailed his fingers down my face, my neck, then yanked my wrap aside to cup my breast in his hand.

"Ah, yes," he said very softly, and lifted his eyes to my face. "How soon short hours make one forget. You pleased me well, Tirzah, and I achieved good union with the One through your body. You will return tonight."

His fingers brushed over my breast one last time, his eyes unreadable, then he pulled the wrap across my nakedness and turned aside, walking out of the workshop without another word.

Every face in the shop, including Yaqob's, was averted from me.

I had never been so utterly humiliated in all my life. My face flamed, but it was as much with anger and hate as it was with shame.

I knew why Boaz had done it. Yaqob would never believe me now if I told him that Boaz had not bedded me, or had shown no sign of wanting to bed me. Boaz's actions just then had been those of a man intimately acquainted with a woman's body.

I remembered how we had regarded Raguel, how we had pitied her, called her "Poor Raguel" behind her back, and my eyes filled with tears as I turned away.

FOURTEEN

As demanded, I went back that night. I washed and clothed myself in the white dress, used the kohl Isphet gave me to emphasize my eyes, then walked alone to the gates of the Magi's compound. The guards let me in without a word.

I hesitated outside the open doorway, then walked through. "Excellency?"

"Good. You are here."

He sat back from his desk, and I fetched the water and washed his hands and feet, drying them, then rubbing in the fragrant oil. When I had finished, he indicated the chair at the side of the desk, waited until I had picked up the stylus, then resumed his lessons.

He made me redraw and explain all he had taught me the previous night. I struggled to remember. I had spent some seven hours at this desk last night, and much of what I now recalled for the Magus was vague and imprecise.

When my stylus slipped in my nervous fingers he shouted, and I cringed, half expecting him to strike me. But he only watched me, his eyes very careful, then asked me to draw some further figures that he had only touched on briefly before.

These, at least, satisfied him. "Good. You have not disappointed me."

I blinked in amazement—and some very faint gratitude that I should have pleased him. I loathed the characters, truly I did, but I was craft-trained, and I took a professional pride in doing my best at whatever task I was set.

"Tonight," Boaz continued, "I will instruct you in the art of constructing simple words with the characters you have already learned. See, here is your name again—do you understand how it is constructed?"

I glanced at him, and was surprised to see that his face held no scorn or animosity.

"Yes," I hastened to reply as I saw a flicker of irritation at my hesitation. "I understand, Excellency."

"Then draw it yourself."

I did, and he seemed satisfied. "Now, my name. What characters would you use to construct that?"

I frowned. "Excellency?" It was a long word, and I was not sure of some of the characters.

He laughed. "Boaz!"

I almost dropped the stylus in my utter astonishment, not only at the laughter—unforced and easy—but that Boaz should be *able* to laugh. Then, completely forgetting my loathing of the man and his manipulations, my own mouth twitched. Excellency, indeed!

I drew the characters, and he nodded, his amusement fading. He took me through several other words, then had me lay down the stylus.

"Tirzah. You must not fear what I have just taught you. Yes, I can use words as sorceries, as numbers and symbols, to work my will, but I do not intend to teach you to do so. Nor will I make you write unwitting sorceries. That is not why I have asked you here. Do not fear the stylus so much."

I relaxed still further, a dangerous thing to do, and smiled. "Thank you, Boaz."

The change was instantaneous.

"You will call me Excellency!" he hissed. "If you dare presume again—"

"No, Excellency!" I stumbled, falling from the chair to the floor and my knees. "Forgive me!"

He turned back to his desk. "Very well. You may go. You are too tired to learn any more tonight."

"Thank you, Excellency," and I fled.

Isphet welcomed me home gladly, and gave me the herbal to drink. I lay awake for hours, trying to make sense of what had happened. He had smiled and laughed at my foolish incomprehension, and we had then sat in comfortable companionship as he taught me my first words. During that time I had not been frightened, angry, or even resentful. Then . . .

I stared at the darkened ceiling. I understood what I had done wrong. I had presumed. I had stepped over that danger-edged invisible line of what was acceptable and what was not.

I drifted into sleep, and that night the chorus of the frogs in the reed banks rang loud through my dreams.

The next day I managed some time with Yaqob; I think the whole workshop had conspired to give us this chance. We found ourselves alone in the upper workroom as the workshop slowed down for the night.

"Tirzah." He hesitated, then saw the expression on my face, and held me close. Poor Tirzah, I thought, wondering if he pitied me more than loved me.

"Tirzah, I must ask . . . about you and Boaz . . ."

Yes, I thought, yes he does. He cares.

". . . if you think you will be able to glean anything from Boaz or his quarters . . . Raguel was so useful, and if you could find us *something* that will enable us to understand him, understand how to destroy him and escape from this place . . ."

I walked a few steps away. "I don't know, Yaqob. His rooms are so bare, so barren . . ."

Yaqob seized me by the shoulders and turned me about. "He doesn't say anything about weapons, or patrols?"

He saw the look on my face, and dropped his hands.

"It's not why he requires my services, Yaqob."

"I'm sorry." Now it was Yaqob who walked away. He sat down on a bench, then looked up at me. "Tirzah, despite Boaz's presence I believe we will have a chance at a successful uprising—"

"But the extra soldiers. And no patrol works to routine anymore, Yaqob!"

"Listen to me, Tirzah! I think I have found another man who will serve as well as, if not better than, Ishkur—a gang leader called Azam. He is ruthless, and determined, and he hates all Magi as much as we. The stonemasons have pledged me their support, as have the carpenters and water-carriers. Soon I will have Gesholme united behind me. Boaz will falter. He must. He will make a mistake, or become complacent."

I shook my head. I did not think Boaz would make a mistake, and the word "complacent" did not equate with the sense of danger that hung about him.

"By the Soulenai, Tirzah! You *know* that Threshold will be the death of us all, eventually. Don't you *want* to escape? Don't you *want* our children to be born free?"

I burst into tears, and he held me tight again, stroking my hair, kissing my forehead. "Tirzah, we rely on you. You can deliver us Boaz. Make sure that you do it."

A week passed, and then two. Boaz required my presence every second night, and on several occasions we worked almost until dawn.

He pushed me to learn as fast as I could, and I found it easier with each succeeding night. Soon I could write to his dictation, and that pleased him, save when occasionally I misformed the characters, or did not get their edges as straight and as clean as he desired them. He gave me small pieces, scraps, to read, and I tried to make my voice smooth and pleasing, for he snapped whenever I stumbled over a word.

I was still very wary, but I chose to trust that he would not give me sorceries to form or to read, and I bent my entire will to learning the art of writing. In their own way, letters and characters were fascinating, and I enjoyed the challenge of learning some of their mysteries. Besides, here was a skill I could surely use to help Yaqob; perhaps one day Boaz *would* be careless enough to leave patrol rosters about, or perhaps a list of the location of weapon caches.

And perhaps not. Boaz gave me only meaningless passages to decipher. Sometimes he played with me, handing me items regarding Gesholme and Threshold to read. My eyes would brighten, skimming ahead over the text, trying to see how useful this might prove, then I would realize that he had given me nothing but absurdities, and I would look up to meet his cold eyes.

"Do you spy for Yaqob?" he asked one night.

"Excellency, what do you mean?"

"Does Yaqob question you about what happens between us?"

At least that I could answer directly. "No, Excellency. He assumes he knows . . . and he does not want to know the details."

"Slaves own nothing," he said, "not even their own lives. Yaqob should not expect to have any claim to your love or your body."

I bowed my head and did not respond, but I was angry. Love was a gift freely given, not demanded or owned. My body might not be mine anymore, but I reserved the right to bestow love as I wanted.

He didn't laugh again in my presence. What I had seen so briefly on my second night in his room had been a momentary aberration.

"Tirzah, Orteas has work he must finish here. Will you assist me in the Infinity Chamber?"

I laid down the piece of glass I'd been caging. Zeldon and Orteas tried to shield me from the Infinity Chamber as often as they could, but they felt the horror as much as I, and it was not fair to them that they shoulder this burden.

We walked quickly along the streets to Threshold. Almost the entire southern face had been glassed now, and it shone in the sun. The glass completely covered the mouths of the shafts as they led inward, but sometimes . . . sometimes in the evenings when the sun did not shine so directly I thought I saw flashes of light across the blue-green southern face, as if there was a fire within that sent light surging upward through the shafts.

The interior of Threshold was cool, but I was not grateful for the escape from the heat. Every time I came in here the feeling increased that somehow Threshold was alive. Its shadow stretched darker day by day, and its mouth seemed to yawn wider every time I approached it.

When would it need to feed again? Five. Ta'uz had said it would be five, and I wondered at the significance of the numbers. How could he have predicted the three?

I followed Zeldon up the passageway. Colors swirled, but the glass did not speak.

"Zeldon, do you feel anything from these walls?" I whispered.

"No. There is nothing. The glass on these walls was mixed and crafted in Ymelde's workshop, and she tells me that she put nothing into its crafting that could have killed it."

"It is Threshold, then," I said, and wished I hadn't spoken. Even if there were no guards or Magi about, Threshold itself could hear. How much did it know about my involvement in the plot to kill Boaz, or Yaqob's part, or Zeldon's? Had we been spared *only* because Threshold was somehow restricted to three that day?

"Yes," Zeldon said, "it is Threshold."

And, because we neared the Infinity Chamber, we fell silent.

Several workers were waiting with the portions of glass to be attached, and a Magus, Kofte, was standing with a dreamy expression on his face as he ran tender hands over the golden walls. He straightened as soon as he saw us, and his face assumed its normal arrogance.

"To work!" he snapped.

It was painstaking work, and Zeldon and I focused as closely as we could on the task at hand, for that way we dulled the despair of the glass already nailed to the wall.

Concentration helped, but even that wavered when, with each succeeding panel we helped attach, the panel added its horror to that of the rest of the glass. The instant a panel was laid against the stone that would hold it, its whispering screamed into fright, and then into . . . into something else. Something else that continually fed the glass's despair and kept it at fever pitch. I knew that some of these panels had been here over a year, and yet their screams were as barbed as the first day, their anguish even worse.

I wished I could understand, wished I could help the Soulenai understand.

I straightened, easing my back, as the last panel was fastened in place, and looked about. Kofte was still here, but he was ignoring us, turning his attention again to the walls. My eyes trailed over the inscriptions, and then stopped. Caught. I had reached a passage I could read.

I held my breath, stunned. I had never thought that I might be able to *read* this dreadful writing! Read, but I could not understand all of it. Although I could form the words in my mind, and could have mouthed them had I wanted to, I could not understand the meaning of the majority of them. They were foreign. Hard. Incomprehensible. But there were one or two words . . . a phrase . . . some that I *did* know.

I dropped my eyes, relieved that I had not been able to comprehend most of what I had read. What would have happened had I spoken them aloud? Would sorceries have sprung into action? Would Infinity have reached out to seize me?

I jumped as Zeldon dropped his hand on my shoulder. "We're finished, Tirzah," and we turned as one to bow for Kofte as he dismissed us.

The next day I approached Isphet. I needed to talk to someone about what was happening—but not her. This saddened me more than my inability to talk to Yaqob. Since my arrival, Isphet had become a good friend, a friend *she* thought I would be able to turn to with any problem. Over the past two weeks she had pressed me to talk of how I felt about Boaz, about his use of me, but to do that would deepen and complicate the lies already thriving between us.

"Talk to me," she would say, stroking the hair from my forehead. "It will help."

I would turn my head away so she could not see the deceit in my eyes. "I cannot, Isphet. I'm sorry."

And so I would take her herbal brews and drink them uselessly down, for Yaqob had lost all desire for me while he thought I bedded with Boaz.

Initially I did not talk to Isphet because I feared what Boaz might do when he found out. Now I could not talk to her because I feared the suspicion that would flower in Isphet's face when she realized what *was* going on.

Boaz had been more than cunning. I was increasingly isolated from my friends and my lover, trapped in a web of lies he had forced me to construct. There was no one I could safely talk to. Except . . .

"Isphet, I would like to touch the Soulenai, and let them touch me. But I want to be alone when I touch them. Will you aid me in this?"

Since my induction into the Elemental arts, Isphet had allowed me to touch the Soulenai on a number of occasions. Each time she and several others had been with me, and I had reveled and grown in the experience. But now I needed to do this on my own.

"Why alone, Tirzah? What is it you want to say to them that cannot be said in front of myself, or any other Elemental who joins the rite?"

"I . . . I . . ."

"What is it you have to hide, Tirzah? I do not like secrets in my workshop!"

"I am confused, Isphet, and I am afraid, and I do not like it that others should hear of my intimate problems when I speak of them to the Soulenai. Isphet, please!"

She could read the truth in what I said, but she was still hurt. "You can always come to me, Tirzah. I have been through what you have."

"Isphet, please. Just this once. It will give me peace."

In the end, she chose to trust me, and for that, I thought, I would always love her.

Behind one of the furnaces was a small, almost totally enclosed alcove, but there was space enough for me and a bowl of glass. No one would know what I did there, and Isphet took care that none saw our preparations.

She was a master of the Elemental arts, and I marveled at her skill. Not just in the preparation of the molten glass, but at her ability to carry a bowl that weighed almost as much as she did and contained the heat of the sun within it.

Yet not a trickle of sweat ran down her brow as she laid the bowl before me, nor were her hands so much as reddened when she withdrew them from the glowing metal sides.

"Undo your hair," she said curtly, still displeased with me, and I hastened to comply. Then she placed several pots beside me that contained the powdered metals I would need.

"Do not be too long, for I know not what will happen if a guard or a Magus appears. And"—she hesitated, and her voice softened—"be careful."

Then she was gone.

I had learned well from Isphet, and I knew what to do. I stared for a very long time into the glass, knowing now that the reason it stayed molten was because I *needed* it molten, then I passed my hand over in a great arc.

The glass swirled, and I felt myself drawn into its motion.

My hand passed over again, and blue flared within the glass, then red, gold, and green as I added successive powders.

The colors sang, soft and sweet, and I let myself be seduced into their embrace.

"My friends," I whispered, hardly aware of my voice, and I saw into the Place Beyond.

Tirzah.

I wept, for it was all I could do for the moment, and the presence of the Soulenai enveloped me.

Tirzah! What's wrong?

At least that I could answer, and I told them all that had happened since our plan to kill Boaz had gone so disastrously wrong. It was a relief just to talk, to tell, and when I had finished I found my tears had dried and I felt calm and refreshed.

You tried to murder Boaz? That was rash. It would be dangerous for you to try again.

That was no casual remark. It was as close to an order as I had ever heard the Soulenai mouth.

Tirzah, we do not think it is such a bad thing that this Boaz has called you to his side.

But I cannot see the good in—

Sometimes it is not always easy to see the reason or the goodness within the reason, Tirzah. Persevere. Wait to see what he reveals of himself.

Reveals of himself?

Wait. Tirzah. Wait.

He means to use me. I do not like it. I think he wishes me to betray myself and my friends.

They did not comment on that.

If he speaks of himself, Tirzah, then listen. And you say he teaches you to write. How unusual. For what purpose, Tirzah?

I cannot tell. But—

But?

But perhaps this art of writing will help us understand why the glass screams within the Infinity Chamber—and perhaps even help us understand what it is that so infects Threshold.

Tell us!

I paused to collect my thoughts and gather my courage. I would have to speak those words I had seen within the chamber. Briefly I told the Soulenai of my experience.

They were wary, as I had expected them to be. But they were also so desperate to understand what was wrong with the glass they eventually asked me to mouth some of the words . . . *but be careful, Tirzah, for we do not want you or us ensorcelled.*

Yes, I know. I saw the word "Infinity" in two places, but I was not surprised to see that there.

No. What else?

I saw the word "bridge."

Bridge? Bridge to what?

Infinity, I suppose. Isphet has said she supposes that Threshold is being constructed as a means for the Magi to step into Infinity.

There was a long pause. *What else, Tirzah?*

A phrase. There was one entire phrase I could read and which made sense. All the rest was gibberish.

Yes? A phrase?

It used the word "bridge" again. It read ". . . *from the Vale across the bridge to . . .*" There was no more, for the panel ended there.

The Soulenai shrieked, and I reeled back in my tiny alcove and struck my head against the brick. My head swam, and I managed to retain contact with the Soulenai and the Place Beyond only with the utmost effort.

What have I said? What have I done?

Not you, sweet Tirzah, not you! Oh! What have they done? What can we do?

What is it?

Oh, Tirzah, we fear very much that the Magi have unleashed something that not even they will be able to control. The Vale . . . the Vale . . .

What is the Vale?

It is a place of darkness and despair, Tirzah. We will not go near it, nor do we wish to talk of it. No wonder the glass screams. Does the Infinity Chamber touch the Vale? Does it?

I do not understand . . .

But they were gone, and I blinked and looked about, and noticed that the glass had cooled and the colors had mottled, so I bound my hair, and stepped back into the workshop.

FIFTEEN

Tonight," he said, "we will do something slightly more difficult. You can form characters well enough, and have read the trifling pieces I have handed you. Now, something more challenging, I think."

We sat by one of the tall windows. It was open, letting the night fall inside. Beyond the verandah was an octagonal pond, thick with lilies and flowers, and the cool breeze wafted in a gentle fragrance that mingled with the scent of the oil on Boaz's feet and hands. It was very quiet, and I found it hard to believe that we were wrapped about by a community of thousands of slaves.

Boaz rose from his chair and moved across to one of the cabinets. He was dressed only in a loose wrap of vivid blue cloth, knotted about his hips and falling in soft folds to his ankles. He wore no jewelry, no metal. I had never seen him dressed so casually before, and it disturbed me. This Magus did nothing on impulse.

He retrieved a small scroll bound with flax thread and brought it over to me, then sat back down opposite, leaning back in his chair. The only light came from a lamp on the wall behind him and the brilliance of the moonlight that fell through the window, and his face lay in shadow.

"Read."

I fumbled the flax knot, then rolled out the scroll with uncertain fingers, for he had never let me handle anything this fine before. The papyrus was delicate yet strong, and characters had been inscribed upon it in bold strokes.

I recognized the writing. It was Boaz's, but without quite the beauty I had seen him write before me.

"I wrote that when I was nine," he said. "Read it."

My eyes skimmed the words. At first I thought it was nonsense, then I realized it made horrifying sense.

I cleared my throat and read, praying my voice would remain steady and not irritate him with a stumble.

One, three, nine, eighty-one. A form in itself. Three lines of three, nine lines of nine, the square of beauty, breed into more beauty. Life is numbered from conception to death, rising from and declining into the One. There is beauty in numbers. This beauty is called Regularity, and its essence is Predictability. Everything else is unworthy. Eighty-one, nine, three, One. Life is numbered, all elements of life can be reduced to numbers, life is nothing but the predictability of numbers. There is nothing but numbers. Nothing. Nothing but the One.

I stopped. I could go no further. Tears filled my eyes.

"I was nine when I wrote that. The age of beauty I think, for nine is a special number in itself. An age when a child comes into realization."

His voice was distant, remembering. "Tell me what you think of it, Tirzah."

I answered truthfully. "I find it sad, Excellency."

"How so?"

I hesitated.

"Speak, do not fear me."

"I find it sad, Excellency," I said slowly, "that a boy so young should find life so sterile."

I waited for the outburst, but it did not come. Instead he leaned across the space between us and lifted the scroll from my hands. He ran his eyes over the first passage, then rolled it up and put it on the floor beside him.

"I do not understand," he said, and I wondered if he was jesting at my expense. But whatever his face could have told me was hidden in shadow. "I do not understand why you should find these words sterile. Are not numbers beauteous? Does not their contemplation provide one with the answers of life?"

"Excellency, I found it sad that a boy of only nine years could have written that. A child of that age should be out discovering the wonders of life, playing with his fellows."

"And were you out playing with *your* fellows at that age?"

I was silent.

"No. You were not. You were inside discovering the beauties of glass, while I was inside studying the numbers and their forms. You caged, I calculated. Which of us is right, Tirzah? Who has seen the most beauty?"

He was moving the conversation into dangerous territory, and I tried to deflect him. "Excellency, how is it that you can use numbers, cold formulas, to explain the myriad wonders of life, to explain life itself?"

The question was a risk, but I had kept my voice respectful and slightly puzzled, and he accepted it.

"Numbers are the building blocks of life, Tirzah. All is ruled by numbers, and all are generated from the One and decay back to the One. Let me demonstrate."

He stood up and took my hand, forcing me to my feet. I tensed, but he only led me out the door.

Kiamet faded away from his post, giving us privacy.

Boaz kept my hand in his. "See this potted vine?"

I nodded. At our feet was a large terracotta pot with a fat-stemmed vine in it. The vine's stem grew up a verandah post, leaves branching off it, until it disappeared into the darkness beyond the light.

"See." His voice was very soft in my ear, and I could feel the warmth of his body. "There is a leaf at the base of the stem. Yes?"

I nodded.

"And then the stem twists once, and another leaf. Then it twists twice, and there is another leaf. Then three times, and yet another leaf. Then five twists, before a leaf, then eight, then thirteen, then . . . well, I could go on. But the progression is one, one, two, three, five, eight, thirteen, twenty-one, and so on. Predictable. Do you understand the predictability in that progression?"

"Yes," I said slowly. "The next number is obtained by adding the previous two numbers."

"Yes, very good. Now."

He pulled me over to a bush growing just beyond. He leaned down and broke off a small branch. "Look, here is where it branches out from the main stem, then it divides twice, then three times, then five . . ."

"But I thought it was one, one . . ."

He smiled. "The main stem is the first one, then this broken stem the second one, then it launches into the twin divide."

He threw the branch away. "There are other progressions in nature. You will find that many plants divide one, two, four, eight, sixteen, and so forth. Is it not wonderful? Life *is* dictated by numbers. There are examples everywhere."

He paused, and studied my face in the moonlight. "Ah, but I see you yet resist. *We* are composed of nothing but numbers and our forms are dictated by mathematical and geometrical formulas—not by the whim of gods or fate."

"I cannot believe you, Excellency."

"Then I shall prove it to you." He lifted one of my arms, and slowly ran his fingers from the base of my neck over the beaded collar of the dress, then down my arm to the tip of my middle finger. His touch was very soft.

"From the base of your neck to the tip of your longest finger, your arm is *exactly* half your height. As are your legs. Exactly. But, Tirzah, as measured from the tip of your beautiful head to the soles of your feet, where does your body divide exactly in half?"

I was silent.

Boaz's hand slid to my waist, firm and very warm. He pulled me gently against him, and my eyes widened.

"Not there, Tirzah." His hand slid slowly down over my belly, rucking up the material of my linen dress slightly. I shivered. "Whether a man or a woman, their body divides into two at the organs of sexual pleasure and generation."

I thought he would move his hand down yet farther, but although the pressure of it increased, he kept it still. I could not look away from his face.

He laughed softly. "Appropriate, is it not? At that point where a body is precisely halved, so two bodies join to form one and, eventually, one body will divide to create two lives. No wonder, perhaps, that some Magi seek a woman to find perfect union with the One."

He lifted his hand from my belly to my breasts. "And the body is halved again, quartered, at the breast. Do you want me to go on? There are still further fractions we might explore."

I couldn't speak. I was terrified that whatever I said, however I moved, would only encourage him further . . . and yet . . . He was so very close, his hands so very sure, and the scent of the oil I had rubbed into his flesh was so very strong. I could feel his heart beating through the wall of his chest. I wondered if this night he would finally bed me, and I wondered that I felt no revulsion at the thought.

A hand shifted to my hair.

"You have such beautiful hair, Tirzah. It is like trapped sunlight. I am so glad that you leave it loose when you come to me." He took a strand of hair and pressed it to his mouth, and I could feel his breath on my cheek. I closed my eyes and let myself relax. It would be bearable.

He kissed my forehead very gently, then my ear, then trailed his mouth down my neck. "Do you wear it loose like this when you go to the Soulenai?"

And, by the Soulenai, I was so demented by that stage I almost said yes.

But some instinct made me hesitate even as I was mouthing the word . . . and my eyes flew open, horrified, and I very gently disengaged myself from his arms. "What do you mean, Excellency?"

"You do not know what I mean by Soulenai?"

"No." My breast was heaving, but I hoped he'd put that down to frustrated desire rather than fear.

"Just as well, my sweet"—and his eyes and voice were frigid—"for I would have killed you had you answered 'yes.'"

Oh, by all the gods and Soulenai and damned numbers and cursed fractions in existence, I hated him at that moment! He had so very nearly trapped me, using my own weakness to do it. And with that "yes," not only would I have killed myself, but probably all those I loved in the workshop as well.

He watched me steadily, then waved me back inside the room. "Sit down, Tirzah."

I sat down, finally regaining my composure.

He sat also, and his face retreated into the shadows. "I am fully aware that someone tried to kill me that day Ta'uz died. But I am in perfect union with the One, and Threshold protected me. Tirzah, who planned my death?"

"Excellency, I have no idea. It was an accident, surely?"

"Was it perchance those Elementals who practice their arts within Gesholme?"

"Excellency!" I pleaded, and my voice broke on the word. He knew my guilt, I was sure of it. All he had ever wanted to do was use me to trap the others in the workshop. *Dung lizard!*

"Tirzah, listen to my warning." His voice slid cold and sharp from the shadows. "I know full well that more than those who died planned my death. If I find one piece of evidence that indicts anyone, *anyone,* then I will have them summarily killed. Do you understand?"

"Yes, Excellency," I whispered.

We sat for what seemed a very long time. I was tense, not daring to move, breathing as shallowly as I could.

Then Boaz visibly relaxed, and his voice warmed. "I have frightened you, Tirzah. I am sorry."

He rose, startling me, but he walked over to the cabinet and poured wine into two wooden goblets, handing me one and sitting down again.

He had never offered me wine before, but as he sipped and stared out the window, I raised the goblet to my mouth and took a careful mouthful.

The wine was extraordinary. It was a nobleman's wine, and certainly better than anything I'd had before. I took another mouthful. There was still silence between us, but it was companionable now. Not cold or dangerous.

It was as though I sat with a different man.

My resentment and loathing faded, and I shifted more comfortably in my chair. I drank some more wine, and wondered why he did not use glass goblets. There was so little glass or metal in this room. I drank again.

"Talk to me, Tirzah," he said, and I jumped slightly.

"Excellency?" I was confused. Talk about what? And what would destroy this mood?

His goblet was empty, and now he rose to refill it, bringing the wine pitcher back to refill mine as well. "This silence is eating at me, Tirzah, and you must have questions. Ask me one or two."

I didn't speak, thinking, suspecting another trap. But Yaqob had been pressing me for information recently, and I realized there was something I could ask Boaz that was reasonably safe in the context of our previous conversation. Something that might provide useful information for Yaqob, and perhaps even the Soulenai.

"Excellency . . ."

"Ask what you will, Tirzah."

"Excellency, you have shown me some mathematical progressions, formulas, that rule nature. There is another curiosity I have heard, and I wonder if you might explain it to me."

"Yes?"

I took a deep breath, then leaped in. "One day I heard two Magi briefly mention the numbers one, three, five, seven, eleven. They are another progression, perhaps." I prayed Boaz would not read the lie in my voice, for these were the figures Ta'uz had mentioned in connection with the numbers who would die on site. I only hoped Boaz would not remember the conversation he'd had with Ta'uz, or connect it to my question. Even the lie that I'd accidentally overheard Magi converse was dangerous.

But Boaz paid it no mind. "You have given me only five numbers, and in themselves they do not make a progression. What follows the eleven?"

"I do not know, Excellency."

"Well, then I cannot say what progression those numbers are part of."

"Oh, but I thank you for your consideration, Excellency."

The lamp swung in the night breeze, and I saw a tiny smile tug at the corners of his mouth. "You are being very polite, Tirzah."

I am being very careful, I thought, for I do not want to scare you from this mood. And the next instant I wondered why I'd thought "scare." Why not jolt? Or shake? And *why* didn't I want this mood to end? I hung my head, thinking it best not to respond.

He sighed, and swirled the dregs of his wine about his goblet. "There is only one thing those numbers have in common."

"Yes, Excellency?"

"They are all incomposite numbers, except the One, of course, which exists outside and beyond the others."

I did not have to pretend confusion. "Excellency?"

He sat forward, so I could see his face more clearly. "Incomposite numbers are those which cannot be factored—they cannot be divided except by themselves or by the One. They are thus indivisible."

"Then they would hold a special relationship to the One, Excellency."

"You are very good, Tirzah," he said softly, his eyes keen, and I thought I had gone too far. But he reached for the pitcher and poured himself yet more wine. This time he did not offer me any.

"And you are correct. Incomposite numbers hold a very special relationship to the One. They not only have a direct relationship with the One, they are, in a sense, different expressions of the One."

"So . . . from eleven the next would be thirteen? Then . . . seventeen?"

"Precisely, Tirzah. And then on infinitely. Perhaps we will make a Magus of you yet."

His smile was now wide and open. I had never seen him this relaxed before. Yet I would not relax myself, for that way lay danger. "There is no end to incomposite numbers?"

"No. As with all numbers, they stretch into Infinity."

I felt a shiver run down my spine. Would Threshold continue to eat into Infinity? How would it manage to sate its appetite when the incomposites stretched into the thousands, and then into the tens of thousands?

"You look very dark, Tirzah. Perhaps I have not convinced you of the importance of numbers and formulas in life."

"I think it is beyond me, Excellency. I prefer to understand life through less demanding means."

"And what means might those be, Tirzah?"

The sense of danger swamped me again, but he did not

look at me with the flat and cold eyes of the Magus. They were merely curious, as if he really wanted to know.

"I have my Vilander gods, Excellency. They explain the world and all that occurs in it through myth. Perhaps you would like me to tell you—"

"Not tonight," he broke in, and his voice had a harder edge to it. I visibly tensed, and he relaxed. When he continued, his tone had softened. "But your Vilander gods are very far from you here. It must be hard for you to touch them."

"Yes," I admitted, "they are very distant, Excellency. This sun is too hot for them, and there are no rolling gray seas for them to wallow in."

"But you have a curious mind, Tirzah. You think deeply, and you must entertain many questions. How do you answer them, if your Vilander gods are silent in this land?"

I looked him directly in the eye, and risked a tiny smile. "I ask *you,* Excellency, when you allow."

He stared at me, then burst into laughter.

I was shocked, but his laughter was infectious, and my smile stretched wider.

"You have a lovely smile, Tirzah. It lights your eyes. You should smile more often."

Then he leaned across the space between us and kissed me. He took my face in his hands, but his fingers were gentle, and his mouth tasted of the wine he had drunk. Both his touch and kiss were tender, and very, very sweet. This was not the mouth nor the hands of the Magus who'd sought to trap me under the eaves of the verandah.

Then he leaned back, and the light shone so directly into his face I saw exactly what happened next.

His eyes widened, the fright in them very real. "Go," he whispered hoarsely. "Go, leave me . . . before . . ."

But I was still trapped by the lingering sweetness of his kiss, and I was not quick enough. As I hesitated a change swept over him. The Magus resurfaced, coldness replacing warmth and humor . . . and then fury boiled forth.

"Get out!" he shouted. *"Get out!"*

And I fled, sending the chair crashing to the floor in my haste to leave.

My mind was in turmoil, and it was a very long time before I slept. I had talked to two people this night, the Magus and the man. And the Magus did not like the man very much. Underneath the chilling, eminently dangerous face of the Magus lay a man whom I thought was the very antithesis of the Magus. I wondered when the walls of the Magus had been constructed, and I remembered the scroll he'd shown me. Even by nine he'd stepped onto the path of the Magi, had been seduced by the numbers and the power of the One, and in succeeding years he had built walls so thick that whoever Boaz really was had little chance of escape.

But he did surface occasionally. I thought hard, furrowing my forehead in the darkness of Isphet's quarters. Boaz would only let the face of the man show when he thought it was safe . . . when he thought I had been so thoroughly cowed and frightened I would not attempt to take advantage of him.

The second night I had gone to him I had fumbled in my attempts to draw some of the figures and characters, and he had shouted at me until I'd cringed against the desk.

Then he'd relaxed and laughed when I'd tried to write "Excellency" as his name. But the moment *I'd* relaxed, and called him Boaz, he had instantly reverted to the Magus, and had scared me back into submission.

Tonight he'd watched the effect his threats had on me, then relaxed, sure I was so chastened I would attempt to take no advantage if he softened toward his true character.

And, oh, I'd been so cautious, and had not presumed even when he'd not only laughed, but kissed me. My response had been hesitant and more than careful, and I had not pushed the kiss beyond what it had asked itself.

Then something had frightened him, had scared the Magus back into control.

It had not been my actions, but his. *He* had been the one to presume, to overstep the bounds, and the Magus had been furious—at himself more than me, I think.

I drifted toward sleep, hating the Magus, but wondering about the man. After that shared laughter and the sweetness of the kiss, I think I would have answered any question honestly.

But the Magus never had the chance to ask it, because Boaz had thought to warn me.

SIXTEEN

Yaqob put his arm around me, and pulled me into his body. I relaxed against him, relishing his closeness and warmth. It had been too long . . .

Boaz had not called me back for over a week, and I thought he'd been so disturbed by what he had revealed of himself that I might never be called back again. Well, perhaps I would not mind overmuch. Yaqob's touch was good, and for the first time in weeks I allowed myself to dream a little. When we finally won our freedom we could have all the time we needed together; his mouth brushed my hair, and I reminded myself of how much I loved him. I could not wait to be his wife in freedom.

We were in the upper room of Isphet's workshop. Zeldon had hurried in from a visit to one of the neighboring workshops, and had asked Isphet and Yaqob to join us in our caging room. Now Isphet sat at the table with Orteas and Zeldon, while Yaqob and I relaxed on a bench set against the wall.

"A new boatload of slaves arrived two nights ago," Zeldon said, and Isphet shrugged.

"New slaves arrive all the time."

"But on this boat were four glassworkers. Four men who are skilled in the art of caging."

All of us sat forward, and I felt Yaqob's hand tighten about my shoulder.

"Are they . . . ?" He hesitated to put the danger into words.

"Elementals?" Zeldon had no such compunction. "No. They are not."

"Have you seen their work?" Isphet asked. How could men who were not Elementals cage with any degree of skill?

"Yes. After collecting the potash from Izzali, he mentioned the new workers, and took me to meet them. They already had yesterday's work spread before them, and I inspected it. It is well formed, but it has no life. The glass does not sing like that made by Elementals."

He paused, and looked at me. "It was caged glass meant for the Infinity Chamber. Izzali's shop has also been firing the golden glass. Boaz is spreading the work about."

"Spreading about both work and those who can cage," Isphet said. Her professional pride had been wounded that another workshop had also been given the task of firing the golden glass. "Why?"

I wet my lips. I should have said something about this earlier, but there had been no time, and both Yaqob and Isphet had kept their distance.

"He does not trust this workshop," I said. "He suspects us in the attempt to kill him. I think that if he becomes certain he will have us killed. But, until now, he could not afford to. This workshop was too important."

"How long have you known this?" Yaqob snapped, and I felt the tension in his body. "You have not been to Boaz's quarters in a week!"

"He told me this the last night I was there, Yaqob. I'm sorry. I should have said . . . but there was no time . . . and I have hardly seen you . . ."

Yaqob looked to Isphet, then they both exchanged glances with Zeldon and Orteas.

"Tirzah," Yaqob said very gently, "Isphet tells me you are keeping secrets. She says that she can almost smell them about you."

"I . . ."

"Secrets, Tirzah," he continued. His hand stroked my arm, but it did not comfort me. "And yet you tell us nothing of what goes on in Boaz's quarters. Until a week ago you spent many nights with him, longer than Raguel ever did with Ta'uz, and we wonder why. Now we find out that Boaz clearly suspects us—"

"You knew that already," I said. "Why else would he visit this workshop and warn us about practicing the Elemental arts?"

"But we did *not* know he realized that the falling glass was no accident but an attempt on his life, and connected it with this workshop," Yaqob said angrily. "Does he suspect a planned revolt? Have you told him the details?"

"Yaqob!" I pulled away from him, tears in my eyes.

"Some women are indiscreet in a man's bed," he said. "Are you one of them?"

I stared at him. I remembered how the Magus had wrapped me in his arms, had stroked me and kissed me, and had almost beguiled me into betraying not only myself, but all those within this room. Perhaps I *was* weak.

"No," I whispered. "Yaqob, how could you ask that? You were the one who insisted I go to his bed. How can you suspect me?"

"Then tell us what you do for so many hours and nights with the Magus," Isphet said. "*Tell* us!"

Should I tell them that he teaches me to write, and kisses me with tenderness?

No, how could I? "He uses me—"

"For eight or nine hours, Tirzah?" Isphet said. "No Magus needs that long to commune with the One."

"And sometimes he requires me to sit in silence. On a stool, as Ta'uz required of Raguel. And"—this at least I could tell them—"he tries to tell me something of the way of the One."

They accepted that, and Isphet even smiled grimly, remembering.

"He begins to relax about me, now. The last time I was with him he said something that might be useful."

"And *now* she thinks to tell us," Yaqob said, but his tone was mild.

I told them of the incomposite numbers, and of their peculiarly strong relationship with the One. "They are, he said, different expressions of the One."

"And they stretch into Infinity," Yaqob muttered. Everyone was appalled. Seven would die, then eleven, then . . .

"He has also mentioned a Vale, but I do not know what that means." Something curled and died within me at such a blatant lie. But I could not say that I had read the inscriptions on the Infinity Chamber. If I confessed that, then I would have to confess I could write as well as read, and then they would wonder just how far I'd fallen under the power of the One.

And Yaqob would never hold me so close again. Damn you, Magus Boaz, I thought, *damn* you for your manipulations!

The three men shook their heads, but Isphet frowned.

"Isphet?" Yaqob said. "What do you know?"

"I have heard of the Vale only briefly, when I was a child," she said slowly. "The elders within our community in the hills—the Graces—are so steeped in the understanding of the Soulenai I sometimes think they spent more time gazing into the Place Beyond than they did looking at this world. My father trained with them in his youth. He mentioned a Vale, and I think he must have had the knowledge from the Graces. The Vale . . ."

Her voice trailed off as she tried to recall exactly what it was her father had said. "The Vale is a place, I think, that harbors darkness and shadows. Yet it contains power. My father really did not like to speak of it. It is not a prison, but it is a place that is deliberately sequestered from this world and the Place Beyond. It does not have anything to do with Elemental magic or the Soulenai. It simply exists somewhere."

"And yet apart from you, none of us here has heard of it," said Zeldon.

Isphet looked up sharply. "The Graces of the hill community have far more understanding than most Elementals, Zeldon. We are workers, they sages."

"Tirzah," Yaqob said, "in what context did Boaz mention the Vale?"

"Ah, it was something to do with the Infinity Chamber. And a bridge."

"A bridge?" Isphet cried. "By the Soulenai! Do the Magi indeed intend to touch the Vale through the Infinity Chamber?"

"We need more information," Yaqob said. "Tirzah, why hasn't Boaz asked you back for this week?"

"Um . . . it is my monthly time," I said, and managed to blush.

"It hasn't stopped them before," Isphet muttered, but said no more about it.

"Well then," Yaqob said, "he'll ask you back soon. Tirzah,

this news of the incomposite numbers is disturbing. And the vague mention of the Vale is even worse. Are you *sure* he's said nothing else of help?"

I shook my head.

"Then you must do your best to find out more," he said. "With new workers to cage for the Magi, Threshold is only a few short months away from completion. Soon we'll be asked to begin work on the capstone. Then . . ."

He shivered. "I will speak to Azam within the day. I fear we shall have to bring forward our plans."

Then he smiled, and hugged me tight. "And then we'll be free, Tirzah, running across the plains toward Isphet's magical hill home, leaving Boaz lying dead and forgotten behind us."

I tried to smile for him, and was glad when he leaned forward to kiss me.

SEVENTEEN

He called me back within a day, and to the workshop it appeared as if it had indeed been my monthly flux that had kept him distant. When I went to him I found only the Magus, aloof, easily pushed into rage, and very, very careful.

"You were impertinent to so flaunt your body before me, girl," he said as I washed his hands and feet my first night back.

"I will never do so again, Excellency," I whispered.

"And then to *kiss* me!" he said. "Did I not make it clear that I have not Ta'uz's weakness?"

"I am sorry, Excellency!"

"You were repulsive, Tirzah."

"I know, Excellency."

Satisfied, he set me to a translation of a Geshardi treatise on the properties of the square, and then sent me away the instant I dared to yawn over the dry text.

But he called me back the next night, and then the next, until I was so tired Zeldon and Orteas had to let me sleep through the mornings.

"And what does he say?" Yaqob asked me one afternoon as we stood underneath a canvas awning. I leaned close to him, and touched his body, hoping he would make love to me, but he shifted irritably and I dropped my hands.

"He says nothing," I said truthfully. "He is cold and distant and does not think to natter on about what patrols he will send where on the morrow."

Yaqob did not laugh at my poor attempt at humor, and led me silently back to the workshop.

Within the week, the addition of four more glassworkers had its effect. We no longer had to work such long hours, and one afternoon I actually found myself with little to do.

I wandered down to chat with my father.

Druse was inspecting a dozen goblets one of the Magi had asked him to make. They were lovely, of rich ruby glass, and my father had done well.

He smiled as I admired them, then reached down to a shelf underneath his worktable.

"Tirzah, look. This is one that did not fire as cleanly as the others. Can you do something with it?"

He placed a rough goblet into my hands. It had been blown, but not finished, and I could see why. The glass had fired into amber rather than red, and the walls of the cup were too thick for a Magus to be asked to wrap his fingers about.

"I didn't mean it for caging," Druse said, "but rather than throw it away . . ."

I kissed him on the cheek. "It would give me pleasure to work something other than that cursed glass for the Infinity Chamber, Father. Thank you."

I took it back to the upper room. Orteas and Zeldon were supervising glass placement within Threshold. I sat cross-legged on the floor by the open doorway to the balcony, turning the cup slowly over in my hands, listening to it speak, understanding its weaknesses and strengths, wondering what I could do with it.

I found myself remembering the tenderness of Boaz's kiss. I thought of the man hidden behind the Magus, and I smiled to myself. Then I realized that Boaz only had wooden goblets in his quarters. He would appreciate one of glass, and this amber glass was lovely—and would look beautiful in his hands.

I wondered what design he would like, and I remembered how his fingers had caressed the glass I'd caged for him in Setkoth.

Back at the worktable, I reached for the wax marker, hesitated, then sketched a design on the goblet of leaping frogs among river reeds. One frog peeking out mischievously from behind the reeds; another leaping upward as if he wanted to dive into the goblet itself; one sitting, as if in the contemplation of mysteries; and two chasing each other about the reeds, their faces stretched in friendly grins.

I imagined, as I worked, that I was surrounded by the croaking of the frogs as their song floated up from the Lhyl, but it was bright afternoon, and the frogs only sang at dawn and dusk.

Not once during that long afternoon, as I began the painstaking work on the Goblet of the Frogs, did I wonder why I should be taking so much care and expending so much effort on a gift for a Magus. Nor did I ask myself why I went to so much trouble to hide it from the curious eyes of Zeldon and Orteas, or why, on successive days when I had free time, I only worked the goblet when I was alone.

One day Boaz surprised me, and all who heard his summons, by ordering me to his quarters midafternoon.

Stunned, I stared at the guard who had delivered the order, then nodded and went back to the tenement building to wash and change. It felt strange to walk the streets dressed in the linen dress in the revealing light of day, and I felt the weight of eyes as I passed: there goes Tirzah, poor Tirzah.

I looked up at Threshold, avoiding the pity of the passersby. The southern and western faces were completely glassed now—and the sight would have been supremely beautiful on any other building.

As I watched I thought I saw bright trails of light flicker underneath the plate glass, almost as lightning forks. I frowned, and looked again.

There, a flicker, and a flash farther down, perhaps from the mouth of one of the shafts.

Then I heard the rough voice of a guard, and I dropped my eyes. I had reached the gate to the compound, and the guards gave me a cursory glance and let me through.

This was the first time I'd been inside the compound during the day, and I slowed my pace a little to satisfy my curiosity. The gardens were uglier now, for darkness and moonlight did much to hide their rigid geometry. Even the trees had been trimmed into precise shapes, and the pathways had been raked into crisp lines and right angles whenever a bend appeared.

Boaz's residence also looked less pleasing by day than it did by night. I had grown so used to seeing it only in the pastel lights that softened its lines, and now I realized that it was stark and uncompromising—as uncompromising, perhaps, as the soul of the Magus.

Fifteen paces from the house I stopped, stunned. When first Boaz had summoned me I had wondered briefly that he'd not taken over Ta'uz's residence, which was larger and much grander, and situated in the center of the Magi's compound. This house was stuck against one of the boundary walls, and its low verandah made it appear secretive and sly.

And safe.

That thought brought me to an abrupt halt.

This was one of the few buildings on the entire site that *was protected from Threshold's shadow!* The wall of the Magi's compound was high, and this house low. It was in constant shadow—but the shadow of the wall, not of Threshold. Adding to its security was the enveloping verandah. Raguel had said that Ta'uz spent long hours staring out the windows of his house at Threshold. Boaz could not do that here even if he wanted to; both verandah and wall hid Threshold from sight—and hid the house from Threshold.

I began to think of all the times (and they were rare) when I had seen even a hint of the man hidden within Boaz. They always occurred within this house, never outside.

Within the house, where he was safe from Threshold.

I realized I was not only staring, but shaking as well, and I forced my legs to move. Boaz might be watching my approach. Even now he could be working himself into a murderous fury at what he might well perceive as my reluctance to obey his orders.

I hurried forward, and stopped at the doorway. "Excellency?"

"Tirzah"—he stepped out from an inner room—"you are late."

"I had to hurry back to my tenement to wash and change, Excellency."

"Then wash my hands and feet, and sit at the desk, and do not waste any more of my time."

"Yes, Excellency."

He set me once again to translating the Geshardi treatise on the square, and I bent over the papyrus, trying to write with as much neatness and precision as I could. I heard Boaz sit in a chair behind me, then the rustle of papyrus as he unrolled a scroll to study.

I worked in silence for perhaps two hours, for I could see the shadows lengthening in the garden outside, and the distinctive shadow of Threshold stretch farther and farther across the compound.

Except that it never touches this house.

"You are not concentrating."

He was standing directly behind me and I could not help a start of surprise. I had not heard him rise.

"I have almost finished the treatise, Excellency. See, I am on the very last passage now."

He picked up the sheet on which I had been writing and studied it briefly. "Ah yes, I can see that. I will be glad to be finally able to read this treatise."

"You cannot read Geshardian, Excellency?" Again he had so surprised me I asked a question without permission.

"The northern languages are coarse and unrefined, girl, and I have never wasted my time on them! Do you understand?"

"I understand, Excellency." So this was why he'd taught me to write. Few within Ashdod would have any command of these languages. I wondered that he would even think to find a northern treatise interesting.

"You have a question, girl. Ask it."

"Excellency, I did not know that the Geshardi worshiped the power of the One."

"They do not." He dropped the sheet of papyrus back on the desk. "But they have some moderately learned geometricians among them. One day, perhaps, they will come to understand the One." He saw that I had another question. "Yes?"

"You worship the One as a god, Excellency. I had never realized that before."

"It is the *power* of the One we worship, foolish girl, not the One itself. It has no personality within itself. Perhaps the lower castes see the One as a god, Tirzah, for as the number from which all numbers emanate from and then decay into the One resembles Providence. But do not believe for a moment that the One has a mind and a will of its—"

"Excellency!" The frantic shout of a guard cut Boaz off and he whirled about.

"Excellency!" The guard reached the doorway and grabbed at its supports to stop himself from falling headlong into the Magus's apartment. "Excellency . . . Threshold . . . there's a problem . . . you must—"

But Boaz was already out the door, thrusting his arms through his blue robe as he ran. The guard caught up with him, words tumbling from his mouth, and without thinking I rushed out as well.

Five.

Who?

I was not stopped as I hastened after Boaz to Threshold's compound. All knew that he made frequent use of me, and my presence with him was not questioned.

"Where?" Boaz said, and the guard led us up the ramp and into the abomination itself.

About us workers stood still, silent, and pale.

The guard took us only partly up the main passageway before he turned down one of the major corridors that branched off it.

As soon as I entered that corridor I sensed its wrongness— its *increased* wrongness. I could see it, too.

Boaz stopped, and we both looked at the glassed walls. I

hesitated, then reached out a trembling hand, not believing what I was seeing.

"Tirzah?" Boaz saw me as if realizing for the first time that I had followed him, but he did not berate me, for he, too, was now standing by the walls, running unbelieving hands over them.

What had been glass was still warm. It was also very, very dead, and at that I was not surprised.

Some kind of heat, so tremendous that I could not conceive how it could have been generated, had completely fused the glass into the stone of Threshold's walls. The masonry was now clearly visible through this brilliant black substance that was like, and yet unlike, glass.

The entire corridor had been fused in this way. Now it was a tunnel black as night and yet still radiating light down its length.

"This way," the guard said quietly, and led us yet farther into Threshold.

The five workers had been simple laborers, sent in to see why one of the gates had apparently been blocked open. They had moved deep into this corridor, then the gates before them and behind them had slammed closed.

None of the three Magi who stood waiting for Boaz could explain why.

"We were nowhere near the controls, Boaz," said one.

"No one was," confirmed another.

Their words wafted over my head. I was staring transfixed at the five bodies. Whatever heat had seared through this corridor had burned them, although not beyond recognition, for enough remained of their features for me to see that at least they were none that I knew.

And I could certainly see that they had been cooked. They were contorted into shapes of pure horror, their bodies twisted, their limbs flexed, their hands black claws. Their flesh still smoldered, and the smell was wrenching.

I turned away, unable to look anymore. Four or five paces away lay the blackened remains of one of their tool bags, the tools themselves scattered about the floor.

I peered more closely, then walked over, squatting to pick up a hammer.

I gasped, not only at its feel but at its weight. It had been turned completely to stone, as had all the tools. Even wooden handles had been converted into black, glassy stone. Had the glass, melting from the walls and ceiling, dripped down onto these tools? Or had some other force been at work, something I could not understand?

"Boaz?" I said incautiously, but in such a state of horror that I did not think to address him properly, "what has happened to these?"

And I held out the hammer for him.

He cursed and struck the hammer from my hand. It hit the floor with a sweet, clear ring. "What are you doing here, girl! Get back to my residence!"

"I . . . Boaz . . ." I did not move, but overcome by what I saw about me and by the coldness of his eyes, I burst into tears.

"Curse you!" he hissed, and seizing my arms in cruel fingers, bundled me into the care of the guard. "Get her out of here!"

The guard had no wish to linger. He took hold of me with kinder hands, and pulled me down the corridor. As we left I heard Boaz say to the other Magi. "It's even better than I'd dreamed. Far more powerful. Far more."

The guard escorted me back to the Magus's residence. I sat on the chair in front of the desk, the Geshardian geometrical treatise awaiting completion before me, my eyes uselessly blurred with tears.

EIGHTEEN

He came back as night fell. His manservant, Holdat, had been in and laid out a meal, but I had not liked to touch it, and was not hungry in any case.

"Have you finished?" he asked as he stepped through the door.

I nodded listlessly. At some point I had found myself writing without realizing I had picked up the stylus. Startled, I had stared at the page, then shrugged. I needed something to keep my mind busy.

"Then stand up!"

I struggled up.

"How *dare* you presume to intrude!" he seethed, and I blinked, terrified.

"Excellency?"

He stopped in front of me and leaned threateningly close, his finger stabbing at the air between us.

"How dare you follow me from this room!"

"Excellency, I was afraid!"

"Afraid?"

"Afraid that it might be someone I knew lying dead in Threshold, Excellency. I had to know."

He paused, and I did not like the expression that filtered across his face. "The guard said nothing about deaths."

"Excellency, why else would he rush in so pale and horrified? All slaves instinctively fear death and crippling injury on a construction site. It is our lot, and it is what I thought of first."

"Did you think Yaqob lay speared by glass, my sweet?"

That was *exactly* what I had feared—surely Threshold had us marked by now? I opened my mouth to reply, but burst into tears instead, and just as quickly tried to stifle them. I gulped, a shaking hand over my mouth, my eyes wide and terrified.

My fear was clearly evident, and it sated his need to intimidate me into submission. I had presumed too much in following him into Threshold, and I'd had to be chastized and put back in my place.

His expression relaxed slightly, but not before a final barb. "Do that again and I'll pass you across to the guards for their enjoyment, Tirzah, because—by the One!—you give *me* little enough. Do you understand?"

"I understand, Excellency!" I sobbed, my entire body shaking now.

There was a long silence. Then . . .

"Ah, Tirzah. Why cry so? Here," and he handed me a napkin to wipe my face with.

It was not the hand of the Magus.

I scrubbed at my face with the cloth, surreptitiously looking at him. He was still very, very wary, but it was the man not
the Magus who now stood before me.

I burst into fresh sobs, relieved, yet scared I would say or
do something that would cause the Magus to snap back into
control.

Boaz gestured impatiently, and finally snatched the sodden
napkin from my hand. "Go and wash your face. Your kohl has
smeared all over and you look like a five-year-old girl caught
out at some mischief."

As I gratefully wiped the cool water over my face, finally
managing to stem the flow of tears, I wondered if I should
have offered to wash Boaz's hands and feet on his return.

"Excellency?" Unsure of how to phrase the question, or
even if I should just take the initiative, I vaguely indicated the
basin.

"There's no need, Tirzah," and he was beside me, hanging
his overrobe on a peg by the stand, washing his own hands,
taking the towel from me to wipe them dry.

"Good. Now, have you eaten?"

I shook my head.

"Then sit."

It was a plain meal. A bowl of cold, soaked grain. A platter
of fruits. Unleavened bread with a small dish of oil. An assortment of cheeses. A pitcher of wine and two goblets.

He laid some fruit on a plate, broke a piece of bread, sea-
soning it lightly with the oil, spooned some grain beside it,
then handed the plate to me. "Eat, Tirzah. It has been a long
time since your dawn meal."

He passed me some wine. "It would please me if you
drank, Tirzah. And then ate some more."

"Yes, Excellency."

He did not want to talk, which suited me, and we sat for
some time in comfortable silence. I marveled that beneath the
Magus lived such a man, and I hoped that, after the Magus
had so terrified me, the man would linger a while yet. I was
more determined than ever not to speak or move out of turn.

As Holdat materialized to clear away the meal, Boaz
leaned an elbow on the table, took a sip of wine, and smiled
at me.

"What are you thinking, Tirzah?"

"I am thinking that I still have much to learn, Excellency."

"A diplomatic answer, Tirzah. I wish you would make me a clear glass plate that I could fasten in your skull and show me what goes on behind those lovely eyes of yours. Come, sit with me by the window."

He brought the wine over, and placed it on a small table by our chairs. We were very close.

"Talk to me, Tirzah. Do not be afraid."

But it took some courage to say what I wanted, for I was very frightened of losing him back into his shell.

"Excellency, I am wondering why you have asked me here. I know that you do not want to use me"—and something shifted in his eyes at that—"but wish to teach me the skills of writing. Yet surely, somewhere at court or among the servants and scribes of the Magi, there is one who can translate Geshardian for you?"

"Are you still scared of the writing?"

"Sometimes, Excellency." And even more afraid of what Yaqob will say to me when he finds out, as he surely will.

"There is no need, Tirzah. The last thing I want to do is to cause you harm."

I kept my face impassive, but I felt a spurt of hard anger inside. How could he say that when he spent hours threatening me, my friends, and driving me into repeated episodes of sobbing terror? How *dare* he say that when he almost crippled me with pain in the workshop when I refused his bidding?

I turned my face away slightly, lest he see the emotion seething inside. He must be aware of what he did when hiding beneath the robes and demeanor of Magus.

He stood up, and again I jumped, sure that somehow he'd seen my inner anger. "Excellency?"

"Peace, Tirzah. Sit there and wait."

He was gone some minutes, and when he returned it was with the white robe and sash of the Magus gone and the long blue wrap knotted about his hips. In his hands he carried a box, and on his face an expression so wary I wondered if the Magus would emerge at any instant.

"Excellency," I cried softly, leaping to my feet, "let me carry that for you."

But he snatched it away, his eyes alarmed. Dismay thudding my heart, I dropped to my knees. "Forgive me, Excellency! I only thought to help."

"Get back in your chair, Tirzah," and I was relieved to hear that, although harsh, he did not use the voice of the Magus.

I crawled back, my heart still pounding uncomfortably. He sat down as well, and stared at me steadily.

"If you ever reveal what I am about to show you, Tirzah, I *will kill you.* Do you understand?"

And what made that threat so frightening was that it came from the man Boaz, not the Magus.

I believed him utterly, and my belief showed on my face. "Yes, Excellency."

"Good." He sighed, then relaxed, staring at the box, his fingers gently tapping.

I understood we had reached the point to which he'd been directing me ever since he'd first ordered me to his quarters. Now that we had arrived, he was in no hurry to proceed.

His long fingers still tapping gently, gently, gently against the lid of the box, he leaned his head against the high back of the chair and regarded me. It was a pleasant inspection, and I relaxed and took some more of the wine.

"Tell me of your northern lands, Tirzah."

"Excellency, where shall I begin?"

"With the land itself. I have never seen it."

"Viland is very flat, Excellency. Windswept. It is a narrow strip of land running north–south. There are wild gray seas to the west, great mountains and forests on our eastern borders."

"And the people. Is your coloring usual among northerners?"

"Yes, Excellency. All Vilanders are fair-haired and blue-eyed."

"And are all the menfolk as handsome as you are beautiful, Tirzah?"

I blushed, and he grinned.

"They hide behind great beards, Excellency. It is difficult to say."

"Another diplomatic answer, Tirzah. You have been wasted in craftwork. What of Geshardi? You speak the language well. Have you ever been there?"

Now there was an edge to his voice. Geshardi was what he'd wanted to discuss all this time. Questions of my homeland had been part gentle detour, part ruse.

"I learned the language from the traders that my father and I dealt with, Excellency, but I have never been there."

"Surely they described it to you."

"Geshardi lies beyond the western forests of Viland's border, Excellency. The traders spoke of a milder climate than ours, and gentle hills that rolled into the distance, covered with soft gorse and low trees and abounding in deer and hare." I paused, then gave him what I thought he wanted to know. "The Geshardi traders had light brown hair, rather than the Viland fairness, but they generally had blue or gray eyes. We are of cousin races."

I hesitated again. "They did not have great beards, Excellency, and they were fair of feature and smooth of tongue."

He was silent a long, long time, his eyes very distant. I took the opportunity to study the box. It was quite large, and extremely well crafted. I peered closer, but could not quite make out the wood. It almost seemed to be made from Jusserine, a rich, dark red timber that grew in the forests that divided Geshardi from Viland.

"My father was a Geshardi Prince," Boaz said eventually.

I could not think of anything he could have said that would have stunned me more. *Boaz's father came from Geshardi?*

My eyes narrowed. How could this help Yaqob? And then I felt my stomach clench with self-hatred at so treacherous a thought.

He was looking at me again. "My mother was Chad-Nezzar's sister."

"Yes, Excellency. I have heard you are the Chad's nephew." I looked at him more carefully now. His face and arms were tanned from the sun, but the skin of his chest and belly was much paler than I'd seen on any of pure southern blood. And his gray eyes . . .

"She'd been married in her youth to an Ashdod nobleman. I have an older half brother, Zabrze—heir to the throne now. When her husband died, Chad-Nezzar had her married to a Geshardi Prince at Ashdod's court to conclude a trade alliance.

"They were married in a flurry of trumpets, clinging silks, and carefully applied kohl. They retired to secluded apartments where they stayed, as is tradition in Ashdod, for seven days and seven nights, before emerging to further banqueting and a score of invitations to hunt.

"My father was, apparently, a man of action, and the seven days and nights spent in seclusion had left him thirsting for adventure."

Boaz slid his eyes my way again, and they were deeply amused. "Although he had not spent those seven nights in total inactivity, Tirzah, for I was made on one of them." He looked back to the dark of the night outside. "On his first hunt, down the great River Lhyl, he grew so excited he stood up in the boat to sound the trumpet, lost his balance, and toppled into the water. A great water lizard took him."

"Oh, Excellency, I am so sorry . . ."

"I never knew him, and that saddens me, Tirzah, for I think he was a man worth the knowing. My mother became hysterical when she heard. In seven days he had won her heart, and she never recovered from his loss. Within the year she had given birth to me, and when I was six she died. Of despair, I think."

My eyes had filled with tears, and Boaz had to collect himself before he could go on.

"This box contains my father's wedding gift to my mother. She treasured it, for it was all she had left of him, apart from me, of course. It contains . . . a book."

And suddenly I knew why the writing, why the reading, why the translating. Boaz wanted to read the book, but couldn't, so he had trained me to do it for him.

I vaguely wondered why he hadn't simply asked me to teach him the Geshardian tongue.

"She told me, and at the age of six I wasn't old enough to understand completely what she'd meant, that he had seduced her with tales from this book. She could not read it either, during her lifetime no one else from Geshardi came to Ashdod, and all she had were the memories of the tales he'd read to her. There was one . . ."

"Yes, Excellency?" I could only whisper now, and the tears were running down my cheeks.

"There was one in particular that I loved, and which she told me time and time again. But it has been thirty years since her death, Tirzah, and the tale has all but gone from my mind. Tirzah, would you read it to me?"

"It would be my honor, Excellency."

He sighed, and undid the catches on the box, and lifted out a large book.

My breath caught in my throat as he handed it over. It was very, very beautiful. Bound in calfskin, the cover and spine had inlays of precious metals and gems set amid copper and gold wire and bronze studs.

I reached out my hands, and took the book.

And almost dropped it. Not only because of the weight, but because it spoke to me.

Lovely woman, hold me, touch me. Come, do not fear me. Lovely woman, I am yours, kiss me, soothe me, hold me, touch me . . . touch me . . .

How I sustained my composure I'll never know.

Touch me, soothe me, let me love you, love you, let me lie down beside you, let me touch you, love you . . .

The book was a work of great Elemental cantomancy. Greater than any Elemental magic I'd witnessed or felt under Isphet's tutelage. What I was hearing through the elements of metal and gems in the book was not the voices of the elements or even of the Soulenai, but . . . but Boaz's father's voice, his soft seductions as he'd bedded his new wife . . .

Lovely woman, let me hold you, touch you, love you . . . Oh! Lovely woman!

Questions about Boaz's father and his relationship to the book raced through my mind, filled it, consumed it.

Had he made the book? Did he have any understanding of what the book was? Was *he* an Elemental Cantomancer himself?

I blinked away my tears, the voice fading now as the book throbbed with the heat of their passion. My hands trembled, but I steadied them and studied the book anew. It was very old, ancient, and Boaz's father could not have made it. Perhaps he had just acquired it as part of a trading deal, and knew none of its magic. Perhaps he'd had no idea that the book had absorbed the passion of their wedding night, and had kept it alive though the man and the woman had died.

Perhaps. Perhaps not.

Did *Boaz* know what this book was?

If he noticed any of the emotions surging through me he gave no sign.

"Tirzah. Open the book. Please. In there is a story. Please read it to me."

I opened the book. Inside the writing was exquisite, drawn in vermilion and edged with gold, spreading across smooth creamy parchment—vellum, not papyrus. The characters were unusual, but I could read them. There was a listing of contents, and my eyes skimmed down it, wondering which tale Boaz wanted me to read to him.

"Excellency? Which one?"

And then my eyes found it, and I had no doubt about which one Boaz would name. Which tale it was that had haunted both his childhood and manhood.

"The Song of the Frogs," he whispered.

NINETEEN

I raised my eyes and looked at him, knowing then that stronger magic than fate had enslaved me and brought me through so much hardship to this man and this moment in time.

Was it this book?

"As you wish, Excellency," and I turned the pages and began to read.

The Song of the Frogs

It was a long time ago. A time when mists clung thick to form and voice. A time when all peoples, all races, all creatures lived in happiness and sharing.

It was this same world we live in now, but different.

The peace did not and could not last because it was perfect, and all know that perfection is a dream but never a reality. One race turned against another, then they united to turn against a third, and when all save a few were exterminated, those few crept among other peoples and whispered words of discord and hate.

War spread with the cruel relentlessness of a malignancy.

Because war thrived, peoples learned to live among it. Cultures, societies, and religions adapted. Sometimes war raged year after year, while other years were spent in peace—or what passed for it. Some races were decimated, others, more fortunate, more adaptable, more warlike, flourished.

But among all races there was one people known as the Soulenai, and they found it difficult to adapt to this new word and world of war.

Oh, gods. I risked a glance at Boaz, but the name seemed not to perturb him.

The Soulenai were masters of magic, Cantomancers of renown and skill, but they were peace-loving, and the thought of waging war made them nauseous.

They believed at first that if they took no sides, if they extended goodwill to all, then none would have reason to wage war on them.

But their lands were invaded, their children slaughtered.

So they thought to move far away, journey to a land where there was no war.

And so they did. They found a peaceful if largely dry land, covered with ten thousand pebbles, but a land where they could flourish again with work and effort. Yet within a decade war had found them, and decimated the land where the Soulenai settled. Dry land became utter desert, field turned to rock, furrow to chasm. Even if steel did not pierce their bodies, many among the Soulenai laid down and died because of their great sadness.

Those left alive wept, wondering if they were cursed.

As they wept, a great river rose from their tears, running

through the pebbles and the cracks in the rock and following the course of the chasms, dividing the desert, and giving life along its banks.

The Soulenai sat on the banks of the river and ceased their weeping, but their hearts still sorrowed. No matter where they went, what they did, war would follow, and eventually all would die. What use the beauty of the river when none would be left to enjoy it?

But as they grieved anew, their sorrow dry-eyed now, a song rose about them. It was an ugly song, and the Soulenai thought it suited the harshness of the desert and rock about them.

One thought to ask, "Who sings?"

"We do!" And ten thousand frogs lifted their heads from the banks of the river and saluted the Soulenai.

"What strange creatures are these?" the Soulenai asked, for none had seen frogs before.

The frogs introduced themselves, and then made great glad cry.

"Soulenai Saviors! For millennia we were locked inside a myriad of pebbles, trapped, as if by sorcery. But then came a wet such as we had never dared dream, and it was your tears. The river formed, and we sprang into life. Thus for you we offer our song."

The Soulenai smiled, glad that they had helped at least one race. "We thank you, Friend Frogs. You sing a beautiful song."

The frogs laughed. "You think it ugly, but we do not care. Soulenai Saviors, our song is a gift, and we would tell you how to use it."

"A gift?"

"We will give you a land where you may live in peace forevermore, Soulenai Saviors."

"Oh! What is this land?"

"We know it only as the Place Beyond."

I stopped, pretending to pause to wet my throat with wine. This was dangerous. I risked another glance at Boaz. He sat with his eyes closed, his breathing gentle, and I could not tell his thoughts. Magus waiting to trap, or man yearning for the comfort of his lost mother and unknown father?

"Please, go on," he said, and opened his eyes. They were bright with tears.

I returned to the tale.

The Soulenai were cautious. The frogs sang of hope, but the Soulenai had seen hope dashed before.

"See!" cried the frogs, and opened their throats in song.

The Soulenai saw. They saw a land where the mists still lingered. They saw a land of sea and stars, plunging cliffs and sweeping plains. A land where they would not be disturbed. They saw a land of such peace that it was magic in itself. It was a land where eternity laughed. A land where the unborn frolicked with the dead and yet no one knew the difference between them.

"We think we like this land, this Place Beyond," said the Soulenai. "But how do we reach it?"

"Follow our song," cried the frogs. "Listen, understand, let our song rock and soothe you, let it touch you, touch you, touch you. Let it hold you, touch you, love you."

And so they did.

The Soulenai followed the path of the frogs' song, for they were of such magic they could understand the song, and they went into the Place Beyond, and none have heard of them since.

But I think that if you let the Song of the Frogs rock you and soothe you, if you let it hold you and love you, then you too may be able to reach this Place Beyond, for it is surely a wondrous land.

"I think that is where my father took my mother," Boaz said into the silence. "I think that he understood the Song of the Frogs. I think that is why my mother died of grief. She had lost not only her lover, but the Place Beyond."

"Perhaps that is where they are now, Excellency," I said softly.

"Perhaps, Tirzah, perhaps." He sighed. "I wish *I* could understand the Song of the Frogs. I think I would like to visit this land called the Place Beyond."

Even now I still thought of entrapment, but I also thought of something that needed to be asked.

"Excellency?"

"Yes?"

"Excellency, what was your mother's name?"

Boaz stirred in his chair, and took the book from my hands, replacing it in the box.

"My mother's name was Tirzah." His eyes were still on the box.

Such emotion overwhelmed me I found it hard to speak. "Excellency, why give me your mother's name?"

"For the frogs you carved me that day, Tirzah."

And yet he had dashed them to the ground. Killed them. Would I ever understand this man?

"Tirzah?"

"Yes, Excellency?"

"It would please me if, in my bed, you would call me Boaz."

And so I did.

He did not take me into the Place Beyond, but he transported me nevertheless. Yaqob and I had never had the time nor the privacy to do our love justice. Boaz and I had ample of both. And Boaz also brought laughter, which Yaqob had never thought to do. He teased me with his hands, his mouth, his body, until—driven to wantonness—I pleaded with him to make an end to it and mount me.

"An end to it?" he said. "When we have the night before us?"

But he did as I asked, and with the sweetness and tenderness he'd given me in that kiss, until I pleaded with him *never* to make an end to it. By that time, even he was too breathless for laughter.

An end to it there had to be, and it brought me as much release as he—which surprised me, for I had not realized that a woman could gain as much satisfaction from a bedding as a man.

He did not leave me, but lay sprawled heavy across my body, gently kissing, stroking, whispering . . .

. . . *hold me, touch me, soothe me, love me* . . .

. . . until we both drifted into sleep.

We slept, then we woke and Boaz, still heavy atop me, resumed where he'd left off, and it was faster, harder, and more frenetic than our first loving, but it was as good, and this time my cries made no coherent words.

We slept again, and when I woke, it was to find the Magus had returned.

TWENTY

I grabbed for the sheet, not wanting the Magus to so witness my nakedness, but he tore it from my hand, then seized my arm, half dragging me from the bed.

He was robed in his full vestments of office, his hair tightly clubbed back into its queue, his eyes full of fury.

"Filthy whore!" he hissed. "What have you done?"

I could say nothing, fearful that whatever I said or did might cause him to kill me.

"Did you think to subvert me into subdividing the One, as Raguel did with Ta'uz?"

My eyes widened, and his mouth thinned in satisfaction. "Yes, word of Ta'uz's disgrace reached us back in Setkoth. Think not to so pollute me or the One."

He hauled me closer. There was nothing in his face of the man who had been with me the night before.

"Nevertheless," he said, his voice now soft, "I did achieve good union with the One. Perhaps I should have explored this avenue of meditation previously."

Those words hurt me more than his hands. Boaz had left the One far behind him when he brought me to his bed. But I could understand why he lied to himself.

He wrapped his arm about my shoulders to hold me tightly against him, then placed his hand over my face. His fingers gripped me painfully, and I struggled helplessly against him.

"I can make sure that you will not conceive," he said. "*Absolutely* sure—"

"No, Excellency!" I cried. "There are herbals I can—"

"Absolutely sure," he whispered, and the power of the One flooded my body.

Nothing I had felt before prepared me for this. Even the pain he'd caused me in the workshop had been inconsequential compared to what he did now.

My breath racked in for a scream, but I was in such agony I could not let it go. The power seared through me, concentrating in my belly, roping about like a blade out of control. It was surely tearing me apart.

Another surge, and my body jerked about in his arms. I don't know how he managed to hold me, for I was convulsing uncontrollably by now.

"Absolutely sure," I think I heard him whisper from very far away, then he dropped me on the bed.

I came to perhaps an hour later. I whimpered, for the pain was still almost unbearable.

"You will get dressed, and then you will get out."

My hands clenched at the sheets and I dragged myself to the side of the bed. My body screamed at the abuse it had taken and at the abuse I was now subjecting it to, but I had to get out. *Had* to.

My vision blurred, and I groped about for my dress, pulling it over my shoulders. Then I struggled to my feet, bent almost double, one arm wrapped about my belly, the other feeling along the wall for the door.

"I will summon you again," he said, and I stumbled out into the blessed sunshine.

Kiamet carried me back to the tenement building. For that I will be everlastingly grateful to him. He had kind hands and an even kinder voice, and I think he said a number of unkind things about Boaz on the way.

Isphet was appalled, as were the other two women of our quarters.

"What has he *done?*" she whispered as she lowered me onto my sleeping pallet.

"Ensured I will not subdivide the One," I said, then I fainted.

She washed me, and fed me a drink that eased much of the pain, then wrapped me in blankets and let me lie back down.

"You must stay here today," she said. "Not even Boaz would insist you make an appearance at the workshop."

"Thank you, Isphet," I said, and grasped her hand. Apart from wanting to know what he'd done to hurt me so badly, she'd asked no further questions.

"Sleep," she said.

I woke in the early afternoon and lay for some time, not thinking, not wanting to think. Much of the pain had subsided, but when I lifted the blankets I saw that my belly was deeply bruised, evidence of the internal hurt.

I wept then, for I was sure that he had utterly destroyed any chance I would have for bearing children. It was my penalty for witnessing what I had.

"Tirzah?"

The door to the internal courtyard opened and a figure slipped through. "Tirzah?"

"Yaqob!" and then he had me in his arms, soothing me and crying with me.

He saw the bruises, and the hurt in my eyes, and he rocked me in his arms, and promised me a death for Boaz that would pain him ten times more than he had pained me.

But that gave me little comfort, for I was not sure, even after what he'd done to me that morning, that I wanted him to die.

"Yaqob, how did you get here?"

"Shush, love," he murmured. "I was careful. Everyone thinks I'm in Threshold, laying glass. But, after what Isphet told me this morning, I had to come . . ."

"Oh, Yaqob!" I sobbed anew, and he kissed me, and let me weep.

"I have to go," he said after a while. "I dare not stay any longer."

"I thank you," I whispered. "But go now, for I could not bear it if you were seized on my account."

He kissed me again, and smiled for me, although his eyes were grim, and then he was gone.

I lay for perhaps another hour, then I struggled into my

wrap, combed my hair into some semblance of order, and carefully, carefully, made my way out into the street. I blinked in the sunshine. It seemed strange that everything was carrying on as normal.

But there was something I had to do. Something I had to destroy as Boaz had all but destroyed me this morning.

Very slowly I made my way to Isphet's workshop.

She was appalled that I had left my pallet.

"You need at least a day and a night, Tirzah. And we can manage without you today."

"I will not stay long. There is something I must do."

And she let me go.

Some of the workers nodded to me as I crossed the floor toward the stairs, and Druse caught at my elbow, fearful to hug me. "Daughter . . ."

"Shush, Father. I will be all right. Let me go now."

And he did.

The stairs were hard, but the pain was receding with every hour that passed, so I managed them with reasonable dignity. Zeldon and Orteas put their arms about me, their voices murmuring, and I let them hold me for a few minutes, then I gently disengaged myself.

"Let me go now, there is something I must do."

I went to the place where I had secreted the goblet. I had wrapped it in thick rag and cloth, and Zeldon and Orteas could not understand what was in the bundle I carried, but they did not pry.

I went back down the stairs, and made my way toward the furnace.

What I would do would kill the glass, and for that I was truly saddened, but it would have to die. I couldn't let it live now. Not after what he'd done.

Neither could I unwrap it, for I did not want to hear its soft whispering, asking what I did to carry it so close to the heat and flame.

"Tirzah? What is that you do?" Isphet asked behind me.

"Think not that I intend to kill myself, Isphet. Please, leave me be."

And she faded back into the workshop.

The heat of the furnace was very hot on my face, but it was comforting, and I realized why Raguel had liked to work so close to the fires. Somehow they would have scathed away so much of the hurt to which she, too, had been subjected.

I was so close to the flames now that they seared the tears from my cheeks. I lifted the bundle in my hand and stepped up to the great doorways. Beyond them, red and yellow and orange flames and streaks of heat rippled and writhed, so intensely alive they called to me.

I prepared to cast the goblet in as Raguel had once cast in the bundle that represented her child.

Sweet, sweet Tirzah, let us touch you, touch you, hold you, soothe you, love you.

"No!" I cried and raised the bundle.

Sweet Tirzah, let us love you and hold you, let us soothe away the hurt, let us speak to you, talk to you, talk to you . . . talk . . .

"No!" I sobbed, but I had lowered the bundle in my hands, and my head drooped.

Talk to us, Tirzah, let us love you, touch you, soothe you . . .

And there was nothing I wanted more. Nothing.

My entire body racked with sobs now, I clutched the bundle to my breast and fled into the tiny alcove at the rear of the furnace. There I curled up into a tight ball, wrapping myself about the bundled goblet.

Soothe you, soothe you, love you . . .

And they did, although to this day I'm not sure how they managed it. After a long time I unwrapped the goblet, and turned it over and over in my hands.

The Goblet of the Frogs was all but complete. There was some fine sanding to be done among the river reeds, but the frogs were finished, and the lacework of the cage was fine and strong, and it was the most beautiful thing I had ever created.

The amber frogs were alive, crawling through the reeds, their eyes black and glistening with sympathy, reaching their cool, moist toes through the reeds to touch my hands and stroke my skin, then, suddenly shy, hiding among the waving reeds until their courage returned and they reached forth again.

Hello Tirzah.

The voices of the Soulenai, speaking to me through the mouths of the glass frogs.

I dashed away the final tears. *Greetings, Soulenai.*

This is a beautiful goblet, Tirzah. Deeply magical. Do not destroy it.

No. No, I won't.

You carved it for . . . him.

Yes. But I do not think I will give—

Shush, and listen to what we have to say to you, Tirzah.

I kept my silence.

We watched and listened last night. We were pleased at what we heard.

They were silent for a while, and I thought they must still be overcome by what they had heard and witnessed. After a long time they spoke again.

That is the Book of the Soulenai, Tirzah.

Your book.

Yes, Tirzah. Be quiet. Let us speak, but we must of necessity be brief, and we cannot tell you it all. Listen. Boaz is an Elemental Cantomancer.

No, no, it cannot be—

Yes, it can be, Tirzah, and it is. His father used that book to make him, spun magics about his conception and about the woman he made him in, and created an Elemental within her womb. Of course, he did not expect to be eaten by a water lizard within days of the conception. The boy was born and grew without his father to guide him, grew in a sterile and polluted environment where the Magi seized him and corrupted him as a child.

I thought of the scroll he had written as a nine-year-old child. Perhaps the Magi made their move when his mother died. And they never "understood" what they had in their care.

He was a Prince at court, Tirzah. The Magi seduced him in the hope that through him they could extend their power over the Chad and his heir. He has exceeded their expectations. Boaz has become a Magus of great power and purpose and influence and he works well for their cause. For Threshold.

But . . .

But underneath all of this lay the makings, the blood, of an extraordinary Cantomancer, Tirzah. The growing boy, trying to be at one with the One, was horrified by the whispers he heard about him. Horrified by the talents he displayed. So he buried them deep. Buried his true self deep.

I thought of his residence. It was bare of anything that might whisper to him. Few metals, no gems, no glass. Wooden goblets.

Tirzah, the Magus is in almost full control. Only rarely does Boaz relax enough—and only ever with you—to reveal his true nature. Yet even with you such revelations frighten him. Terrify him.

"There is no hope for him. He will *never* let the Cantomancer through." I spoke aloud now, wanting to deny Boaz with my voice.

There is hope, Tirzah. There must be hope, for Boaz is the only one with a chance of destroying the horror that Threshold is becoming.

What do you mean?

He is Magus-trained, and you have felt yourself the degree of the power of the One that he commands. He understands Threshold in a manner that we, or you, cannot. Yet he is also a Cantomancer. He will be able to wield powerful magic on that day he learns to combine both sides of his nature. He must be the key to Threshold's destruction.

My mouth twisted bitterly. *He will never destroy—*

You must persuade him, sweet Tirzah. You must make him see who he is, teach him not to fear his hidden self, open himself to the elements, to us, to the Song of the Frogs.

He will never listen to me. He will never let himself be who he truly is. You know what he did to me. You know.

Yes, we know, sweet Tirzah, but there is hope.

Now I did laugh bitterly. *Hope? Hope? After what he put me through? He will always deny his Elemental side. Always.*

We believe not, Tirzah. Think, if you will. Think. He has kept the Book of the Soulenai, even though he must have known it was crafted of Elemental magic. Yes?

Yes, I said reluctantly.

He could have, should have killed you this morning, Tirzah. What true Magus, fully in control, would have let a woman live who had seen enough to think him an Elemental? Who knew that he kept an Elemental talisman? And who he knows must be Elemental herself?

What he did was bad enough.

Yes, yes it was. But even that was not as bad as it could have been.

Oh? And how much worse could it have been? He has destroyed any chance I have of bearing children. My womb has been rent and shredded.

No, Tirzah. He has hurt you badly, but he stayed the worst of the power. Your womb will recover, although it may take months, even years, to do so.

I was crying now. Even if my womb did recover, it would not lessen the betrayal of what he had done.

Tirzah, if someone visits such pain on another person, then one day that pain will rebound on them. It is the price he will eventually have to pay. Tirzah, he could have killed you, he could have permanently crippled you, but he did not.

I shook my head, not wanting to forgive him.

You do not have to forgive him, Tirzah. That is something he will have to seek from you himself. But listen to us. Listen. There is hope for the Elemental within that cruel hoax that calls itself Magus. Has he not hidden himself from Threshold? Has he not kept the Song of the Frogs alive in his heart for years and years? Tirzah, you must work to help him accept his true heritage. He's struggling within himself now, screaming for help. Be the one to give it to him. Help him. And you know as we do that there is only one person he will let help him. You.

The Magus is too powerful . . .

You must find a way, Tirzah. Do all you can. Be there. Go back when he calls you. Finish the goblet and give it to him.

He destroyed the other glass.

Then we must hope that he will not destroy this one. Tirzah, do this for us. Help him, for he is the only one who can destroy Threshold—and we do not believe any of you yet realize what a terrible thing Threshold will eventually become. Help him. Soothe him, hold him, love him. Promise us this. Promise.

Yes, I promise.

I cried for a long time, then I grew sick of my tears and resolved to weep no more. I sighed and walked through the workshop, up the stairs, and sat down at the worktable with Zeldon and Orteas.

Lifting a sanding strip, I sat for the five hours it took me to finish the goblet.

Zeldon's and Orteas's eyes widened at the sight of the glass, but they did not speak, and neither did I.

TWENTY-ONE

I did not see Boaz for several weeks, which did not surprise me. He had revealed so much, so dangerously, that he would not call me again until he felt in full control. Until the Magus felt invulnerable.

But I was alive, and continued to live, and for that I suppose I was grateful.

My injuries healed as best they could, although when I pressed with my fingers all I could feel of my womb was a hard lump instead of soft, pliant flesh. I wondered if the Soulenai were right in saying that one day I would bear children, but all I could do for now was hope.

I did not tell Isphet or anyone else of what the Soulenai had told me. To do so I would have to reveal all, and I was locked too deeply into my secrets now to let a single one go. Besides, I wanted time to think. I wanted to see Boaz again. Be sure.

I went back to work with the glass, often helping out with the mixing and firing of the blue-green plate glass, as much of the work for the Infinity Chamber had gone to Izzali's workshop. Soon we would begin the capstone. And then Threshold would be all but finished.

The plating now spread down the eastern face. Early one morning I went with Yaqob and a worker called Fust to help with a particularly difficult section of the glass. It would be my first time on the glass face, and I was a little nervous. But I wanted to go. The kindness of those within the workshop was stifling me.

Yaqob was cautious, but I was agile enough, and not afraid of heights, and he would be there to help me. And it would be nice to have some time together. Boaz confused me, and Yaqob was so straightforward. He had no hidden depths to tug at my own soul.

It was a lovely morning. As we used the ropes hanging from the peak to pull ourselves up, I laughed at Yaqob's jesting and at the middle-aged Fust's panting behind me. Even Threshold's danger seemed mute, distant. We climbed to a spot two-thirds of the way up the face, and as we finally eased ourselves into a safe position, waiting for the glass to be winched up to us, I looked out over the landscape.

It stunned me. I hadn't realized I would be able to see so much. Neither did I realize it would be so beautiful.

To the east the great Lhyl River wound its serpentine way through the land, green reed banks lining its path, irrigated fields and gardens stretching out about half a league on either side. Beyond them stretched league after league of desert, patched here and there with a stand of date palms about a spring or well. Far distant I thought I saw a slow caravan wending its way north. I wondered if it carried slaves, or more inanimate cargo. I returned my gaze to the river. Several graceful riverboats plied south along its waters. The Lhyl was a wonderful gift to give the land, I thought. No wonder the frogs had sung for the Soulenai.

"Look," Yaqob said, and pointed north. There lay a smudge on the horizon, a distant haze. Setkoth. Closer than I'd thought, but still a good half day's travel by riverboat.

To the immediate east and south of us lay Gesholme. It looked even uglier from above than it did from within. To the southwest, hidden by Threshold at my back, lay the compound of the Magi. It made me think of Boaz, and then Yaqob nudged me.

He pointed down this time. Far below, their forms puppet-like, a group of workers fastened plate glass to the ropes that would be used to haul them upward. Beside them were several Magi, Boaz among them.

I shouldn't have been able to distinguish him from this height, for his clothing and head of black hair were virtually identical to the other Magi about him. But his movements were so familiar, the sweep of his hand, the way he shifted his weight from hip to hip, that I knew it was him.

I closed my eyes, took a deep breath, then opened them again.

"Boaz?" Yaqob asked softly at my side

"Yes, to the left. See?"

"He spoils the beauty of the morning, Tirzah."

I nodded, opened my mouth to say something, then there was a shout above us, and all thought turned to the glass that fellow slaves were now hauling upward.

The glass climbed ever higher, and we made ready to receive it, securing our feet in their notches.

Threshold's shadow winked.

It was so brief, but I was sure. I felt it in the pit of my stomach as well as saw it, and I knew.

"Yaqob!" I cried, terrified, and he wrapped his arms about me as tight as he could—as if that could save me had I been chosen. He, too, had seen and felt what I had.

Who?

The glass sliding upward passed over the mouth of one of the shafts. As it did so there was a burst—an *explosion*—of heat and light from the mouth . . . and the massive plate of glass melted.

Melted into the vicious black substance I had seen coat the walls and ceiling of the corridor that had cooked the five.

Seven. But who?

Mostly the poor men who slaved below to haul the glass skyward, and one donkey-handler standing close to them.

Great gobs of molten glass poured down and spattered the men.

They took agonizing minutes to die, and I think Threshold had planned it that way. The glass seared great chunks off their skin and flesh. One man had his face eaten away, another half his chest. Another yet lost the flesh off his arms, and ran screaming about the compound, waving the blackened sticklike objects about. Apologetic whiffs of smoke drifted from them.

I leaned in against Yaqob and hid my face, and he held me tight until the screams and howls had been silenced.

Only then I dared look down again.

Boaz was staring up at me.

I was shaking, and could do no work. No one could, the day's glass had been destroyed and more would have to be transported to the site.

By the time we got down Boaz had gone.

Yaqob saw a tall, athletic man of early middle age in the crowd of laborers milling about the compound, and he gave a slight nod of his head.

The man responded and disappeared into the throng. Yaqob, Fust, and I walked silently back to the workshop.

The athletic man joined us there in the midafternoon when the fuss had died down.

His name was Azam, and he was the one who Yaqob now depended on to bring the laborers behind his plan for revolt. Azam was a striking man, keen eyes, aquiline face, graying hair. I thought he looked anything but a laborer, and wondered if he had been born into slavery or had been subjected to it through misfortune.

Again we met in the upper room.

"Threshold has worked in our favor this time," Azam said.

"How so?" Yaqob asked.

"Among the laborers there grows the sense that they are just fodder for Threshold's appetite," Azam said. "I have spread the word about the incomposite numbers, about how they grow into Infinity itself and how all of us, eventually, will die. Yaqob, almost to a man, they are now committed to you. Even if Threshold takes me, they will still follow. They know that if we revolt many will die, but they also know that many will escape, and that is enough."

"Azam, that is good news."

"And I have even better, Yaqob."

"Yes?"

"Last night one of my men discovered a site where the guards store spare weapons."

"Azam!" Yaqob leaned forward. "Tell me!"

As Azam described the location of the weapons, I watched the faces about me. They had lost all suspicion of me since Boaz had abused me so badly, and now did not hesitate to talk before me.

And yet if only they knew what secrets I held.

I longed to tell them that Boaz had been born an Elemental Cantomancer, and that he hid a kinder face behind that of the Magus, but they would have regarded me with astonishment that would have rapidly deepened into suspicion. None but I had ever seen what the deception of the Magus hid, and they would never, never, believe that he was a Cantomancer. Has poor Tirzah fallen in love with her captor, they would wonder, and then say that such a thing is not unknown.

And if she has, then will she betray us to him? Then they would be silent and distrustful of me, and that was the last thing I wanted.

If Boaz *could* be persuaded to accept his Elemental heritage, then surely I'd be able to persuade him before Yaqob's plans for revolt ripened into action. And then he could help us. We could all escape together, and no one need lose their lives.

If Boaz could *not* be persuaded before Yaqob led his revolt, if the Magus remained in tight control, then he would be a hopeless case, and I would tell the Soulenai so. And we would flee into the night and into freedom without him.

Whatever, I wanted to know what Yaqob was up to. I wanted to know when and how he planned to launch his strike. I would never betray him or any of my friends to Boaz, never that, *never*. But I hated to think that they might murder Boaz when I was within days of persuading him to help us.

That would be . . . a shame.

"Tirzah?"

I jumped, so absorbed in my thoughts I'd lost track of the conversation. Isphet.

"Tirzah, all of us hate to ask this, you know we do, but do you think Boaz will call you back?"

Again I wondered if all they wanted me for was to collect information for them. Then I dismissed the ungracious thought. Boaz had ignored me these past weeks, and all—Isphet and Yaqob more than most—had been kind and generous to me.

"Sooner or later, yes. He said he would." I sighed. "It's just that I displeased him so greatly the last time I was there . . ."

Yaqob's arm was about me again. "One weapons cache is not enough, and it is too well guarded at the moment for us to have a real chance at it. Tirzah, you know how desperate we are for weapons. If only you could find out where other caches are, and the number of guards that patrol them. If we had more weapons, we would have a real chance. A *real* chance."

"I know, Yaqob."

"Well." Isphet smiled. "We mustn't stand about here idle all day. Azam, take care that you're not seen on your way back."

He nodded and left quietly.

"Yaqob, Tirzah. I wonder if you could collect some more potash from Izzali's workshop?" She smiled at us. "There is no need to rush. Take your time."

We took our time. Yaqob led me to one of our favorite haunts, a small space used for the storage of water urns and in a relatively isolated alley. He drew the canvas across the opening, then pulled me into his arms.

"Tirzah, it has been so long." His voice was rough with desire, and I tried to relax. It had been several months since Boaz had first called me to his quarters, and Yaqob had not made love to me in that entire time. Perhaps it was only now that he trusted me, was sure of me, perhaps that was all he needed to regain his desire.

He pressed me hard against a wall, pulling my wrap down, his hands at my breasts, my back, my buttocks, his mouth hard, demanding.

I tried to relax—had I not let him do this countless times before? But I was tense and uncomfortable, and Yaqob was not yet so consumed by his desire he could not feel it.

"Shush, love, it's all right. I won't hurt you. Come on now, relax, relax."

I tried, gods know I tried, but when he pulled me down to the floor and settled his weight upon me, I cried out and tried to push him away.

"No, Tirzah, it's too late," he said. "I can't stop now. Please, let me . . ."

But this time I was not prepared to put up with the discomfort and the indignity of the dirt anymore. With the last of my strength I managed to roll away from him.

"Yaqob, I'm sorry . . . but it hurts . . . it hurts . . ."

He grabbed me again, rolling me back, and I thought he would force me. "You said the pain had all gone. That you were healed."

"Yes, but I didn't realize . . . until I felt you . . . Yaqob, please, it hurt me."

He cursed and rolled completely away, sitting with his back to me. After a long time he spoke over his shoulder. "Tirzah, I'm sorry. But I thought—"

"It's Boaz," I said, "it's what he did to me."

Yaqob sighed and helped me up. Thinking he understood what I meant. "When he's dead it won't matter," he said. "It won't hurt then."

That night Boaz sent for me. I was half expecting it, for Threshold had frightened everyone that day, and the Magus would surely be feeling in total control.

But it was late, and our quarters were asleep when the guard banged at the door.

"Open!" he cried as Isphet sleepily made her way to the door. "Open up!"

"Yes?"

One day, I thought, I will master that imperious "Yes?"

I was up and halfway into my dress by the time Isphet came for me. She leaned forward and kissed my cheek. "Be careful, Tirzah. Be very careful."

I returned her kiss and paused long enough to give her a quick hug. "Thank you, Isphet," and then I was gone.

Outside in the still night air the nerves struck. My stomach churned, and I had to clutch my arms about me to keep them from trembling.

"What's wrong?" Kiamet asked.

"Nothing. The night air. It's cold."

"He's in a bad mood. Be careful."

I stared at him, wondering at his kindness. I also wondered how much he'd seen and heard from his silent post on the verandah.

Kiamet didn't say anything else, and delivered me to Boaz's residence.

Again I shivered, hesitated, then walked to the rectangle of light.

"Excellency?"

"Enter."

I went in, bowed, then collected the pitcher and water and washed his hands and feet. He was silent, staring. I kept my eyes down, my breathing as gentle as I could, and hoped that I would not rattle the pottery or spill the water. I sensed he was waiting for a slip—any slip.

I did not give it to him, and eventually he handed me the oil to massage in.

The fragrance was soothing, but I did not let it relax me.

He took the vial back, put it on the desk. "Get up."

I rose.

He stared at me, so fully the Magus I could feel as well as see the power of the One radiating from him. "Have you learned your place?"

"Yes, Excellency."

"Good. Then take off your dress and wait for me in the bed. I shall join you shortly."

He left me lying there for close on three hours; still, tense, terrified. He sat at the desk, his stylus scratching back and forth, back and forth, back and forth.

Every few minutes my eyes drooped closed, then I would open them wide, scared I would slip into sleep. That would have angered him more than anything else. It would have been a presumption.

Eventually he sat back, wiped then put away his stylus, rose, and extinguished the two lamps, leaving only faint moonlight to illuminate the room. He walked over to the bed and stood looking at me.

I didn't know what to do. I had not covered myself, and I wondered if that was a mistake. But just as I was about to reach for the sheet he turned aside and disrobed, hanging his clothes over the back of a chair.

He sat on the side of the bed, sighed, then rubbed his eyes with his hand. When he dropped his hand I could see that his face was very weary.

"I had to do it, Tirzah," he said, and the coldness had gone from his voice. "I had to."

"I know, Excellency," I whispered.

He nodded, hesitated, then lay down beside me, but not touching me, as tense as I was. "Tirzah . . ."

Then he sighed again, and rolled over and gathered me into his arms.

I kept very silent, and kept my responses very passive, not wanting to do anything to frighten him. Yet even so, it was good.

Again I woke to stare into the eyes of the Magus. Distant, derisory. I tensed, waiting for the pain.

But it didn't come. He handed me my robe. "Get dressed."

I scrambled into it, then hesitated, unsure as Holdat entered and laid out a meal of bread, oil, and cheese with a pitcher of goat's milk.

Boaz sat down, then waved to me to sit and eat.

Every move I made I thought I'd drop something, clatter something else, and how I forced some of the bread down I don't know. The milk was easier.

"I have decided that this union with the One through the use of a woman's body does have some merit," he said.

In the present tension that was almost too much, and despite the danger sliding about the room I had to bite my lip to keep from giggling inanely. Some merit, indeed. Well, I suppose the Magus had to justify himself however he thought appropriate. I dropped my eyes to the plate. "Yes, Excellency," I mumbled.

"I have decided to explore it further."

I looked up, wondering what he was leading to. He was looking at me very carefully, and I realized that he was as unsure of himself as he was of me.

"But I cannot keep Kiamet scrambling about Gesholme every time I need to find you."

I took a deep, unbelieving breath.

"So I have decided that you will move into these quarters. There is a small closet at the rear that you will inhabit whenever I have no use for you."

I let my breath out slowly. "Yes, Excellency." I doubted I would ever see the inside of this "closet."

"Apart from the capstone, the caging work is almost complete, and the six other cagers can do that. I think I will keep you at work here. There are several other Geshardi treatises that I would like translated."

"Yes, Excellency." Emotion soared through me, but I kept my face bland and submissive. The Magus would never have allowed this, never. Were the Soulenai right? *Did* he want me to help him?

"Do you have any questions?"

"Excellency, I have some small items that I will need from my quarters, and there is something I would like to collect from Isphet's workshop."

"Slaves have no possessions, Tirzah."

I dropped my eyes, unsure again.

"But you may go. Be back here by midmorning."

"Thank you, Excellency." I rose, bowed, and walked outside, trying to keep my gait from springing with hope. He had shown me something of his true self again last night, had shown some regret for his actions, and yet this morning the Magus had not felt it necessary to exact retribution for my witnessing of such fragility. In fact, for a Magus, he had been quite pleasant.

And to share his quarters! *No* Magus ever did that with a woman!

I wondered, hoped, if the man so long denied was sliding closer and closer to the surface. If one day the Magus would dare to let him free.

As I passed Kiamet I smiled and winked, and then laughed at his shocked face.

I sat at the translation for most of the afternoon. It was an even drier treatise than previously—is any given line composed of a finite or an infinite number of dots?—but I sat happily, and the hours flew by.

Boaz spent the entire day at Threshold. Holdat brought me a light meal after noon, and I thanked him, and he looked surprised at that, but managed to return the smile before he left.

I hummed a little as I worked. All within the workshop were stunned by the news I was to move into Boaz's quarters. My father had hugged me, and told me to be careful. Isphet had been quiet, and Yaqob's eyes had darkened into unreadability, but both had thought this a good opportunity for them. Surely I would find out something of use.

And so here I was, and I hoped it would end well. I would live life on a dangerous blade-edge, ever careful not to provoke the Magus, but ever hopeful that he would relax more and more until I would spend most of the time with that man who had shown me his father's book.

I thought I would like that very much.

There was a step at the door, and I turned about—careful with my movement.

Boaz. He removed his outer robe, then asked how the translation went. He felt no need for harsh words.

"Excellency, it is going well."

"And do you find it fascinating, Tirzah?"

"Ah, Excellency, it is a truly astounding piece of work."

"Really, Tirzah? Then I must have given you the wrong treatise to translate."

My eyes flew to his, but they were blank, and his face was devoid of humor. I looked back at the desk.

"You may sit on the verandah, Tirzah, or stroll the gardens, until Holdat brings the meal."

"I thank you, Excellency."

I returned from the verandah when I saw Holdat approach with his covered tray, and this time he was the first to smile. But I noticed he wiped it from his face before he stepped inside.

The meal passed silently. Boaz served me himself, and that gave me the courage for what I had to do. There would be no good time, only a worse than usual time, and this was not one of those.

After Holdat had removed the remains of the meal, Boaz waved me to the chairs by the window. On the way I lifted a bundle from a shadowy space among the papyri rolls on the shelves that ran the length of one wall.

He saw, and tensed.

I dropped to my knees before him and bowed my head. "Excellency, forgive my forwardness."

"You should know better, Tirzah."

But his voice was tight rather than angry, and I looked up. "Excellency. I know that on many occasions I have angered you when you have only tried to teach me what is right, and for that, I crave your pardon. Excellency, I have learned so much from you that I find it hard to express my gratitude. I have not the words for it, but perhaps this will demonstrate something of what I feel."

And I held the bundle out for him.

I think he accepted it only because my hands shook as I held it out, and he could see the fear burn bright in my eyes.

I *was* afraid, because what I gave him now presumed so much that he might well retreat into a fury that could kill me.

My heart thudded as he slowly unwrapped the cloths, then they fell free, and he turned the Goblet of the Frogs over in his hands.

His eyes were downcast, and I could not read them, so I looked back to the goblet. For me it sang, and I wondered whether Boaz could hear it, too. I could almost see the frogs move; I could almost hear the Soulenai hold their collective breath.

Boaz took its weight in one hand, then held it up so that the amber glass sparkled in the light.

He was going to dash it to the floor!

"I dropped the other one," he said quietly.

"Yes, Excellency."

"And I have every right to do so with this one."

"Yes, Excellency. Slaves own nothing."

He tormented me for a moment more, then finally lowered it, and I (as the Soulenai) let out my breath. Again he rolled it between his hands, studying it intently. "Why the frogs, Tirzah? They are ugly brutes to decorate a goblet with."

"Their song is comforting, Excellency. It is the first sound I wake to, and the last I hear at night."

"But now *my* voice will be the sound you will sleep and wake to, Tirzah!"

"Yes, Excellency. Please, I do beg your—"

"Oh, be quiet," he said, "and take this ugly piece of glass and put it back on the shelf where it won't irritate my sight."

"Yes, Excellency. Thank you, Excellency."

And so a month passed. Boaz never revealed himself to the extent he had that night he'd had me read from the Book of the Soulenai, but neither did he revert to the hateful man who'd torn me apart the following morning. I think that I had earned some measure of his trust, for he could find no way in which I'd taken advantage of that moment of abhorrent weakness I'd witnessed. But he could still remain cold and distant with me for days on end. Then I would silently continue at whatever translation he gave me, and I learned his habits so that I could anticipate his every need. Gradually he would warm back into disinterest and occasional rebuke.

As I suspected, I was never banished to the closet (in reality a small storeroom at the rear of his house). He let me roam about his residence as much as I liked, as in the gardens close by. The room I knew so well was the main chamber of the house. Several smaller rooms ran off it, and they contained nothing of interest. But at the back of the house lay something I had never suspected—a charming bathing house. It was verandahed like the house, and was protected by the wall, and in the evenings Boaz would ask me to bathe with him in the great, square bathing pool. It was tiled in such vivid emerald glass that the water glowed as if lit from beneath, and the water was delightful after the heat of the day. No one else used the pool, and we had complete privacy. Often I dived down to the bottom of the pool to lay my hands and cheek against the glass, feeling its cool joy, until Boaz would dive to fetch me.

But it was at night, in the darkness and intimacy of the bed, that he let me get closest to him, in both emotional and physical senses. Sometimes he would lie and talk for hours, very quietly, telling me stories of the court. Never personal, never dangerous, but stories that showed me glimpses of the man he truly was.

I never asked him questions. Nor did I ever call him Boaz.

Sometimes he would ask me to tell him of life in Viland. As I spoke, he would roll closer to me and fold me in his arms, and I would lay my head on his chest and fight to keep my voice expressionless. He never asked me questions about Geshardi, but on these nights he would always make love to me with such sweetness and tenderness I would sometimes cry afterward, and this he did not seem to mind very much at all.

On the mornings after this sweetness and tenderness he would be terse and cold, and I had to be extremely careful. He would eventually relax, sometimes over a day, sometimes taking two or three. But relax he would.

On occasion it was the chilling Magus who lay down beside me, but he would roll over and go straight to sleep, pretending I did not exist. He never "used" me, he never "communed" with the One through me. The Magus never laid a finger on me.

And the Goblet of the Frogs stayed on the shelves. I never saw him handle it, or even look at it, but he did not break it— and I noticed that it collected no dust.

He occasionally allowed me to visit Isphet. Sometimes he insisted Kiamet accompany me, sometimes he asked Holdat to go with me. Rarely was I allowed to go back to Isphet's workshop or her quarters alone, and generally only when Boaz knew Yaqob would be busy at Threshold.

Either he still distrusted Yaqob, or he was jealous of him. I realized that I hoped it was the latter.

One day a week Boaz made me accompany him on his inspections of Threshold. Only the gods know what everyone thought about the Magus dragging his mistress through the site after him, but they kept their eyes downcast and their faces respectful. On these tours Boaz was always very distant, sometimes to the point of spitefulness. It hurt, until I realized that he only ever relaxed with me in the privacy and safety of his residence (his safe residence), and he was unlikely to present anything other than his Magus face to me, or to anyone else, where Threshold could see.

By the end of the month the plating on the northern face had begun. Isphet told me that Orteas and Zeldon were busy with the plates for the capstone, as were those workers in Izzali's workshop. The Infinity Chamber had been completed, and now no one was allowed in there save the Magi.

Almost finished, Threshold was changing, and I did not know what to do about it.

The exterior blue-green remained unchanged, and the last time anyone had seen the Infinity Chamber it had still been golden, but the rest of Threshold's internal spaces were turning into slippery glazed black. Any tools left inside overnight were stone in the morning.

None of the Magi seemed concerned, and Boaz always appeared delighted with the progress.

"It's even better than I'd dreamed," he had said on that day he'd first seen the black corridor and the five blackened bodies. "Far more powerful. Far more."

And while Boaz gradually relaxed with me, he never hid his delight in Threshold. I wondered one evening, as he and another Magus sat laughing and drinking on the verandah, if he would ever be able to let go his addiction to the power that was Threshold.

If, finally, the lure of the threshold would be too great.

TWENTY-TWO

I was tidying the desk when first I noticed it. Several other Magi had spent some hours here the night before (I'd sat quietly in a corner, rising only to serve wine as it was needed), talking to Boaz about the final date for the completion of Threshold, and passing about several papyri rolls and bundles. Eventually Boaz had sent me to stroll the gardens for an hour or two as they discussed more private business, and when I'd returned the Magi had gone and Boaz was asleep in bed.

It was a scrap of papyrus paper only, and I might have put it to one side had not the word "weapon" leaped out at me.

My heart beat faster. This was no idle notation regarding mathematics or geometry.

Almost instantly I dropped it, whipping my head up, certain I would see Boaz standing in a doorway or window, watching me.

But I was alone. Boaz was at Threshold, Kiamet with him. Even Holdat was busy elsewhere in the compound.

I picked the paper up again and read, my heartbeat now scudding painfully fast.

I knew Boaz had frustrated Yaqob time and time again; first by ordering the search that had discovered the blades Yaqob and his fellow plotters had built up over many months, then by constantly moving the soldiers' various weapon caches about the site.

What I had here was the location of a temporary site. Over two hundred lances, five hundred swords, and a hundred pikes were being moved there today and stored for a week only before they'd be moved somewhere else.

I put the paper down, shaking.

It was not a particularly large cache, but that in itself was tempting. I knew Yaqob and Azam only wanted to know the sites of the caches so that on the day they rose against the Magi they could seize the weapons. It was a risky plan. Yet here was a cache of weapons that if seized now could be hidden about Gesholme. One or two swords here, a pike or a lance there. In a search many might be found, but many others would not.

I looked at the location again. It would be so easy for them. Perhaps only one or two guards to dispose of, and two dozen men could spirit the weapons away in a few minutes.

And, oh! They'd be so useful. It would mean the difference between an uprising doomed to failure and one that might just succeed.

"Yaqob," I breathed, and stumbled back to the bed.

What should I do? *This* was what Yaqob had thought I might find all along. *This* was the information he'd wanted.

And *this* was exactly how Boaz might set out to trap me. He was a careful man, so very careful. He would never leave information like this lying about.

Yet it was only a scrap, as if it had fallen unnoticed from a sheaf of papers. And there *had* been a large number of papers passed about last night.

"Yaqob," I whispered again, and rested my head in my hands, thinking.

Was there still enough of the Magus in Boaz to try to trap me like this? Yes. But what if it wasn't a trap, what if I *did* tell Yaqob, and he succeeded in his uprising because of it? Would I betray Boaz by revealing the location of the weapons? Or would I betray Yaqob by remaining silent? I didn't know what to do. It was like trying to outmaneuver a viper. Either way and it would strike.

They had a week. I could think about it for a day or two, then tell them. Watch Boaz, see if he watched me more than usual.

The more immediate problem was what to do with the scrap of paper itself. In the end I burned it. If Boaz *didn't* know about it, then he wouldn't miss it. If he *did* know it was there, then he would expect me to burn it anyway.

"Damn you, Boaz," I muttered as I watched it burn to untraceable ashes. "Damn you whether you planted it or lost it!"

I disposed of the ashes, then went about my usual routine, and watched Boaz as closely as I could without raising suspicion.

But he gave me few clues. The only one, if clue it was, came on the third day of the week when he gave me permission to visit Isphet's workshop unescorted. I was somehow not surprised to find Yaqob there.

"Tirzah!" He took my hand, and smiled, but made no move to kiss me. "You look, well, pampered."

I colored. Boaz was growing bored with the white garment I wore each day, and so I now had several dresses, of varying degrees of richness but of the same cut and fashion as the white sheath. Today I wore a lemon-colored affair with dark green and red patterns about the hem and breast, hanging from a red- and gold-beaded collar. My skin glowed with over a month of good eating and a comfortable bed. I had discovered a new kohl of light gray that complimented the blue of my eyes. I looked like a woman content with her lot.

That was, I suppose, a mistake. I should have turned down the corners of my mouth and reddened my eyes before I let Yaqob see me.

"*He* does not 'hurt' you then, I see," he said flatly, and I winced.

"Yaqob, please . . ."

"Tirzah." Now Isphet stepped up and kissed my cheek. "What news?"

"Oh, I grow bored with my—" By the Soulenai themselves, I almost said "translating," and then thought, did they *know*? Holdat was a slave himself and had contacts outside the compound of the Magi; even the guard may well have gossiped. "Ah, I grow bored with my life of enforced idleness, Isphet. I long to be back here with you."

I hoped they would not read the lie in my face. I enjoyed their company, and I liked to visit, but I was also growing accustomed to the little luxuries of life with Boaz.

As I was growing accustomed to Boaz himself. Even his distant Magus persona. I was, I realized, settling into life with him. If I had to, it was going to be very, very hard to let go.

"I hope," Isphet said rather carefully, "that you do not grow so accustomed to your life of idleness you have forgotten what it was like to live and work the life of a slave?"

"And," Yaqob said, fingering the fine cloth of my dress, "you have not forgotten what it is that we all strive for."

"Freedom," I said in a small voice.

He nodded. "Tell us."

"Oh, Yaqob, there is not much to tell. We rise every morning, Boaz goes off to Threshold, I dust and doze until he comes back, we eat, we go to bed." I gave a shaky laugh. "I might be the wife of any boring citizen were it not for the robes and the manner of a Magus that Boaz wears."

Yaqob and Isphet looked at each other.

I took refuge in anger. "He tells me nothing! He does not trust me! Would you prefer that he beat me, hurt me as he did that one morning, than leave me in relative peace? Do you think to distrust me because I seek only to please him and humor him? Do you—"

"*Hush,*" Isphet said, and looked ashamed, which only made me feel worse. "I'm sorry, Tirzah. It must be hard for you."

"Well," I said, "I don't know if this is of any use or not . . ."

"Yes?" Both Isphet and Yaqob leaned forward.

"Boaz and his fellows have been discussing the date for completion of Threshold. There's to be a Consecration Day."

"When?"

"Eight weeks from last fifth-day. A big ceremony. They were *very* specific about the date. It's important for some reason. I think Boaz has been so jumpy over past months because he thought Threshold might not be ready in time."

"Thank you, Tirzah," Yaqob said. "That might well prove to be useful. Eight weeks. We don't have much time. Is there anything else?"

"No."

On the way back to Boaz's, *our,* residence I tried to justify my silence. I was only protecting Yaqob. If it was a trap, then he would die. But even if it wasn't, well, it would be a mission fraught with danger, and many might well lose their lives. Kiamet might be stationed there that night (although he'd not been moved from his post in months), and he had treated me with such kindness I'd not like to see him hurt. Yaqob might seize a weapon and do something foolish.

Like try to kill Boaz. I shuddered and hurried inside.

Five days passed.

It was very late one evening. Boaz had been genial if not exactly friendly all day, and I had great expectations for the night.

"Excellency, how does that feel?"

We were on the bed, Boaz lying naked on his stomach, me, also naked, kneeling beside him. I was slowly rubbing oil into the muscles of his back and legs. I don't know who was receiving more enjoyment from it, Boaz or me.

He murmured contentedly.

"Have I missed a patch, Excellency?"

"No." He rolled over. "Put the vial down, Tirzah."

I smiled and did as he asked, waiting for him to reach for me. But he didn't.

"Tirzah," he said, "I have had a worrying week."

"Excellency?"

"It seems I have misplaced a most important piece of papyrus."

My smile froze to my face.

"It contained information that, had it reached certain slaves, would have caused great trouble."

"Excellency, I don't know what you mean."

"No, Tirzah, I think that you do. Tell me."

I fought for time to think, turning a corner of linen over and over in my hands. He *knew*. But should I confess? Or continue to pretend ignorance?

"Excellency." My voice was very low, but I looked him in the eye. "I burned the paper. I realized its danger."

"Why didn't you just give it back to me, Tirzah?"

"I panicked, Excellency. I thought that if you knew I'd seen it, then you might think I might pass the information back to . . ."

Oh, gods, trying to watch every phrase I spoke throughout the day was a trial I could do without!

"To who, Tirzah? To Yaqob?"

"To any who might betray you," I said softly.

He seized my wrist. "I needed to know if you would betray me."

I was furious that he had again set out to entrap me . . . but at the same time I realized I had passed a crucial test. He could never have known if I owed my true loyalty to him or to Yaqob. Now I had shown my hand, and perhaps now he would trust me more.

"Do you still lie with him, Tirzah?"

"Not since you first summoned me to your residence, Excellency."

"Good," and he pulled me down to him. "Very good."

And I had a feeling that I had passed two tests that night.

TWENTY-THREE

I waited as Boaz questioned the foreman in charge of the plating, then fell into step behind him as he moved slowly around Threshold, his face upturned as he scanned the pyramid. I wondered how he could see it, for the sun glinted so fiercely off the glass that it must surely have hurt his eyes.

The wind ruffled my dress, and I smoothed it down. This was a particularly becoming dress, a deep violet with a delicate gold pattern running through it. I smiled as my fingers felt its silkiness. I wondered if I could persuade Boaz to obtain a crimson gown for me, for I thought it might suit my coloring very well.

I looked about. Scores of workers were now engaged in laying paving and tiling about Threshold rather than working on the pyramid itself. Hundreds more laid a great avenue from the riverbank through Gesholme to Threshold; many buildings had been destroyed to make way for it, and hundreds of slaves now slept in the open, or crowded into neighboring tenements.

Seven weeks to Consecration Day, and the preparations proceeded apace.

I smiled surreptitiously at a young man who was paving several paces away. He was particularly handsome, and I could see the admiration in his eyes as he looked at me.

I sighed. This was boring. I don't know why Boaz insisted I come with him for these inspections. Perhaps he only wanted to display me. That brought a small smile to my mouth, and I shook my hair out still farther. Boaz liked my hair long and loose, and it was growing out nicely. Would it take a month to reach the small of my back? Or only three weeks?

Several other Magi brushed past me and walked with Boaz, talking quietly. They smiled and nodded now and then; all were pleased with Threshold.

We'd reached the southern ramp now, and Boaz led us up toward Threshold's mouth. The skirts of my dress bunched in the stronger wind, and I frowned as I tried to make them lie smooth and becoming. Perhaps I should have picked something more serviceable to wear on this inspection.

Then we walked inside.

"What are you doing here?" Boaz asked sharply, and I looked up, startled, thinking he spoke to me.

But a group of workers were standing before him, obviously about to leave after completing some task.

"Some of the glass had broken in the main eastern shaft, Excellency," the leader mumbled.

I looked over at them and grinned. My father was among

them, although gods knew what he was doing with this group. But workers were often assigned to secondary tasks if they were free from their main occupation, and perhaps this was the case with Druse.

"Well," Boaz said, "you should have been gone an hour ago. I wanted the interior clear for this inspection. I won't—"

He stopped, and stared, as did I and the other Magi, the foreman, and sundry guards with us.

Every one of the men in the group, my father included, had whimpered. Frightened. Lost.

I frowned. What was going on? Boaz hadn't come close to losing his temper, and . . .

. . . and then some instinct made me count the men in that huddled, subservient group.

Eleven. The next incomposite number after seven.

"No," I whispered. "Father, please, come away from there . . ."

Boaz looked at me sharply, then back at the men.

"Father!" I cried, and took a step forward.

Boaz gestured, and Kiamet grabbed me.

"No," Boaz said. "No. There is nothing we can do."

There was nothing he *wanted* to do.

The group of eleven men were trembling now, their eyes wide, terrified. Druse blinked, then stared at me. *"Tirzah!"* he screamed, and reached out a hand.

I wailed, and tried to free myself from Kiamet's hold, but he was strong, and held me easily.

"Tirzah!" my father screamed again, then began to die.

Threshold was enjoying itself. It had tasted death on four occasions now, and had learned that the slower and more terrifying the death, the sweeter the eating.

I twisted and screamed, as everyone else looked on with either horror or interested curiosity while the men died.

Gradually, sickeningly, Threshold turned them to stone.

First their feet. They were all barefoot from walking the delicate glass of the shaft, their sandals left behind at Threshold's stone doorstep. Thus their feet were on stone, their *bare* feet, and Threshold seeped into them through their soles.

The flesh of their feet turned gray, then dull. The wrongness spread upward in crumbling, creeping, writhing snakes of gray, up their shins, their calves, their thighs.

The men were in agony. They twisted and turned, trying to escape, but they could not, for their feet were stone, fused into Threshold.

The gray, relentless, crept farther. Their hips, their bellies, and now the men's screams were tearing them apart inside, for I saw a great gout of blood spurt from one of their mouths. The man took breath to scream, and he choked on it, then he took a great breath again, and his eyes bulged and he gagged and vomited, and what he vomited was shards of rock.

I wanted to look away, I wanted to turn and hide my face in Kiamet's chest, but I could not, for there was my father dying before me, my father who loved me and who had raised me and who, despite his faults, was beloved to me.

"Is . . ." he whispered, and his voice was harsh and grating, as if he'd forced it through a roughened throat. "Is . . ."

Gods! He was trying to call me by my birth name!

He could no longer breathe, for the stone had claimed his chest, and the veins in his neck bulged and spasmed, and then they faded into gray, and his eyes, still staring at me, bulged, blood trickling from the corner of one of them, turning to tears of stone down his cheeks, and then one eye popped, and then, I think, it was over, for his face was nothing but a carving . . . a carving of a man who had died in such agony he would wear the face of it into immortality.

Silence.

"Such power!" whispered Boaz, and that broke the horror that held me.

"You cold-blooded lizard!" I screamed. "Is there nothing in *your* veins but stone?"

He turned and stared at me. Everyone did, and I think my voice must have reached those scores of men who stood on or about the ramp, staring at the eleven rock-frozen bodies.

"That was my *father* who died before you, and all you can do is stand there and whisper your admiration?" I had no sense of danger. None.

"Threshold is an abomination, Boaz! Destroy it! You have it in your power. *Destroy it!*"

His face darkened in fury, and he opened his mouth to shout, but I forestalled him.

"Look what it is *doing,* Boaz! Is it good that it destroys and kills? Is *that* good? Do *you* enjoy that? Is this what your *father* would have wanted?" And, oh, by the Soulenai themselves, I should have realized this was going to accomplish nothing at all but *my* destruction.

I freed an arm from Kiamet's clutches, and I waved it about in a grand, sweeping gesture. "How can you stand here and declare your admiration when at the same time you yearn to understand the Song of the Fr—"

He hit me.

My head slammed back into Kiamet's chest with such force I must have bruised him.

Then Boaz seized my hair in rough fingers and jerked my face back to his. It was roping with fury and the power of the One.

"It is well that the caging work is all but finished," he seethed through clenched teeth, "because now I can well afford to rid myself of the more troublesome of the cagers!"

He threw my head back against the guard. "Take her to the hold, Kiamet, and lock her up. No food. No water. Tell me when she's dead."

I heard him step away. "And get someone to throw these lumps of useless rock in the Lhyl. Well away from the dock. I don't want the boats to damage their keels on them."

The cells in the compound's hold had been constructed of thick stone to hold the most rebellious of slaves. There was no window, and what fresh air and light reached me filtered in through a gap between two blocks of masonry high in the northern wall.

There was a thick, wooden door, barred tight. Nothing else. No pallet, no blankets. And no water. Not even a bucket in which I could relieve my needs.

I curled into a miserable ball and cried. My father was dead. And it was all my fault. The Soulenai had entrusted me to persuade Boaz to accept his Elemental heritage, and destroy Threshold. But all I'd done was relax into a comfortable life as his mistress. I'd stroked my soft gowns, and eaten the fine food. I'd practiced for hours drawing kohl about my eyes and rouging my lips. I'd strolled the gardens and watched the fish flash in the ponds. I'd worked at the translations, and *enjoyed* the challenge—the damned ensorcelled *writing*! I'd been soft and submissive, and wallowed in the Magus's approval. And at night I had put to the back of my mind the canker in my belly that was my ruined womb, and flaunted my body before him, desperate to have him seize me and bear down on me.

All this I'd done, and meantime Threshold had grown.

And eaten my father.

I had betrayed Druse and the Soulenai, and I had betrayed myself. I had *prostituted* myself for a life of ease and leisure.

I curled up and hoped that death would come swiftly.

But it did not. The cell baked during the day, and froze at night. By evening on the first day my throat was rasping, crying out for water. I did not care. I continued to weep, losing more precious fluids by doing so.

The night dragged on for an eternity. I think I became delirious at one point, for I believed myself trapped in Infinity, and I cried out for Boaz to save me, to come rescue me, and then reviled myself for such weakness.

Morning came, and it was a relief. There was a noise outside the door, and I thought that it would open, but it was only a changing of the watch. So I sank to the floor and lay staring at the stone wall before me.

Was Druse condemned to lie in the mud of the river bottom for eternity? Raguel's soul had been lost because we did not have the remains of the body to farewell into the Place Beyond. Likewise Druse's soul would be lost. He had not been an Elemental, but that would not have stopped Isphet farewelling him into the Place Beyond.

Would Druse's soul stare out of stone eyes at the murky life of the river for eternity?

"I'm so sorry," I whispered hoarsely, but that was little consolation to offer a soul so abandoned by his daughter's weaknesses.

That day was a nightmare. The cell became almost an oven, and my thirst became a raging beast in itself. By late afternoon I was sitting against the door, banging on it, pleading, shouting with what voice I had left for just one drink, just a small one, Boaz would never know . . .

I wanted to die, but not like this. I wanted a swift sword thrust. Easy. Gentle.

And so during the early evening I begged and pleaded for that.

The guards were silent.

My throat swelled so I could plead no more, and I fell into another delirium, to wake shaking and freezing in the depths of the night.

I struggled up, sobbing in great, dry gasps.

I blinked, then blinked again. Faint moonlight filtered in through the crack in the masonry, and it glinted upon something on the walls.

Ice.

I thought I must be hallucinating, but eventually I reached out and touched it . . . blessed ice. I scrambled to my knees, almost falling over, and licked the stone, crying again as I felt the moisture seep through the swollen tissues of my throat, blessing whatever gods had sent this to me.

Shivering, shaking with cold and fever, I crawled about the walls, scraping hands, chin, nose on the rough rock, licking, licking, licking like an animal, not caring that I sucked years of filth from the walls along with the moisture.

I did not want to die.

The day passed, but it took forever to do so, and I lay on the floor, my once beautiful dress now snagged and ruined and stained, and I begged the sun to go down and the night to fall.

When it did I managed to raise myself to hands and knees, a true animal now, and I waited for the ice to form.

I thought it would not do it. I ran my tongue about the walls, seeking, thinking that it would not get cold enough, worrying that my rough tongue would prevent the ice from forming, but eventually I found a slick of moisture and I broke into sobs, and then spent an hour trying uselessly to stop them, not wanting to waste the fluid.

Another day passed, and another night, and then perhaps some more days and nights, but I am not sure, because then I slipped into death.

"She is dead, Excellency. See?"

I heard this as if in a dream, but I did not open my eyes, for they were gummed closed. And anyway, I *was* dead, and I no longer felt any curiosity.

But strange, though, that the voice should have sounded so much like Kiamet's. Had Kiamet followed me into eternity? Such a nice man. So kind.

A hand grasped my shoulder and rolled me over. My head lolled and struck the stone floor. That hurt, and I was angry. Pain had no place in eternity.

A step, and then someone knelt by my side.

Silence.

"You are a fool, Kiamet. She still breathes."

"Excellency, I was *sure*! It's been eight days. No one—"

"Get out, Kiamet, and close the door. Do not open it until I call."

"Yes, Excellency."

Not dead, then. I would have cried if I could.

He knelt there a long time, and I thought he was waiting for me to die. Then a rough hand grasped my hair and pulled my head forward, and this time I managed a croak of protest.

"You *stupid* girl," he said, and I thought I heard his voice break. But that must be wrong. A product only of delirium. "You stupid, *stupid* girl."

And then water splashed in my face.

Someone carried me back to his residence. Not Boaz, because he would never have allowed anyone to see that. Perhaps Kiamet. Yes, I think it was Kiamet. I was placed on Boaz's bed, and even then I thought that unusual, for I must have been filthy. Then Boaz's voice.

"Get out, and let no one in."

"Yes, Excellency," and I heard Kiamet's steps retreat.

Still I had not opened my eyes, for I thought that would break the spell. I was wrapped about in fever and pain and, I believe, very close to death. I was trying hard not to let anything interest me lest I begin to fight to live.

He leaned over the bed and tore the dress from me, throwing it aside with a murmur of disgust. My body was caked in dried sweat and blood, abraded and bruised with my nightly forages across the walls for moisture; the flesh was a shade somewhere between yellow and gray.

At least that's what it had looked like when last I'd inspected it, and that was . . . how long ago? Two days? Three? I doubt the intervening time would have improved its appearance.

Then he gathered me into his arms, forcing me to cry out softly, for his touch was rough, and my entire body ached and throbbed. He carried me through the room, then into a back room. The temperature was cooler here and I tried to think . . . where?

He dropped me.

I grabbed at his arms but I was weak and I failed.

The next instant I was enveloped in cool, fragrant water, and I had to fight to the surface, gasping and spluttering as my head broke through. He'd brought me to the great bathing pool.

"You *do* want to live then." He'd jumped into the pool as well, and I felt him grasp me and hold me upright. "Then *live,* damn you. Live!"

I gulped at the water. He'd trickled some down my throat in the cell, but this . . . this . . . I took another great gulp.

"That's enough." He seized my hair again and forced my mouth away from the water. "Too much at once and you'll kill yourself. Do you understand?"

"No, Excellency, I do not," I managed. "Tell me why, Excellency, I should fight to live when it will only give you one more chance to try to kill me?"

That little speech was almost too much, and I gagged, the water I'd drunk roiling about in my stomach.

He pulled me closer, supporting me in the deep water. "Tirzah—"

"Drown me now!" I said. "It will save you the trouble of a greater effort later!"

He stared at me, and opened his mouth to say something, but was halted by Kiamet's—dear, sweet Kiamet's—entrance.

"Excellency"—the man was almost on his knees—"Excellency, I have presumed, but I thought . . . someone skilled in healing . . . herbals . . ."

"Isphet!" I gasped.

And then Isphet was in the chamber, bowing, then throwing a bag down on the tiled floor. "Excellency," she said, and raised her head. Her eyes widened in horror at the sight of me. Without waiting for the command from Boaz she jumped straight in.

"We will wash her, Excellency, then put her back to bed. Kiamet, get out. Excellency, you will have to support her while I wash."

And both men did as she ordered.

Later, when Boaz had carried me back to the bed, Isphet gave me a small drink, then rubbed soothing unguents over my entire body.

"Excellency," she said, turning her head slightly to where Boaz stood silent and unreadable at the foot of the bed, "she must be fed small drinks every half hour for the rest of the day. This evening, if she is well enough, some bland food. I will mix a herbal that will help ease her pain, and then another to make her sleep dreamless through the night. I will stay with her—"

"No," Boaz said. "You have done enough. Mix the herbals, then get out."

Isphet drew an angry breath, but dropped her eyes and acquiesced. "Very well, Excellency. But she needs care. If—"

"I will arrange it."

"Then call me if you need me, Excellency." She rose and busied herself for a while mixing the herbals and putting them to one side in two pitchers. Then she gave me another drink, and soothed the hair back from my brow.

"Tirzah," she said, her eyes swimming with tears. "Live."

I tried to smile for her, and grasped her hand. "Thank you, Isphet. I shall do my best."

"Well"—a smile trembled through her tears—"at least today I've managed my first decent bath in six years."

That did make me grin, and she wiped her tears away, stood, bowed at Boaz, and left.

There was silence.

It was an uncomfortable day, for many reasons. I had been so close to death when Kiamet had carried me back to Boaz's residence that I was aware only of a myriad troublesome discomforts about my body. As I recovered, took a firmer grip on life, they flared into spears of agony. But I lay quietly as the pain spread, not wanting to give in to it, not wanting to give Boaz the satisfaction of knowing I suffered.

He sat at his desk, engaged in his infernal scribbling. As distant as if leagues separated us instead of paces. He had a small hourglass on the desk, and when it indicated time for me to be watered, he would do so. Holding my head, allowing me small sips of the honey-sweetened water Isphet had mixed for me. Silent, watching.

In the late afternoon he came over to water me yet again, then paused as he read the pain in my eyes.

"You should have said something."

"I did not want to disturb you, Excellency," I said, with little respect in my voice.

He sat down on the bed and lifted me up, supporting me with one arm as he fed me Isphet's analgesic mix with the other. When I had finished he lowered me back to the pillows.

"I will wait," he said, and so he did, sitting with me, holding my hand between his, gently rubbing and stroking.

The pain eased and, grateful, I slid into sleep.

I woke in the early evening. I did not think I made a sound, but Boaz knew, and he came over.

"Threshold must be missing you, Excellency. You have spent the entire day with me."

His mouth tightened. "Can you eat something?"

I nodded, and he left the room. I heard him speak quietly to Holdat, and I heard both he and Kiamet ask after me.

I almost smiled. Boaz must have felt under siege.

Holdat returned with some mashed fruits such as mothers feed teething babies, softened yet further with a thin syrup. He smiled at me, then left.

Boaz fed me like a baby. I tried to push his hand away, but he gestured irritably, and so I let him hold the spoon. Perhaps it assuaged his guilt.

I finished the fruit, mildly surprised that my stomach did not rebel.

"We must talk," he said.

"If you wish, Excellency."

"Stop calling me Excellency in that tone of voice!" he snapped.

"Then what would you have me call you? How much sweetness would you have me inject into my voice?"

"In this room you may call me Boaz. Outside, Excellency. Although if you cannot inject some *respect* into your tone then I would prefer you call me nothing at all."

"I remember that once before you asked me to call you Boaz—in this bed. The next morning you sent me into convulsions of agony for the presumption."

He was silent at that. Then . . . "I was afraid. I had been . . ."

"You had been honest, Boaz. Honest enough to let me see something of who you really are. But I think that if you are going to be so honest in future I'd prefer to be somewhere else. I cannot survive another of your attacks."

"If you want me to stop hurting you," he said, "then stop giving me reasons to!"

"What? Nothing forced you to show me that book! Nothing forced you to—"

"What were you *thinking* of, to stand there, in the midst of Threshold, and shout those things at me?"

"I was thinking that I had just seen my father die a death that should not be visited on the worst criminal. I had seen *eleven* men die such a death, not to mention the others who have died. I was thinking that my beloved father had cried out to me to save him, and I could not. I was thinking that all you could do was admire Threshold's power. I—"

"Threshold would have let none of us live if I had let you say any more."

"Threshold certainly would not have let us live if you had stood there and admitted I was right," I said quietly.

He glared at me, then stood up, pacing about the room, his robes swishing angrily. Then he sat down at his table, picked up the stylus, and began to write.

Scratching back and forth, back and forth. The evening

darkened into night. Holdat came and took the tray, but did not smile this time.

Scratching back and forth. Back and forth.

Finally Boaz threw down the stylus and dropped his head into his hands. He sat like that for a few minutes, then his shoulders shuddered, and he stood up.

I expected him to come back to the bed, but he walked over to the shelves, and lifted out the Goblet of the Frogs. He stood looking at it, then, finally, came over to me.

"I sat for over eight days with this goblet turning over and over in my hands," he said, his eyes on the glass. "I thought that when Kiamet brought word of your death I would raise it and throw it against the wall. I thought that might ease my pain.

"But when Kiamet did come to me, his eyes sunken and his skin as gray as if *he* had spent those eight days in that cell, and he said, 'Excellency, I think she is dead,' then through my pain I thought I heard the frogs cry out."

"What did they say, Boaz?"

He took a deep breath, and raised his eyes to mine. I do not think I have ever seen such pain in another human's eyes. "They said, *Hold her, soothe her, touch her, love her, hold her, soothe her, touch her, love her.* And"—he broke off and collected himself—"and I put the glass down, unbroken, whole, and rushed to you. Tirzah . . ."

He put the goblet to one side and he lay down beside me, wrapping his arms about me. "Tirzah, that is all I have ever wanted to do. Hold you, soothe you, touch you, love you. *All* I have wanted to do."

"You heard the frogs?" I said.

He was silent.

"Boaz," I said eventually, "there are other means and other ways to power than that which the One and Threshold offer."

If I was to be allowed to live, then no longer would I ignore my promise to the Soulenai.

"I will not revert to childish dreams, Tirzah." His voice was hard now, and I felt his body tense. Then he relaxed, and he forced some humor into his voice. "I can see that all my preaching at you about the One has come to naught."

"Numbers and rigid parameters do not hold the beauty I

crave, Boaz," I said softly. "One day, if you like, I will tell you how I understand the world."

He thought about that, then abruptly rolled away and sat up. "One day, Tirzah. But not now. I do not want to know now."

He picked up the pitcher that held Isphet's sleeping brew, and poured out a measure . . . into the Goblet of the Frogs. "Come now, it is time you slept."

I smiled as the glass touched my lips (*let us hold you, soothe you, love you*), then drank obediently. A dreamless sleep would be good. "Boaz?"

"Hmmm?"

"Why does the Infinity Chamber touch the Vale?"

He stilled, but he did not retreat into a chill. "How do you know that?"

"Boaz, you taught me to read."

"Ah. Well." He thought about it. "The Vale contains the power that we need, Tirzah."

"It is dark power, Boaz. Surely the deaths . . . the manner of deaths show that. Do you know what you do?"

Now he did retreat into distance. "Nothing will dissuade me from Threshold, Tirzah. No childish hopes. No childish myths. Nothing. I have worked toward it most of my life. I am not going to give up on the dream now."

He would not speak again, but he sat with me until I drifted into sleep.

In the morning, he went back to Threshold.

TWENTY-FOUR

Threshold was, I thought, the mistress against whom I could not compete. Over the next few days I tried, softly, gently, to persuade him to see, to *admit*, the wrongness of Threshold, but he refused. Threshold was the culmination of everything that he, as countless other Magi, had worked toward. He told me that I could not understand what power it would bring, nor would he attempt to explain what that power was.

I gambled on the fact that Boaz had grown tired of trying to kill me and so, somewhat nervously, I trampled all over what had previously been forbidden ground. I never mentioned the word "Elemental," but I asked him to tell me of his mother, what she had told him of his father, and if he'd ever heard any other tales of the Soulenai. I talked to him of my love for glass, and while I never quite said that it whispered to me, I went dangerously close to it. I asked him time and time again what it was the frogs had "seemed" to say to him, and then, as he was holding me each night while the sleeping draft took effect, I would ask him to whisper the words back to me again and again.

Boaz bore all of this with varying degrees of patience . . . or impatience. Sometimes he would ignore me, often he would stalk off to Threshold. Sometimes he would tell me to go to sleep—and once, exasperated, he fed me the sleeping draft so that I *did* fall silent. Sometimes he would let me talk on as he sat at his desk, and sometimes he would talk.

I think in the three or four days after I'd been dragged from the cell, Boaz came to a decision within himself. I did not think it went far enough, but it was an improvement on what had been. Boaz would admit to himself that his true nature was not quite the cold, calculating Magus face he showed the world. He had warmth and humor, and he would no longer deny that. He had ordered me to his residence, and then asked me to his bed, not to use me, but to love me. He would admit that. His Magus side would just have to learn to live with it. With me he would be himself, and not expect me to pretend that I saw someone or something else. Now he discarded completely the robes of the Magus while he was with me and wore the simple blue wrap.

Despite all this progress, Boaz would not yet admit any Elemental magic within himself. Perhaps he did not even recognize it, and I thought it would need even more time before he could be brought to see it, let alone accept it.

I wondered how much time we had.

More worrying was the fact that his fascination with Threshold, and with the power it promised, had not dimmed.

Perhaps he relaxed and laughed with me, perhaps he allowed himself to remember how much he loved his mother and mourned the tragic loss of his father, but none of this was going to interfere with Threshold or its needs.

I do not think that anyone beyond Boaz's residence had any idea of the profound changes within him. Outside the safety of his home, Boaz remained the chilling, calculating, indifferent Magus. It was safer that way.

Certainly this was the face he continued to show Threshold, and even Isphet, who came once every day, had no idea of the changes my brush with death had wrought in the Magus.

I was young and I recovered relatively quickly. Eight days in bed to match the eight days I'd spent crawling about the cell, and then I got up. I was weak, but I was whole, and the experience had effected no profound physical changes. Even my womb remained the hard, dry canker it had been. I had hoped that somehow all the fluids Boaz and Isphet had forced down my throat, and the hours I spent soaking in the bathing pool, might have softened it. But apparently not.

Well, Boaz had not changed so much that he would allow me to subdivide the One, and so I sighed, and put all thought of children from my mind. This was not the place anyway, and I was still a slave.

On the ninth night, as we sat by the window, I asked Boaz to show me his father's book again. "Would you like me to read from it? There are many other stories within it, and I, at least, would like to explore them."

He sat and thought about that for a while. Old habits were hard to overcome. But he eventually fetched the box and laid it in my lap.

"It is not too heavy for you? I can bring the table over . . ."

"It is not too heavy, Boaz. I thank you."

I examined the box closely. It was very finely crafted, so finely that I knew I had yet to meet the craftsman who could match it. The original ruby shade of the wood had darkened almost to black. But it had been well cared for, regularly oiled, and it was in good condition. I ran my fingers over the hinges and lock. They were of a bronze alloy, and they whispered sleepily to themselves. They were so old I think they had no interest beyond their own slow dreaming.

I opened the box, and Boaz took it from me as I lifted out the book.

"It is so beautiful, Boaz."

"Yes."

"You have kept it all these years, and carried it about with you."

"Normally not. I have a residence in Setkoth—not the house you came to—and usually it lies in a locked cupboard there. It lay untouched for many years. But after I saw the frogs that you carved that afternoon . . . it reminded me . . . and when I prepared to come to this site I brought it with me, even though I could not read it."

"But you thought I might be able to."

"Yes. Somewhere in the back of my mind lurked the knowledge that you and your father were here, and perhaps one of you might again read me the story."

I grinned. *"One* of us?"

"You." He was relaxed enough to return the smile. "Read to me now."

And so I did. I read again the Song of the Frogs, and halfway through Boaz got up and fetched the Goblet of the Frogs from the bookcase. He sat there, turning it over and over in his hands as the story ran to its close.

Hold me, soothe me, touch me, love me.

The lovely voices rippled about the room, and as my own voice died we sat and listened to them. I knew he could hear them as well. I *knew* it.

"I am always comforted by those words," I said. "Surely you must be, too."

Silence.

"Yes," he replied, reluctantly.

"It is what your father sang to your mother. It is, I think, part of the Song of the Frogs."

"Yes."

"Do you think," I said slowly, "that if one day we understood the entire Song, if perhaps you sang it to me one night, we could reach this Place Beyond?"

"Do not press too far, Tirzah."

"I am past fearing you, Boaz."

He sighed. "Be careful. Between us and in this place there are words you can say that cannot be said anywhere else."

"Certainly not in Threshold's shadow."

Irritated now, he stood up and stared out the window. Then he poured a measure of wine into the goblet. "You are well enough now, I think, to stomach some of this."

He fed me a mouthful of the wine as he had fed me over the past days, and I swallowed it and smiled as he then drank from the goblet. He sat, pulling his chair close, and we shared the wine companionably for a few minutes, sharing from the Goblet of the Frogs.

"Would you like me to read another story, Boaz?"

"Yes, I think I would like that."

And so I opened the book randomly, and read a tale. It was a tale of the very early Soulenai and how they had discovered their magic. They had, it seemed, grown an affinity to metals and gems and a fascination with and love for glass.

Again, very dangerous, and when it was done Boaz rose and poured another goblet of wine and drank it all himself in four large swallows.

I had pushed far enough this night. I closed the book, patting it gently in thanks, and put it back in its box.

"Boaz? Where does this go?"

"I'll put it on the cabinet here. Perhaps I will ask you to read from it again one night. And perhaps, now that your translation has been laid to one side—" we had both abandoned the pretense I was there to translate dry geometrical treatises—"you can read from it yourself during the day."

Boaz wiped the goblet and put it beside the box. Not back on the crowded shelves.

Then he fetched a small box from a locked drawer in the desk.

I had never seen inside the drawer before, and I had certainly never seen the box.

As on the first night when he'd sat with the box containing the Book of the Soulenai on his lap, so now he sat, distracted, his fingers gently tapping the box.

"Tirzah, if I give you this box and its contents, will you promise me never, *never* to tell me what you do with it?"

"Of course, Boaz. What is it?"

He handed the box over and I took it in trembling hands. I felt sick, apprehensive, as if I somehow knew the importance of what lay within.

I opened it . . . and stared until my eyes blurred with tears.

Inside lay three locks of black hair, tied with thin golden wire . . . and a lock of hair that had been completely turned to stone.

"I know," he said slowly, "that . . . others . . . sometimes like to have a body, or a remnant of a body that they can farewell properly . . . Look," and he pointed. "This lock is Raguel's."

I swallowed, and had to grasp the box firmly to stop my hands from shaking.

"And this, Ishkur's."

I took a shaky breath.

"This . . . this one belongs to Ta'uz," he said.

My eyes flew to his face.

"Tirzah, I do not know how they regarded each other, but they died together, and I know how I feel about you. I thought . . ."

"Thank you, Boaz," I whispered, the tears sliding free now.

"And this." He picked up the stone curl. He did not have to explain who that belonged to. His fingers closed over it. He stared at his fist and a change came over his face.

Something happened. I do not know how else to explain it, but something happened in that room.

When he opened his fingers, there, nestling in his palm, was a lock of graying blond hair.

He put it back into the box and closed the lid.

"You did not see that," he said, and for the first time in many, many days I heard a trace of danger in his voice. "Nothing happened."

"Nothing happened, Boaz. But I do thank you for this box. Once I have . . . emptied . . . it, I think I shall use it for my kohl sticks."

He let his breath out. "Yes, that sounds a suitable use for it. Tomorrow you may visit Isphet in her workshop, I think, but I do not want to know what goes on there, and I do not want you to be gone too long."

Kiamet escorted me to the workshop, clucking all the way that I should not be embarking upon such an excursion yet.

"I shall retreat into the darkness of insanity if I cannot walk about, Kiamet, and it is not that far."

He waited outside. "Do not be long," he said, and there was fear in his face.

"Kiamet, I shall be as long as it takes. Wait. Do not come in after me."

He nodded, and looked unhappy.

Two steps inside the workshop door I was enveloped in a gigantic hug.

Yaqob! I was surprised, not only at the vehemence of his embrace, but because I had not thought of him in days. Many days. Poor Yaqob.

I kissed him gently and asked him to set me down.

"Soon," he whispered fiercely. "Soon we'll have you free from that piece of sun-rotted beetle dung. I will kill him myself."

"Yaqob! No!"

"No?" His arms loosened about me. "No?"

"No. I, ah, I mean that we have to be careful. Sure. When do you plan your uprising?"

"Soon," he said, and kissed my cheek. "Soon."

"When?"

"Shush, love. We'll warn you beforehand. Tell you to be ready."

I wanted to question him further. Surely he wasn't going to do anything without telling me! But the others were crowding about, touching, kissing, telling me how much they loved me.

Eventually Isphet rescued me and took me upstairs with Yaqob and Zeldon.

"What is that you carry, Tirzah?" she asked.

"Oh, Isphet!" I opened the box and showed them the hair. "Locks from Raguel, Ishkur, Druse . . . and Ta'uz!"

Unless I had actually come out and said Boaz was an Elemental Cantomancer, I doubt I could have shocked them more.

Isphet, her hands shaking, reached out and took the box

from me. She stared at it, then raised sharp black eyes to my face. "How?"

Oh, but I was going to be glad when all this pretense was over. "One of the slaves in the compound has helped dispose of most of the bodies. He snipped these from their heads."

"Druse?" Yaqob asked. "How? We all saw him."

"As they dragged his body away,"—I did not have to pretend the heartache in my voice—"a stone curl crumbled off. The slave picked it up and, overnight, away from Threshold, it reverted back to its natural state."

"Which slave?" Isphet asked.

Oh, damn her! "I do not know his name, Isphet. A slave. Middle-aged. I hardly saw him in the darkness."

"And Ta'uz?" Zeldon said. "*Ta'uz?* Why would we want a lock of his—"

"They died together, Zeldon," I said, my voice tight with the strain of this deception, "and they created a child together that we sent into the Place Beyond. I thought it fitting that perhaps we send him with the mother of his child."

"And no other locks?" Isphet probed. "These are all he collected?"

"Damn you, Isphet! These are *all* he gave me! I know not why he took a lock from one and not another. Perhaps he knew they might mean something to me, perhaps sheer happenchance! If you like, I shall take the box back and throw—"

"No. No, I am sorry, Tirzah. I did not mean to sound ungrateful. I wonder when we can farewell them?"

"Now," I said. "We will not be disturbed. Boaz is busy at Threshold and does not expect me back for an hour or more yet."

Isphet looked at me again, her eyes sharper than ever.

We farewelled them with due reverence and much gladness into the Place Beyond. I like to think that Ta'uz was surprised, but glad to be sent to such an eternity, and his daughter was there to greet him.

A land where the unborn frolicked with the dead.

And the murdered with their murderers. But I think such

concepts had been left far behind in that wondrous place. Druse was surprised as well, but grateful, and I was grateful—no, more than grateful—that Boaz had given me this chance.

The Soulenai watched and nodded at me. They would have seen through the Goblet of the Frogs what Boaz had done with the stone curl.

Persuade him, sweet Tirzah. Only he can destroy Threshold.

After the swirling colors had slowed and then mottled, I turned to Yaqob. "When? I can hardly wait. I need to know."

"Shush, Tirzah," and I tolerated his kiss. "Before Consecration Day. It must be before then."

"Yes, but *when*?"

"It is safer for you not to know. I fear each night that Boaz will beat you to such agony that you will let slip—"

"Yaqob! I lay in that cell for eight days and I did not 'let slip'!"

"Hush, love. Yes, I know. But I fear for you with him. Believe me. I *will* rescue you. Have you heard any more information that might be useful?"

Back at the residence I rested for an hour, for the afternoon's activities *had* tired me. Then I prepared for Boaz's return.

He did not come back until it was dark, and that suited me well.

"Has not Holdat laid the meal?" he asked. "I am tired, and hungry, and do not want to wait."

"Shush, Boaz, and come with me."

I led him through the house into the lovely vaulted bathing chamber. It was redolent with the scent of candles, and night-blooming wisteria that wafted in from the gardens. I had opened the windows, but only slightly. No one could see in. Candles floated in the pool, flickering soft shadows about the chamber and across the water.

A small table had been laid for a meal, with wine, but only one goblet, that of the Frogs.

I led Boaz to it, and removed his robes before he sat down, wrapping and knotting the blue cloth about his hips. Then I pushed him into the chair, and washed his feet and hands as he had once insisted I do before we commenced the writing lessons.

"Is his Excellency feeling more relaxed?" I asked with a smile.

He nodded, his eyes as shadowy and intimate as the chamber.

Then I sat down and served him; a reversal of roles, for it was normally Boaz who served me. I cut choice meat from the fillet of cold honeyed lamb, then laid seasoned bread, stuffed vegetables, and a tart fruit next to it.

"Are you not going to eat?" he asked as I picked up a knife and cut his meat for him.

"I have eaten. Let me feed you."

And, as he had fed me, so now I fed him, but using my fingers rather than cutlery, and wiping his mouth with the corner of my dress rather than a napkin.

"Drink," I said, and poured wine into the goblet.

He did so, but then put the goblet to my lips so that I might drink as well.

Hold me, soothe me, touch me, love me.

"I have read another tale from your father's book this afternoon, Boaz," I said. "Would you like me to tell it to you?"

"Very much."

"But not here, I think. Come, bring the wine."

I stood pitcher and goblet by the pool, then slipped from my dress.

His hands fell to the knotted cloth at his hips.

"No," I said, "let me." And I folded the wrap away from his body.

The water was cool and very fragrant. I took a cloth and washed him down, smiling as he reclined against the side of the pool, sipping from the Goblet of the Frogs.

Hold me, soothe me, touch me, love me.

"Why?"

"Because I wanted to say thank you for the box, Boaz. My kohl sticks look very good in it. Now, shush, I want to tell you a tale."

I put my arms about him and rested my head on his chest,

floating gently by his body, and I told him a tale about the Soulenai that held no dangerous overtones, but only spoke of their love for each other and for their brethren and their hopes for a peaceful world. And when I had finished I took his hands, and put them where I thought they would do the most good.

"Hold me, soothe me, touch me, love me," I whispered, and this he did.

TWENTY-FIVE

In two days the capstone would be laid, the following day Threshold would be consecrated to the power of the One. Today Chad-Nezzar, the majority of his court, most of the nobles, all of the Magi, and thousands of spectators were due to arrive from Setkoth.

I was very nervous. I dreaded the completion of Threshold, dreaded that day when it would flood with power. But I also dreaded its completion because that would trigger Yaqob's revolt. While I could *sense* that preparations proceeded apace for it, I had no idea when . . . or how.

I looked about for Boaz, but I could not immediately see him. At home, with me, he relaxed more and more, but of what use was that if the Magus still reigned beyond the verandah? He was still no closer to admitting, let alone exploring, the Elemental side of his nature.

In fact, as Threshold slid close to completion, he was further from it than ever. He was so enthralled by Threshold, by the power it promised, that he had put aside thought of anything else. Over the past few weeks he had not touched the Goblet of the Frogs, nor let me read to him from the Book of the Soulenai.

The Soulenai fretted as much if not more than I. At night I heard them whispering from the Goblet of the Frogs, but Boaz slept on soundly.

I sighed and shifted, smiling my thanks to the boy behind

me who held the shade above my head. The sun was a great red orb in the sky, seeming almost to writhe in a haze of heat.

I was waiting just outside the gates of Gesholme, standing inconspicuously underneath the wall. Before me the stone wharf gleamed in the sunshine. Slaves had spent four days washing, sanding, and sweeping to make it fit for the abundance of royal and noble feet set to alight upon it. Guards, their weapons and armor gleaming, the various tassels of their units fluttering in rainbows of color in the breeze, stood to either side of the wharf. Before them ranged Magi, some two dozen, their blue and white robes immaculately arranged, their hair rigidly cubed into queues.

Boaz had allowed me to stand here to witness Chad-Nezzar's arrival. The Chad, as everyone else with even a tenuous claim to distinction, was arriving for the laying of the capstone and would stay for Consecration Day. Threshold had been eight generations in the making and had consumed much of the wealth of Ashdod. I suspected that everyone arriving, whether Magus or noble, was here to grab what power was there for the offering.

I hoped they were truly prepared for what *might* be offered them, because Threshold's shadow had been thickening by the day.

No more had died since the eleven. Thirteen next, and I thought I knew what Threshold had planned for Consecration Day.

A movement, and Boaz stepped through the gate and onto the wharf. He was the Magus, all the Magus, and he ignored me. I wondered how he would explain my presence to Chad-Nezzar. Perhaps he wasn't going to. Perhaps I would be cast back to the tenements for the duration of the royal visit.

But I didn't think so.

Boaz moved to talk quietly with the captain of the guard, then with one or two of the Magi, making sure everything was in readiness.

All slaves had been removed from sight for the day, locked into the closely guarded tenements (all save me, and I now existed in that no-man's-land between slavery and servitude). I wondered what Yaqob was thinking. Surely he would have to give up his plan for revolt now that Chad-Nezzar and a large part of his army floated only a few minutes away.

Surely they didn't have the weapons or the stupidity to battle the imperial soldiers. Surely.

I looked back through the gates. The avenue that Boaz had constructed through Gesholme toward Threshold stretched completed, lined by ranks of soldiers. I knew that one day Gesholme would be razed to the ground (for what use were slaves once Threshold was finished?) and that colonnaded avenues and vistas would surround the pyramid.

Then Threshold would stand free of any reminders of the sweat and pain expended to build it.

I wondered if then the frogs would still chorus at dawn and dusk.

A shout distracted my meanderings, and I looked back at the wharf. Everyone stood tense and expectant now, gazing up the Lhyl. A great riverboat hove into view about the sweeping curve in the river, and I gasped in wonder, for at first I thought it was an apparition.

All riverboats that I had seen were constructed of great bundles of reeds tied together, and I supposed this one was too despite its massive size, for it had the usual graceful sweep of line and the high prow and stern. But the sides of the boat were covered to the waterline by great drapes of silk and gauze, gold and vivid pinks with spangles of sky blue and silver sparkling here and there. How the rowers' oars ever managed to function without becoming entangled in the materials I do not know.

Above, three largely decorative sails bulged in the breeze, one each of rich blue, crimson, and emerald, each striped with ribbons of pure gold.

Great streamers and banners fluttered from the masts, bells and chimes sounded, and clouds of incense drifted about, presumably to keep both insects and the smells of mass-packed slavery from the royal nose. Musicians played from the bow of the boat, and I could see a pet monkey scampering among them.

It was the most beautiful man-made sight I had ever seen.

This boat was followed by scores of others, some small, some approaching the royal barge's size, all decorated to some extent, even the soldiers' boats.

Men moved to catch mooring ropes, and rowers shipped their oars so that their paddles reared to the sky in a glistening, silent salute. I backed up against the wall, feeling utterly insignificant amid such glory.

A ramp slid to the wharf, and Boaz stepped forward. A small honor guard marched off the boat in rigid formation, stood to each side of the ramp, and thrust their spears into the sky.

"Glory to the immortal Chad!" they roared, and the refrain was taken up by every guard and soldier whether on boat or on land. "Glory to the immortal Chad!"

I noticed the Magi kept their mouths shut.

The not-so-immortal Chad stepped into view at the top of the ramp. His flesh was even more studded, pierced, and encased in jewelry than on his previous visit, and he wore a headdress of bronze and copper, inlaid with more jewels than the rest of him combined.

He swayed as he stepped onto the ramp and for one moment I thought he would topple into the Lhyl, but Chad-Nezzar obviously had a lifetime of such minor brushes with disaster behind him, and he recovered in regal style and proceeded down the ramp with as much dignity as he could muster.

I was grateful I was far enough away not to hear the chatter of his metals and gems, for I could well imagine their excitement at this scene of pomp and majesty.

Boaz stepped forward and kissed one of the assortment of jewels on the hand Chad-Nezzar offered him, welcoming his uncle to Threshold with a speech carefully composed to demonstrate that while the Magi owed him respect (and more yet, perhaps, to his treasury), they considered him a guest invited only through the benevolence of the Magi themselves.

While Chad-Nezzar accepted these words calmly enough for the moment, this was not, as I was to discover, quite how the Chad thought of himself.

Once the formal greetings and flowery phrases had been mouthed, both Chad-Nezzar and Boaz relaxed.

"You have done well, nephew," Chad-Nezzar said, waving a hand about, and Boaz inclined his head.

Whatever Boaz was about to say was halted by the arrival of another man at the head of the ramp. "Zabrze!"

My own interest sharpened. Zabrze was Boaz's older half brother, son of his mother's first marriage. And heir to the throne, as Chad-Nezzar had never taken a wife.

Well, what woman would let Chad-Nezzar near her with that armory of metal to prick and scratch?

Zabrze may well have been heir to the throne of Chad of Ashdod, but his appearance and bearing were in complete contrast to Chad-Nezzar's.

He was an extraordinarily striking man. In his mid-forties, he was lean and fit, dark-skinned, dark-eyed, and dark-haired. He was undoubtedly a Prince, but Zabrze used bearing and assurance to radiate this fact, not half the royal treasury. He wore a knee-length wrap of a dark blue striped with gold knotted about his hips, and a broad gold band about his upper right arm. His hair was braided, tied with gold wiring, and swept back into the nape of his neck. But that was it. Even his feet were left bare.

He stepped from the ramp and gripped Boaz's hand. The affection was obvious, and I realized that only the formality of the occasion kept the brothers from embracing each other.

Zabrze was followed by a woman some six or seven years younger than he. Handsome rather than beautiful, but radiating the same assurance as her husband, she was dressed in a fine white linen dress hanging from a collar made of threaded gold beads draped about her neck and extending over her shoulders. As she moved I saw she was some eight months gone with child.

Fear gripped me as Zabrze took the woman's hand and Boaz smiled and bowed to her. Zabrze had brought his pregnant wife to *Threshold?*

I heard Boaz call her Neuf. It was an elegant name for an elegant woman, and I sighed and put my moment of fear from me, wishing I had even a tenth of that elegance and assurance.

Sundry other nobles and dignitaries alighted from the boat, but my interest was truly only in Zabrze and Neuf. With Chad-Nezzar, Boaz led them through the gates and down the avenue, servants scurrying to shade the group with tasseled parasols and waft incense before them lest the scent of slavery reach their royal nostrils.

I stood by the wall and waited until I found an opportunity to slip back to Boaz's quarters.

On the way I stood momentarily transfixed, staring into a dark alley. I could hardly believe what I was seeing. One of the officers from Chad Nezzar's army was chatting quietly and extremely surreptitiously . . . with Azam.

My stomach turned over, and I hastened away before they saw me.

Azam?

The royal entourage, as many of the nobles, were accommodated within the compound of the Magi. Chad-Nezzar, Zabrze, and Neuf were quartered in Ta'uz's old residence. Other nobles and guests slept aboard their riverboats. Most of the vessels had sleeping quarters, for Ashdod's nobles liked to spend many weeks each year floating in grand processions on the river, sometimes hunting, sometimes banqueting, sometimes intriguing. The eight thousand soldiers who had accompanied Chad-Nezzar erected a spreading camp about Gesholme and the riverbanks.

My initial relief at the arrival of these soldiers had dimmed. What did an officer of the imperial army have to say to a slave?

And a slave who was Yaqob's right-hand man in his quest for freedom?

I sat alone in Boaz's quarters all day, alternatively fretting about Azam and nervously wondering what I should do and say, should I come face-to-face with Chad-Nezzar or Zabrze and his wife.

Boaz stayed with his family and did not return until very late at night.

I rolled over as I felt him lie down beside me. "Boaz?"

"Go back to sleep, Tirzah."

But I wanted to talk. "I did not know you were so close to Zabrze."

"We were close as children. He looked out for me at court. But when I was seven or eight he was close to eighteen, and spending more time with the army than with me. We grew distant."

That was not what I'd seen on the wharf, but I let it pass. I snuggled close to him. "I have heard that Zabrze commands Ashdod's army."

"Apart from those under *my* command, Tirzah."

"Is he a good commander? A popular commander?" I asked.

Boaz hesitated for a very long time. "Zabrze is a *good* commander," he said finally. "But the army is large, and to many, perhaps, he is a distant figure."

I wondered about the officer I'd seen whispering with Azam. "And he is heir. But he does not share your uncle's predilection for banding and studding."

"He is a man of relatively plain tastes." Boaz paused. "He will be a good Chad."

"His wife is very elegant," I said wistfully. "But I am surprised that he should bring her here when . . ."

"She bears children with ease. This will be their eighth."

"Eight! Then you have almost a squadron of nephews and nieces!"

Boaz laughed. "Yes, and I am pleased Zabrze elected to leave them in Setkoth. Four nephews, three nieces, and whatever they're growing now. Zabrze is doing his best to ensure the succession."

"Threshold must be very important to draw so many royals and nobles hither."

He was silent, suspecting that I was about to embark on one of my increasingly unsubtle frets about the structure. But not tonight.

"Boaz, why the impatience to have Threshold finished by a set day? Surely a month or two more would not have hurt?" He had driven everyone on site hard for the past months, and the past five or six weeks in particular.

"There is only one day each year that we could hold Consecration Day," he said. "If we had not been ready for that day, then we would have been forced to wait another year." He gave a short, hard laugh. "And I do not think I could have waited that long. So close, and to be forced to wait a year."

A year, I thought. A year to draw him so deep into love he would eventually accept his Elemental heritage, even if only for my sake.

"What is so special about the third day from now, Boaz?"

I felt him fidget. "It is the day of the year when the sun reaches the zenith of its yearly voyage through the sky. In three days' time the sun's strength will peak at noon, and for an hour it will shine stronger than at any other time of the year."

"Threshold depends very much on light, doesn't it?"

"Yes."

His reply was curt enough for me to edge onto another topic, although just as dangerous. "Boaz, what will happen to all the slaves on site after Consecration Day? You will not need them here."

"Worried about your 'friends,' Tirzah? Worried about what I will do with you?"

"Shetzah!" I had picked up Ashdod's curse words along with its milder language since I'd arrived. "Of course I am worried about *all* of my friends. They mean a great deal to me; I would not have survived without their love and help. I wonder if you are thinking of throwing them to the great water lizards!"

"You actually do worry about that, don't you? Well, fear not, sweet Tirzah, they are far too valuable to waste. We'll recoup much of their value through resale. They'll be sent to the marketplaces of Setkoth, perhaps even Adab and other northern cities, within the next few weeks."

"Boaz—"

His arm slid about my waist and pulled me down to him. "And I admit I cannot wait to see them gone, Tirzah. For then I know I will have your undivided affection—"

"You have that now, Boaz," I said quietly.

"And," he said fiercely, "I know I will not have to watch the shadows about me for assassins and rebels. *When* do they plan their move, Tirzah?"

"I have been isolated from the slaves and tenements since I came to live with you, Boaz. Think you that they whisper to *me* of their hopes for freedom?"

"Curse you, Tirzah," he whispered. "You shall not see your friends again. Your life is with me now."

"Boaz!"

"There is *no* need! I shall instruct Kiamet and the other guards that you shall not leave this compound unless with me."

"Boaz—"

"Do not presume too much upon the familiarity I have allowed you over past weeks, Tirzah. I am too close now to risk losing Threshold to *anyone*."

I frowned, puzzled. What did he mean by that?

But then his arms wrapped yet more tightly about me and his voice softened. "Come now, Tirzah. I have spent all day watching my tongue about simpering courtiers. I do not want to have to snap at you, least of all places here, in bed. Come now." His hands grew gentler. "Come now." And he put his mouth to better uses than talking.

"Boaz! What are you doing abed? I thought we might stroll the gardens."

"Zabrze!" Boaz, as I, had been almost asleep, and now he lurched into a sitting position. "What—?"

"Ah," Zabrze said softly, walking from the doorway over to the bed. "Now I see. This is a most unusual situation for a Magus, is it not, Boaz?"

I rolled over and reached for a robe, thinking to leave, but Zabrze himself stopped me, sitting on the bed and staying my arm. "No. Do not move. I should have thought before such a rough intrusion. But, Boaz"—and thankfully his eyes slid away from my nakedness to that of his brother's—"I was sure that I would find *you* alone."

"What is it, Zabrze?"

"I wanted a quiet word with you, brother. But now is definitely not the time." He smiled at me. "I know I would not want to be disturbed from such a woman's bed. No. We can talk later."

He rose and walked toward the door.

"Zabrze!"

"No," Zabrze said. "Later, brother. What I have just seen needs careful thought, methinks."

And then he was gone.

TWENTY-SIX

The next evening, the evening before the ceremony to lay the capstone, Boaz entertained his family.

For a royal gathering it was a relatively informal affair. Several servants helped Holdat cook and set up a table in the pool chamber. It was laid with the best platters and glass-ware, and golden knives and spoons glittered.

The Goblet of the Frogs was conspicuous by its absence.

The only illumination was from scores of scented candles floating in the water, and I threw water lilies and droplets of oil in as well, to add yet more beauty and scent.

Guards ringed the house, but at a respectful and discreet distance. It was very quiet and very serene, and I surveyed the chamber one last time before Chad-Nezzar, Zabrze, and Neuf were due to arrive. Then I turned to go.

Boaz stood in the entranceway, immaculate and invulnera-ble in his Magus robes.

"I want to keep this private," he said. "The last thing any of us needs is a dozen servants to upset the eye with their bustling. Holdat will serve the meal, you the wine."

And then he was gone.

My throat choked with nerves. Serve wine to a Chad of Ashdod, a Prince and his wife? But I was only a humble glassworker!

But I had Holdat to guide me, and I could not do much wrong so long as I kept myself as inconspicuous as possible and didn't spill the wine. I was used to serving Boaz, and I did well enough with his family. Chad-Nezzar largely ignored me, initially Neuf eyed me curiously, but not overly so (Zabrze had not told her, then), and then proceeded to ignore me as well, while Zabrze regarded me with unreadable black eyes and then followed the example of his wife and uncle.

For the early part of the meal I spent most of my time sitting on a stool in a darkened corner of the chamber, slowly relax-ing, and moving to fill a goblet only when needed. Holdat did all the serving, taking plates silently and efficiently, offering platters or napkins according to occasion. I admired his skill, and wondered where Boaz had found him. Perhaps in Setkoth, for I could not imagine that Gesholme would have need of such skills.

Boaz and his family ate well and enjoyed, as far as I could tell, inconsequential gossip about courtiers and happenings in Setkoth. They did not raise their voices, save to laugh at the misfortune or social blunder of a courtier, and they patently

kept clear of any contentious topic. Indeed, Neuf directed
most of the conversation, leaning now close to her husband,
now close to Chad-Nezzar, now resting her slim hand on
Boaz's arm and smiling into his face.

I wondered uncharitably if all those nieces and nephews
were of such distant blood relation to Boaz. Neuf exuded an
unmistakable sensuality beneath her elegance, and I resented
her every time she directed it toward Boaz.

While the conversation proceeded amicably enough
through the meal, Chad-Nezzar's metals and gems kept up
a conversation all their own. As I passed to and fro about
the table, I would hear them chatter about this and that, but
on one occasion I was astounded to hear them whisper of
their love for Chad-Nezzar himself. He was an old man, although yet vital, and they did not want him to die. I lingered over Neuf's and then Zabrze's goblets, trying to
catch more.

Ah, they loved him, not so much for himself, but because
they were afraid that when he died their happy community
would be broken up. Chad-Nezzar had, apparently, been thus
enmetaled and bejeweled for decades, and the metals and
gems had grown fond of one another. Would the Prince
Zabrze wear them when he inherited the throne?

Sadly, no, they thought, and I silently agreed with them.
Long live Chad-Nezzar, if only for the Elementals' sakes.

As the evening progressed I found my services required
more and more. All the men drank, if not heavily, then constantly. Voices rose and laughter sharpened.

Neuf finally rose from the table. "My husband. Tomorrow
will be a long day, and I have two to sleep for now. I crave
your indulgence and"—she turned to Chad-Nezzar—"the
permission of the Mighty One to retire."

Chad-Nezzar waved his hand. I suspected he did it so often
to show his jewels to their best advantage; as far as his jewels
were concerned, they loved the slow, graceful rides through
the air.

"You have it, my dear."

"Neuf," Zabrze said. "The girl can escort you back."

His eyes drifted in my direction. "And perhaps the girl
might like to give us her name. I have a curiosity to know."

I opened my mouth, and then closed it. Should I give them my birth name? It would be far less surprising than if I said . . .

"Tirzah," Boaz said. "Her name is Tirzah."

Everyone, save Boaz, stared at me.

"Tirzah?" Chad-Nezzar said slowly. *"Tirzah?"*

Neuf looked at me, then at Boaz. "Well, well," she said. "A strange name for a slave girl, Boaz. I was not aware slaves were permitted to wear the names of nobles. This site is more relaxed than I had originally thought."

I had no idea what to do, but I decided that if Boaz had started it, then he could finish it. The choice of name was not my fault.

"She had a cumbersome name common among the northern savages," Boaz said. "I thought to give her something prettier."

"But the name of my *sister*?" said Chad-Nezzar.

"I should point out," said Zabrze with some degree of amusement, "that I was curious about the girl's name because she enjoys a . . . well, shall I say, a reasonably intimate relationship with Boaz."

Neuf's eyes jerked back to me. "A presumption, girl—"

"My presumption, name and relationship both!" Boaz snapped at his sister-in-law. "Leave her alone."

"Boaz," said Zabrze, "I like not your tone of voice."

"My Lords and my Lady," I hastened, "I will leave—"

"Assuredly, girl," Neuf said, and stepped to the door. "You shall accompany me to my quarters. This *moment!*"

"Return when Neuf has released you," Chad-Nezzar said. "I think we shall *all* want some more wine after this episode."

Neuf shot him a black look, then stalked from the chamber, I hurrying after her.

She did not speak until we reached the residence. Then she turned to me under the swinging lights of the verandah.

"You are a very foolish girl."

"Great Lady, I—"

"He is a Magus. He has no time for you."

"Great Lady, I—"

Sharp fingers grasped my chin and angled my face to the light. I wondered if I was going to ever be allowed to get past the "I."

"Perhaps it's your northern blood. *Shetzah,* but he's ig-

nored all the other flesh paraded before him over the years.
It's the only explanation."

More than you think, Great Lady, I thought. More than you
think.

Her eyes narrowed suspiciously, and her fingers tightened.
"Or are you a plant? There to destroy him? Whatever, you're
dangerous."

I opened my mouth yet again to protest, but this time she
did not let me get even one word out.

"Don't you see what is *happening*, girl? Don't you *know*?"

I kept silent, still.

"Boaz has remarkable talent . . ."

I wondered if I dared a nervous laugh.

". . . and he has worked hard, studied even harder, to reach
where he is today. He has dedicated his life to the One, to becoming the greatest Magus who ever lived. Now he is within a
few short days of accomplishing his dream and we find out
that, lo! he's risking it all for some underfed and outspoken
slave girl."

She must have seen the anger in my eyes, for she gave my
chin a rough little shake. "Many Magi plot to undo him, girl.
Perhaps not those who have been at this site and who already
know of you, but many of those who have come down from
Setkoth would be more than happy to take advantage of this
weakness. Believe me, I know. Intrigue is what I specialize in.
I do not want to see Boaz lose it all because of a passing lust
for a light-haired northerner. Do you understand?"

"I understand, Great Lady."

She dropped her hand, but not her eyes. "I wish you did,
girl, I wish you did."

And then she was gone.

Shaking, I walked back to the pool chamber. There were
shades and complications here that I did not understand.

On my return, Boaz gestured impatiently for me to fill the
goblets, and I hurried to the table, my mind still on Neuf's
warning. Then their conversation shifted all thought of Neuf
far to the back of my mind.

Chad-Nezzar and Zabrze had grouped themselves on one

side of the table, facing Boaz on the other. Anger, only partly born of the amount of wine consumed, drifted between them.

They were talking of Threshold.

"I am remembering," Chad-Nezzar drawled, "that when the Magi first approached the then Chad, Ophal . . . what, Zabrze, how long was it now?"

"Almost two hundred years, Mighty One," Zabrze said, his eyes on his brother.

"Quite," Chad-Nezzar continued, "two hundred years. The Magi promised Ashdod great riches from Threshold's construction. And yet all that stone monstrosity has done is beggared this nation."

"It has been a monumental construction, Mighty One," Boaz said, and I noted the formality that had been absent earlier. "Of course it has soaked up the riches of a nation. Be assured that it will give more back."

"I surely hope so, Magus Boaz," Chad-Nezzar said. "I also know that the Magi promised Chad-Ophal that there would be power for the taking when Threshold was complete. Is that the case?"

"Assuredly, Mighty One," Boaz said carefully.

"But for whom, brother?" Zabrze asked. "For whom? Is Threshold the means to power for Ashdod, or for the Magi?"

Boaz waited a long time before he answered. "Threshold promises power for all."

"*Kus,* Boaz!" Zabrze leaned back in his chair and took a great swallow of his wine, watching the effect his obscenity had on Boaz. "Forgive me if I think that Threshold holds great power for the use of the Magi and the Magi *only!*"

Back in my corner, I thought vaguely of how uncomplicated my life had been before this night.

Chad-Nezzar watched the brothers carefully, but did not say anything. It was better, perhaps, if Zabrze had this out with Boaz.

Now Zabrze sat forward over the table. "Share its secrets with us, Boaz," he said. "Tell us *how*! *What* we can expect."

"Power, Zabrze. But beyond that I would find it difficult to explain. Its mathematical formulas are far too complicated for the amount of wine you have consumed."

"Boaz," Zabrze moderated his voice. "Forgive my suspicions. I would trust you with my life. Normally. But . . ."

But now the lust for power is infecting everyone, I thought. Everyone.

". . . I wonder if your ultimate loyalty rests with the Magi rather than with your family. Perhaps it would be best if the Chad finds someone else to conduct the Consecration Day ceremonies. I—"

He got no further. Boaz leaped to his feet, stared at Zabrze, then turned to his uncle. "Mighty One! There is *no one* more qualified than I to consecrate Threshold. I demand—"

He stopped himself. "I *beg* you to allow me this honor. For Tirzah's sake if not for mine."

I realized with a start he spoke of his mother, not of me. Yet for *this* Tirzah's sake, I thought, I would prefer you so far from Threshold on Consecration Day you could not even remember what shape the building is.

"Forgive Zabrze," Chad-Nezzar said. "He is sometimes rash, and perhaps he has been too hot-tempered tonight. But, Boaz," he said carefully, "I do share his concerns. I would not want to think that all I am going to witness two days hence is the handing over of all power within Ashdod to the Magi. Boaz, answer me this, *what can we expect?*"

Holdat and I had so pressed against the wall by this stage we had almost melded with it.

"What, Boaz?" Zabrze asked softly. "What?"

Boaz looked into his goblet, thinking. Then he raised his eyes. "Threshold has been built so that it can tap into the power of Creation," he said.

There was not a sound in the room. Chad-Nezzar and Zabrze were stunned.

"All life is governed by mathematical and geometrical parameters, formulas. Three hundred years ago a group of Magi, far more learned than others, realized that Creation itself—or the power that Creation drew upon—could be reached via a bridge constructed of the appropriate mathematical formula. The Magi who first realized the possibility did not achieve the formula in their lifetimes, but over the next three generations other Magi worked hard at the problem."

He waved a hand tiredly, an unconscious imitation of his

uncle's mannerism. "Eventually they solved it. Threshold is that formula. It will tap into the power of Creation."

"This sounds very fine," Zabrze said slowly. "And yet I know that many Magi argued that Threshold should not be built. There were divisions within the ranks of the Magi. Deep divisions."

"Some were nervous, frightened," Boaz admitted. "Then. Not now."

"Too late, *now*," Zabrze muttered, and I looked consideringly at him. Was the sharing of power the *only* thing he was worried about?

"Not now that we are sure Threshold will work," Boaz said, looking into his brother's eyes.

Zabrze had lost his patience. "Work at *what?* What *will* happen when this damned formula of yours taps into the power of Creation?"

"It will propel us into Infinity, brother. Immortality."

No wonder Boaz would not be deflected from his purpose. Immortality was a heady prize.

But at what price? No one thought to ask that, and I was certainly not prepared to peel myself off the wall to do so.

His words shocked Chad-Nezzar and Zabrze into a moment of profound silence.

Both men reacted very differently. Chad-Nezzar's face flushed with excitement. He was an old man, and had thought only of enjoying whatever power Threshold offered for another five years, perhaps ten at the most.

Now, everlasting life beckoned.

The chant with which he'd been greeted on the wharf would become fact, not flattery.

Zabrze was uncertain. He saw the greed in his uncle's eyes, he saw the need in his brother's, and then he looked up and saw the fear in mine.

"Think of it!" Chad-Nezzar babbled. "With immortality, I could rule the *world!*"

"Then do not think of asking anyone else to lead the Consecration Day rites," Boaz said softly. "Who else can you trust to pass this power over?"

"Yes, yes, the rites are yours! Zabrze! Immortality! What greater prize can there be?"

Chad-Nezzar obviously had not yet thought that an heir to a throne might not appreciate contemplating that the present incumbent enjoyed eternal life, but I think that was very far from Zabrze's mind, too.

"Happiness," Zabrze said. "Contentment. Love."

He looked very, very sad.

They talked for an hour more. I served wine, but I think Boaz and Chad-Nezzar hardly knew I was there. Zabrze glanced unhappily in my direction once or twice, and he drank no more. I do not know if Boaz had ever thought about *not* sharing the power Threshold would grant, but now he seemed committed to the idea of sharing it with his uncle. Perhaps Boaz, as Neuf had been, was worried about the rebellious Magi, and preferred to have Chad-Nezzar's army with him rather than against him.

Eventually, Chad-Nezzar decided he had to take his metal and jewelry to bed and stumbled off, Zabrze's arm about him for support.

"Tirzah?" Boaz said.

"I will help Holdat clean up, Boaz. I will be with you shortly."

"Tirzah. Holdat. I trust I have your discretion. There were words spoken here tonight . . ."

It was Holdat who replied, and with the unconscious dignity sometimes only slaves can command. "We are yours, Excellency," he said, "and we will not betray who you are."

"Well, see that you don't," Boaz said, and left the chamber.

We had all but finished when I saw a movement at one of the windows.

Zabrze.

"The garden," he said, and led me to a relatively clear area, but I glanced behind me. "Great Lord," I said, "I would feel better if we . . ." and I pointed to a spreading, dense ipacia tree.

"You don't like Threshold," Zabrze said, once we were under the branches.

"No. I fear it. Great Lord, it has such a sense of wrongness about it that I fear very greatly what will happen."

"Tomorrow?"

"Yes, and on Consecration Day, when Threshold comes into its full power."

"I have heard," he said slowly, looking out over the gardens, "that there have been accidents."

"Accidents are common to construction sites, Great Lord."

"Don't dissemble with me," he snapped. "Tell me!"

"Threshold is taking lives, Great Lord. No one is safe, whether Magus or slave."

I hardly knew this man, yet I trusted him without hesitation. I told him what I knew about the incomposite numbers and the manner of the deaths. "Ta'uz was concerned about Threshold. So it took him, Great Lord."

Zabrze was staring at me in horror. "And Boaz cannot see this?"

"Boaz will not admit any wrong, Great Lord. You saw him this evening. He is thrilled that Threshold can so demonstrate its power."

"You have risked much, Tirzah"—and the name rolled strangely off his tongue—"to talk so."

"You are his brother, Great Lord, and I can see the bond between you. I want to help him."

"And you are very outspoken for a slave. Perhaps it is your northern blood. No slave bred in Ashdod would be so familiar."

I was silent, but not concerned. Unlike Neuf who had mouthed true threat, Zabrze was merely being curious.

"I was not always a slave, Great Lord. In Viland, my native home, my father and I were forced into slavery through debt."

"Some are enslaved through debt," Zabrze said softly, "and some through vision of power."

"Great Lord, your wife. Please, it would be better if she were back in Setkoth."

His smile died. "Why, Tirzah? What did she say to you?"

"It is not that, Great Lord. But I fear for her. She is vulnerable at the moment . . . the child . . ."

"Perhaps you are right. But Neuf has a mind of her own. Come now, what *did* she say to you?"

"She was upset at my naming, Great Lord."

"It was a shock, Tirzah. Go on."

"She fears that my presence will threaten Boaz. That I will be used as an excuse by some Magi to strip him of his power and influence."

"Neuf sometimes thinks too much about Boaz," Zabrze muttered, then raised his voice. "She may be overly fearful, Tirzah. If Magi *were* to move against him they would do it through Chad-Nezzar. He was shocked only by your name, not by your presence. And I think Boaz enjoys his full support. Especially after what he told him tonight."

Zabrze paused and studied me carefully. "Neuf has good connections."

"She said that she specialized in intrigue."

He laughed. "You'd think that with all the children I'd given her she'd specialize in *their* welfare. But, no. Neuf will always find time for intrigue. She has as many friends among the Magi as she does among the court, and Boaz owes a great deal to her support over the years."

I thought it best to remain silent.

"And thus to you, Tirzah. Are you sure the only reason you beg me to send Neuf back to Setkoth is to remove her from Threshold's influence?"

"Great Lord, I—"

"Liar, Tirzah. But do not fear. I think that Boaz would find it very difficult to look past you. I know that I would."

I stared sharply at him, but neither his face nor his voice held any trace of seductive intent. Zabrze was only being kind.

"So, Tirzah, a Vilander. What was your birth name?"

I told him.

Zabrze made a face. "Well, I can well understand why Boaz stripped you of it. I cannot think of an uglier name. It's even worse than his father's."

"I did not know at first that Tirzah was your mother's name. It was a long time before Boaz mentioned it to me."

Zabrze did not speak for a while. "Does he talk to you of his father?" he asked finally.

"A little, Great Lord."

"A little." He sighed. "A 'little' is not good enough for Avaldamon."

My eyes widened at the name. Avaldamon? It was a *beautiful* name! "You admired him."

"Yes, a great deal. He was"—and Zabrze looked at me very carefully—"a most unusual man."

"So I have come to realize, Great Lord."

"He took care to talk to me at court, even well before there was any thought of a marriage between him and my mother. He had gray eyes—Boaz's eyes—and they sparkled with humor. Especially whenever he was near Chad-Nezzar."

My mouth curled in a tiny smile, and I do not think Zabrze failed to notice.

"I was a lonely boy, nine or ten then, and Avaldamon spent hours talking to me of, well, of strange things. I do not think many at court appreciated just how unusual he was."

I stared across the garden, listening to the chorus of the frogs.

"My mother loved him. She thought him strange and foreign at first, but I saw her face when she and Avaldamon came out of their seven-day seclusion." He grimaced. "I wish that one day a woman would look at me like that."

Poor Zabrze, I thought.

"I was on the boat the day he died."

"Oh, Great Lord!"

"I think, after all I have lived through since, that still remains the worst day of my life. Tirzah, will you understand when I tell you that at the instant the *cursed* great water lizard wrapped its jaws about Avaldamon . . . the riverbank screamed?"

"What . . . ?"

"The frogs screamed, Tirzah. It was noon, and yet the frogs screamed."

I was close to tears. "I understand, Great Lord."

"Yes," he said quietly, "I think that you do. Tell me, Tirzah," and now he forced some jollity into his voice. "You were free once. Did you have a trade, or were you taken for your beauty only?"

"My father—he was one of those killed by Threshold, Great Lord—and I were glassworkers. I cage."

"Hmm." He nodded. "And to cage at your age requires special skills. Am I right?"

"It requires a close affinity with the glass, Great Lord."

"Yes, of course." Zabrze changed the topic, steering us

into mildly less dangerous waters. "My mother was devastated by Avaldamon's loss. She almost died then, I think, except she soon realized she was with child, and that gave her hope. She loved Boaz, but he was not enough to replace Avaldamon, and so she died anyway. I really don't think she had any other option.

"Poor Boaz. Orphaned by the time he was six. He was a sensitive boy, like Avaldamon, and he took our mother's death very badly. I was sixteen or seventeen then, and I spent as much time with him as I could, but . . ." He shook himself, and I could see that the guilt of not being able to be there for Boaz still grieved him. "Boaz, poor child, would spend his days wrapped about his father's only gift to him."

"The Book of the Soulenai," I said without thinking.

"I did not know its true name. But the Soulenai were the subject of many of the stories. They and the Place Beyond."

He saw the question in my eyes. "My mother told me. I know she told Boaz some of the tales and she told me one or two as well. If you know of it, then I presume Boaz still has it?"

I nodded.

"Well," he continued. "Boaz missed his mother very much. Increasingly I was away, but I should have been there, I *should* have!"

"Great Lord, we can never be all that we wish."

He laughed bitterly. "Such a *wise* head for a slave! Well, perhaps slavery makes for increased wisdom. I imagine that with your looks you have endured . . . well, that you have endured. But Boaz. The Magi got him. He was vulnerable, and more than useful to them. They offered him comfort and a place to turn to when he thought he had no one and nowhere to go."

"I saw a piece he wrote when he was nine. It was . . . sad."

"Yes. He had sold his soul to the One by that age. Lost."

"He is a very powerful Magus, Great Lord. He has exceptional command of the power of the One."

"He has used his father's talents to bad ends. He has been transformed from the boy his mother birthed. Tirzah, will you do what you can for him?"

"What I can, Great Lord. But I fear it is already too late. I do not know what to do."

"Do your best, Tirzah. Do your best. For Avaldamon, for she whose name you bear, and for Boaz himself."

And then he was gone.

I stood there for a very long time, wondering at the unexpected ally I had found. But what good would it do me? I felt that Zabrze had no idea what to do, either. He was almost as frightened of Threshold as I was, but was constrained by his inability to speak out or to act on his fears.

Who, beyond a slave, would believe him?

And, having listened to him, who beyond a slave would *trust* him?

Zabrze, as I, was fighting against the greed of immortality.

I walked slowly back to Boaz's residence, then remembered too late that I'd seen Azam talking with one of Zabrze's officers.

I wheeled about, and thought about running after Zabrze, but it was too late. He would be back with Neuf by now, and she certainly would not welcome my intrusion. I wondered at her indifference to Zabrze. He was a man I could have loved very easily.

But then I was a slave, with a slave's tastes, and I knew not what noble women desired in a man.

Boaz was in bed waiting for me, but waiting only to douse the last lamp. He was cold-mannered and impatient, and I could see the Magus hungering for the morning. He turned his back to me once I climbed in beside him, and thus we spent the night, Threshold crowding the bed between us.

The next day the beast was capped out.

TWENTY-SEVEN

It was done with great ceremony and majesty, and I have a feeling that, of us all, Threshold enjoyed it the most.

The capstone was massive—fully fifteen paces square at its base, rising pyramidally some fifteen, as did the Infinity

Chamber. The capstone was also caged in golden glass as was the chamber, with the same inscriptions and formulas writhing across its sides.

The capstone was the outer expression of the inner chamber.

I turned my head aside as we passed it. I did not want to have to read a single word of its foulness.

Most people on site had come to witness the capping out of Threshold. Two walls surrounding Threshold had been razed; it now lay open to the countryside to the north and the river to the east. Walls still surrounded the compounds of the Magi and the slaves.

North of the pyramid spread the vast majority of the army Chad-Nezzar had brought with him; other units were ranked down the avenue leading to the wharf, while others yet complemented the usual guards and soldiers detailed to keep the slaves in order.

The slaves were situated to the northeast, sitting cross-legged on the ground, huddled shoulder to shoulder in a mute pack. They were hemmed in by guards, walls, and by Threshold itself.

Everyone else—Magi, nobles, and other guests, including me—were arranged neatly in Threshold's forecourt. Again I was placed inconspicuously to the rear, this time standing against the wall of the Magi's compound. Just on the other side, I knew, lay Boaz's house.

I was struck by the crazed thought that if things got too bad, I could just scramble over and hide deep within his house. Perhaps at the foot of the pool. Threshold would never see me there. Would it?

Kiamet and Holdat stood with me; Kiamet ostensibly to guard, but he had become such a friend to both Holdat and myself that I think had we decided to run, Kiamet would have cleared the way for us.

But there would be no escape. The wall was too high and smooth to scramble over, and there were too many bodies packed in front and to the sides of us.

Thirteen.

I wondered who.

I could not see much of what was happening on the ground as there were hundreds of Magi and nobles in front of me. I knew that Boaz, as Master of the Site, would conduct this rite, and Chad-Nezzar, as monarch, would make a polite speech. Then everyone would sit and watch several hundred slaves sweat and strain to raise the capstone. There would be polite gasps of wonder and awe, and then the slaves would be herded back to the tenements to consider their fate. The army would engage in some spectacular parades and displays, and the nobles and Magi would repair to a capping feast within the Magi's compound. So it was planned.

Except that events did not go according to plan.

I heard Boaz's voice, distorted at this distance, but full of the power of the One. He gave an impassioned but not overly long speech about the glory that was Threshold.

I wondered what Zabrze was thinking, and if Neuf was with him or if he'd persuaded her to sail back to Setkoth.

I heard Chad-Nezzar make a polite speech in return.

Both Boaz and Chad-Nezzar made remarks about the power that Threshold would bring *all* within Ashdod. As they spoke I could see the shivers of anticipation and greed down the backs of those Magi and nobles directly in front of me. Perhaps many were not sure of the exact nature of the power that would be on the offing, but power was power, and they all wanted great handfuls of it.

As Chad-Nezzar finished, the slaves set to work.

The capstone was fragile but heavy—its internal structures were built from metal struts and thick, clear plate glass. Engineers had built a ramp running up the southern face of the pyramid, and up this the capstone was to be run. The slaves were mostly assigned to long ropes that pulled the capstone skyward; as they leaned their backs into the ropes, marching down the avenue, so the golden glass slowly rose.

I heard the foreman's shout to the slaves to pull, then horns, drums, and cymbals sounded; the capstone was to be raised to music.

Not only music. As I saw the peak of the capstone rise above the heads of the crowd, hundreds of Magi broke into song—a slow, resounding chant that followed the beat of the music.

So the capstone rose, inching up the ramp to Threshold's peak, sent on its way by sweat and labor and a slow, bleak chant. The capstone glittered in the sun, the reflections almost painful, but I found it hard to look away.

An hour passed, perhaps two. The chant continued.

Finally I forced my eyes to Threshold's peak, trying to break the trance that had gripped me. A group of slaves waited there to shift the capstone into place and mortar it in.

"Oh," I murmured, and Kiamet took my arm.

"Tirzah? What is it?"

"Nothing, Kiamet. It is all right."

He could tell from my tone that it wasn't, but he let his hand drop and turned back to Threshold.

The capstone was almost at the peak now, and the thirteen men prepared to secure it.

Did Boaz realize? I wondered. Had he *deliberately* picked thirteen to stand atop Threshold?

The chant stopped, and a great shout went up from among the Magi. "Hoi!"

And then again, "Hoi!"

The thirteen had seized the capstone and were edging it into position.

"Hoi!"

In a minute, perhaps less, it would slide into place.

Then one of the slaves shouted. I could not hear him, not above the shouts of the Magi, but I saw him gesticulate wildly.

I was too far away to see, but I imagine that slave had a look of horror on his face.

He slipped and fell, and then the slave next to him slipped, and then the slave beyond . . . The last three or four tried to break away, but it was too late. Threshold would not let any of them go.

Inexorably Threshold pulled each one under the still moving capstone in the space of four or five breaths. It was a disgusting, horrific sight that stunned even the Magi into silence.

The harsh grating as the capstone settled was clearly audible.

Threshold had cemented its cap in place with the flesh and blood of the thirteen.

Then the true horror began.

Blood began to trickle down the four sides, spurting from

underneath the capstone. Then great gouts of it issued forth, far more blood than the thirteen bodies could have contained. It oozed relentlessly down the blue-green glass until Threshold was covered in it.

A pyramid of blood.

I turned aside and gagged, and Kiamet held me close, covering my eyes.

But I could still smell it—the warm, coppery scent of fresh, sacrificial blood.

I finally managed to escape back to Boaz's house. I think I was supposed to help at the feast, but I did not care. I could not smile and pour wine after what I had just witnessed.

I suppose the banquet went ahead because the Magi were close to ecstatic at Threshold's continuing exhibition of power. Now it not only ate, but *manufactured* blood!

I thought of all those glass shafts and corridors within Threshold, and wondered if they now ran with blood.

I heard voices, and sat up from the bed where I'd been lying. It was full night now; somehow I'd managed to lie unmoving for most of the afternoon and evening.

The voices were those of Boaz and Zabrze.

"Curse you, brother!" I heard Zabrze shout. "Is your heart stone? Is your mind crazed? What was that today but *evil*?"

"You have not the training," Boaz replied. "And thus you cannot see. The power of the One moves close to awakening. Infinity beckons. Be glad."

They were within the lights of the verandah now, and I could see that Boaz looked as calm as Zabrze looked furious.

"Boaz—"

"*Nothing* is going to deflect me from Threshold now, brother! *Nothing!*"

He stalked inside.

Zabrze stared after him, then looked at me, his eyes pleading. Then he wheeled about and disappeared into the night.

I slowly got to my feet. "Boaz?"

"Don't you start too, Tirzah!"

"Boaz, perhaps Zabrze is right—"

"*Tirzah!*"

"What building weeps blood, Boaz?" I shouted. "That is no building, that is—"

"It is Threshold, curse you!"

"It is not right," I said softly. "I do not care what you call it and I care not for what power you think it will give you. *It is not right!"*

"I've had enough," Boaz growled, and seized me by the wrist.

Stop! Stop! Stop! the Goblet of the Frogs cried from the cabinet. *Stop! Stop! Stop!*

"No," Boaz whispered. "No, I do not think I will," and he hauled me from the room.

Kiamet moved to join us, but Boaz rounded on him and snarled, and Kiamet, shocked, stumbled back to the verandah.

"Boaz? Where are we—"

"Threshold," he said, and his grip tightened about my wrist until I thought he would grind the bones to useless shards.

"Boaz! You're hurting me!"

His grip lessened, but it was still tight, and I could do nothing to free myself.

He pulled me through the compound of the Magi—feasting was still going on in some quarters, but the noise and festivities were muted—then down the streets of Gesholme to the avenue stretching toward Threshold.

"Boaz! No!"

"Yes, you stupid fool!" he said. "Look!"

Reluctantly I raised my eyes. Threshold stood bathed in the light of a full moon. Nature was surely blessing the pyramid, I thought numbly, for a full moon to shine so bright before the heat of the sun of Consecration Day.

It was beautiful. I had to admit that, but it was a cruel beauty. The blood had gone now—absorbed, perhaps—and the blue-green glass shone like a calm sea under the moon. A calm sea, but with deadly inner depths. The capstone gleamed, and I had a presentiment of how it would look when the full power of the sun struck it.

Lights, bloodred, flickered underneath the glass sides.

Threshold was waking.

"Just over twelve hours," Boaz said beside me, "and it will awaken completely."

"Are you sure that's what you really want, Boaz?" I asked.

He ignored the question. "Come, I will show you Threshold's full splendor."

He pulled me farther toward the pyramid.

At its base an officer stepped forward. From his insignia I noticed he was from Zabrze's command.

"Excellency," he said, and bowed deeply. "How may I help?"

"Stand guard. Watch. Let no one near who is not Magi. *No one.*"

"At your command, Excellency!"

I was almost rigid with fear now, and my legs stiff, but Boaz dragged me yet farther toward Threshold. I was sure he would lead me to the ramp, but at the last he turned aside and led me to the spine connecting the southern and eastern faces.

"Up," he said, "and if you won't climb yourself then I'll damn well carry you."

His voice was cold, distant, and despair swept me. This was not Boaz anymore. This was the Magus rampant. Threshold had won.

Small steps were cut into the spine.

"No," I whispered. Not the capstone. No.

Boaz hauled me up the first twenty steps, then, scared he might let go, I made an effort myself. The climb was steep, and Threshold high, and within fifty steps I was panting, a combination of effort and terror.

It took us almost half an hour to reach the top, and by then the moon had sunk toward the horizon, casting half of Threshold into deep shadow. There the bloodred lighting underneath its skin flickered even more virulent than on those faces still exposed to the moonlight.

A small ledge ran about the capstone, perhaps a pace wide. Boaz let me go, and I instantly leaned against the capstone, sinking my fingers into the gaps in the caged lacework, praying it had been fastened securely to the inner wall.

The glass screamed at me, screamed at me to rescue it, screamed to me that if I would not rescue it, then I must kill it.

Smash us! Smash us! Smash us!

But I lacked the courage or the means even to do that, and I closed my ears and mind as best I could to the despair of the glass. I wanted to let go, but I couldn't, for then I was sure I would fall.

Boaz stepped farther along the ledge, easy and confident. To distract myself from the glass, I made the mistake of looking out. Instantly nausea swamped me.

I hastily lowered my eyes . . . and saw the remnants of a crushed foot at the join of the capstone and Threshold.

I whimpered, frantic, wondering what I could do to escape, and looked back to Boaz. Perhaps if I pleaded. . . .

But Boaz was lost. He was standing at the northwest corner of the pyramid facing into the emptiness, head back, arms extended, robes flowing in the night breeze.

I had thin-soled sandals on my feet, and through them I imagined I felt a throb, then another, and then I knew I was not imagining it.

"Boaz!" It was only a whimper again, but he heard it and turned.

"Feel it?" he asked. "*Feel* it?"

"Yes. Yes, I do. Boaz, please may we go down now? Please?"

The throbbing grew more powerful.

"Soon," he whispered, looking at the sky. "Not long. Be patient."

Then, "Tirzah? Look."

Boaz pointed to the side of the pyramid in the shadow of the moonlight, and then beyond that.

I followed his finger . . . my heart stalled, then raced.

Threshold's shadow stretched for almost half a league across the plain behind it. A rectangular shadow. Rectangular.

I thought I was going to be sick.

Boaz strode back to me and seized my arm. "Down."

I sagged in relief, and might have fallen had it not been for his grip, but I rejoiced too soon.

Boaz hauled me down the steps, and how we didn't tumble to our deaths during that mad descent I'll never know, then he pulled me to the ramp.

No! "*Boaz!*"

"I want you to understand once and for all," he said. "Once and for all."

I let my feet slide from underneath me as we neared the top of the ramp, hoping that it might slow Boaz down, or even stop him. But he only cursed, bent down, and gathered me into his arms.

I was even more trapped than before.

Threshold winked as we passed into its mouth.

I wanted to close my eyes, but I couldn't. I was going to my death, I was sure of it.

Threshold's internal glass walls were now all the black, shiny substance. Thin red forks of light flickered underneath them. I remembered how the glass had been fused into the stone in this process of turning glass into black, and I understood that the red light flickered through stone as well.

Flesh now, perhaps.

Boaz climbed without pause through the main passageway. The light was eerie. Moonlight reflected down the shafts and seeped into the corridor, but it had been corrupted on its way down and was now pink-tinged and thick.

The air smelt coppery, warm.

"Almost there," Boaz whispered.

I glanced at his face. It was the face of a man I did not know, and one I instinctively hated. I understood that Threshold would do this to all it enthralled. Not human anymore, no will of their own.

I closed my eyes momentarily, wishing I could find the time to grieve, but I was too terrified.

The slope leveled out and Boaz set me down on my feet.

"Are you ready?" he said. "Ready for Threshold's intimate delights?"

"No, please . . . Boaz . . . don't . . . please . . ."

He seized my hand and wrenched me into the Infinity Chamber.

The first emotion I had was of relief. Here the light was soft gold, moonlight filtering through the golden capstone down the main shaft through the chamber's own golden glass. No blood. No coppery smell.

Then I heard the glass scream.

It had never, *never* been this bad before. These were the screams of trapped animals, mutilated almost unto death, pleading, wanting both freedom and death, begging me to help them, screaming . . . *screaming to me to save them* . . . *oh, gods, please, please! Save us! Save us!*

I screamed myself, and blocked my ears.

It did not help.

I screamed again, feeling the glass's agony ripple through my body.

Gods, what would happen here?

"Beautiful," Boaz murmured, and lifted his hands.

I knew what he would do next, for I had seen him do this once before. He was going to open the gates of all the shafts and flood the Infinity Chamber with light.

It would only be moonlight, but it would be bad enough.

I cried out again, almost convulsing with the horror of the glass that ran through me.

He smiled, took a deep breath, and laid his hands upon the glass.

And heard—*felt*—it scream.

I had screamed as he touched the glass, and when he wrenched his hands away from it with a look of absolute horror I thought it was only in reaction to me.

But then I realized not.

His face had lost all color, and his eyes were wide, terrified. Somehow I threw myself across the chamber and grabbed his hands, slamming them back against the glass.

"Feel it, Boaz! *Feel it!*"

And he did. He tried to break away, and I don't know where the strength came from, but I managed to keep his hands pinned against the glass.

Save us! Save us! Save us! Save us!

The glass was screaming . . . and it was screaming to Boaz. *Boaz!*

Save us! Save us! Save us! Save us!

"No!" he moaned.

It comes! It COMES! Save us!

He finally wrenched his hands from beneath mine. *"No!"*

"Boaz, please," I whispered. "We've got to get out of here. Please. Please!"

"Tirzah?"

"Boaz, come on, now. Come on." I tried to keep my voice gentle. "Please, come now."

I grasped one of his hands between both of mine. "Come on, now."

He was so shocked by the horror that the glass had flooded into him that he could not resist me. Very, very gradually he moved.

"Come on, now."

We had to get out. Surely Threshold had realized what had happened? But perhaps it was concentrating so much on its own burgeoning power that it had ignored us.

I led Boaz down the corridor as fast as I could. But that was not fast enough. I wanted to run, but he was stumbling and resisting now as before I had stumbled and resisted.

"Come *on*, Boaz. *Hurry!*"

Threshold's mouth loomed before us. I was sure that it would snap closed as we passed under it into the clear night air, but finally we stumbled out.

"Excellency?" the officer said, worried by Boaz's face.

"The climb," I said. "And, well, the privacy. He could not resist the chance to commune with the One. And so now he's breathless."

The officer winked, and let us go.

TWENTY-EIGHT

I led Boaz through the streets back to the Magi's compound. It was very quiet now. Everyone was in bed to rest for Consecration Day.

"Let no one in," I said to Kiamet, and he nodded. I wondered when he ever slept, but now was not the time to ask.

I led Boaz over to the bed and sat him down. His face was expressionless, his eyes dull.

"You heard the glass," I said.

He looked up. "What?"

"You heard the glass scream, Boaz. It wants you to save it."

"No."

"*Yes!* It was screaming to *you*!"

"No!" His eyes were wild now, and he stood to face me. "What you speak is—"

"Truth, Boaz. What I speak is truth."

"No. I heard nothing. I—"

"*Shetzah!*" I flung my hands in the air. "How long are you going to deny that you are an Elemental, Boaz?"

He cringed at that word.

"Say it, Boaz. We're safe enough here. Threshold can't hear us or see us." My voice was much, much softer. "Why else pick a residence so shielded from Threshold's eye? Why else save to hide your Elemental leanings?"

"*No!* I am a Magus . . . a . . ."

"What you *are,* Boaz, is an Elemental Cantomancer. I am Elemental, too. Don't deny that you don't know that."

"No, Tirzah. Stop. You're condemning yourself. I'll have to kill you—"

I laughed. "Go ahead, then. Kill me."

He cursed and turned away. "I do not believe you. I cannot be this . . . Cantomancer."

There was a slight step outside on the verandah, but I assumed it was Kiamet at his post.

"Oh? Thus speaks the man who kept the locks of the dead? Thus speaks the man who turned stone to hair? Thus speaks the man who keeps and treasures the Book of the Soulenai?"

"No! I do *not* want to hear any more." Boaz flung himself away from me.

"She speaks truth, brother."

Zabrze! I looked at him gratefully. Maybe Boaz would listen to him.

But he had no intention of listening to either of us. "Out! I want you both out!"

"No," Zabrze said quietly. "I've had enough, and I've heard enough to know Tirzah has, too. Boaz, the time has come to admit who you really are."

"Kiamet!" Boaz shouted.

"He will not come, Boaz," Zabrze said. "Kiamet is my man."

That stunned me as much as Boaz. Kiamet?

"Has Kiamet been spying on me for all these months?" Boaz said.

"Looking out for you, Boaz, and keeping watch. But 'spying'? No. Kiamet owes his loyalty to me but has not reported on the activities within this residence. Although"—Zabrze glanced at me—"I wish I *had* asked him to do that. It might have saved me some surprises on my arrival."

"We were in the Infinity Chamber, Great Lord," I said. "The glass in that chamber screams with despair. It is . . ." I shuddered. "Tonight Boaz laid his hands on the glass and heard it. It screamed to him to save it. Great Lord, only an Elemental could have heard it."

"Boaz," Zabrze said, "you *are* an Elemental. Listen to us."

Boaz opened his mouth to deny it yet again, and I turned away in disgust.

Boaz, Boaz, Boaz.

I twisted back. It was the Goblet of the Frogs. I looked between the two brothers. Boaz had clearly heard it, for his eyes were riveted on the glass, but Zabrze was only staring irritably at Boaz.

That answered one question. I had thought Zabrze might be Elemental, too, but that call had been so strong that even the weakest Elemental would have picked it up.

Boaz, Boaz, Boaz.

Not many voices. One.

"No!" Boaz screamed, and leaped for the glass.

It flared. Light seared through the room, and Zabrze and I both cried out.

"What?" Zabrze murmured.

"The goblet is Soulenai magic," I said, blinking my eyes, trying to clear them, frantically searching for Boaz. *What was he doing?* "It calls to Boaz."

There was a faint tinkling, and I thought that Boaz had managed to shatter the glass.

"No!" Not my voice, but Boaz's.

He was crouched by the cabinet, his hands over his face. A man stood before him, with his hand reaching down.

Boaz.

Not a man but a specter, woven of mist only.

"By the gods!" Zabrze cried. "Avaldamon!"

Boaz's head jerked up, unbelieving.

Boaz. The specter's hand drifted closer, and Boaz, shaking, reached out his own.

Boaz. Listen to the frogs. Learn their Song. Follow the path it shows you, for it is all that will save you. Listen, Boaz. Accept. Destroy Threshold.

And then he was gone.

I rubbed my eyes, wondering if he'd ever been there at all. I'd never heard of this—but what power Avaldamon commanded to so visit from the grave!

"Avaldamon!" Zabrze whispered, and then he stepped to his brother's side, knelt down, and embraced him.

I think it was Zabrze's embrace, even more than the fleeting apparition of Avaldamon, that shattered Boaz's resistance. He broke into harsh sobs, and Zabrze rocked him back and forth.

Boaz finally blinked, as if waking from a dream. "Tirzah?"

"Boaz!" I dropped beside him, and added my arms to those of Zabrze's.

"Boaz, listen to me now. The Soulenai say that you are the only one who can destroy Threshold."

"Oh, no, Tirzah. I cannot—"

"You are Magus trained," I said, repeating what the Soulenai had told me. "You understand the power of the One. You understand Threshold. And you also command such great"—I kissed his cheek—*"wonderful"*—now I kissed his forehead—"Elemental power, you can counteract whatever Threshold truly is. *You* are the key to Threshold's destruction."

Boaz slumped against Zabrze and myself. "My father . . ."

Zabrze glanced at me. "Avaldamon was an Elemental Cantomancer, Boaz. He told me this. Why, I don't know, for such a confession was more than dangerous in a world where the Magi ruled. But perhaps even then he had an intuition of his own death and knew that *someone* had to be told."

Boaz raised his tear-stained face to Zabrze. "And you accepted it?"

"Avaldamon had been kind and understanding in a court where very few were, Boaz. I trusted him. And I admired him beyond any man I have met since. His powers were astounding—he demonstrated some to me—and yet his compassion was overwhelming. He was"—Zabrze's mouth twisted cynically—"a bright contrast to the Magi at court."

"And to what I became," Boaz said very quietly. "How is it that you did not tell me this earlier?"

"I was gone so long from court when you were young, Boaz. When I returned it was to find that the Magi had claimed you. I . . . hesitated . . . to stand up in court and shout that you were the son of an Elemental Cantomancer."

Even Boaz had to grin weakly at that.

"Come," I said, and pulled both men to their feet. "Let us sit where it is more comfortable. You are both too old to squat so abandoned on the floor."

It was a bad attempt at humor, but Zabrze and Boaz seemed grateful for it. They sat at the table, and I lifted the boxed book and the goblet down and placed them before Boaz.

"You always knew, Boaz," I said. "You did."

It was a relief for him to finally admit it.

"Yes, although for a long time I did not realize what it was." His voice was very quiet, and he kept his eyes on the box. "I felt so abandoned when my mother died. I had no one to turn to . . ."

I glanced at Zabrze. The man's face was distraught, and I touched his hand.

". . . and one day a Magus came to talk to me. He said that the power of the One was a wondrous thing and that if I opened myself to it then I would never be alone. It sounded . . . a relief. I threw myself body and soul"—his mouth quirked at the unintentional pun—"into the study of the One. It appeared to be everything that I needed. Solace. Company—the company and community of the Magi as well as the One. Power. That appealed to me."

"Maybe you were yearning to understand your own power, Boaz," I said, "and misunderstood the yearning."

"Maybe. Whatever, it did not take much to push me into a singular dedication to the One. I learned easily, the Magi were proud of me. Even Chad-Nezzar was, I think, for I was an orphan boy who had no grand inheritance. Let the Magi have me, he said, and take care of my education."

"When did you begin to realize that there were depths to you that were different?" I asked. Now both my hands were wrapped about one of Boaz's.

"About twenty. I realized that when I touched certain things—glass, metal—they whispered to me. I knew what it was immediately. And I knew that Elemental magic was bad, corrupt, foul. So I believed myself to be bad, corrupt, foul. Tirzah, Zabrze, you'll never know what years of horror I went through. I built walls and fortresses that I hid behind. I became the perfect Magus. It took me five, six, seven years, but I did it. Eventually I believed that I'd killed whatever it was that had so corrupted me."

"But you still dreamed of the Song of the Frogs," I said.

"Rarely, Tirzah. Or maybe I so blocked the dreams from my conscious mind that I do not remember them. I was inviolate. The perfect Magus. Until you carved those cursed frogs for me in Setkoth."

Zabrze looked puzzled, and I told him briefly how I'd carved the glass on my arrival in Setkoth. He nodded, and told Boaz how the frogs had screamed on his father's death.

"Well," Zabrze said eventually, sitting back. "What to do now?"

"Destroy Threshold," I said firmly. "We must."

Boaz was silent.

"We *must*," I said again. "Will you not yet admit its wrongness, Boaz? Will you yet deny it?"

He dropped his eyes. "No. No, it is wrong. But apart from physically pulling Threshold down . . . I cannot think how . . ."

"Boaz," I asked, "what is Threshold's wrongness?"

"It is the power that it draws upon, I suppose," he said.

"The Vale," I said, remembering.

"The Vale?" Zabrze asked. "I have only barely heard of it."

"It is," Boaz began slowly, thinking it through, "a well of

power. The Magi have known of its existence, and have known of the power it contained. We always thought it the well of Creation, the void out of which the universe and all it contains sprang. We thought to tap it. Threshold—or, more correctly, the Infinity Chamber—would then become the bridge into Infinity and immortality."

"Boaz," I said, my horror mounting. "What if something were to come through the other way? What if something in the *Vale* used Threshold as a bridge into this world?"

Silence.

"Damn you, brother!" Zabrze said, and grasped Boaz by the arm. *"What have you done?"*

"Am *I* to blame for the entire history of Threshold?" Boaz snapped, wrenching his arm away. "Threshold was conceived and begun long before Avaldamon arrived to beget me. I have overseen the final days of its completion, nothing else! Do not blame Threshold on *me!*"

"Then oversee its destruction, brother!"

Boaz looked out the window. "Too late, Zabrze. It has begun."

I turned to look outside. Dawn light was filtering through the hanging vines about the verandah. How long had we been talking?

"What do you mean, 'too late'?"

Boaz looked back to Zabrze. "Threshold will awaken to its full power when the sun is directly overhead. Noon. When light will flood the Infinity Chamber. There is nothing we can do to stop the process now."

"But I thought," I said, "the rites . . . surely if you do not conduct the Consecration Day rites . . ."

Boaz shook his head. "The rites were for two purposes only. One, for show. Everyone expected *some* sort of rite once Threshold was completed. The Consecration rites were designed to fit that need. The rites would be grand to make the Magi look grander. And two, and far more importantly, the rites were designed to have at least some of the Magi in or near the Infinity Chamber when the sun seared through. We wanted to be first."

"Thus your insistence that you conduct the rites," I said quietly. He had been going to leave me. Leave me for Infinity and all it promised.

" 'Insistence' is too pleasant a word for it, Tirzah. No, whichever way you look at it, the lack of rites is not going to make the slightest bit of difference to whether Threshold finally awakes or not. Whatever happens, once the sun reaches its full strength . . ."

"So we physically destroy it," Zabrze said firmly, and Boaz laughed harshly.

"*Destroy* it, Zabrze? It has taken eight generations to build, and we have some six hours to pull it down."

"I have an army."

"And do you trust them? The power of the One is strong among the military. The Magi have been cultivating it for years, decades, anticipating that Chad-Nezzar might try to use the army to seize Threshold for himself. And the promise, the *thrall,* of power is going to make many stay their hand."

Zabrze was tellingly silent, and I thought of the respect the officer on duty at Threshold had shown for Boaz last night.

"And," Boaz said quietly, "I doubt very much that Threshold would allow itself to be destroyed. You have seen demonstrations of its power. If any came near it with a mallet . . ."

"Nevertheless," Zabrze said, "we must try."

And then I remembered one of his officers talking so quietly with Azam. "Great Lord . . ."

"Yes, I know," he said. "We must make use of Yaqob."

Again silence. This man *would* make a great Chad, I thought, for he constantly outwits all those about him.

"Yaqob?" Boaz asked, a decided edge to his voice.

"Boaz," I said gently. Boaz disliked Yaqob for many reasons other than that he might be an Elemental. "The slaves will fight to destroy Threshold. They *know* full well how wrong, how dark, it is."

"And they are planning a revolt, anyway," Zabrze finished.

"And why does *that* not surprise me?" Boaz muttered. "But how is it that you know this, Zabrze?"

"*Shetzah,* Boaz! I cannot think how you can spend so much time in Setkoth and still be so unaware of court intrigue!"

Zabrze leaned forward. "I came down here fully expecting trouble—from several quarters. I'd heard the rumors about Threshold, about the 'accidents' on site, so I certainly expected trouble from the pyramid itself—I did not realize then how bad it would be. I also knew that Chad-Nezzar had a tenuous idea about seizing Threshold for his own use, and I knew that the Magi and the power of the Magi had infiltrated much of the army, how much I wasn't sure, but enough that I no longer trust much of my command. And then, here we were sailing into an encampment of slaves unsure of their future. Of course I expected some kind of revolt, or at least a plot for one!"

"And so you came prepared to put that down?" Boaz asked.

"No," Zabrze said, staring at his brother, "I came half expecting to use them as allies."

"I saw one of your officers talking to a man I know is involved in the plot," I said.

"Yes."

"But how did you know so quickly?" I asked. "Your men had been here barely two hours before I saw—"

"I told Prince Zabrze, Tirzah," said a voice, and I looked about, wondering when the shocks were about to stop.

"I told him."

"Kiamet?" Boaz said, his voice angry.

"My brother is Azam," Kiamet said. "No one knew that. No one."

Gods. I dropped my face into one hand.

"Kiamet has been a very useful man," Zabrze said quietly. "Very."

"Azam pressured me for information," Kiamet said. "But I would not give it to him. I"—he hesitated, his eyes pleading to Boaz for understanding—"I would not betray you, My Lord."

"But you did not hesitate to work for my brother," Boaz said bitterly.

"Oh, Boaz, be sensible!" Zabrze said. "You should have realized! Kiamet was not one of those guards who has been here under Magi influence for years. He came down with the soldiers when Chad-Nezzar came here some months ago. He has always been my man."

"And yet, Boaz," I said, thinking it through, "there is much he could have reported to Zabrze about both you and me, but did not. Think about it. He has been more loyal to us than is immediately apparent."

Kiamet shot a grateful look my way. I returned it. He could have told Azam about what I'd been doing in this residence, what I'd been learning. But he had not.

"It has not always been easy," Kiamet said simply.

Boaz nodded, accepting it. "Now what?"

"Now we see just how many we *can* rally to aid us," Zabrze said, and stood. "Perhaps if we can raise a thousand or more then we might mount an assault on Threshold itself. Smash the capstone, even the Infinity Chamber. Stop it."

"But—" Boaz began.

"But if we can't"—Zabrze looked at me—"Tirzah? If we can't?"

"Then you must do what your father told you, Boaz," I said. "You must listen to the Song of the Frogs. Understand it. Learn it. Learn who *you* are. And then perhaps you *will* be able to stop whatever it is that Threshold will become at noon."

"And how, pray, will I learn to understand the Song of the Frogs?"

"I have some friends, Boaz."

"Yaqob!" He spat the word.

"Yes, and Isphet, and a dozen others. They will help you. There is a place that Isphet knows. A community where the ways of Elemental magic are still strong. Among them are Graces, elders of power who *can* teach you." I looked at Zabrze. "Great Lord, if you can't destroy Threshold, then I will have to get Boaz away from here."

Zabrze nodded. "Can you get him to your friends now?"

"I think so. Boaz, here, take this," and I handed him the box containing the book.

He quickly wrapped the Goblet of the Frogs in a robe and held it close.

"Kiamet," Zabrze said, "go with them. Make sure they are safe. Then go to Azam, as we planned."

Kiamet nodded.

"And Tirzah?"

I looked up.

"Stop calling me Great Lord. It is slightly ridiculous in the situation."

I nodded, smiled, then Kiamet and I hurried Boaz out the door.

TWENTY-NINE

We walked slowly, confidently, Kiamet and I slightly behind Boaz. Two or three of the Magi called out to Boaz, and one stopped to chat to him about the preparations for the rite.

He was curt and impatient with them. But that was normal for the Master of the Site, and none who talked to him realized that it was because he was nervous.

Just as we reached the gate, there came a shout behind us.

"Excellency!"

We jumped, and I saw Kiamet's hand slide toward his sword. But then he relaxed.

Holdat.

"Excellency!" Holdat panted. "What is it that you do?"

Boaz opened his mouth, no doubt to snap, but Holdat took the box from his hand, managing to fawn and bow at the same time.

"Excellency! You must let me carry that for you!"

"It is a good idea, Excellency," Kiamet said softly.

I regarded Holdat fondly. No doubt he would astound us shortly with the revelation that he was Zabrze's long-lost twin brother.

But no. Holdat whispered to me as we marched through the gate and into Gesholme that he had seen and heard some of what had transpired in Boaz's residence during the night. "And I was not going to let you go without someone to cook for you, Tirzah!" He winked.

I suppressed a smile. It would be useful to have Holdat

with us. If we escaped. My good humor faded and I risked a glance over my shoulder at Threshold. It loomed bright and confident in the morning.

The sun was well above the horizon.

"Curse it, Tirzah, which way?" Boaz's soft voice cut through my thoughts.

I bowed slightly, thinking that everyone from Threshold to the lowliest slave must have their eye on us, and led the group down a street, and then into an alley. My stomach churned; it was weeks since I had been home to Isphet's tenement. What would she say? What would she do? *Would* she help us?

We arrived without incident. Kiamet, as would have been natural in normal circumstances, stepped to the door and hammered on it. My mind jumped back to the night of my arrival when Ta'uz had led me here.

There was a soft scuffling inside, as there had been then, and then Isphet threw back the door.

"Yes?" she inquired.

But I could read her eyes now, and they said that she believed I had betrayed her. Why else would the Master of the Site arrive so precipitously at her door?

She stared at me, her expression flat and hostile, then looked at Boaz. "Have you come to find fodder to make up the seventeen, Excellency?" she asked. "Does Threshold require further feeding today?"

Boaz ignored her as Kiamet whispered in his ear, then disappeared down the alley. Gone to Azam, I supposed.

As soon as Kiamet left, Boaz returned his attention to Isphet.

"Let me enter," he said, and pushed past her. I was quick behind him, then Holdat, still clutching the box.

"Isphet," I said as she closed the door. "It is not as it—"

"You bitch!" she hissed. "You have betrayed us. Why? For what? Does he pat you on the head? Feed you sweetmeats? Do you roll over and let him scratch your belly?"

"Isphet—"

"She has *not* betrayed you, Isphet," Boaz said. "She has risked her life more than once to save you."

She glared at him. "What do you want?"

Kiath and Saboa had retreated to a corner, sure the rest of their lives could be measured in hours at the most.

"We have come to help you escape," Boaz said.

"Isphet, Boaz needs training. He is an Elemental Cantomancer. We need you to help us get to—"

"What?" Isphet tried very hard to laugh. "What? Have you been out in the sun too long, girl? Is this some elaborate trick? Some—"

"Oh, be quiet, woman!" Boaz snapped. He was fast regaining his equilibrium as his own shock faded and his acceptance hardened. "Why do you suspect a trick? If I wanted to destroy you, as all other Elementals within your workshop, or destroy Yaqob and Azam for the planned revolt, I would have done it without a word or warning shout and you would *all* be dead by now. Let Tirzah talk!"

Isphet just stared at him, more shocked now that he'd named Yaqob and Azam so surely.

"Sit down, Isphet," I said, and led her to a stool, pulled one up beside her, and started to talk.

I talked until the sun shone strong through the windows. Boaz sank down on the floor, his back against a wall, his eyes never leaving Isphet's face. Holdat stood close by, his arms folded, the box at his feet.

"It was Boaz," I finished gently, "who gave me the locks of hair. He transformed Druse's stone lock to softness, and he told me to go to you with them."

Isphet looked at me, then to Boaz. I did not blame her for disbelieving.

"And yet," she said, her eyes still locked on Boaz, "he also filled you with so much pain you will never bear children, and threw you eight days into a hole that left you all but dead. Tell me, Tirzah"—her eyes swept back to me—"why I should trust you after you have kept so many secrets. Why?"

"I can give you no other reason, Isphet, save our friendship. Please, trust me."

"Kiamet, my guard," said Boaz, "has gone to Azam. Your little uprising shall have more support than you ever suspected. Prince Zabrze will aid you if you will help him destroy Threshold."

Isphet finally managed to break into harsh laughter. "After all these years, *Excellency,* slaving over the hot glass, you now tell me we're all going to march up to that cursed pyramid and *smash* it?"

"Isphet," I began again, thinking to tell her of the Book of the Soulenai, but then the courtyard door burst open and Yaqob, Azam, and Kiamet stepped in. Yaqob had a wild look to his eye, and he, as Azam, was armed.

"Yaqob!" I leaped to my feet, Boaz rising more slowly, his eyes on Yaqob.

"Azam came to fetch me with a wild tale that Princes were allied to slaves and that Magi were Elementals in disguise," Yaqob said. "I almost did not believe him, save that now this Kiamet joins us, and a unit of imperial guards wait for us in the alley, and I see that this maggot"—he spat at Boaz—"has managed to crawl out of his dung hole to sit and chat to slaves. Isphet, what have they told you?"

I cringed at the "they."

"That Boaz is an Elemental Cantomancer . . ."

Yaqob's eyes widened. Kiamet had very obviously not used that term.

". . . and that now he and Zabrze wish to aid us in our struggle for freedom. I do not know what to think."

"I would smell 'trap,' " Yaqob said, "except this is so elaborate that I wonder what its purpose could be. The light entertainment before the true fun of awakening Threshold? Eh, Boaz? Do the Magi and Chad-Nezzar himself wait outside to burst into applause as I lead my sorry band out to fight for freedom? *Eh?*"

"Yaqob—" Boaz began, but Azam broke in.

"We have not the time for this, Yaqob. Isphet, stay here, and lock up safe until we come for you. If it looks bad, then flee for the Lhyl. You may have a chance of stealing a boat." He paused, and looked about. "Yaqob, Kiamet, come with me."

But Yaqob was staring at me. "Tirzah," he said. "Do you remember what once I told you?"

"Yaqob?"

"I said, Tirzah, that on the day we fought to freedom, you and I, I would leave Boaz dead behind us."

And before any of us could react he drew his sword and lunged the distance between himself and Boaz.

I screamed and lunged myself, but there was nothing I could do. Boaz was surprised and unarmed, and all I saw was a flash of steel as Yaqob sank his blade into Boaz's belly.

"That," Yaqob snarled, his face close to Boaz's, "is for the pain and the grief you have caused Tirzah and I."

Then he stepped back, wrenched his sword free, seized me, and gave me a hard kiss. "Soon, Tirzah," he said, "soon." And then he was gone.

I beat Kiamet to Boaz's side only by an instant.

"Boaz!" I cried, wrapping my arms about him as he sank to the floor.

Behind I heard Isphet push Azam out the door. "Go!" she said. "Go! There is nothing you can do here."

Kiamet was helpless. He had been trained to inflict such wounds, not aid them, and Isphet laid a hand to his shoulder and literally hauled him away. He sank to the floor some paces away, his mission to aid Azam forgotten.

Boaz had still not said a word. He wore a stunned look on his face as he stared down at his hands wrapped about his belly. Blood was seeping through his fingers.

"Boaz!" I wailed again. "Isphet, *do* something!"

"Stupid, stupid, stupid," she muttered, and I think she was referring to the whole of life with that word, not just the tragedy playing out before our eyes. "Stupid! Tirzah, take his hands for me, keep them away. I need to look . . ."

She tore at his robes, using a small knife we used for gutting fish to cut them away. "Kiath, tear up some bandages. Now!"

Isphet exposed Boaz's belly, and I stifled another cry. Yaqob had struck him slightly to one side of his navel, a neat clean wound that nevertheless bled profusely.

Boaz moaned, as the first pain nibbled in at his shock.

"Isphet!" I cried, and she turned and struck me hard across my face.

"Shut *up,* girl! I don't need you moaning as well!"

She probed quickly, then took the bandage that Kiath handed her. "There's not much I can do now, Excellency . . .

Boaz . . . except stop the bleeding. Later I'll explore it more. See what damage has been done. But a belly wound . . ."

She didn't have to tell any of us how dangerous that was. "It depends on what Yaqob struck on his way through. Tirzah, help him sit up, I need to wrap this about him. Good."

Boaz grunted as I leaned him forward, then relaxed back once Isphet was done. "Isphet," he said, his voice hoarse with deepening pain and shock. "Get Tirzah away from here if—"

"I'm not leaving you!" I said. *"Not!"*

"No one's going anywhere yet," Isphet said. "Tirzah, press here . . . yes, that's good. Maintain that pressure. It will help stop the bleeding."

She sat back on her heels, her face pale and smudged with blood across the chin where she'd wiped one of her hands. Her eyes drifted between Boaz and myself. "It seems," she said softly, "that Yaqob has more to be concerned about than whether or not the Magus plans to foil his uprising."

"I live for Boaz, Isphet. I have for months now."

"Then it is a shame you neglected to tell Yaqob that your affection for him has dimmed, Tirzah! He is too good a man, and has been too good to you, to be thus treated. You have given him the hope and the dream to get through many a dark day. Now . . ." She looked at Boaz with utter distaste. "Now he will take the news hard."

"Then I hope he doesn't take it out on me again," Boaz muttered, and his hand fluttered over the red-tinged bandage about his belly, "if this was only the result of a mild distemper."

"Rest," Isphet said abruptly, and she rose, walked to the far side of the room, and sank down to her sleeping pallet. Her eyes never left us.

"Boaz?" I whispered. "Boaz?"

"Hmm?" He was drifting in and out of consciousness.

"Boaz, don't leave me."

"Perhaps Isphet was right. Yaqob would be better for you . . . after all I've done . . . Yaqob would be better . . ."

"Boaz," I whispered, *"don't leave me!"*

We sat for an hour or more, waiting for we knew not what. Kiamet and Holdat had dropped to one side of Boaz, helpless, but lending me strength through their presence.

Eventually Isphet rose and came over to us. Boaz was now asleep—or unconscious—and she told me to relax the pressure on his belly.

"He tore you apart with his power, Tirzah," she whispered. "And now he suffers likewise. It is not a coincidence, methinks." And she was gone again.

I lowered my head and wept, remembering what the Soulenai had said to me.

Tirzah, if someone visits such pain on another person, then one day that pain will rebound on him. It is the price he will eventually have to pay.

"No, no, no," I whispered. But it was too late. I could only hope that the price he would have to pay would not be *too* great.

Time passed, and the room grew hot. Boaz sweated and tossed in my arms, and I whispered to him fooleries that I'm sure only deepened his fever. Holdat fetched a damp cloth and wiped Boaz's brow, and I smiled briefly at him, grateful.

"Fighting," Isphet said, breaking into my thoughts.

I raised my head, listening.

I did not hear anything immediately, then heard the faint noise of shouts, and the ring of steel against steel. "Zabrze has had to fight his way through to Threshold," I said listlessly.

"And we fight with him." Isphet was standing now, a hand and an ear to the door. "Kiath. Go to the roof and tell me what you see."

Kiath slipped out the courtyard door, and I heard her quick steps on the stairs.

She was gone a long while, and meantime the sound of fighting grew closer. Isphet glanced at me and at Boaz from time to time, her face worried. Where was Yaqob? Azam?

Would we have to move without them?

Gods, no! I prayed. How would we move Boaz? He could *not* be moved.

Damn you, Yaqob, I thought, that you be so unwilling to accept the help handed you! Damn your jealousy! But then I wondered if the blame for Yaqob's actions should be laid at my feet, not his. Had I been wrong to keep silent for so long?

Kiath returned.

"Well?" Isphet snapped.

"There is heavy fighting in the streets to the west of us," Kiath said. "I do not think Prince Zabrze managed to get close to Threshold. His men, and those of us who fight with him, are being forced back."

"Where is the sun, Kiath?" I asked. "How high?"

"It waits but an hour until noon."

"Isphet!" I cried, forgetting my earlier concerns about leaving. "We've got to go! If we're still here at noon . . . !"

"There's worse," Kiath said.

"Out with it, girl!"

"Gesholme is afire."

We all stared at her, and I realized even Boaz had his eyes open. Afire! Oh, gods!

"Then we have no choice," Isphet said, and squatted down by Boaz. She grasped his face in a rough hand.

"Magus, can you walk?"

"His name is *Boaz*," I said softly, but my eyes were hard.

Isphet ignored me. "Well?"

"If I have help, yes," he replied.

"Well, you'll die if you stay here. Kiamet, help him up." And she rose and bundled several belongings into a blanket, speaking swiftly to Kiath and Saboa.

Boaz did not make a sound as Kiamet helped him rise, but his face paled, and I grabbed him, thinking he was about to faint. Holdat fussed about us, but I told him to look after the box. "And the goblet, too, if you can manage it."

He nodded, wrapping both goblet and box in a blanket Kiath handed him, and then Isphet was at the door.

"Ready?"

We all nodded save Boaz, he was concentrating too hard on staying upright.

"Isphet," I said urgently as she opened the door.

"What?"

"Please, we've got to stay out of Threshold's shadow as much as we can. Keep to overhangs and narrow alleys. If it sees us . . ."

She stared at me, but she understood. "Very well. Come on now, the alley is clear . . ."

Clear of people, but smoke drifted down over the rooftops,

and the sounds of fighting some three or four streets distant
clattered about our ears.

"Hurry!" Isphet hissed.

"What about the others?" Saboa asked. "The tenements are
packed."

"I've no time to save the world," Isphet snapped. "This
sorry band will take all my effort."

But she banged on doors as we passed, shouting to occu-
pants to get down to the river.

We stumbled along, Kiamet taking much of Boaz's weight
as he concentrated on putting one foot ahead of the other, his
arm tight about my own shoulder. Please do not die, Boaz, I
prayed. Please. Please.

We reached the end of our alley and Isphet waved us to a
halt. "Down here, I think," she muttered, indicating a street
branching to our left.

"But," Kiamet began.

"I *know* it's longer," she said, "but it's also clearer, and
frankly I prefer an extra quarter of an hour in clear streets
than lying dead in crowded ones."

I glanced worriedly at the sky, looking for the position of
the sun. But smoke was thick overhead now, and all I could
see was an indistinct haze.

And so we stumbled on. Isphet led us well, taking twisting,
narrow alleys and passageways that I barely knew existed.
Bands of other slaves passed us, some armed, hurrying to the
fighting, others like us, fleeing flames and the action behind us.

I wondered what Threshold thought of all this.

"Boaz!" I whispered as a thought occurred to me. "With all
the smoke drifting overhead, the sun won't have a chance to
break through!"

Boaz mumbled a reply, his face ashen and sweating, and it
was Kiamet who answered.

"The wind blows from the northeast, Tirzah. Threshold
will be clear."

Isphet stopped us underneath an overhang. "Tirzah, Kiamet. Strip that blue robe from Boaz." She looked me in the
eye as I was about to protest. "We're nearing the river. There
are undoubtedly hundreds of slaves about. What they will do
if they recognize Boaz I cannot say."

Appalled that I hadn't thought of this myself, I pulled the blue robe and sash from Boaz as Kiamet supported him, gathering them into a bundle and further loading down the long-suffering Holdat. Boaz's white under-robe was stained with blood and dirt, but that was good in as much as it further disguised him.

"Kiamet, bear with me," I muttered, reaching for the dagger in his belt. I cut Boaz's queue off with two quick slashes, and threw it away, mussing his now shortened hair. Then I rubbed dirt about his face.

"Quick!" hissed Isphet, and we were off again.

There were burning buildings close to us now, and the smoke was thick and choking. Embers and sparks flew through the air, and tears streamed from my eyes.

Shouts and screams and the clash of steel echoed from around a corner, and Isphet waved us to yet another uncertain halt.

"I do not know what to do," she said. "There is fighting ahead of—"

Abruptly half a dozen men lurched into our alley. Two were slaves, the others wore the armor and insignia of the imperial army. One wore little more than a blue wrap, rent and bloodied, and a gold band about his sword arm.

"Zabrze!" I cried. "Oh, Zabrze! Help us! Please!"

"Tirzah?" He stumbled closer, and I saw that he had sustained a number of nicks in his chest and arms. "*Shetzah!* Is that Boaz?"

"I have not had a good day, Zabrze," Boaz muttered, barely able to raise his head to look at his brother.

"*Damn you,* Kiamet!" Zabrze snarled. "What were you doing to so allow this—"

"There was nothing any one of us could have done," Isphet said, restraining Zabrze by the arm as if she thought he might strike Kiamet. Zabrze stared at her, then pulled his arm free.

"It was a rash action fueled by long-held hatreds," Isphet continued, utterly calm in the face of Zabrze's anger, "and, surely, he should have expected something of the like. But what is happening, Zabrze? We know nothing save of the fighting and fire."

Zabrze glared at her familiar use of his name, but knew this was not the time to fuss. "Most of the army remain loyal to Chad-Nezzar, who remains *totally* loyal to the power promised him by the Magi and the power of the One through Threshold."

Zabrze threw a simmering glance at Boaz, but was too worried about him to comment further. "I have a few units behind me, no more. We tried an assault on Threshold, aided by Azam and Yaqob and some two thousand slaves, but it was no use. We got no further than the gates to the pyramid's compound, and have been beaten back street by street."

He looked at me. "It's the river, Tirzah. Escape. There's nothing more we can do. We've got to get Boaz to safety."

"It must be close to noon, Zabrze."

He nodded distractedly. "Yes. I'll help you get through, but . . . but Neuf . . ."

"Oh, gods, Zabrze!" I cried. "Where is she?"

His face looked haggard. "Still in the compound of the Magi, I think. I'll have to go back for her."

"Zabrze! You can't . . . it's too late . . . too dangerous!"

"I can't leave her here!" Zabrze shouted. "I *won't* leave her here!"

A dozen other armed men joined us, Azam among them. "Great Lord. We must get to the river."

Zabrze nodded. "Yes, yes. Take this group, and mind that you cause no further hurt to my brother. I think he is the only one who will ever be able to destroy that abomination!"

Yet more men joined us, and I felt more hope than I had for a long while. The sound of fighting still reached us, but it had drifted off into another street.

"The way is clear," Isphet said.

"Then hurry!" Zabrze shouted. "I'll join you as soon as I can." And he dashed off back the way we'd come.

Without thinking I handed my share of Boaz's weight to one of the imperial soldiers. Boaz was safer now than he had been all morning, and though it broke my heart to leave him, I owed Zabrze too much to let him run back to his death for that woman. And I wanted him alive and with us, for I knew he was going to be as important to Boaz's ultimate survival as Isphet or anyone else.

"Isphet," I gasped, "look after Boaz! Promise!"

She nodded. "What . . . ?"

"I'll be back," I cried, and then I was off, bunching my skirts about my knees as I ran after Zabrze.

I caught him as he turned the corner into a blind alley.

"Stupid woman!" he cried. "Get back with—"

"You'll be caught by a sword or a falling tenement if I let you wander about Gesholme by yourself! And that won't save Neuf. Come on! This way!"

And I grabbed his royal hand and pulled him in the opposite direction.

It was a nightmare run.

Smoke lay thick about us, and I tore lengths from the bottom of my dress so Zabrze and I could wrap them about our faces and keep some of the smoke from our lungs. There were people about the streets, but most of them were milling aimlessly, disorientated by the smoke and the heat and the thickening darkness above us.

Threshold, stretching its shadow.

"Zabrze!" I cried as I looked back to see him with the same confusion darkening his eyes. "Think of Neuf, or of Boaz. But don't let Threshold confuse you! Resist it!"

He shook his head, then nodded. "Which way?"

"Down here. *Fast*, Zabrze!"

The gates to the compound of the Magi were unguarded and we stumbled through unhindered.

"Where was she, Zabrze? At your residence?"

I saw him nod—the smoke was not so bad here, and when I glanced northeast I saw that Threshold stood clear and sun-drenched. Soon. Soon.

The residence, as the gates, was unguarded, and I supposed that all soldiers and guards were in the streets, either protecting Threshold or fighting the rebels.

"Where?" I gasped.

Zabrze took the lead, pushing past me and leading me down a central corridor. He checked rooms as we passed, but no sign of Neuf.

We would never find her if she'd fled to somewhere else.

But she hadn't. We eventually discovered her hiding in a pantry off the kitchen. Her eyes were wide and frightened, and her hands trembled as she clasped them before her.

"Zabrze! What's going on! I heard rumors that you had led men against the Magi?"

"No time to talk now," Zabrze said. "If you stay here you'll die. We've got to get down to the river."

Neuf saw me for the first time. "Girl! What are you—"

"*Shetzah, Neuf! Hurry!*" And Zabrze dragged her, stiff and resisting, into the kitchen.

"Zabrze," Neuf said in a firmer voice. "I don't want to go with you if you are going to lead me off on some wild insurrection. I won't do it. I'll stay here. I'll be safe here. I'm not going to go with slaves . . ."

Zabrze cursed again, far more foully this time, and swung Neuf into his arms. She gave a wail of protest, but he ignored her. "Tirzah. Out. Go."

I wasted no more time, thinking that it would have been no great loss if we *had* left the cursed woman to her fate.

I raced from the residence, then through the Magi's compound and into Gesholme, Zabrze panting behind me. Put her down and make her run herself, I thought, but that would only be counterproductive, because I knew that Neuf, placed on her own two feet, would refuse to take any step that might bring her closer to the river.

The streets were calm now. Even the smoke was drifting away, although I could still hear flames crackling somewhere.

I stopped, worried. "Zabrze . . ."

"Tirzah," he panted, stopping briefly beside me. "It's close to noon, and I want to be as far from Threshold as possible. Come on, girl, I want to *live*."

And so we fled.

No one hindered us, although we passed through a number of units of imperial soldiers who were, I think, still allied with Chad-Nezzar and Threshold. But they were staring behind us—toward Threshold.

"Don't look, Tirzah," Zabrze said, covering a protesting Neuf's eyes with one hand. "Don't look!"

I had no intention of looking, and led us into a series of narrow, dark alleyways that would get us to the river out of the sight of whatever was happening behind us.

Just as we were covering the last hundred paces or so, Threshold awoke.

There was a blinding flash of light that sent Zabrze and myself crashing to the dirt. The sun must have reached its peak, pouring its strength through the capstone into the Infinity Chamber and charging Threshold with power. I can imagine what happened—the entire pyramid would have burst—*exploded!*—into light. Anyone looking at it must surely have been temporarily blinded.

The bridge to the Vale was complete.

And something crossed over.

The stillness that hung over the site was now so dense I could feel it pressing against me, trying to keep me to the ground. Zabrze still held Neuf tight in his arms—she was unprotesting now—and he and I fought through the oppression, crawling close to the northern wall of the alleyway, praying that whatever Threshold now was it would not see us.

Behold, creatures, and see your god!

I wailed, and went rigid with horror. The voice had penetrated every structure of the site—yet without sound.

"Tirzah!" Zabrze whispered. "Please, we're so close!'

I got to my hands and knees and crawled a few more steps.

Behold, creatures, and tremble at the sound of your god!

And Threshold shrieked and roared.

I gagged, dry retching, and I heard Zabrze crying a few steps ahead of me. Neuf had fainted, and she was now a dead weight in his arms. I scrambled over to him, and he freed one arm from Neuf and wrapped it about me, and we lay there as the dreadful sound roared about and through us.

Behold, creatures, and know your god! Know that I am the One, and know that I call myself Nzame!

"Nzame?" Zabrze whispered. "Couldn't it think of anything better?"

I would have laughed, except I was crying too hard. Zabrze's words had broken the spell about us, and we somehow rose to our feet, Neuf now moaning quietly in her husband's arms, and stumbled down the alleyway toward the Lhyl. Behind us Threshold continued to speak.

Behold my power, and subject yourself unto it!

To my right I caught glimpses of the main avenue, and saw scores—hundreds—of people crawling toward Threshold.

Come, humble yourself before me and power unimaginable shall be yours for the asking.

"Nzame! Nzame!" Thousands took up the shout.

And then I stopped, unbelieving. Chad-Nezzar was running down the avenue toward Threshold, screeching and screaming.

"Nzame! I am yours! Take me!"

He was tearing off great chunks of jewelry and metal bands and chains as he ran, casting them to each side. "Nzame! Nzame!"

As he tore the chains and jewels from his body, little gobbets of flesh flew off as well, but in his ecstasy Chad-Nezzar ignored them. "Nzame! Nzame! I am yours! Yours!"

Zabrze caught me by the hair and hauled me away from the sight.

Come to me and adore me!

"Yes! Yes!" The screams rent the streets.

Do as I ask and Infinity shall be yours.

"Nzame! Nzame!"

Feed me. Feed me. Feed me.

And there was a dreadful crackling sound behind us. Neuf was on her own feet now, sobbing, one of Zabrze's arms tight about her waist, his other hand still tangled in my hair, dragging me forward.

If not for him, I think I would have been lost.

The crackling intensified, and I screamed.

"Hurry, Tirzah! The boats are leaving!"

I do not know where that scream came from, whether from Zabrze or from those in the boats themselves, but we were close enough to the wharf now to see that yes, indeed, all the boats were pulling away, oars dipping and glistening.

Terrified faces stared from the boats. Not at us, but beyond us.

The crackling was now a great roar rushing toward us. Rushing to catch us, to eat us.

Feed me! Feed me!

I felt something . . . something *wrong* snatch at my heel and I wrenched it away, taking two more huge strides to the edge of the wharf, my eyes frantic.

Trapped. All the boats had gone.

Behind me the *wrongness* lunged.

And missed, for Zabrze's hand, still tangled in my hair, pulled me after him when he jumped into the water.

We hit in a gigantic crash of cool green water. I thought of the great water lizards, but I thought they might be a relief after what had almost got me on the wharf.

I struggled to the surface, thinking that one or other of the brothers was always throwing me into deep water, then hands reached down from a small craft and we were hauled aboard.

I crouched on the deck for a minute, retching out the river water I'd swallowed, then I thought to look up as the bank slid by.

To the north Threshold gleamed.

Beyond it, in a circle some five hundred paces wide, everything had been turned to stone. Everything. Houses, ladders, the remaining boats moored to the bank, even birds that had been caught on the ground.

Of people there was no sign.

I looked one more time upon Threshold.

It winked.

THIRTY

The expanding stone circle had caught the other side of the riverbank as well, but only for a few paces. The dividing line was unbelievable. On one side grass stood carved into stone, tangled into a gray, brittle mass. On the other it waved in the wind and sun, except for those few strands that had been caught half in, half out of the perimeter of stone. These tugged mournfully at their stone parts, as if they could somehow be dragged back into life.

The Lhyl had not been touched, flowing as cheerfully through stone banks as earthen. But the reed banks had not been so lucky. All those within the circle had been encased in their granite enchantment. I wondered whether the frogs had been caught as well. Flee, I thought, flee before Threshold—Nzame—thinks to eat yet more.

The small craft that had picked us up ferried us to none other than Chad-Nezzar's royal barge, still wrapped in its silks and banners.

Azam leaned down from the deck to help us up, Kiath at his side.

"Boaz?" I asked as soon as I was safe on deck.

"Alive," Kiath said, which did not reassure me greatly, and she then helped Neuf who was still spluttering and retching.

"Isphet's got him in the main cabin," Kiath said, an arm about Neuf's waist; Neuf herself was too wretched to complain about this treatment. "Come inside and we'll give you dry clothes."

"Go on," Zabrze said. "I'll join you shortly."

Kiath led us into one of the cabins, gratefully cool and dim. Isphet, forgetting her earlier anger and distrust, enveloped me in a great hug. "Tirzah! We thought you were lost!"

"*I* thought I was, too. Isphet, this is Neuf, Zabrze's wife. She's—"

"Oh!" Isphet muttered. "Not another invalid!"

I left Neuf to Isphet's tender care, wondering briefly at the sparks likely to fly between those two, and hurried over to a bed in the corner. Saboa rose as I approached, kissed my cheek briefly, and stood back. Holdat, I noticed, was huddled in dark shadows at the foot of the bed, still with his blanket-wrapped bundle.

Boaz was awake, and tried to smile for me. But pain and fever raged within his eyes.

I sat on a stool by the bed, and took his hand. "We have escaped, Boaz."

"I thought I had lost you, Tirzah, when you dashed after Zabrze like that. Don't leave me again."

"I cannot imagine the nuisance you two got into as children, if this is the trouble you create now."

He lifted his free hand and stroked my cheek. "What happened? I heard . . ."

I told him what I could.

"Nzame? I do not know it," Boaz said slowly.

"Well"—Isphet's sharp voice came from behind us—"you have summoned it, and I hope Tirzah speaks the truth when she says that you have the arts to send it back again. Tirzah, here, get out of those clothes."

She handed me a dry robe, and I changed, wringing my hair out and toweling it dry.

"Boaz?" I asked softly.

"The next day or two will tell, Tirzah. But that is a bad wound. If the sword perforated his bowel on the way through, then he's dead. We'll never be able to stop the infection." She paused. "And already you can see the fever in his eyes."

I stared at her, terrified. I couldn't lose him now! *Damn* Yaqob! Whatever I was about to say was halted by Zabrze's entrance, Azam behind him.

"Where is this Isphet?" Zabrze asked.

"Yes?" Isphet inquired.

"Ah." He swung to face her. "So *you* are she. Well, Isphet, I am told that we must head for some rag-torn community in hills to the southeast of here. A community where Elemental magic is still strong and Boaz can learn what he needs to know."

"I don't know that—"

"Isphet," I said. "You planned to head there anyway. And the Soulenai say that Boaz is the only one who can destroy Threshold—we shall have to contact them so you can hear for yourself. Zabrze has already demonstrated his willingness to help us. If you still think that this is some elaborate device to—"

"No," she said tiredly. "No. I must trust you, I suppose."

"Many of the imperial soldiers fought for us, Isphet," Azam put in. "And many died."

"Yes, yes. Well, we can travel the Lhyl for a way. But most of the journey will be hard and long. The hills are far distant."

Zabrze frowned at her. "These hills. I know only of an insignificant range beyond the Lagamaal Plains at the southeasternmost border of Ashdod and the Great Stony Desert."

"Yes. Those are where we will go."

"But no one lives there, Isphet. No one. The geographers say those hills are barren."

"Barren? In places, yes. In other places they can be surprising. You do not know of the Abyss?"

"The Abyss?"

"You shall see when we get there. You do not know as much about your country as you think, Zabrze. Now. These hills are at least a two- or three-week trek across the Lagamaal Plains, a dry and inhospitable country. And we have . . . how many with us?"

Azam looked at Zabrze, as if unsure whether to defer to him or not, then answered anyway. "There are thirty or thirty-five craft with us, Isphet. Maybe four, perhaps five thousand people. Slaves, soldiers, servants. Even one or two nobles. And—" he glanced at Boaz—"at least one Magus."

"Magus no more," Boaz said quietly.

"Well," Neuf broke in. "I demand to be returned to Setkoth."

Zabrze opened his mouth to speak, but was forestalled by a voice from the doorway.

"You'll travel where we go, you sorry bitch, and if you don't like it, then I'll happily cast you overboard for the water lizards to eat."

Yaqob. He jumped down the three or four steps and looked about the room. "You'll all do as *I* say here. I led the revolt, and the vast majority of people in these boats are slaves. *I* will take command."

He stared at Zabrze defiantly.

"No," Zabrze said very softly but very dangerously. "I do not think so, Yaqob. You have no experience of command—"

"I led the revolt!" Yaqob shouted.

"No," Zabrze replied. "You didn't. Oh, you planned and talked about it for many a long month, but your revolt was always in the planning and never in the doing. It took me, through Azam, to give it the impetus it needed to see some life. You're a fine man, Yaqob, and a brave man, but you are no leader."

"How can you—"

"How can I say that? You are too hot-tempered, Yaqob, and you let emotion overwhelm your good sense. Look!" Zabrze's finger stabbed in Boaz's direction. "There lies the man—the only man—who can ultimately save us from

Threshold, and you try to murder him in a fit of pique! Now you leap into this cabin, snap at a woman who is frightened and unsure, and demand that all bow at your every word. No! I will not have it!"

Yaqob spun to face Azam. "My friend . . ."

Azam looked at Zabrze, then back to Yaqob. "I am sorry," he said, "but Zabrze is—"

"Isphet?" Yaqob all but shouted.

The cabin was very, very quiet now. She looked for a long time at Zabrze, and he at her. Something passed between them, but I could not understand what.

"Zabrze has a cool head," she admitted finally, "and he has the ability to command. Yaqob!" She grabbed his arm as he clenched his fist. "Yaqob, our situation is desperate. We need to take advantage of everything we have. Zabrze can command this disparate force."

"And I cannot?"

"No," she said softly, "I believe you would have trouble, Yaqob."

Yaqob stared at Isphet, then pulled free of her, exiting the cabin as suddenly as he had entered it.

"Damn," Zabrze muttered. "I wish I didn't have to do that."

"There was no choice," Azam said. "Besides, you *are* Chad now."

Zabrze blinked. The thought had very obviously not occurred to him. "Chad-Nezzar—"

"Chad-Nezzar is either dead or running demented about Threshold's stone temple," Isphet said. "Chad of nothing save his own slavery to Nzame. Whatever, he's no use. You are Chad, Zabrze, although"—her mouth twisted very slightly in a smile—"you'll forgive me if I leave mouthing the pleasantries and flatteries for a more suitable occasion."

Zabrze smiled at her, then turned to his wife. "Neuf? Are you well? You understand why we can't go back to Setkoth, don't you?"

She let him fold her in his arms. "Our children . . ." she whispered.

"I know, Neuf," and his voice broke. "But it's too dangerous to try to get back past Threshold—Nzame now controls all southern approaches to Setkoth, as well as the majority of Ashdod's army. There's nothing we can do."

Isphet managed to organize food for us all as the afternoon faded. We ate sparingly, not sure what we had with us until a thorough search among the boats was done. But grain fields were sliding past us, and Zabrze did not think it would be too hard to requisition some if we needed it.

"Isphet," Zabrze asked, "how long upon this river do we travel?"

"I do not know it well," she said, "but I remember that after we'd traveled the great dry land we came to the Lhyl at a place where it broadened into great marshes. There was a lake . . ."

"Ah," Zabrze said. "The river empties into Lake Juit, perhaps five days south of here. And from there southeast?"

"Yes. A long journey."

"Can you find the way? How old were you when you traveled to Setkoth?"

Her eyes flashed. "I can find the way, Zabrze. I was, oh, twenty, twenty-one. My husband and I were both glassworkers, and we went to Setkoth to ply our trade."

"How did you fall into slavery?" I asked.

"We bought passage on a small fishing boat," she said, and her voice was hard. "The captain thought to earn extra by handing us over to slavers one night. They sold us to the Magi at Threshold. We never got to Setkoth."

"And your husband?"

"He died the first year in Gesholme," she said. "During the wet season fevers are common."

Zabrze nodded, his eyes sympathetic, then he turned to his wife and quietly encouraged her to eat some of the bread.

I moved back to Boaz's side. Isphet had brewed an analgesic herbal (one of the few things she bundled into the blanket on leaving the tenement had been her store of herbs), and we'd given it to him an hour ago. Now he was asleep, although he occasionally murmured under his breath, and his skin was ashen and sweaty.

I felt his forehead. It was hot.

"Tirzah," Isphet said quietly behind me. "We can do no more for now. Go up on deck. Sit a while, get some air. I'll watch him."

I nodded, touched his forehead once more, and climbed up on deck.

The air was cool and pleasant on the river, and I relished the clean smell, and the openness. Irrigated fields stretched to either side of the banks, and water fowl moved softly among the reeds. Fish splashed, and I saw the shadowy form of one of the great water lizards slide into the river at our passing.

The evening chorus of the frogs was gentle, and puzzled . . . as if they missed the voices of their stone-clad comrades to the north.

Behind us, in a colorful string, came the other boats of our flotilla, disappearing into the dusk. Azam had climbed down into a smaller boat an hour or two earlier, and was now wending his slow way through the fleet, finding out exactly who we had with us, what they had, and informing them where we were going and, no doubt, who led us.

I took a deep breath. Yaqob. He must be on board here somewhere. I looked about, then asked one of the men wandering past. A slave—a *free* man now, I corrected myself—by the look of him. He pointed to the very prow of the boat, and I thanked him and walked forward, my steps slow, unsure.

"Yaqob?"

He sat on the small platform the musicians had occupied when Chad-Nezzar had docked at Threshold's wharf, and he rose as I approached.

"Tirzah." He faced back to the river.

We stood side by side, looking at the tranquil river before us. Neither of us said anything for a while, unsure of ourselves.

"Well," I said eventually, "it seems that we are free, Yaqob. I almost never imagined that we would—"

"*I* never imagined that you would one day betray me like this, Tirzah," he said, and turned to look me in the eye. "I knew a gulf was growing between us, but I thought it was only because you felt self-conscious about your role in

Boaz's bed. But I have watched you since this morning. Watched you closely."

"I came to love him, Yaqob. I'm sorry."

Oh, gods, what a stupid, trite thing to say.

"After all he did to you? Tirzah, I cannot believe that you can stand here and say that *our* love is dead because of a man who has caused you such pain, who tried to *kill* you! I don't understand. Boaz is—"

"Boaz is not the man he first seems. Yaqob, listen to me! Underneath that Magus exterior lies a man of such sweetness and tenderness that I could not help but love him. I wanted to free him as much as you wanted to free all of our friends in slavery. Yaqob, he is an Elemental too! He—"

Yaqob did not want to hear, and turned away.

"Yaqob! You do not deserve what I have done to you. But take your retribution out on me, not him . . . please!"

Yaqob spun about and seized my shoulders. "I don't want retribution, Tirzah! I only want *you*!" He leaned his head close to mine, but I twisted my face away before he could kiss me.

"No. No, it's over, Yaqob."

"I never thought to stand here on my first day of freedom and listen to you mouth such words," he said. "I built my life around you, Tirzah, I wove all my dreams with you as their center. And yet here you say . . . it's over."

He dropped his hands and walked away.

I sat by Boaz's bed during the night, and all the next morning. The fever tightened its hold, and by noon of the next day he was sweating, moaning, and tossing about.

"Tirzah," Isphet said. "There is nothing we can do. He cannot fight the infection."

Earlier we'd sponged him down, and been appalled at the angry red streaks that had spread across his belly and down his flanks. His belly was swollen, tight, and hot; internal bleeding aggravated by infection.

"Tirzah, come away." Isphet's hands tightened on my shoulders. Zabrze moved to take my place by Boaz's side as Isphet led me out into the fresh air.

"Tirzah, he's dying."

"No!"

"Tirzah, he is *dying*! Accept that! There is no herbal I can give him, *nothing* I can do. Now you must accept it. We can try to make him comfortable, but to be honest with you I do not think we'll be able to do that for much longer. He won't keep anything down . . ."

I burst into tears, and Isphet hugged me tight. "I never knew how much he meant to you," she whispered, stroking my hair, rocking me to and fro. "You hid it so well. So well."

"I wish he could understand what I say to him," I sobbed. "I want to tell him that I love him—I've never really told him that—but he won't hear, he won't hear . . ."

"Shush, Tirzah. He knows. I'm sure of it. Now, you must sit up here awhile. Zabrze needs time to say good-bye, and I will watch with him. If Boaz worsens I'll send for you, but for now you need to rest. Look, here is Holdat, he will take you to a shaded corner."

She passed me into Holdat's care. The man looked almost as woebegone as I felt, and he slid an arm about my waist and led me to the rear of the cabins so we could sit in the shade of their awnings. Kiamet was there, too, and we sat quietly for some time.

"Tirzah," Kiamet finally said. "This is a strange request, but perhaps it will make you feel better, and I know it would surely comfort Holdat and myself. When you and Boaz sat by the windows at night, sometimes you would read tales to him from the old book. Holdat and I"—he glanced shamefacedly at his friend—"would stand just out of sight, on the other side of the wall, and listen. Tirzah, would it comfort you to read from the Book of the Soulenai again?"

"Not the Song of the Frogs," I said.

"No, not the Song of the Frogs. But there must be many others that you've not touched yet."

"All right. Holdat, do you still have the box—"

But Holdat had already retrieved the box from wherever he'd stored it, and lifted the book into my lap. I ran my hands over it, feeling its age, feeling its soft whispering, then, as I had been wont to do with Boaz, I opened it at random.

It was a story I had not yet encountered, but that was not

unusual, for the book was very large and I'd not had time to read through it completely.

"Oh," I said, "it is a sad tale, about the death of a king."

Silence, and I could sense Kiamet and Holdat look at each other.

I took a deep breath. "But Isphet says I must accept . . . accept that Boaz . . ."

"Tirzah," Kiamet said. "Perhaps it is best not to read—"

"No," I said sharply, then apologized for my tone. "I think I *will* read it, Kiamet. Maybe it will give me some comfort."

And so I read. I was proud of the way my voice held steady, for the tale opened with the tragic wounding of a great and good king in a battle not of his making.

And so his servants bore him home, and his people made much ado, and prepared as best they might for his death. He was wounded sore, a belly wound . . .

I almost faltered there.

. . . that stretched from navel to groin. The surgeons stitched it, but evil spirits had entered with the sword, and the king made much moan and burned with fever.

As he sank toward final death, the man who tended the frogs by the river appeared at the castle door, and begged to be allowed to see the king's surgeons.

"I have a good powder," he said. "One the frogs told me of."

"Oh, gods," I whispered, and stumbled in my haste to read further.

The king's servants were not disposed to allow so humble a man access to such eminent folk, but he prevailed, and eventually the frog keeper stood before the surgeons.

"What have you there?" asked the senior of the group.

"Powder," said the man, "that will drive the heat and evil spirits from the king's belly and make him whole again."

The senior surgeon smiled derisively, but a junior stepped forward and said, "How is this powder formed, good man?"

"In the river, between the reeds, where the waters lie still and warm, can sometimes be found a thick slime that has, at best, a loathsome odor. I collect this slime, and dry it, and grind it, and thus form this powder."

"I have heard something of this," said the junior surgeon, and spoke quickly to his fellows. They were uncertain, but because they were desperate, they decided to try it.

"Break open his wound," cried the frog keeper, as the surgeons hurried away with his jar of powder, "and sprinkle some inside. Mix portions in fluid, and dribble it into his mouth! And . . ."

"And *what*?" Holdat said.

"And by that time the surgeons had hurried to the king's bedside and saved the king's life," I said. I bent and kissed the cover of the book. "Thank you, thank you."

I gave the book back to Holdat, then looked to Kiamet. "Is Azam's small craft still tied to this vessel?"

"Yes—"

"Then why do we tarry here, Kiamet? Escort me to the reed banks."

Isphet was incredulous. "*These* . . . ashes?"

"In his wound and in his mouth, Isphet."

"By what authority?"

"By the authority of a book, Isphet. Later I shall show it to you."

"You can *read*, girl?"

I almost hissed in frustration. "That is neither here nor there, Isphet, not when Boaz lies a-dying in that bed."

"Zabrze?" Isphet turned to him.

"*The* book, Tirzah?"

I nodded, and so did he. "Let her be, Isphet."

"Bah!" But she stayed by me. "What are you doing?"

"This is powder, Isphet, not ashes, and I shall sprinkle it in his wound, then mix some in your analgesics and drip it into his mouth."

I unwrapped his wound, then recoiled as the stench struck. It smelt even worse than the slime Holdat and I had just gathered.

Now green and yellow had added their evil colors to

Boaz's flesh. His belly was so swollen he looked five months gone with child, and the skin was so tight and hot I thought it would split without much provocation. The wound seeped pus from underneath a thick black scab.

"Isphet, what can I use to lift this scab?"

"I'll do it, girl. Ugh!" And we both recoiled from the bed at the foul effluent that poured out as she lifted the scab.

I took a deep breath from several paces away, then stepped forward and sprinkled the powder until the wound was covered in it. Isphet was by my side with some cloths and a fresh bandage, and we wasted no time in cleaning and rebandaging Boaz's belly.

"Holdat?" I called softly, and he was by my side, the Goblet of the Frogs in his hand.

Isphet looked at it carefully. "Zeldon told me that you'd caged a beautiful goblet, girl. This is it?"

I gave it into her hands and watched her face as she heard the frogs whisper. "Oh, Tirzah, it's wondrous!"

As she held the Goblet of the Frogs I poured in a measure of the analgesic herbal, then slowly added pinches of the powder. I wasn't too sure how much to add (and damn those surgeons for hurrying away before the frog keeper had time to shout the exact measurement), but I kept adding until the brew had a slightly bitter taste. Any more and his mouth would reject it.

Then I sat down, dribbled portions between his lips every few minutes, and waited.

Time passed, but I refused to leave Boaz's side.

It was late into the night when I began to notice the difference. His breathing eased, and he slipped into a sleep that was sound, not tormented. Isphet finally persuaded me to rest for a few hours, keeping vigil by Boaz herself, dribbling the rest of the mixture into his mouth.

I thought I would not sleep, but I did, and woke only when Isphet put her hand on my shoulder.

"Is he . . . ?"

"Still asleep, but better. I want to rest myself, but wake me at dawn, and we'll clean and perhaps sprinkle a little more of that powder in his wound."

"Maybe it *has* helped, Isphet."

"Maybe," she admitted. "Now get out of that bed and let me sleep."

I sat down by Boaz, and smiled. He was breathing deep and easy now, and the fever had broken.

I kept to my task dribbling in tiny portions of the mixture, but now my relief had let tiredness edge in, and after a while I laid the goblet to one side and rested my head on my arms. Just for a few minutes, I thought. I'll just close my eyes for a few minutes.

I woke at the pressure of his hand on my hair.

"Boaz!"

He smiled. "Listen. Can you hear it? It is the dawn chorus of the frogs."

Later that day, I let Isphet sit and examine the Book of the Soulenai. She was slightly nervous of it until she felt its soft murmurings, and the fact that I was able to read it she passed over without further comment. As the book sat in her lap I leaned over her shoulder and turned the pages one by one, trying to find the story of the dying king. It was no longer there.

THIRTY-ONE

Three days later we drew close to Lake Juit. As I stood with Boaz and Zabrze at the prow Zabrze told me the lake was named after the pink and scarlet Juit birds who prowled the marshes at its perimeters.

"The lake is huge," he said, shading his eyes as he stared south. "No one has ever sailed all the way about it."

"And the marshes at the lake's borders extend for farther leagues," Boaz added. This was the first day he'd risen from his bed; he was wan and thin, but his eyes and skin were clear,

and his belly flat and cool once more. The wound had
scabbed over with pink healthiness, and though he leaned
heavily on my shoulder, I did not think it was because he had
such great need of my support.

"The marshes are thick with reeds that trap hot, humid air.
They are often shrouded in mist at dawn and dusk," Boaz
continued. "The water's depth varies from over a man's
height to only an arm's length deep. It is safest to use a flat-
bottomed boat and pole to get about in them."

"Not that anyone really does," Zabrze commented. "It is
too easy to get lost among the never-ending reeds. Sometimes
fishermen go into the marshes looking for marsh eels. Many
have never come back. Fallen over the edge of the world, I
think. Or trapped with the gods in some Elysian paradise."

"It must be easy to hear the chorus of the frogs within the
marshes," I said, and leaned still closer to Boaz. He recovered
with each breath he took, but my own wounds at his close
brush with death had scarcely healed over.

"I think we could land at any point from here on." Isphet
now joined us, Azam with her. Neuf remained resting in one
of the cabins; she was still weak from the flight through
Gesholme. Yaqob, two days ago, had decided to travel in one
of the other boats. It was sad that he felt he had to do so, but
both Boaz and I were more relaxed with him at a distance.

Zabrze thought for a while, then looked at Boaz. "No,
Isphet. We shall sail another day or so, methinks. Until we are
very close to Lake Juit."

"That will take us perhaps a little too far south," Isphet
said. "We joined the Lhyl about a day's journey north of the
lake. I think it best if—"

"Isphet." Zabrze reached out and let his fingers graze her
cheek. Isphet's eyes flashed, and I'm sure I looked as startled
as Boaz and Azam did. "Bear with me. There is a small landing there, too small for this number of craft, and we shall
have to regiment them carefully lest they crash into one another and frighten the frogs, but there is a small landing . . ."

He looked to his brother. "Boaz. Surely you know of what
I speak?"

"Many of the nobles have residences dotted about Lake

Juit," Boaz said. "It is very pleasant down here with the breezes that sweep off the water, and it is far from court intrigue." He grinned at Zabrze. "Zabrze comes here but rarely, and Neuf has not been once!" The grin faded. "But our mother loved the country and the lake. She inherited a house almost on the shores of Juit itself, at the junction of river, marsh, and lake. It was where I was born and where I spent the first three or four years of my life. I have never been back since."

"We both have emotional ties to that house," Zabrze continued, "but that is not the only reason I wish to dock there rather than higher up the river. The house is large, but more important is the land attached to it."

"The Juit estate is the largest in the family," said Boaz. "And it has kept us well fed and clothed at court year in year out. It will provide us with many of the supplies we'll need for our journey."

"We are almost five thousand, Zabrze," Azam said. As with most of the former slaves, his skin now shone with the burnish of freedom, and the lines around his eyes and mouth had relaxed to be more reminiscent of laughter than strain. "Even a rich estate will have trouble feeding that many."

"It is better than nothing, Azam," Zabrze replied. "And perhaps I'll send some of this lot fishing . . . yes!" He laughed, and slapped Azam on the back. "That's what I'll do. Dried fish may be unappetizing, but it should get us to Isphet's reclusive home!"

The next day at dusk we docked at the landing of the most beautiful house I have ever seen. To the south I could see the initial expanses of Lake Juit, to the west the great swathes of marshes, while to the east stretched the estate.

The house was set back from the riverbank some eighty paces, on a slight rise. It was constructed of river mud-brick, and the walls had been glazed but left unpainted so they glowed russet red in the setting sun. It was long and low, roofed in dried and bound river reeds, their color faded to a soft amber over the decades. Shaded verandahs encased the northern and western aspects, on the other two aspects the roof beams had been extended and were supported by brick columns several paces out from the walls; they were covered with flowering creepers. The windows and doors were thick-paned with crystal-clear square patchwork glass edged in dark green.

"Oh, Boaz!"

"It is very old," he said. "Very. Every generation or so the roof is re-reeved, but otherwise it needs little maintenance. The rooms inside are dim and cool. I remember it so well."

"And yet you never came back?"

"It was too close to the frogs for the Magus," he said, and then grinned and pointed.

A man was hurrying down the path from house to landing. Elderly but sprightly, he was furious.

"No notice?" he cried. "No notice, and you bring the entire court? Who is this? Which one? Zabrze? Boaz?"

He came close enough to see who lined the decks of the nearest boats, and he stopped, his jaw hanging open. "Who *is* this come to visit?"

"Me and my realm," cried Zabrze, leaping the distance between boat deck and the stone landing. "Have you no respect, Memmon? Must I give ten days' notice?"

"Memmon is the overseer," Boaz murmured at my side. "He comes to Setkoth once a year to deliver the accounts for our inspection, but in reality, I think, to see what mischief Zabrze and I are up to. He would be equally furious if we'd given six months' notice but were five minutes late."

Zabrze laid his hand on the man's shoulder and talked quietly into his ear. Memmon eventually shrugged, nodded, then proceeded apace back up the path.

"He goes to rally the servants and field workers," Zabrze called. "Come now, put down the ramps!"

And the first three boats, all the landing could cope with at one time, began to do just that.

I loved the house the instant I stepped inside it. This was a home, loved and full of cherished memories. Even Neuf regained some of her color—and some of her hauteur—as she walked through the front door.

"It could do with a second level," she muttered, hands kneading into the small of her back as she looked about, "and those verandahs really must go."

Zabrze and Boaz both broke out into hard-voiced protest, and I smiled and left them, exploring on my own.

I peeked apprehensively into the kitchens, then grinned to see Holdat already there, deep in animated discussion with the chief cook over a steaming pot. The room had tall windows looking across the fields rolling into the distance, and I could see the small figure of Memmon directing people as they disembarked. Field workers were hurrying about with canvas and poles; some tents could be erected by full dark, but the night was so mild I doubted many would mind sleeping in the open. They would soon have to get used to it, anyway.

There were reception rooms, dining halls, and sleeping chambers—and a bathing pool in a verandahed enclosure—but before I could explore all of these delights Boaz found me wandering in one of the corridors and guided me back to the main part of the house.

"Zabrze needs to see us," he said. "There's trouble."

Trouble had appeared in the form of a half-starving and half-mad slave from the building site. He had fallen from one of the boats as our flotilla had fled south and had then hidden in the river, close to the stone reed banks, until evening. That night he'd found a small boat that was still reed—it had floated free in the haste of our escape and had not been turned to stone—and he'd set sail after us.

When the wind had died, he had rowed. I do not think he had rested much in the past few weeks. To have caught up with us within half a day of our own docking spoke of the desperation of his efforts.

"I have news," the man, Quebez, said, "of Threshold." And so Azam brought him to the house.

We congregated in one of the airy front rooms. Neuf was there, sitting close to Zabrze, I as close to Boaz. Isphet and Yaqob sat by one of the windows, Azam stood by the chair in which Quebez sat. Zeldon, who'd traveled in one of the smaller boats, now stood, arms folded, by the door to the gar-

den. Apart from Quebez, we provided, I supposed, the head
for the great body of people sprawled outside in Memmon's
hastily arranged camps.

"Great Lord," Quebez had unerringly picked out Zabrze as
the leader of our group, "I have . . . I heard . . ."

Azam rested a hand on Quebez's shoulder. "If you would
prefer to rest an hour or two . . ."

"No, my Lord—"

"Call me Azam," he said gruffly, but I thought he might
have to get used to such titles from those outside.

"No, I must speak now. I must tell of what I saw."

We were silent, and Quebez took a deep breath and related
the horror he'd witnessed while hiding in the river.

"I thought my life had ended as the last of your boats sailed
without me. Either . . . Nzame . . . or one of the great water
lizards would be sure to get me. But somehow I escaped.
Somehow."

Was it the frogs, I wondered, watching out for him?

"I clung to the reeds of stone, and as I clung *its* voice sifted
through my mind. It spoke to those who had succumbed.
They must have been grouped about its skirts in a mass, for I
saw no one in the streets whenever I dared raise my head for
breath, yet I could hear many thousands call its name, *Nzame!*
Nzame! Nzame! Thousands.

"Nzame demanded many things of those who proclaimed
their adoration for him. He demanded that he be fed. He demanded that many would be needed to feed him, for his appetite was that of the One, and it was ever increasing."

"The incomposites," I murmured, and Boaz nodded.

"Increasing," Quebez said, "into Infinity. Never ending, always expanding."

I felt Boaz shudder and I glanced about the group. Everyone, even Neuf, looked shaken.

"Nzame said that as he was fed, then so would his power
grow, and so the stone would spread in its circle about him, its
diameter increasing according to the incomposite he was fed."

"*Shetzah!*" Zabrze said. "Does that mean what I think it
does?"

"He said"—and Quebez's voice faltered—"that as the incomposites grew, then so his stone would stretch across the land. Everything in it would be stone. Everything subjected to his will."

"Nzame will not only turn Ashdod into stone, he'll also eat everyone in it!" said Azam.

"Not quite," Quebez whispered. "Nzame said that there would not be enough people in Ashdod to sate his appetite, nor turn the entire land to stone. He would need more."

"And how does he intend to get these 'more'?" Zabrze asked quietly.

"Neighboring realms will provide the fodder, Great Lord."

"Oh?" Zabrze said. "And does he expect that once word spreads of Nzame's presence our neighbors will gladly send their peoples to feed the beast's hunger?"

Quebez shook his head. "Nzame has help, Great Lord. Thousands screamed his name and hurried to pay homage at his feet. Many thousands. An army."

"An army can be defeated—" Zabrze began.

"Not this one, Great Lord. Nzame had changed most of them. As dusk fell and as I paddled down the Lhyl, I turned for one last look. I had moved only just in time, for a score of what had once been men were milling about on the landing."

"What do you mean—'had once been'?" Boaz said.

"Nzame had turned them to stone, My Lord. Shambling, crumbling, moaning men of stone. *They* are what he will send to do his will."

There was complete silence.

"As I swam, almost hoping by this stage that a water lizard would get me, I heard Nzame shout one last word."

"Yes?" Zabrze asked.

"Setkoth."

Azam took Quebez to the kitchens for food, then returned. We had not spoken a word in his absence. I dared not look at Zabrze and Neuf. They had seven children in Setkoth.

It was Zeldon who finally spoke. "Boaz. Tell us, who is this Nzame? Is it—he—truly the One?"

"No. The One has no personality or mind, and it certainly would not *name* itself. Nzame has appropriated the concept of the One to himself, but he is not the One."

"Then who is he, brother?"

Boaz looked as stricken as Zabrze. "He, or it, has come across from the Vale."

"The Magi are worse than fools, Boaz, to have constructed such an abomination," Isphet said. "What do you have to say for yourself?"

"I say that I will do my best to right the wrong in which I played a part, Isphet."

"*If* you are this Cantomancer that Tirzah tells me you be."

"Then teach me, Isphet! I can do nothing groping about in the dark as I am now!"

Isphet opened her mouth to respond, but Zabrze stopped her. "Enough! I want your thoughts on what to do now, not where to lay the blame."

"Boaz *must* be taught," I said. "The Soulenai have said he will be the one to halt Threshold . . . Nzame. Isphet, *can* you teach him?"

"I can teach him the fundamentals of the Elemental arts, but *if* he has the potential for cantomancy then he needs the Graces to instruct him. Only they have the power. I must take him home."

"We *all* must go," Zabrze said. "All of us. This house is too close to Threshold for safety—"

"No!" Neuf cried. "I will not go any farther—"

"Damn you, Neuf!" Zabrze grasped her by the shoulders so he could force her to meet his eyes. "*This house is no longer safe!* I will not have you and our child put at risk!"

She dropped her eyes, acquiescing.

"Zabrze," Azam said, "is there anything we can do to stop Nzame and his army now?"

"The majority of the army stayed at Threshold. With the slaves who also stayed, Nzame will have ten thousand to work his will for him. Here? I have but some few hundred soldiers and some four thousand men and women who have few weapons and lack the skills to fight stone . . . damn it! *None* of us have the skills to fight an army of stone men. How does one kill stone?" He laughed harshly. "I do not know!"

He sobered. "No. We cannot fight now, not until Boaz can give us something to fight with. But what I can do is warn. If you agree, I want to send some two score runners—messengers—about Ashdod and our neighboring states to tell of what has occurred. To warn, and to ask for help."

"And do you think we'll get that?" Yaqob asked. He had been very silent, but his voice was even and reasonable. He looked calmer within himself, and I wondered if Isphet had been talking to him.

"Yes," Zabrze said. "I think at least one of our neighbors will help us. Darsis, a state to the east, has a large and well-equipped army, and we have always been on good terms with it."

"Not if Nzame begins to eat its citizens," Zeldon muttered, and I threw him an irritated glance.

"And I have always been on good terms with its Prince, Iraldur," Zabrze continued. "If I send personal messages, then I hope he will aid us. It will be in his best interests to do so, anyway. Brother"—he turned to Boaz—"perhaps these Soulenai believe you can destroy Threshold when no one else can, but you need to get into it alive and in one piece. Give me some months, and I believe I can rebuild a force that will do that for you."

We then discussed what needed to be done to prepare our thousands for their trek across the Lagamaal Plains to the southeast. Neither Zabrze nor Boaz knew this area well, and they questioned Isphet closely about the conditions.

"Water?" Zabrze asked. "It will be difficult to carry enough water for five thousand."

"We should carry some, but we can find it. Food is scarce, though. There are hares across the Lagamaal, but not enough to feed five thousand. And unless you develop a taste for mice, beetles, and snakes . . ."

There were some camels and mules we could use as pack animals, but not all that many; the home estate could provide some, and Zabrze thought he'd be able to purchase more from neighboring estates.

"We shall have a few score," he said, "but those people who are fit enough shall have to carry packs as well. What horses we have I want to save for our messengers."

Then Zabrze called Memmon in. The estate, it seemed, had great grain reserves, enough to feed us for three weeks, but little else.

"Fish," Zabrze said. "I want us ready to go in five days. I dare wait no longer. Azam, Zeldon, can you organize groups to go a-fishing over the next three days? And others to dry the fish."

They nodded.

"And reeds to be dried and woven into baskets," Zabrze continued, "and—"

"And all this can be organized in the morning," Isphet said. "There is something else I want to do while we are here, and it is best I speak now. Boaz"—and she swiveled a little on her chair—"I have heard tell how you are an Elemental. How the Soulenai wish you to train as a Cantomancer to destroy Threshold. Well, I have yet to see any great demonstration of your skill, and you have yet to be presented to the Soulenai themselves. Before I commit us to a trek across the wilderness, and before I expose my home people to possible danger, I want *confirmation* of who and what you really are."

Isphet was right. Boaz was still the Magus in many people's eyes, and it *would* be best if his true arts were demonstrated.

"In two days I want to induct Boaz into the arts of Elemental magic . . . *if* the Soulenai accept him. Yaqob, will you speak to the other Elementals among us? Dawn, on the second morning from tomorrow."

Yaqob nodded, and after some desultory conversation we rose and ate the meal that had been laid for us, then prepared for bed. We would all be kept busy over the next few days.

"Boaz? Tirzah?" Yaqob stopped us as we walked to the sleeping chamber assigned us. He was stiff and apprehensive, and we stiffened in response. I noticed Boaz's eyes slide to Yaqob's hands, as if expecting another attack.

"I should apologize for what I—"

"No," Boaz stopped him. "No, you should not. For many months I shamed both you and Tirzah with my words and actions. As I lay slipping in and out of consciousness, as you and Zabrze fought to right some of the wrong I had caused, I heard Isphet tell Tirzah that as I had torn Tirzah apart with my power, so I suffered likewise. She did not think it a coincidence, and neither do I. Perhaps other hands besides yours guided that sword into my belly, Yaqob. There is nothing you should apologize for. Nothing."

Boaz paused, searching for the words. "If anyone needs to seek forgiveness, then it is I. Yet it is not something I can ask for, Yaqob, only something I can earn. I hope that eventually my actions will go some way toward negating the evil and unhappiness I have helped propagate."

"Boaz," I murmured, and took his arm, wishing he had said this to me in private, but knowing it had to be said before Yaqob.

Yaqob stared at Boaz, then at me. "Destroy Threshold," he said, "and treasure Tirzah."

He hesitated awkwardly, then walked away down the darkened corridor.

We watched him go, and I hoped that a corner had been turned here this evening.

Among the thousands who had fled Threshold there were only some three dozen Elementals. I realized that this number must be close to the total number of Elementals the building site had held. Over the years, Isphet had managed to gather the majority into her workshop. She was special, and most Elementals had gravitated to her.

This morning I, as all the others, was about to find out just how special.

I wondered what Isphet would use to summon the swirling colors and initiate the rite when she no longer had the molten glass.

The night before the dawn rite Isphet talked quietly with several of the boatmen from the estate, and when we rose in the chill predawn darkness it was to find that eighteen small flat-bottomed punts awaited us at the landing. We all climbed in without speaking, two to a punt, and Boaz took the pole and pushed the punt he and I shared away from the landing. I watched him carefully, thinking it might be too much for him, but Boaz coped with ease.

Isphet and Yaqob led the procession of craft into the lake. We kept silent, letting the sounds of the awakening land soothe us. Mist drifted across the lake, tangling in the great reed banks to each side, but it was not thick, and as rose light stained the eastern horizon the reed banks retreated, and we

found ourselves in open waters that were still shallow enough
for the poles.

Isphet drew us to a spot so deep within the lake that the
reed banks were a green line in the distance. She indicated
with her hands, and the boats maneuvered into a great circle
and poles were shipped. I thought we would drift out of position, but perhaps the magic was already strong about us, for
the circle remained complete.

Again at Isphet's signal, those of us still seated rose and
faced inward, the boats hardly rocking. We were all clothed in
robes of pale hue, no jewelry, no belts or sashes. Hair was left
to flow free and be caught by the cold breeze.

All eyes were on Isphet. She was dressed in pure white,
and with her black hair flowing over her shoulders, and her
extraordinary dark eyes I thought she looked a witch.

She surely commanded all of us.

We were still, our gazes riveted on her.

Slowly she raised her arm, then, in an abrupt motion, cast
her hand over the water before her in a great arc.

As one, millions of pink and red Juit birds launched into the
sky from the reed banks, their wings making a great roar over
the lake. I stared at Isphet, thinking that the undulating pink
and red rising behind her looked like a great sheet of flame.

Then a different movement caught my eye and I looked
down. The water contained within the circle of our boats was
swirling in such great motion it was like a whirlpool, though
none of the boats at its edge moved. Dawn light had spilled
over all of us now, and I could see that the green water
whirled to black in the pit of its circle.

Isphet moved again, casting her powdered metals into the
water, and color swirled there: blue, then at Isphet's command, red, then gold, and finally a brilliant emerald.

"Feel," she whispered about the circle, "feel the colors . . .
listen . . . listen . . . listen, Boaz, can you feel us listening too?"

Yes.

Yes, he did. He was one of us, and not frightened as I had
been when first submerged in the power of the colors. He let
the power embrace him effortlessly, completely.

Yes.

I could hear a rushing—the water, increasingly maddened—but I ignored it, letting the power submerge me as well.

Then the Soulenai were among us.

I shuddered, for their presence was different—stronger—from what I'd ever felt before. Far more vigorous.

Submit, Boaz, I felt Isphet urge, *let their power and grace suffuse you, enrich you.*

As I leaned my head back, eyes closed, letting their presence filter through me, I felt Boaz do the same.

Again he accepted without hesitation.

Submit . . . This time the Soulenai spoke, and I could feel the curiosity as they rippled through Boaz, exploring, touching.

He accepted it all.

They moved through each of us, and between us as well—something I'd never felt them do previously.

I opened my eyes. Were the Soulenai walking among us? It felt like it, oh, it did, because this was power such as I'd never felt before. They were vital in this place, very strong, and I wondered why.

Then they spoke.

The Elemental arts are dying about the land. War has arrived once more, and the land again turns to stone. Eventually, even the Song of the Frogs will die. Then all will be lost. We charge you gathered here with the reversal of the stone and with the renewal of the land. You are all beloved, and you will all have to shoulder the responsibility of the resurrection.

But there are some among you who will have a greater burden than the others. Listen, and know. Isphet . . .

And the Soulenai *did* move among us, I could both feel and see them now. A glow surrounded Isphet, and I could only barely distinguish her form within it.

Isphet. You are so strong, so beautiful, and you have kept hope alive in a place of stone and death. We thank you for that, and we would charge you with a further duty. You travel back to your home. That is good. Speak with the Graces, seek their counsel. Isphet, you will become a Cantomancer of great skill, and your task will be to illume a nation. You will have the chance given to few others.

We all felt her shock. Isphet had never thought herself worthy of aspiring to the highest level of Elemental magic, to become a Cantomancer, but I was not surprised. She deserved this honor.

Your task will become clearer as the months and years go by, Isphet. Will you pledge to remain true to us and to your task . . . will you illume?

I do so pledge, she whispered, and we were honored to witness for her.

Yaqob. Now the glow surrounded Yaqob, and tears of joy—and some of relief—sprang to my eyes.

Yaqob. We ask of you much the same as what we asked of Isphet. From the Graces you will learn the arts and skills of the Cantomancer. Yaqob, you have suffered disappointments and maybe will suffer more. Use disappointment to create strength and forge compassion. You shall instruct, and your task shall become clearer as year passes into year.

And they asked of him the same pledge as they had of Isphet, and he gave it and we so witnessed.

Tirzah.

Such great beauty infused me that I cried out, but the love of all those about supported me and I accepted.

Tirzah. Learn with the others, yet what you learn will be incidental to the powers you already command. You will be a great Cantomancer. Few shall surpass your power. Yet, like Yaqob, you shall suffer loss. Do not let it overwhelm you, Tirzah. Resolve to live through it. Do you pledge to remain true to us and to your task, Tirzah?

I do so pledge. I felt the Soulenai caress me, but it gave me little comfort. Loss? Loss?

Boaz, you are the fourth, and you already know much of your task but, again, as the weeks unfold it will become yet plainer. You will learn the skills of the Cantomancer, and you will attain power that even your father could not have dreamed of. Even he, so given to adventuring, will fear the places you shall explore. Boaz, even more than Tirzah, you must learn the paths. Understand the Song of the Frogs, understand its implications. Do you pledge us this to do?

I do so pledge. I could feel Boaz's emotion. With that

pledge he cast off the remaining barriers the Magus had built. *I do so pledge.*

Then behold, Boaz . . . behold . . .

And that command extended to all of us. We had a brief glimpse of the Place Beyond—the briefest of glimpses—then I became aware of a man standing in the center of the whirlpool.

He smiled at Boaz, and I saw that it was Avaldamon.

He was more substantial than when he'd appeared so briefly in Boaz's residence, yet still wraithlike. An apparition only, not flesh.

He held out his hand, then took a step, then another, and he walked across the water to the boat.

He was breathtaking, not only in feature, but in the power and knowledge that shone from his eyes. He lifted a hand, caressed Boaz's cheek, then pulled his son to him. For that fleeting moment of embrace, Avaldamon appeared to be fully fleshed, and Boaz later told me that he'd held a man in his arms, not a wraith.

Be blessed, Boaz. He turned from Boaz and swept an arm about the entire circle. *Be blessed, all of you.* And then he was gone.

The whirlpool died, and we sat down, but we made no attempt to move, or to touch the one next to us. We sat there for many hours, I think, until the sun blazed overhead and a curious Juit bird swept over Isphet's head and woke her, and then us, from our trance.

Everyone, not just the four of us who had been singled out, had been altered by our experience.

We sat, blinked, and smiled. Hesitantly we touched the person next to us, then leaned over to embrace those in the next boat.

There was laughter, and soft, glad tears . . . and then a voice spoke.

I see you. I see you, and I know you.

We stilled, hearts thudding.

That voice had come from the north.

Nzame.

I hunger for you.

THIRTY-TWO

Minor miracles were accomplished in five days. The lake had proved abundant; each day men and women sat on the riverbanks gutting and scaling fish, then leaving them on racks to dry. As it came closer to the day of our departure, more fish were either smoked overnight, or baked with grain to form nutritious fish cakes that could be eaten without need for further cooking.

Others wove tight reed panniers for the mules and camels, or to be carried on the backs of the strong. And most of us were strong. There were no children among us, nor pregnant women (save Neuf), for the slave camp had tolerated neither of those. The baskets were packed with the fish or grain, and what fruits, cheeses, and herbs the estate could provide. Anything else we would have to forage for on our journey.

Isphet had told us that the Lagamaal Plain was arid, but not a desert. It would be hot during the day, cold at night. Sandals were repaired, and some new ones made. Few had clothes apart from the simple wraps allotted to slaves, so Zabrze ordered that the riverboats be stripped of their drapes and banners, and these be used to provide everyone with flowing robes and cloths to wrap about our heads and necks to keep the sun from us. I smiled as I thought what Chad-Nezzar would think to see former slaves arrayed in such finery, but then the smile died as I remembered what Chad-Nezzar had become himself.

Nzame's ability to see and speak to us so far to his south had appalled everyone. Zabrze, once told, paled and sent yet more scouts scurrying east and west with pleas for assistance. He sent none northward.

Zabrze had debated whether we should start our journey a day or so earlier than he'd planned, but decided not to. Nzame might have the ability to see great distances, and he might have an army of stone men, but they may yet be busy in Setkoth, and Zabrze thought that few boats would be able to carry great numbers of them.

He decided we should begin our journey well prepared rather than flee into the night and starve within the fortnight.

Neuf had been very quiet, and Isphet was worried about her, for she was fading emotionally and physically. No one, not even Zabrze, knew quite what to do. Neuf had been vibrant and healthy when she'd alighted from the boat after her journey from Setkoth to Threshold, but I felt that the shock of Consecration Day, together with her worry over her children's fate, had sapped her will to live. She was not the unfeeling mother Zabrze had intimated.

She carried within her what was likely Zabrze's only heir. Isphet told me the baby was healthy, but privately she worried about the birth.

"Neuf says the babe is not due for another five or six weeks. I pray that she is right, and I pray that we are not still on the trail when she goes into labor."

We left early one morning as the Juit birds rose flamelike into the sky and the frogs croaked their dawn chorus. Zabrze had asked Memmon to come with us—many of the estate workers had decided to accompany us to safety—but Memmon had refused. He said he would stay and keep the estate in order for when either Boaz or Zabrze returned, and nothing would change his mind.

As we stepped onto the path east I turned and looked behind me. The house was so beautiful, and the river, lake, and marshes even more so. I hoped that somehow Lake Juit would escape Nzame's feeding frenzy. I tried to picture this beauty turned to stone, and my eyes blurred with tears.

"Come," Boaz said. "Come on, Tirzah. Let us look to the future and not the past."

"I was hoping that house *would* somehow be my future, Boaz. Will you bring me here to live if somehow we survive the next months and years?"

"Assuredly, my love," he said, and kissed my brow.

Isphet, Zabrze, Boaz, Azam, myself, and two or three others led the trek. Sometimes Yaqob joined us, but he generally kept to the midsection of the column.

Neuf sat on a mule directly behind us where Isphet could keep an eye on her. She smiled whenever someone turned to check on her progress, but otherwise I think she just stared listlessly.

Most on foot had panniers strapped to their backs, even Zabrze walked with a load of grain and fish cakes. Boaz's load was lighter than mine—in the dark hours before we set out I'd loaded some of the grain he carried into my pannier. I still distrusted the strength of the scar on his belly, and I did not want it to split and reinfect so far from the healing slime of the Lhyl. I had several pots of the powder with me, and others stored in sundry panniers throughout the column. But I would prefer that Boaz stay healthy and not be in need of saving a second time.

For the first day, and well into the second, we walked through the fields on the estate. It was pleasant, and not overly hard, even in the heat, for the robes and wraps about our heads kept us cool, and a light breeze came up from the river.

On the third day we moved into uncultivated land. Isphet angled us northeast, and said that if we kept to an easterly direction we should pick up the first of the markers on the trail to the mountains.

"Markers?" Zabrze asked, striding by her side.

"Few of us would ever leave the mountains to come to what we called the low river lands," Isphet explained. "Perhaps four or five people a year. The trail is hard, and it is even harder should anyone become lost. So our people constructed markers through the Lagamaal to guide us between the river and hills."

"Will they still be there? It has been many years since you passed this way."

"The markers have been there for hundreds of years, Zabrze. I doubt they have given up and died in the ten or eleven years since I left."

Given up and *died*? Isphet would not explain, but as the day passed I noticed worry lines crease her forehead, and their depth only increased as we walked into our fourth day.

There was no trail now, only that provided by the sun and stars, and I hoped Isphet knew what she was doing. The ground was hard and littered with shards of rock and small pebbles. Every so often a stand of larger rocks appeared, some four or five paces high, and Isphet said they were the remnants of mountains so old they had worn down to these crags.

I smiled at that.

Low, twisted trees with dark green spiky leaves provided us with little shade but did give us good fuel for our fires, and tufts of tough, wizened grass poked out from between the stones.

"If we run out of food," Isphet said, "we can survive for some time on the tubers at the base of those grasses, although if a person eats them for longer than a week they risk death from their slow poisons."

There were creatures about, too, which we normally only saw at dawn and dusk. Hares, thin and rangy, and the snakes and beetles that Isphet had spoken about. They did not bother us, for we were very many thousands of feet trampling through their plains, but we checked our blanket rolls at night and our robes in the morning, fearful lest some cold-skinned reptile had snuggled into their warmth.

As noon approached, Isphet stood and muttered, peering into the distance as she shaded her eyes.

"There it is!" she cried, although none of us could see anything out of the ordinary. "There!" And she hurried through the grass and over the stones.

We followed at a more leisurely pace, relieved that Isphet had found whatever it was she looked for.

Some forty or fifty paces on, Isphet knelt before a low mound of rocks. I looked at it curiously, but could see nothing that set it apart from the many other mounds we'd passed. Isphet was slowly running her hands over the rocks, then stopped about midway down the eastern face of the mound.

"Ah," she breathed, scrabbled about a little, then drew out a small, dull gray metal ball.

She rubbed it between her hands, warming it, and whispered to it. She listened, her head cocked, then her face creased in a broad smile.

"The ball tells me who has passed and what has happened in the immediate vicinity over past months. Boaz, you feel. Listen."

She handed him the ball. He concentrated, then smiled. "The hares have been mischievous, but not much else."

"Yes." Isphet handed the ball to me, and then to Yaqob who had wandered up.

"Can any Elemental hear it?" he asked.

"Not at first. It must be awoken by one who is already of the mountain community, otherwise it will remain mute, even to an Elemental."

Not only did I hope we didn't get lost, I prayed we didn't lose Isphet along the way.

"And the trail," Boaz said. "It spoke of many things, but not of the trail."

"Ah," Isphet replied. "Again, the ball will only respond to me in this."

She stood and tossed the ball high in the air. It sparkled momentarily, then hit the ground with a greater thud than I would have expected for a ball of its size.

Instantly the loose soil, gravel, and small stones before us began to writhe.

Save Isphet, we all stepped back in horror, Zabrze cursing and stumbling in his haste, and I heard Neuf cry out some paces behind us.

"Be still," Isphet said. "Look."

A narrow path of rock and soil writhed to the east.

"It will lead us to the next marker. Come now, don't fret. The soil will cease moving the moment a foot is set upon it." She secreted the ball amid the marker stones again.

Zabrze swallowed, looked at Boaz and Azam, then waved us forward.

And so we followed a snake of soil and stone through the plain, the five thousand trailing in a long line behind us.

We traveled throughout that day and the next two. Each night we camped at one of the markers, then in the morning Isphet would retrieve the dull metal ball, listen to what it had to say, then toss it in the air to set off the next pathway of shifting soil and pebbles.

Despite the aridity of the landscape and the foot-wearing march, few seemed despondent. Nzame had not spoken again, and Boaz said that he hoped the creature's sight and voice had only extended as far as the lake. Boaz himself relaxed into such lightheartedness that he often had our entire lead group laughing as he made up humorous stories about the communities of hares and beetles that we passed.

His hair he cut even shorter, and he let a light beard grow. It was his way of sloughing off the outward appearance of the Magus, but I thought it made him look like a bandit. When I told him this he grinned, and said that we *were* nothing but bandits, traveling through the plains in such fashion.

Once we'd reached a marker in the late afternoon Zabrze ordered a halt, and we would spread about in a vast camp. Isphet showed us how to search for water in the deep depressions scattered about. If four or five men dug until they reached damp soil, then lined the hole with stones, water would seep through until, by the morning, it was a clear pool, and we could fill our flasks and splash the sleep from our faces.

As dusk fell campfires would twinkle cheerily. We would cook grain, or reheat the fish cakes, and occasionally someone would catch a hare, and then the campfire to whom she or he belonged would have fresh meat. The smell of cooking meat drifting across from a neighboring campfire one night made Zabrze and Azam swear they would catch a hare for us, but the hares were swift and the two men were not in the first flush of youth. We laughed so much the next day when Zabrze tripped and tumbled both himself and Azam to the ground that they grumbled and said we'd have to make do with the scents wafting and not the meat cooking.

Yaqob would usually join us once he'd eaten with his group, and then the discussion would invariably turn to that dawn rite on the lake. We would also discuss Nzame, who and what he was, but we got nowhere with that.

Boaz questioned Isphet closely about the Graces, but she knew little.

"We revere them greatly," she said, "and try not to disrupt their contemplations."

During these discussions Zabrze would remain silent, his dark eyes flitting about the group, Neuf dozing in his arms. I thought they had become closer over the past few days, as if it had been the confines and schemes of court that had kept them at such emotional distance for so many years.

And yet I wondered, remembering that fleeting caress of Isphet's cheek.

Twice I read from the Book of the Soulenai. Isphet and Yaqob were enthralled by the stories, and both admitted that perhaps the skills of reading and writing were not *entirely* bad.

"Except when manipulated and ensorcelled by the Magi," Isphet could not resist saying, shooting Boaz a dark look.

"Perhaps you would like me to teach *you* to read, Isphet," he replied. "And you, too, Yaqob. It is a skill that is only dangerous, as Isphet said, when misused. And any skill can be misused."

I expected Isphet and Yaqob to refuse, but they surprised me. Isphet sat turning a pebble over and over in her hand.

"Among the Graces there are those who have mastered the skills of reading and writing," she admitted. "And there are stores of scrolls and books that have been laid down over the centuries. I think that I might like to be able to read them. If you don't mind, Boaz," she finished hastily.

"It would be my pleasure," he said. "Yaqob?"

"That book is a wondrous thing," he said slowly, looking at it, then he raised his eyes to Boaz. I always tensed at these moments. Yaqob could be so unreadable when he chose, and I wondered whether his seeming acceptance of Boaz was pretense or artifice. "Perhaps I will watch when you give Isphet her first lessons."

Boaz smiled. "Then we will begin tomorrow night."

But that night, the third since Isphet found her first marker, gave us other things to worry about.

Several hours after I had gone to sleep, I was shaken awake by Isphet.

"Tirzah. Tirzah!"

"Mmm?"

"What's wrong?" Boaz said, waking more quickly than me.

"It's Neuf. She's gone into labor."

Boaz and I sprang into instant wakefulness. "What can we do?" he asked.

"*You* can do nothing, Boaz," Isphet said. "But Tirzah will be a help."

"Neuf has always borne her children with ease," Boaz said, but his voice was strained.

"Maybe so, but in a comfortable and secluded birthing pavilion, and not after the stress she's gone through over the past few weeks. Tirzah, *will* you hurry up?"

"Call if you need me," Boaz said, and then Isphet led me to a small stand of rocks protected by two stubby trees. Kiath was there, hanging a small lamp on a low branch. Blankets had been strung between trees and rock to give Neuf some privacy. She lay, supported by Zabrze, his face more strained and worried than that of his wife.

"Really, Zabrze," she said. "This is women's business only."

"*You* are my business, Neuf," he replied. "I'm staying."

And so he did.

The labor progressed rapidly. Isphet relaxed after an hour; despite Neuf's physical weakness she appeared to be doing well.

Close to dawn, Zabrze helped Neuf to squat in the birthing position. Isphet rolled up her sleeves and prepared to assist as best she could. "Bear down," she said, and Neuf glared at her.

"I'm considerably more experienced at this than *you*," she snapped, and Zabrze grinned weakly over the top of Neuf's head at Isphet. I'm not sure if he was apologetic at her words, or relieved at her spirit.

But bear down Neuf did, and with the ease that Boaz had promised the babe slipped clean and sweet from her womb. Isphet cleaned his face and mouth and then lifted him to Neuf's arms.

"A boy," she said, and this time I *knew* that the look on Zabrze's face was one of sheer relief.

"Small, but strong," Isphet commented.

At that moment Neuf gave a small gasp of surprise, one of her hands fluttering to snatch at Isphet's. "Oh!"

"Isphet!" I said. "Quick!" Blood was gushing from Neuf's womb, and I could actually see Neuf's face pale in the dawn light as her life ebbed from her. She collapsed back into Zabrze's arms, and Isphet snatched the baby and handed him to Kiath before Neuf dropped him.

"Isphet!" Zabrze yelled, and his arms tightened about his wife. "Do something!"

We put pressure on the womb, but that was all we *could* do.

Neuf, feeling herself dying, sobbed, and snatched at Isphet's hand again. "Boaz," she whispered.

"Get him!" Zabrze shouted at me, and I almost tripped as I scrambled to my feet and lifted aside the curtains.

But he was already there, having heard Zabrze shout the first time.

"What's wrong?" Then he saw my bloodied arms. "Oh, no . . . no . . ."

He ducked inside the enclosure and knelt by Neuf's side. Zabrze was huddled over his wife's form, crooning her name over and over.

"Boaz." Neuf's eyes fluttered open. "Boaz, this is not where I planned to die. Please . . . please . . . will you bury me according to the Way of the One?"

I remembered that Zabrze had said Neuf had many friends among the Magi, but I had not realized how committed she was to the Way of the One until this moment.

"Please, Boaz, I beg you, don't let me die without knowing that I will have the rites I wish."

"Boaz . . ." Zabrze muttered.

Boaz looked more than distressed. He started to shake his head, but Zabrze shouted at his brother. "Boaz, *don't deny her what she wants!*"

Boaz sighed. "I will do as you ask, Neuf. You will be farewelled according to the Way of the One."

"I thank you," she whispered, and died.

None of us knew what to say or do next. The baby whimpered, as if he realized that his mother had passed on. Zabrze bent over his wife's bloodied form and wept, still crooning brokenly to her.

"I tried," Isphet said. "But . . . there was nothing . . ."

I knelt beside her and put my arms about her, then Boaz spoke.

"She will have to be washed, and she should be dressed in a combination of blue and white."

"Boaz," I said, "surely you're not really going to—"

I was stopped by the fierce look I received from both brothers.

"I promised her," Boaz said, "and I cannot go back on that promise."

We did the best we could. Isphet was distraught, so I sent her to sit with the baby while Zabrze, Kiath, and I washed Neuf's body and dressed her in a blue and white robe given us by one of the other women.

But before we called Boaz back I leaned forward and snipped away a lock of her hair.

"We can have our own rite one day, Kiath," I said, and she nodded.

"Alive, Neuf did not know the wonders of the Place Beyond. In death she will."

Boaz had shaved, and his expression was almost that of the cold Magus once more, but his eyes as he raised them to mine were full of emotion, and I knew this mask would not last.

"Her face will need to be painted with her blood," he said, and I felt my stomach lurch over.

"It is the Way of the One," he said, and I took a deep breath and did as he asked.

That macabre face painting was not the worst of the ceremony. We kept it behind the cover of the blankets, and only Kiath, Isphet, Zabrze, the baby, and I witnessed Boaz farewell Neuf in the manner she wished.

It left a sourness clinging to the back of all our throats.

When it was done Zabrze said a few words; his way, I think, not only of farewelling Neuf, but of grieving for her.

"We shared a marriage for twenty-one years," he said. "It was not passionate, but Neuf and I were a good pairing and we made a companionable couple. She had all that I could give her, except my love . . ."

That was a brutal admission, I thought.

". . . but she had all that she wanted. I wish I could have provided a better death for her. I wish I had not led her to this fate."

Then he turned aside, took the baby from Isphet, and went and sat under a distant tree.

We did not move that day.

Neuf's death cast a pall over the entire column. She had not been well liked, certainly not well known, but any death was sad, especially that of a woman in childbirth, so many people grieved for her.

And she had left such a tiny, helpless baby.

No one else among us had a baby or was even pregnant. Within hours of Neuf's death Isphet was fretting over her pot, trying to concoct something that would be palatable and nourishing.

To lose the baby because there was no milk to feed him would be more than a double tragedy.

"Perhaps if I boil some grain to broth," Isphet said, wiping sweat away from her brow. "No, no, that won't do. Perhaps honey-sweetened water. Tirzah, do you have some honey in your pack? It will keep his stomach full, at least."

Uselessly so. I shook my head.

Zabrze paced to and fro behind Isphet, cradling his son. The baby was wailing softly, and that helped no one.

"Isphet?" Zabrze asked. As he had pleaded with her to save Neuf's life, now he pleaded for his son.

"I can't—" she began, then stopped as a shadow fell over the campfire.

"Masters and mistresses," said a wizened but exquisitely spotless old man, "I crave your forgiveness for this interruption. But I have heard of your problem, and—"

"And *what?*" Zabrze snapped.

"And . . ." The old man held a pot in his hand, and now he took the lid off. It was filled with frothy, white milk.

Isphet squeaked and reached with both hands.

"Where did you get that?" I asked. I think I was the only one left with a voice.

"My Zsasa gave birth last night . . . as well, good lady. She has much milk. But—"

"Zsasa?" Zabrze asked.

"My camel, Great Lord."

"Your camel lived and my wife died?" Zabrze said incredulously. "How is it that a camel—"

"We thank you, good cameleer," I said hastily. "This milk will surely save the babe's life," and I stared Zabrze hard in the eye.

"Yes, yes," he said. "I thank you with my soul for this gift. Excuse my words, I . . ."

"I understand, Great Lord," the old man said, then looked at Isphet. "The milk is very rich. Too rich for a baby. Dilute it with water, half and half, and it will do."

Isphet was already reaching for a bowl, and within minutes she'd mixed the milk.

Still embarrassed by his words, Zabrze asked the old man to join us, and all sat silently about the fire as Isphet took the baby from Zabrze's arms and fed him using a moistened cloth for him to suck from. He was hungry, and eager for life, and he took all that he was given.

"How will you name him, Zabrze?" Isphet asked eventually, wiping the boy's mouth as he lay sleeping in her arms.

Zabrze thought for some minutes. "I will name him Zhabroah," he said eventually. "It means survivor."

That night was the first Isphet went to Zabrze's bed, and that was good, for it was a night he should not have been alone.

Even so, I think the love had been growing between them for a very long time, even before they had met.

THIRTY-THREE

We continued. Day passed into night, and night to day, and Isphet took us from marker to marker. The country grew more arid, and yet there was no sign of Isphet's hills on the horizon; not a smudge, not a cloud.

"We will not see them until we are a day out from them," Isphet said. "They are very low."

We proceeded at a tolerably good pace. The heat was not too fierce during the day and the nights were pleasantly cool. Our food stocks lasted—even Zsasa found sufficient scrub grass to produce the milk for both her calf and Zhabroah— and we found water each evening.

All managed well enough on the march. There were blisters and sore tempers occasionally, but we were fit and used to hardship. Zabrze marched at the head of the column, side by side with Isphet, his robes billowing in the wind. He was quiet, grieving in his own manner for Neuf, and deeply troubled for his other children. Isphet gave him silence and comfort, and the bond they had forged between them strengthened both by day and by night.

The baby thrived. Kiath and Isphet shared care of him, but Zabrze also spent hours with him each evening. He would sit about the fire, his son cradled in the crook of his arm, feeding him milk and water.

Poor Neuf, I thought, not even your son misses your warmth.

As he had promised, Boaz taught Isphet the basics in the skills of reading and writing. She learned quickly, grasping the sense easily enough, but was troubled by the stylus and the characters. Boaz was patient with her—which was far more than he had been with me. But this was a different man, and I should not have minded.

Yaqob watched. He asked questions, and I believe he learned to read as fast as Isphet did. But he balked at the stylus. Yaqob would read, but he would not write. I wondered if that was because he still feared the art, or feared having Boaz watch his first awkward attempts at lettering.

We had been moving for almost three weeks, and though Isphet said nothing, I could sense her worry.

"Isphet," Boaz said finally one night as we sat around before dinner. "When?"

Zabrze, cradling his sleeping son, looked up from the campfire. "We have only three or four more days of food, Isphet. We—"

"I *know* how much food we have left, Zabrze!" she said.

"Has not Azam presented us with detailed reports both morning and evening?"

"Isphet," Zabrze said again. "I have responsibility for five thousand people here, and ultimate responsibility for many more. Another week and some of us will start to die. I want to know what's wrong."

"Nothing's wrong—"

"Yes there is! I have watched you these past two days, frowning at your markers—"

"The trails have still appeared. The soil still snakes—"

"Oh, Isphet!" The baby stirred, and Zabrze rocked him a moment. "Isphet," he continued more quietly, "even the mules in our column know that we are now traveling directly south. Are not your hills more to the east?"

She chewed her lip and dropped her eyes.

"South lies the Great Stony Desert," Boaz said. "Isphet . . ."

She lowered her head into her hand and rubbed her eyes. "I *am* worried," she finally admitted. "We have been making good time, despite our numbers. I thought we would have reached the hills some three or four days ago."

Zabrze looked at her very steadily. "You should have said something sooner, Isphet. How long have you been leading us astray?"

"I have been but following the markers," she snapped, raising her eyes. "I—"

"Hare's done," said Holdat. Boaz had managed to trap it that afternoon.

"Let us eat," I said. "In the morning . . . Isphet, would it help if Yaqob or I, or Boaz, listened to what the metal balls had to say? Perhaps one of us . . ."

"If you must," Isphet said. "But they respond best only to one who has been born among the Abyss." And then she took the plate I offered her and ate sullenly and joylessly.

Isphet stood by the pile of marker stones in the cold dawn light, the metal ball in her hands.

"It tells me that there has been but passage of snakes and beetles in the past month or two. None of my people. No enemies. The way is clear."

She tossed the ball into the air, its form catching the first rays of the sun, and where it fell a line of weaving, writhing soil and stones appeared and snaked into the south. Directly south.

Zabrze shifted irritably. "Isphet—"

"Give the ball to Yaqob," I said, and she handed it over.

He rolled it between the palms of his hands, then closed his fingers about it. "Snakes, beetles, and no people," he said finally as he looked up. "The way is safe."

I took the ball. It told me the same. Sighing, I passed it across to Boaz.

He held it longer than either Yaqob or I had, but he did not appear to be concentrating very hard. His face, his entire body was relaxed, and eventually he looked up at the anxious circle of faces about him.

"It's lying," he said.

"What?" Isphet cried. "It can't be! It wouldn't . . . why? Why? No, you're not right, Boaz. You can't be."

Boaz continued to roll the ball between his fingers. "None of you could detect it, but I also have the command of another power."

"The power of the One," I said. "But how could you use that to tell the ball is lying?"

"Isphet has occasionally let us feel what the other balls along the way have to say," Boaz explained. "They have told us of local gossip, who's been past, weather conditions, where best to find water. They have all appealed to the Elemental in us. They were meant to be used by Elementals."

"Yes, but what has this got to do with—" Isphet began.

"*This* ball," he continued, "appeals to the Elemental magic. All of us felt that. But it also appeals to the power of the One. I could have read this as Elemental *or* as Magus. Any Magus could read this ball and thus tell the way."

"I don't understand," Zabrze said. "What are these balls doing speaking to the *Magi?*"

"They are misdirecting them," Boaz said, handing the ball back to Isphet. "This ball—and no doubt previous balls for some time—is deliberately lying to misdirect any Magus who should attempt to use it. Isphet, would your people, perhaps the Graces among them, know of the events at Threshold?"

"Not the details," she said slowly. "But the Graces are powerful. They would know that something was very wrong. They may well have felt Nzame cross from the Vale. They would know that it was connected with the Way of the One. And, Boaz, they may have felt the power of the One you used when you conducted the rites to bury Neuf."

"Then they would think," Yaqob said, "that whatever went wrong at Threshold was now crossing the Lagamaal, trying to reach them. They have instructed the markers to lie."

"Can you untangle the lies from truth?" Zabrze asked Boaz. "Can you find us the true path?"

"No. These markers have been instructed very well. The Elemental magic used to alter them is very powerful. *I* cannot change it. Isphet?"

"I could not even tell the lie. It fooled me." Her voice cracked. "My own people have been lying to me? Trying to send me to die in the Great Stony Desert?"

"They could not have known who we truly were," Zabrze said gently. "They could not have known that you were on your way home after a decade of exile."

She nodded, and controlled her emotions. "So, what are we to do? We could head southeast by sun and stars, but that is too inaccurate, and we could easily miss the hills and die in these beetle-infested plains. What can we do?"

"Well," said Boaz, "the Soulenai told us I would explore, and so I shall. Isphet, I need to know something about your home. Tell me, does it contain a large body of water?"

"Yes, it does. But—"

"And are there any other large bodies of water between here and your home, or anywhere close to your home?"

"No. Not for many, many leagues."

"So if I constructed an enchantment that searched out water, it would head straight for your home?"

"Yes. Yes, it would."

"Well, then"—Boaz grinned—"easy! Tirzah, where have you stored the Goblet of the Frogs?"

It was in a pack on one of the mules, and I sent Kiamet to fetch it. When he returned I took the bundle from him, unwrapped the goblet, and handed it to Boaz.

"For this," he said very quietly, "we must thank Tirzah, for without the magic of this goblet we *would* truly be lost and dead."

The goblet sparkled in the dawn light, and Boaz wrapped his hands about it as he had the ball. He did not speak, but I felt the same strange sensation run down my back as I had the night he'd changed my father's lock from stone back to hair. The goblet sang softly; all the Elementals in our small group relaxed and smiled at its sweet song.

Boaz covered the top of the goblet with his hand, and I felt the sensation strengthen.

Then he lifted his hand, and held the goblet up so all could see.

The most incredibly ugly creature I had ever seen popped its head over the rim of the goblet. It was so covered by warts and knobs it was almost shapeless. There were narrow slits of black eyes, and a mouth so wide it stretched across about half of its skull. Small padlike feet appeared at the rim, and then the creature heaved itself out of the goblet and hopped away to the south-southeast.

It was a frog, but I had never seen a frog that ugly before. It was also very big, and once it was out I could not understand how it had fitted into the goblet.

About ten paces away it stopped, its great tongue slipping about its lips. It looked to the sky, shuddered, then burrowed beneath a rock.

"It doesn't like the sun," Boaz said, "and will only travel by night. I suggest that we rest while we can, for tonight will be a long . . . hop."

And he grinned at his own joke, and sat down.

We rested that day, and in the evening, as we were eating a meal, the frog emerged from its burrow and hopped to Boaz's side, where he fed it tidbits from his plate.

"Boaz—" began Isphet.

The frog fixed her with a beady eye and burped.

I covered my mouth with my hand and giggled, and then we were all laughing.

"If ever I regain Ashdod, and I rule in regal splendor as

Chad," Zabrze eventually managed, "I will slice the head from the first person who mentions that once I led my people across a great plain by following a frog."

Boaz dribbled some water into the frog's gaping mouth, and it slapped its huge tongue about happily.

Isphet tried her question again. "Boaz, how did you *do* that? I have never seen, or heard of, this ability before."

"I don't know, Isphet. It just felt right."

She shook her head. "The Graces are going to want to take you apart and examine you, Boaz. Be prepared."

"We have to get there yet. Fetizza will show us the way."

We all laughed again. Fetizza was an Ashdod word meaning "lovely dancer."

Boaz looked at his brother. "If ever you get to rule in regal splendor as Chad, Zabrze, you shall have Fetizza to thank. Perhaps you can have her dance at court."

At that moment Fetizza decided enough was enough. She gave a great shudder, angled her head to look at the moon, then bounded off.

"After her!" cried Zabrze. "Follow that frog!"

And thus we did. Five thousand people, scores of camels and mules, all following a great, ugly frog bounding through the stony landscape. Fetizza was fast, and every so often would sit on a rock and wait for us to catch up. She would give a companionable burp as the first person reached her, then off she would bound again.

Occasionally she scurried after a beetle, but generally she kept to her purpose of leading us to the nearest water supply. She was not hard to follow at night, for the moonlight glistened off her slimy skin, and Fetizza constantly croaked in a monotonous undertone, as if telling herself stories to while away the journey.

We followed her that night, and then a second. By the third night there was still no sign of the hills, and food was running low, but spirits were high. The ground had started to rise, and on the fourth night we found ourselves walking up a constant incline.

"Soon," Isphet said, six hours into the night. "Soon." She peered ahead, but still could not see the hills.

But by dawn we could. As the sun rose (and as Fetizza yawned sleepily) we all saw the low, rolling horizon ahead of us.

Isphet hugged Boaz. "Thank you," she said, then smiled excitedly at the rest of us. "A further night of travel, for the hills are still distant, and by dawn tomorrow . . ."

Zabrze gave her a tender smile, then ordered camp set up.

Fetizza led us through the night. Isphet argued that she could find her way on her own now, but Boaz only said mildly that it *had* been eleven years since she left, and who knew what other traps and misdirections her people had set up to confuse whatever enemies tried to find their way through.

"Fetizza will not be misguided," he said, "and she will find the most direct route."

Isphet subsided, but she was at the forefront of the column the entire night.

The landscape was, if anything, becoming more barren the farther we walked. We'd seen the last of the stubby trees some two nights previously, and even the grasses were thinner and more sparse as the ground rose. The incline was not steep, but our way was made troublesome by increasing outcrops of head-high rock.

Isphet restrained herself from running ahead, but I thought that if we weren't there by morning, then she might well lose all patience and shout at Fetizza.

It made me reflect about my own homeland. I really didn't care now if I never saw Viland again. There were no fond memories associated with that thin, cold strip of northern land . . . and my father was dead. There was no point in going back. Did Isphet have parents? Brothers or sisters still living? What else could drag her so impatient into a landscape that made even Viland look enticing?

"What do you think we will find?" I asked Boaz as night lightened toward morning and we tackled yet another slope littered with rocky outcrops.

"I don't know. I hope her people can teach me what I need to learn. The mystery that is the Song of the Frogs. What it is that infests Threshold. How to destroy it before it turns life itself to stone."

"I dread the thought of going back," I said quietly.

"Oh, Tirzah! No. It will be my—"

"No, Boaz," I said. "I will not remain behind. Wondering. You will tie up my future, too, when you walk back into Threshold."

Again I had that overwhelming sense of loss that I'd once felt standing at Threshold's mouth. Oh, gods, I prayed silently. Not Boaz. *Not Boaz!*

We heard a shout, then a scuffle ahead. Fetizza had bounded into a narrow canyon, Isphet close behind.

A man emerged from the rocks and seized Isphet. He wrenched her about, one arm tight around her body, the other holding a gleaming blade to her throat.

Fetizza was sitting just behind them, yawning at the interruption.

"Take one more step and she dies," the man said. "You have no place here."

Everyone froze, and Zabrze raised a careful hand. "My friend, we mean you no harm. We seek Isphet's people— Isphet is the woman you hold so tight in your arms. Please, let her go."

The man stared at Zabrze. He was young, perhaps four or five years older than me, with dark hair, but light eyes. Gray eyes. He was dressed in a short tunic and trousers bound close to his legs with thongs. He wore leather shoes rather than sandals. "Who are you?"

"I am Zabrze, Prince of Ashdod . . . Chad now, I suppose. I lead these people"—and he waved slowly behind him—"to safety from—"

He got no further. The man looked from Zabrze to the line of people that stretched down the hill and halfway up the one behind it.

"You have been sent to destroy us!" he shouted, and his hand tightened alarmingly about the knife. "By *it!* We knew of your approach, we knew—"

"We have come to learn how to destroy Nzame," Boaz said quietly, and he moved slowly to Zabrze's side. "Your people have the skills and the teachers that we need."

"You know its name," the man said. "How can I tell that you are not its servants?"

"We come from Threshold," said Zabrze. "We were there when Nzame first spoke."

"Then how did you escape? No one could escape that evil. The echoes of its powers have disturbed us even here. And nothing but evil could have found these hills. Nothing—"

"Nothing but Fetizza," Boaz said and clicked his fingers. Fetizza bounded back to him.

The man's eyes followed the frog's movement but he said nothing.

"There are many Elementals among us," Boaz continued. "We need training. And the woman you hold *is* of your people. Do you not know her? Isphet?"

"Evil could have borrowed any name to cross the Lagamaal Plains," the man said.

Boaz sighed. "Listen to me. Take Fetizza back to your people. Let them examine her. She—"

"No!" the man shouted. "It is a trick! Begone! You do not—"

"Shetzah!" Zabrze cried. "I could overpower you now and we'd simply continue following the frog. But no. I have stood here and reasoned patiently. Well, now I have had—"

"I *will* slit the woman's throat!" the man hissed. "Attack if you wish, but it will be at the price of her life!"

"Enough," said a mild voice, and an older man stepped into view. He was in his fifties, perhaps early sixties, and had the pleasant face and manner of a master craftsman. He was not as dark as most southerners, with brown hair and beard peppering to gray. His hands and face had a craggy aspect, and his eyes were hazel.

There was nothing in his clothes or even mannerisms to set him apart, yet the man was surrounded by an immense aura of serenity.

"Let her be, Naldi. I apologize that I did not warn you of their identities, but until last night we were not aware of exactly who it was crossed the Lagamaal toward us."

Naldi let Isphet go so hurriedly he almost dropped the knife, and as Isphet moved away from him he took the other man's hands and kissed them.

Isphet stumbled away from Naldi, her face white, her hands to her throat. She did not look at the older man who had arrived to save her. Zabrze grabbed her and wrapped his arms about her protectively. "Are you hurt?"

She shook her head, leaning close against him.

Zabrze raised his eyes to the older man before him. "Who are you?"

"My name is Solvadale," he said, and reached out a hand to Zabrze.

Isphet gasped and turned in Zabrze's arms. She inclined her head in a deep show of respect. "Grace! My name is Isphet. I came from the Fortieth Step—"

"I know you and I know to which Step you belong, and I will speak with you momentarily, Isphet," Solvadale said. "Zabrze?"

Zabrze took the man's hand and gripped it firmly. "We mean you no harm."

"I know that," Solvadale said. "But we could not get word to Naldi, nor to the other sentries, in time. I apologize again, to both you and Naldi, for this embarrassment."

Naldi bowed his head, obviously honored that one like Solvadale would offer him an apology. Now that he relaxed I could see that he was a pleasant-looking man, of normal dark aspect for this southern land. He held out his hand for Isphet, a sheepish smile on his face. "If I'd known . . ."

She accepted his apology and clasped his hand, but she did not move away from Zabrze.

As Naldi stood back the Grace took Isphet's face in one hand. "You have been a long time gone, woman. Where is Banwell, your husband?"

"Dead, Grace. Ten years, now."

"Ah, I am saddened. He was better than a good man."

Isphet nodded.

"And you have changed, Isphet. You have shouldered a great deal of responsibility. And . . . you have been sent to illume."

Isphet's face was as shocked as I think mine was. "How did you know?"

"The Soulenai spoke to us last night," Solvadale said. "They told us of many things."

He walked past Isphet to Yaqob who had joined us. "Welcome, young man. What is your name? Ah, Yaqob. A good name. Yes, we can make something of you."

And then to me. As with Isphet he took my face in his hand. "You have come from very far away, girl. What is your name?"

"Tirzah."

Solvadale smiled. "A beautiful name. A beautiful woman. Blessed."

Elder Solvadale certainly wasn't wasting any breath on explanations. He turned directly to Boaz.

"We have been waiting many, many years for you to come to us. How are you called?"

"Boaz."

"Ah, Boaz. A noble name your mother gave you." Solvadale's eyes narrowed as he took Boaz's hand. "You are a very unusual man, Boaz. You have strong Elemental magic in you, very strong but very raw. And something else . . . please, tell me what it is."

Solvadale knew exactly what it was, but he wanted Boaz to say the words.

"I was a Magus, Solvadale. But that is behind me now."

Solvadale nodded slowly, his face unreadable. "Magus. But behind you? Oh, I hope not. I hope not. And what an unusual frog that sits at your feet, Boaz. But enough of that; the frog and her mysteries we can discuss later. Now we—"

"Now," Zabrze said with more than a touch of exasperation, "can I crave your indulgence for my five thousand. We are tired and hungry and we need to talk, you and I."

It wasn't until Zabrze spoke that I realized I'd never wondered how Isphet's people would cope with such an influx.

But Solvadale did not seem too concerned. No doubt he knew the exact numbers of people, camels, and mules standing behind us.

"It will take some time to get all of you into the Abyss," he said, motioning down the canyon. "Maybe all day, for it is a slow and sometimes dangerous trip. But you are right. We need to talk, Zabrze. As we walk, perhaps we can talk about Avaldamon. You were one of the last to see him alive, were you not?"

THIRTY-FOUR

Solvadale strode ahead, keeping such a brisk pace that most of us were puffing within five minutes. I looked over my shoulder to see people and pack animals scrabbling over and about rocks.

"Solvadale!" Zabrze called, and the Grace turned about.

"I am sorry. I did not realize," he said. "I was hurrying because . . . Naldi?" he called.

"Yes, Grace?"

"I would like to take these four, and Zabrze, through to the Abyss. Will you stay and guide the rest? As I pass other sentries I'll send you help."

"Yes, Grace."

"Wait," Isphet said, and as Kiath reached us she lifted Zhabroah from her arms.

"A baby?" Solvadale asked. "Whose?" His eyes flitted about our small group.

"My son," Zabrze said. "And that of my wife, Neuf. She died in his birth some three weeks ago."

"Ah. I thought I did not feel . . ."

And Solvadale strode off again without explaining.

He did not go so fast this time, and we managed to follow him easily enough. The sun crested the ridge before us, and grew hot as it strengthened.

"Soon," Solvadale said as he saw our sweat. "Soon."

I glanced at Isphet. Her color was high, but I did not think it all due to the exercise. She'd put Zhabroah into a sling made from her blanket, and now he nestled asleep at her breast. I smiled to myself. I'd never thought to see Isphet so motherly.

Solvadale led us into a narrow gully. Here even he had to slow down, for the rocks lay tumbled about as if giants had played skittle ball and not thought to pick up their toys. Fetizza was the only one among us who managed with ease, eventually even bounding ahead of Solvadale.

"Soon," I heard Isphet whisper, then she turned to me. "Oh, Tirzah, you are not going to believe what lies ahead!"

I certainly wouldn't have any warning, I thought. Isphet had kept remarkably silent about her hill home, this mysterious Abyss. Maybe its existence was so wrapped in secret she was not allowed to talk of it. Maybe—

Whatever I'd been about to think next died as I stumbled to a halt directly behind Solvadale and Zabrzè. My mouth slowly fell open. Isphet had not said anything because she did not want to spoil our first stunned sight of her home.

About us the barren hills rolled desolately away, north, south, and east.

But not east before . . . not before they had been cleft asunder.

Solvadale had brought us to the lip of a great . . . abyss.

It was clean cut, so clean cut I swear the rock lip along its entire length had the edge of a blade. The Abyss was some fifty paces wide, and stretched farther north–south than I could see; at least a league.

But it was its depth—and what had been *done* with that depth—that so awed and inspired. It plunged for what Isphet would later tell me was twelve hundred and four paces. From the lip, the bottom was hidden in dimness and mist.

I felt Boaz slip his arm about my waist; as much to support himself as me, I think. "By all the wonders in the universe," he said. "Look what they have done to the walls!"

The rock exposed by the cleft was a soft rose pink. It did not fall sheer, but had been carved over what must have been centuries into a myriad of balconies and levels that jutted farther and farther into the chasm the deeper it fell. Steps, I realized, remembering that Isphet had told the Grace she'd come from the Fortieth Step. These Steps began perhaps a hundred paces below us, then plunged down into the mist. Behind them must be homes and schools and halls, carved deep into the rock.

At intervals, arched bridges of pink rock masonry connected the walls of the Abyss, and on several I could see people moving.

"Oh!" I said. "It's astounding!"

"The mist clears," Solvadale said, "when the sun rises to its noon height. Soon, now," he added, checking the sky.

Fetizza sat at the very lip, gripping tightly with her toes, her bright eyes staring down into the Abyss. Suddenly she gave a great croak . . .

. . . and jumped into the open air.

She fell like a stone.

"Fetizza!" Boaz cried, and I wrapped my arms about him; for one dreadful moment I thought he was going to leap after her.

"Be still!" Solvadale commanded. "She will come to no harm. What was she commanded to seek, Boaz?"

"Water."

"Oh." He winked at Isphet. "Then she has found it for you. Now, follow me."

He led us back from the brink several paces to an outcrop of rock.

"How is it that I knew nothing of this, Solvadale?" Zabrze asked. "I am well learned, and I have studied maps of this area. Nothing I have seen or heard indicates the existence of this Abyss or your people."

"We hide ourselves and our secrets with great care," the Grace replied. "These hills are hidden well from casual eyes . . . and, casual, most eyes turn aside. Come on now, don't stand about."

Beneath the outcrop lay a dark cleft in the rock, head high and just wide enough for a person.

"How will we fit everyone down here?" I asked as I stepped through and found the Grace waiting at the top of a circular stairwell.

"There are other entrances, wider and more accommodating than this. But this stairwell is the most spectacular. For our small group it will do well."

The bends were tight, and the steps narrow and steep, and I hung tight to the banister about the outer wall.

"Tirzah," Boaz said behind me, "let me go ahead, then you'll feel safer."

I smiled gratefully at him as he squeezed past, and I did feel safer having his body before me. I placed my other hand on his shoulder and risked a glance behind.

Isphet followed me, but her grace and confidence told me she'd probably climbed these stairs ever since she was a toddler. Behind her came Zabrze, and I think his face was as pale as mine.

We climbed for half an hour, then we came to a small landing that opened onto a balcony, and Solvadale led us out.

I gasped with delight. We were some ten or fifteen levels below the topmost Step, and I walked to the railing and looked up. The sun shone almost directly overhead.

When I dropped my eyes, I held my breath in sheer wonder. The mist had cleared, and I could see that a great river wound through the Abyss. A narrow strip of rock bounded it on either side, but the bottom was almost completely covered with the dark emerald water.

"No one has ever plumbed its depths," Isphet said quietly at my side. "The Abyss continues down"—she shot a glance at Boaz—"perhaps even into Infinity."

"It is a site of great power," Solvadale said. "Far greater than you realize, Isphet."

And with that he led us back to the stairs and continued the climb down.

He stopped every half an hour or so, always at a balcony, so we could catch our breath and rest weary legs. Corridors opened off all the landings. Eventually, I guessed, we would be led to quarters in one of the Steps.

The next, as it turned out.

As we stopped at the landing, I automatically moved toward the balcony.

"No," Solvadale said sharply. "Wait. This is where I leave you. Isphet, in the morning you may show your friends about the Abyss. After your noon meal, I would have you bring Yaqob, Tirzah, and Boaz to speak with me and several other Graces in the Water Hall. Do you remember it? Can you find your way there?"

"Yes, Grace."

"Good." He smiled. "Then greet your father, Isphet."

She gave a small cry and whirled in the direction of Solvadale's eyes.

A man emerged from one of the corridors. Gaunt and gray-haired, he had Isphet's commanding eyes and presence.

"Father!" Isphet flung herself into the man's arms, and they embraced fiercely.

Thinking to give them a moment of privacy, I looked back to where Solvadale had been standing, but he was gone. I frowned. He would have had to step past me to reach any of the doors, or even the stairwell.

"A baby, Isphet?" I heard her father ask, and I turned around.

"Ah," Zabrze said, stepping forward. "I should explain."

And so he did.

Isphet introduced her father, Eldonor, to the rest of us, and he clasped our hands with genuine pleasure, even though I could see he was eager to talk with Isphet.

"Solvadale asked me to show you to your chambers," he said. "Follow me."

Eldonor led us down several corridors, spacious and well lit, not only from windows carved into the outer wall of rock, but also from shafts like those in Threshold. I shivered, and turned my mind from the pyramid.

The rock was the same uniform pink throughout—perhaps slightly deeper in color internally than on the outer walls of the Abyss—and glowed warmly in the light.

Eldonor stopped at the entrance to a chamber, and showed Yaqob inside. Two doors down he stopped at another door, and indicated to Boaz and me.

Eldonor was perceptive, for no one had said anything about our relationship. Or perhaps the Graces had perceived from a distance, and had informed him of the required living arrangements.

"Refresh yourselves," Eldonor said, waving about the spacious chamber. "At the end of this corridor is a small eating hall. Please join me as my guest once the sun goes down."

Then he was gone.

The chamber was simply but well furnished, and opening off it was a small room where we could wash. It contained a large sunken bath, and I sighed blissfully when I saw it. In the main chamber were laid out fresh linens and robes, and flowers—pink and gold water lilies—floated in a bowl on a low table.

Boaz and I shared the bath, scrubbing at each other's hair, and laughing as the soap ran down into our eyes. It was good to wash three weeks of accumulated filth from our bodies.

"I cannot remember the last time I had you to myself," he said, kissing the lather from my shoulder.

"But you mustn't get used to it, Boaz," I replied. "I was thinking of offering to look after Zhabroah for Zabrze and Isphet. They cannot truly want to have a crying babe to disturb their rest night and day."

He slipped his hands about my waist. "You are a tease, Tirzah . . . aren't you?"

"Absolutely not, Boaz!" I cried in mock indignation and then laughed as his hands tightened. "Well . . ."

"How much time do we have before dark, Tirzah?" he whispered into my wet hair.

"Enough, Boaz. Enough."

We enjoyed a pleasant meal with Yaqob, Zabrze, Isphet, and Eldonor. He was a good host, never too inquisitive, drawing information from us with the most exquisite tact, and giving as much back himself as thanks. Isphet sat close to him, her face radiant with joy at finding her father still living.

Finally, as we sat sipping goblets of sweet black wine and nibbling tart cheese, Eldonor asked his daughter to describe her life as a slave at Threshold.

He was horrified at what he heard; and he wept a little. Zabrze had not realized how bad it had been, either, and he bowed his head as Isphet, and then Yaqob, talked.

Boaz, for his part, kept his face averted.

Neither held anything back. They talked of their humiliations—Isphet's years spent at the beck and call of Magi who wished to use her, Yaqob's frequent beatings in his youth when he was too outspoken—but they also spoke of their joys—the friendship and support they'd found among their fellow slaves, the delight at the creation of the glass, even though it was for a darker purpose.

"I thought you dead," Eldonor said finally, clearing his throat. "None of us heard anything from you. Years went by. And we thought that if Isphet and Banwell were still alive, then they would send word." He took a deep breath. "Last night Grace Solvadale came to my rooms and said, 'Isphet comes,' and I went down on my knees and wept.

"But Banwell *did* die. I am sorry, Isphet. You loved him well."

She nodded, dropping her eyes and not saying anything.

"Yet he was a rash man. He was the one to decide it would be an adventure to seek a life beyond the Abyss."

"And I agreed, Father," Isphet said. "Do not think to blame Banwell in this."

Eldonor held his silence as a servant refilled our goblets, then departed. How far I had come, I thought, from the belly of that filthy whaler.

"But you have found another love, I see," Eldonor said. "And one more highly ranked than your last. One who will be—perhaps is—Chad."

He shifted his eyes to Zabrze. "You will be a mighty man, Zabrze, ruler of one of the richest realms in the known world. Yet here you bed my daughter, a runaway slave. What do you intend to make of her? Will you enslave her once more? Or shall you make her a mistress? Or a concubine to set beside your next high-ranking wife? Or shall you just cast her off when you regain your realm from the horror that grips it?"

"I shall make her my wife," Zabrze said quietly, holding Eldonor's stare. "No more, no less."

"No," Isphet stumbled. "You can't. I . . ."

"Isphet," Zabrze said, and took her hand. "We both know what there is between us. Will you deny that?"

She was silent, staring at him with her great eyes.

"And"—Zabrze's mouth lifted in a slight smile—"you are more the Chad'zina than all the empresses, begums, regnalias, and matriarchs that it has been my misfortune to entertain over the years. I would marry for love this time, and you will ever be my only chance for that. Come, what do you say?"

Eldonor had relaxed into a slight smile, although Yaqob had a huge grin over his face. Boaz and I, like Isphet, could but stare.

She smiled eventually, but she had to make a noticeable effort at it. I think, had Zabrze not pressed, she would have sat there for hours, battling her shock.

"I say yes, Zabrze. Yes."

His entire body relaxed. "You shall have to redecorate the court with your Elemental ideas, Isphet my love. It shall be . . . interesting."

At that instant I had my first understanding of why the Soulenai had told Isphet she would have the opportunity to illume. As a Cantomancer *and* as a Chad'zina, it would be her task to relight a nation with the mysteries of the Soulenai.

When, very much later, Boaz and I returned to our chamber, it was to find that the bed had been remade.

Boaz grinned wryly. "And what will they think of *us*, Tirzah, that we should tangle the sheets so early after our arrival?"

"They will think we are very much in love, Boaz," I said as I sat down.

"Tirzah." He sank down on the bed beside me. "Zabrze shamed me earlier with such a public protestation of his love for Isphet. He has never treated her with anything but honor, and yet I . . ."

"Boaz—"

"No, let me finish. I have treated you so badly, not once, but often, that I do not know what to do to compensate, or to prove to you how much I truly do love you."

I put my fingers over his lips. "I do not need proof, Boaz."

"Yet I must offer it. Tirzah, I swear that somewhere, somehow, I will prove to you the depth of my love, and how much I crave your forgiveness."

"No! Boaz, that is too heavy a vow." Loss, all I could think of was loss. "I understood you long before you understood yourself. There is no need for forgiveness—"

Now it was he who stopped my lips. "Yes, there is, Tirzah. Yaqob's attempt to murder me showed me how deep *is* the need for forgiveness. Not only yours, but that of all those I've mistreated over so many years as Magus."

I was almost crying now. "No, Boaz. You go too far . . . too far."

"But for now"—he cupped my face in his hands—"I can only beg you, as Zabrze begged Isphet, to be my wife."

"Yes, yes. That is enough, Boaz. It is all I want."

But his eyes were sad as he bent to kiss me, and our love-making that night was more tears than laughter.

I lay still in the morning, feeling slightly ill. Had it been the wine? The bitter sadness of the night?

Then an almost forgotten cramp twisted deep in my belly, and my eyes flew open. I had not had a monthly flux since Boaz had loosed his power through me after the first night we'd bedded. Months . . . many months ago.

Tentatively I probed at my belly with my fingers. My womb, for so long such a hard unresponsive canker, was now soft and pliable.

The cramp struck again, worse than before. Sighing, I wriggled out of Boaz's still-sleeping embrace to attend to myself.

THIRTY-FIVE

After we'd broken our fast, Isphet took Zabrze, Yaqob, Boaz, and me for a tour of the Abyss. At first Zabrze was inclined to grumble, for he wanted to see that all our people had been comfortably settled, and that their presence wasn't going to disrupt the Abyss too much. But Isphet said they could wait for another two or three hours.

"I want to show you my home, Zabrze. This afternoon, while we go to the Graces, you will be free to question as you want. But for now you will follow me."

Zabrze acquiesced.

The Abyss was so wondrous and so bountiful I could not understand why Isphet and Banwell had ever contemplated a life outside it. As we walked about, many people greeted Isphet warmly, some with barely controlled emotion. She had been greatly missed. Yet even to us, the people were open and friendly. They were curious at the influx of newcomers, but not particularly perturbed at the sheer numbers that had climbed down into their midst.

I soon understood why. The Abyss, not simply the chasm but the dwellings opening off it, was massive. There were, Isphet told us, one hundred and ten Steps that dropped a thousand paces and ranged almost half a league along the Abyss. In some places, the corridors and rooms stretched back into the rock for almost an hour's walk.

"We have room for eight hundred thousand people, yet currently we are some ninety thousand only. The five thousand will not overly stretch space," Isphet said. "Although they may have had to dust the quarters assigned them."

"Was the population once much larger?" Zabrze asked. "This complex is so immense."

"Not by much, perhaps some two or three thousand more several generations ago. We did not build this, Zabrze." Isphet waved a hand at the magnificence above us. "About six hundred years ago our forebears discovered it, virtually in this condition. Abandoned. Even now there are areas of the Abyss, complexes deep within the rock, that we have hardly explored. Every year we lose adventuresome young children who try to map the unknown corridors. The Graces understand far more about the Abyss than do most of us. There are areas of the Abyss that only they visit."

"Whoever created this must have been a magical people," Boaz murmured. "Look, Tirzah. The balconies and carved dwellings down the sides of the chasm look like caged lacework."

He was right. It was as if a giant had carved the outer lacework of the Abyss, and left it for tinier people to carve out the inner dwellings.

Isphet led us over one of the bridges across the Abyss and into a large domed hall on the other side. It had been beautifully carved and gilded, and enameled and cut-glass panels had been inserted into the dome.

"You and Banwell were glassworkers," I remarked to Isphet. "So there must be workshops here."

"Yes. The people of the Abyss have a deep love of the crafts and most have proficiency in one or another. The glass workshops, as other workshops, are deeper into the rock. I will show them to you another day."

As we walked I noticed that the complex was lit by light reflected along artfully designed yet often almost invisible mirrors in ceilings and walls.

"Were these crafted here?" Yaqob asked, pausing to admire one.

Isphet hesitated. "Yes, but not by us. They were part of the complex as it was discovered by our forebears. We have not learned the secret of their making."

I imagined that the first thing children were taught was to avoid throwing balls at them. I wondered how many corridors and apartments had been abandoned because the lighting mirrors had been broken.

Over the next few hours Isphet slowly led us through parts of the Abyss. There were schools, libraries, homes, markets—all carved out of the rock. Food was provided by the river, principally fish but also a variety of shellfish and eels, and Isphet said that there were vegetable and grain fields above us, sheltered in the valleys to the east of the Abyss. "We do not spend our entire lives within this chasm."

"Isphet," I said, "I have noticed that many of your people are lighter skinned than most southerners, and with gray or blue eyes. How is that?"

"The people of the Abyss are not a race as such. Indeed, we consider ourselves a part of Ashdod. Although the Chads have completely ignored us." She shot a mischievous glance at Zabrze. "We are a myriad of peoples who have gravitated here over many centuries. What connects us all is our devotion to the Elemental arts. Tirzah, you are proof enough that one does not have to be southern born and of dark visage to be an Elemental."

I nodded. The Soulenai had passed through many lands in their quest to escape war and find peace, and I thought they must have left their blood scattered through most of the known world. I daydreamed a little, wondering which of the Soulenai had wandered Viland thousands of years ago. Was it my mother who had bequeathed me their blood? Druse had shown no sign of Elemental leanings. And Avaldamon. Avaldamon had been Geshardi . . . and the Book of the Soulenai was written in that language.

Finally we found ourselves at the base of the Abyss. The chasm was bathed in sunlight, for it was close to noon. We stood on one of the narrow rock ledges above the water, gazing silently into it.

There was a strong, deep current, although the upper layer of the water was almost still. I could see fish flashing in its depths, and I thought that fishing must be easy where all one had to do was string a net across this narrow waterway.

"The water comes from an underground river that surfaces through a fault in the rock beneath us," Isphet explained. "It travels south through the Abyss, then swings east-northeast once past the chasm. From there I believe it meanders its way to the great sea far to the east."

Suddenly Boaz laughed, and pointed. There, sunning herself on a slight outcrop, was Fetizza. She croaked companionably as Boaz called to her, but did not move.

"Are there any other frogs here?" Boaz asked.

"No," Isphet said. "I don't think so. Fetizza shall have to make do with the company of children splashing about her. Come, it is time to eat."

Once the meal was over, Eldonor took Zabrze off to attend his people, and Isphet led us to the Water Hall.

"Ordinary folk only ever come here at the invitation of the Graces," Isphet explained as she led us through long corridors and then down a series of stairs. "Many of our rites are conducted here, but mostly, so I have heard, the Graces sit here and dream."

The Water Hall was situated deep in the complex. It was circular, and very large—perhaps some eighty paces in diameter. The hall was dominated by a pool in its center; the water was very still, very green. Gilded columns surrounded the pool, rising to a vaulted ceiling that, like the walls and floor, was carved out of the deep pink rock.

As we entered, and Isphet closed the double doors behind us, four Graces walked out from the shadows. They were dressed in simple robes, but all wore such an aura of mystery and assurance that none could mistake their power.

One was Solvadale, and he greeted us softly, kissing each of us on both cheeks. "You are all well rested. Good. Please, step forward and meet my companions."

There were two other male Graces, Gardar and Caerfom,

and one female, Xhosm. They also took our hands and kissed us gently. There were other Graces, Solvadale explained, but many had sworn to total seclusion, and others were so engrossed in mysteries we would hardly see them.

"We are the four who shall be involved in your training," he said, leading us to benches placed in a semicircle at the far end of the pool.

All four Graces had carefully accorded each of us the same degree of respect, but as we sat their eyes kept returning to Boaz.

Once we were still, Solvadale again took the lead. "It is so difficult to know where to begin, so perhaps I, on behalf of my companions who are with me today, will commence with an explanation. Yet even an explanation has no clear beginning. If you find questions that demand to be asked as I talk, then do not hesitate to ask them."

He paused, sighed, then continued. "The Soulenai can at times be obtuse. Sometimes *they* can leave their explanations a little too long before the airing. It was only the night before last that they told us of your impending arrival, although we'd been aware of your existence for some time. I am sorry that the markers had misled you . . . had we known you were so close we would have sent help."

"As it was," Xhosm said, looking at Boaz, "you found enough help within you."

"You altered the markers," Isphet said to Solvadale. "Made them lie. Why?"

"We knew of the trouble at Threshold," the Grace replied, "and we knew something of *what* trouble it was. No, wait, I shall talk of that soon enough. We altered the markers because we feared what might slither across the Lagamaal Plains toward us. Again, I apologize for the trouble that caused you.

"Now, it has been impossible for us to remain unaware of Threshold. We live in relative isolation here, but we do have communication with the lands beyond us. We have watched for the last two hundred years as Threshold rose. For the last eighty, we have known that something was terribly wrong with it. Something dark, yet we could not see what. It is only in recent months we learned from the Soulenai that Threshold was to gain its power by accessing the Vale."

"Will you explain the Vale?" I asked.

"Surely. You will have to know about the Vale, and one day you will see right into it, but that will come much later, after you have completed the major part of your training. The Vale was created at the same time as this physical universe in which we live; it exists alongside it, almost in a different dimension. It is a place that collects darkness into itself, much as the universe collects stars and light."

"I was once a Magus," Boaz said, "you know that."

The Graces nodded, solemn.

"The Magi believed that the Vale contained the power of Creation. Were we wrong?"

"No, not really," Solvadale said. "The Vale is a peculiar place. Although it was created at the same time as the universe, it remains much 'newer,' far more vital. It is somehow smaller, more compact—I cannot explain it more than that—and its power remains close to that which caused the Creation. Creation power has diffused very thinly through our physical universe; in the Vale it is far more concentrated . . . more accessible. Does that answer your question, Boaz?"

He nodded, and Solvadale continued.

"Over the millennia since Creation, the Vale has continued to collect darkness unto itself. Life has formed within it. Dark life."

"Nzame," Yaqob whispered.

"Yes, Nzame is one manifestation of it. When we learned that Threshold would ultimately tap into the power of the Vale, then we understood the nature of the threat. We feared what eventually *did* happen. Something crossed over from the Vale into this world."

"But that is neither here nor there for our present tale," Xhosm put in. "Forty years ago we decided to do what could be done, even though we were not sure of the exact nature of the threat. We contacted Avaldamon."

"Avaldamon was the last known Elemental Cantomancer," Solvadale said. "I will explain cantomancy shortly, but for now just listen. He came to us here, noted our knowledge and heard our fears, and suggested a plan."

"No," Boaz whispered, and I took his hand. Oh, no, surely not. Surely.

"Avaldamon," Solvadale continued relentlessly, his eyes fierce, "said that Threshold was so powerful it would take one skilled in Elemental cantomancy *and* the power of the One to destroy it. A Cantomancer-Magus."

" 'How will we achieve that?' we asked," Gardar said quietly, and his eyes were sympathetic.

Solvadale continued, his gaze riveted on Boaz. "And Avaldamon said, 'I will breed a son with the blood of a Cantomancer yet with the training of a Magus.' Boaz, *listen* to me. That you were planned and bred to save us from Threshold does not lessen for one moment the fact that Avaldamon loved and treasured both your mother and you."

"I was abandoned to the Magi?" Boaz asked. "Left for thirty years to live a lie? To live a life that caused so much suffering? I *cannot* believe this!"

Strangely, Boaz's anger was supported by Yaqob. "He was as much a slave as Isphet or myself," he said. "And yet, somehow, more betrayed even than us."

"And Yaqob and Tirzah and myself," Isphet said, "were we all part of this program, too? Were we 'bred' and manipulated so we too could be 'used'?"

"Not by us, nor by Avaldamon," Caerfom replied. "But by the Soulenai, almost certainly."

There was a very long silence after that. The four of us battled anger, resentment, and bitterness. The Graces sat and watched us, gauging our reactions.

"You should know, Boaz," Solvadale eventually said, "that Avaldamon's death was not part of the plan. It was purely accidental. And catastrophic. It was meant that Avaldamon would stay at court, train you surreptitiously in the Elemental arts and cantomancy. Instead you were left directionless. You have survived unscathed—"

"Hardly unscathed," I said, but Solvadale ignored me.

"—which is a miracle, and gives us hope that eventually you *will* be able—"

"To do what I was *bred* for," Boaz finished, his eyes very, very cold.

"*Shetzah*, Boaz!" Xhosm cried, shocking us all. "We are all placed into life for a reason! Whether a Grace or a Cantomancer or a water-carrier. *All* for a reason, all reasons equally noble. Accept who and what you are. Have the sense for that, at least! Deny it, rage at it, and watch not only your own life crumble, but those of all about you!"

"We will not apologize for what we have done," Solvadale said, "and neither will the Soulenai. Accept that."

It took us a further hour of grating, resentful silence. But eventually, one by one, we nodded. Boaz last of all.

These revelations may have been unwelcome, but they accomplished what nothing else had—they welded the four of us into a tight, intensely loyal group. Many of the grievances that still remained between us this morning had been blasted into oblivion by what the Graces had told us.

Maybe that unity was what they'd wanted to accomplish above all else.

"Very well," Boaz said. "Explain what we are to do and who we are to become. The Soulenai said we were Cantomancers."

"Yes. We shall talk of the Cantomancers now." It was a safer topic than that which had preceded it, and Solvadale relaxed. "Caerfom will now speak," he said.

"There are two higher levels of the Elemental art," Caerfom said. "That of the Grace and that of the Cantomancer. Graces are sages. We think, we study, we advise. Cantomancers are 'doers.' They rarely stay among the community of the Abyss, but travel the world. They are magicians in a manner that Graces are not. Cantomancers can manipulate matter, create enchantments—Boaz, you are the best example of that." His mouth twitched. "Fetizza the frog, indeed."

"And the stone lock of hair," I said quietly, and explained that to the Graces.

They all looked surprised, but Caerfom nodded. "Boaz is extraordinarily talented, it is the strong blood of his father. Even without teaching, much of his talent shines through. Tirzah, you also demonstrate this talent."

"Oh, no. I? Why—"

"The Goblet of the Frogs," Xhosm said. "That is a magical object such as only one with Cantomancer blood could make, and only one with the special talent for creating. You can also read the Book of the Soulenai—until you were born, only Avaldamon had ever read that."

"It is in the Geshardi tongue," I said. "Anyone who can read Geshardi—"

"No," Solvadale broke in. "Only Cantomancers can read that book, and then only those gifted in special ways. Boaz, as Isphet and Yaqob, may never find the talent to do so. The book shall remain in your hands, Tirzah. It has picked you."

"And Yaqob and myself?" Isphet asked.

"You both have Cantomancer talent. Bred by long distant blood links to the Soulenai. It will require only very little training for both of you to demonstrate many of the necromantic skills Boaz and Tirzah have already displayed, although you may never achieve their depth and range."

Boaz spoke next. "You said that Avaldamon was the last known Elemental Cantomancer. Explain why there are no others. The four of us . . . are we the only ones you know of now?"

"Yes," Solvadale said. "You are the only ones known to us. Cantomancers are born, not made, and only born of the ancient bloodlines of the Soulenai themselves."

"You mean we *all* have Soulenai blood in us?" Isphet asked.

"Yes. You have yours from your father. Eldonor trained with us for some years. We thought for a while he would be a Cantomancer, but his blood was too weak. In you, as in your three companions, the Soulenai influence runs thick. We do not know why it surfaces in one generation and not another."

"Perhaps at the behest of the Soulenai themselves," Caerfom said. "Even Avaldamon could not be entirely sure that the child he bred would have the blood. But he should have trusted to the Soulenai."

"We have all spoken with the Soulenai over past months," I said, "yet they have said none of this to us."

"It was not ready to be said, Tirzah," Gardar responded tartly. "Today you have found it hard. How would you have reacted while close to Threshold? How would *Threshold* have reacted?"

Threshold. I lowered my eyes.

"Enough," Solvadale said. "We have wearied you. Come back tomorrow after the noon meal, and we will commence your training. We might not be Cantomancers, but we do have the skills to make one."

"Yes," Boaz said, rising. "Good. I need to learn the Song of the Frogs. I need to understand that."

"The Song of the Frogs?" Caerfom said. "We do not know that. Why is that important?"

Boaz and I just stared at them.

THIRTY-SIX

We sat in the cool of the evening by the green waters at the bottom of the Abyss: Boaz, Yaqob, Isphet, and I. Zabrze was off organizing with Naldi how returning messengers would be able to find the hills and the Abyss safely; Zabrze hoped that over the next few weeks he would get some word from neighboring lands, particularly from Prince Iraldur of Darsis, about help against Nzame.

"What is this Song of the Frogs, Boaz?" Yaqob asked.

I had explained something of the story and the Song to Isphet, but now Boaz and I told the tale of the Song of the Frogs, explained about the goblet, and how frogs had run through Boaz's life and through our relationship.

"The Soulenai told Tirzah that I must open myself to the Song of the Frogs, and Avaldamon told me that I must listen to the frogs, learn their Song, follow the path it shows me. I had thought that when I arrived here . . . that the Graces . . ."

"But there are no frogs here," Isphet said. "No song to listen to."

"Not quite," I replied. "We have the Goblet of the Frogs, the song reverberates through that. And we have Fetizza."

We all looked at the frog. She sat at the edge of the water, apparently in a half doze. If anything, in the past day she had doubled in size and was uglier than ever.

"Fetizza has done nothing but eat since her inception," Boaz said. "And look at her now. If she doesn't move in the next few minutes then I shall be convinced she's become part of the rock."

As if she had heard him, Fetizza slowly blinked her eyes, and hiccuped.

"Did you know what was going to come out of the goblet when you created an enchantment to lead us to water?" I asked Boaz.

"No. I really don't know what I did—and the same applies for when I changed that stone lock of hair, Tirzah."

Fetizza hiccuped again, her entire body rocking forward with the strength of it.

"Then we must trust the Graces," Isphet said firmly, and prepared to rise.

Fetizza hiccuped once more, and this time so strongly she gagged, gagged again, and then almost fell over with the force of a gigantic burp.

A small amber frog crawled out of her mouth, balanced precariously in a sliver of drool on her lower lip, then plopped into the water.

Isphet sank back down, staring.

Fetizza gagged again, rolled her eyes, and spat forth another amber frog.

"Kus!" Yaqob swore softly under his breath.

Fetizza coughed up three more frogs, settled herself against the rock, then went back to sleep.

"Well," Isphet said, rising to her feet, "it looks as though the frogs have come to the Abyss, Boaz."

The five amber frogs splashed about in the water at Fetizza's feet, then they swam out into the center of the river and we lost sight of them.

That evening, very, very faintly, we heard a croaking arise from the waters below us, echoing through the Abyss.

In the morning, a child who'd been watching Fetizza reported that she'd coughed up several more frogs for breakfast. All amber.

"Cantomancers are Elementals, but Elementals who have learned to manipulate the power contained within the elements," Solvadale explained that afternoon as we sat in the semicircle in the Water Hall.

Gardar took over. "The elements, particularly gems and metals, can be used for magical arts because they still contain much of the energy expended at the time of Creation. That is why they whisper and chatter. They are, as much as we, alive. All of you have felt this."

We nodded. Boaz now heard the chatter of metals, gems, and glass as much as I did. He kept the Goblet of the Frogs by our bed, and last night I woke to find him lying quietly, turning it over and over in his hands, listening to its song.

"Cantomancers manipulate that power," Gardar continued, "to effect changes about them. Boaz, you manipulated the power within the Goblet of the Frogs to create Fetizza—who, it seems, is more than a little magical herself. All of you, including Boaz, must learn to recognize and control that power. That is what we will begin with today."

Every afternoon for the next three weeks, the Graces taught us meditation exercises. Exercises to put us in touch, not only with our inner strength, but with the energy force within the elements. The exercises *sounded* simple but they cost us many an hour of effort and the occasional curse before we mastered them. I know Isphet and Yaqob, as Boaz and I, spent hours each evening practicing, and many a night Boaz and I would fall into bed too exhausted for loving.

But we were learning. At the end of the three weeks we could touch our inner strength and the power of whatever metal or glass object we held without apparent effort. Boaz remarked to me one evening that it was like seeing into the soul of the object whereas before we had only heard its whispering.

"Their souls glow with such radiance," he said. "Rainbows of color."

I nodded, admiring his ability. I could see something of that, but only glimpses. Boaz *was* powerful . . . or perhaps each of us saw and felt something a little different.

When the Graces understood that we had mastered the exercises that put us in touch with the elements' life forces, they then taught us to manipulate those forces.

More hours of practice, and many more curses. The meditation exercises had been simple compared to what we were asked to do now. We had to become one with the Elemental object we held so that we could almost merge with its life force.

"But don't let it go too far," Gardar warned, "don't merge completely, because then you risk becoming so *one* with the object that your soul and that of the object will merge . . . and your body will die."

"And then we would have an object, perhaps a metal band, with the soul of a Boaz or an Isphet," Solvadale said, "and that would do neither us nor you much good at all."

This teaching was hard for the Graces, even nerve-racking. They could not demonstrate, because they did not have the skills to do so, and they could not completely observe what we were doing or where we were going. They had to trust we would not overextend ourselves.

"Normally a Cantomancer would teach a Cantomancer," Xhosm said to us one day. "But you have only us. Eventually we hope that you can take on the task of teaching others."

"Hold this solid glass sphere," Caerfom said to me another day, "and ruffle the waters of the pool with the force within it. This should be easy for you, Tirzah."

Anything but. I touched the life force easily enough—I think I could have done it in my sleep—but to *direct* the power was far harder. I ruffled Caerfom's clothes, and I tangled Isphet's hair, but the waters remained disobligingly still.

"We will try again tomorrow," Caerfom sighed, and dismissed us for the day.

Seven weeks after we'd arrived, Zabrze woke Boaz and me late one night.

"Damn you, Zabrze," Boaz mumbled, "*you* may have nothing better to do here than sit about and grow lazy, but Tirzah and I have had a long and tiring day."

"Get up, Boaz, Tirzah," Zabrze said curtly, "and listen to what I have to say."

Boaz sat on the side of the bed, rubbing his eyes, and I

struggled into a sitting position, grasping the sheet to my breast. Were Boaz and I going to be bothered the rest of our lives by Zabrze's midnight intrusions?

"One of my runners came in tonight," Zabrze said.

"And?" Boaz asked.

"And bad news."

There was a sound at the door. Isphet, cradling Zhabroah, came in and sat down next to Zabrze. "I couldn't get back to sleep," she said.

"Get on with it," Boaz said to Zabrze, ignoring Isphet. "*What* news?"

"The man was one of those I'd sent to Darsis. He never got through. He'd taken a slightly different route to the others I'd sent; I can but hope *they* got through."

"Zabrze—"

"He traveled north-northeast, rather than northeast, and so he did not move as far east as the others would have, nor as quickly . . . do you understand what I'm saying?"

"Yes, yes. *Will* you get on with it?"

"Two weeks after he left the Juit estate he heard a rumbling in the night. He leaped to his feet, but he could see nothing, and the noise had disappeared. So he went back to sleep. In the morning he rose—"

"And saw stone," I said quietly.

"Yes," Zabrze said, his voice weary. "About five paces away—to the west—the land and everything in it had been turned to stone. He knew what it was. He'd been at Threshold when . . . well, there was nothing left alive in the land to the west. Nothing. All stone. Nzame has extended his power."

"How far from Threshold was he at this point, Zabrze?" Boaz asked.

"He would have been about three days march from it. Two weeks march from Lake Juit would have put him almost directly east from the pyramid."

"Setkoth," Boaz said.

"Oh, gods," I whispered.

"Yes," said Zabrze. "Setkoth must have been turned to stone long before."

Zabrze's other children would doubtless have been caught in the city by expanding stone. If Nzame hadn't rounded them up and eaten them beforehand. If they hadn't had the foresight to escape.

Zhabroah. Survivor.

"There's more," Zabrze said. "The stone frightened my man so much all he could think of was to get away as fast as he could. He turned directly east and traveled night and day. Five days after Nzame expanded, he sent some of his stone-men a-foraging.

"Luckily my man saw them before they saw him. He hid as they passed, and what he saw made him believe that it was more important to get this news back to me than try to continue on into Darsis."

Zabrze paused, collecting his courage. I glanced at Boaz, and he leaned close and put a comforting arm about me.

"It was a group of thirty-six stone-men. A regular unit. They marched—if you can call it that—in formation, shuffling and crumbling. Their features were malformed and craggy, their legs and arms thick and cumbersome. Their mouths, my man told me, were hung open as if in perpetual despair. They moaned, their heads lolling from side to side . . . moaning, moaning, moaning."

If merely the telling gave Zabrze so much distress, then how badly affected had been the man who'd done the *seeing*?

"They were led," Zabrze continued, "by a man who rode what my man could only describe as a shuffling, shapeless lump of rock, about the size of a donkey. This leader . . . was Chad-Nezzar."

"What?" Boaz and I cried together.

"A Chad-Nezzar not turned to stone, but irreparably altered by Nzame. He was quite mad, my man said. Cackling and singing about power and the glory of Nzame. He stroked his mount of rock, as if it were alive, and called it beloved. His body was scarred where he'd torn his studs and bangles from his flesh, and dreadfully sunburned."

We sat for a few minutes, absorbing the news.

"You shall have to tell the Graces of this," said Boaz eventually.

"Yes. And I shall have to think how I can combat an army of ten thousand stone-men, for Nzame must surely have that many."

"And Chad-Nezzar," I asked. "Has he the experience to lead an army?"

Zabrze shook his head, and opened his mouth to answer, but was forestalled by a voice from the doorway.

Solvadale.

"I heard," he said. "And I do not believe that Chad-Nezzar is just 'mad.' I think that now he may well be an extension of Nzame himself."

THIRTY-SEVEN

We doubled our efforts. Several days a week the Graces added mornings to our daily training sessions.

"Learn," they admonished. "Control."

It took another few weeks, but finally we grasped the skills needed not only to feel the life force within the elements, but to control it and direct it.

"Ruffle the waters using the glass sphere, Tirzah," Xhosm said, and I did.

"Create a square of red linen using the force within this metal ball," Caerfom told Yaqob, and he did.

Solvadale handed Boaz a slim gold chain. "Take the force within this chain and transform it to the sound of bells."

And the Water Hall pealed with a clarion of bells.

"Isphet," Gardar commanded, "use what this silver goblet gives you and weave a basket for me."

And so she did.

Of us all, Boaz was the most powerful, and accomplished his tasks with the most ease, but each of us improved daily.

Whatever object we used, whether metal, gem, or glass (and occasionally pottery, but the soul of pottery was dim and gave us little to work with), it was not altered by our use of its life energy.

"We do not completely understand how," Solvadale said

one afternoon. "Somehow the elements draw more energy into themselves from a primal force that we have yet to detect. They just replace what they have lost through your use."

"We can use anything Elemental?" Yaqob asked, slowly tossing the metal ball from hand to hand.

"Yes. But *some* things can be used for more. Again"— Solvadale turned to me—"I refer to the Goblet of the Frogs. Tirzah has a special talent to create objects of such magic within themselves that they, in turn, can be used for magic beyond, say, that ordinary ball. Even Boaz could not have conjured Fetizza out of that metal ball. A life-form, let alone a magical life-form is . . . difficult."

. We were silent, thinking of Fetizza. Each morning and evening more amber frogs slipped from her mouth. Now hundreds of her children swam and bounded up and down the entire Abyss, and their chorus echoed between the walls at dawn and dusk.

"What of stone?" Isphet asked. "Stone contains elements within it. Yet why can we not hear stone whisper?"

Gardar pulled out a small rock from under his bench. The Graces might not be wielders of magic, but I had yet to discover how they managed some of their sly manipulations.

"Feel it," Gardar said, handing it to Isphet. "Then pass it along."

Isphet held the rock, concentrating, then sighed and passed it to me. I rolled it between my hands, seeking, but knowing I would find nothing. I passed it to Boaz.

"Stone is dead," Solvadale said. "Even though it contains many elements, minerals, and sometimes even gems, there is something in the process whereby stone is formed that deadens whatever life it contains. You will never be able to use stone."

"Yet Nzame uses stone," Boaz said. "He turns land and life to stone . . . and his stone walks."

"We do not know why." Solvadale sighed. "Boaz, you have turned what Nzame created from stone back to hair. How? What did you do?"

"I am not sure. I only knew then that Tirzah needed her father's hair to farewell him, not a stone abomination. I just held it."

"If we knew, Boaz," Yaqob said, but with no trace of re-crimination in his voice, "then we might know how to com-bat Nzame's stone-men. How to turn stone to soil and life again."

Boaz lifted his head, nodded slightly at Yaqob, then looked at Solvadale. "You said that eventually you would tell us more of Nzame. More of the Vale. Will you do so now?"

Solvadale hesitated momentarily, sharing a glance with his fellow Graces. "Yes. Yes, we will. We can teach you no more. It will be your task to further develop what you have . . . and use it against Nzame."

And the Song of the Frogs? I could almost hear Boaz thinking. Will you tell me where I can learn to understand that? *How* I can use it against Nzame?

"It is time for you to see, and to use, the Chamber of Dreaming," Solvadale said.

They took us to the rear of the Water Hall, to a door that none of us had noticed previously. Behind it stretched a long corri-dor, carved deep into the rock of the Abyss.

We reached a series of steps, which the Graces led us down, then along another corridor, longer even than the first, then down yet more steps.

"We are very deep within the rock," Caerfom said quietly. "Once down these next steps we will enter a chamber that Graces regard as a place of mystery, but that Cantomancers regard as a place of power."

The four of us shared glances that were at once apprehen-sive and excited. Solvadale beckoned, and we followed the Graces down a further series of curved, pink rock steps.

Then we entered the most incredible chamber.

It was a roughly circular natural cavern, carved out by the passage of water over millions of years. Water tumbled from a fissure high in one wall to a pool in the center of the cham-ber, then flowed into a darkened tunnel in the opposite wall.

"This is where the river emerges from the rock," Caerfom said, then pointed to the tunnel. "And there it flows to emerge into the Abyss."

But while the water was wondrous, it was not the most re-markable thing about the chamber.

The walls were encrusted with every gem possible to imagine, and flowing down their surface were rivulets of metals, some pure, some oxidized. Their iridescence lit the chamber with a soft glow.

The energy, the *power,* within this cavern was astounding.

"We come here to contemplate," Solvadale said. "But you can do more. My friends, I have brought you here for two reasons. First, so that you may experience the wonder and power of the Chamber of Dreaming, but second so that you may use the power within the chamber to understand more of the Vale and of Nzame. It is easier to show you than to explain . . . but a warning."

I dragged my eyes away from the incredible walls to Solvadale. His face was composed, but his eyes were worried.

"What we are about to do here will call tremendous power into use . . . be careful of it. You are yet inexperienced; do not overstep the bounds of your learning." He took a deep breath. "Use of this power will also almost certainly attract Nzame's attention. Be wary of him.

"Now, Isphet, I want you to lead this rite as you have led so many."

"You want me to use the water."

"Yes. But instead of using metal powders to cast into the water, you will use the power of the elements surrounding you."

"Yes, I understand."

"Good." Solvadale paused and looked about at us carefully. "The four of you must combine the power you have and that you draw from the walls. In this rite you must act as one. Lean on each other, draw strength from each other. Can you do that?"

Eventually we all nodded.

"Yes," Boaz said, "we can do it."

"Isphet," Solvadale said, and took her hand. "Normally in any Elemental rite you would contact the Soulenai. Touch the borders of the Place Beyond. Today I do not want you to do that."

"Then what . . . ?"

"Today, as the waters swirl and you meld power with your three companions, I want you to touch the Vale."

She physically recoiled from him. "But the Vale is dark . . . evil."

"Touch, I said, not enter. I want you to do this—and it must be brief—because it is going to be one of the only ways you will understand Nzame. I could spend a day telling you what I know of the Vale and of Nzame, but it would be a poor thing compared to the knowledge and understanding you will gain with a momentary touching of the Vale itself."

"It is dangerous," Boaz said.

"Yes, it is dangerous." Solvadale's eyes were very direct. "But you will all face danger at some point, and I do not want to shield you here. Draw power from the elements about you in this cavern, but more importantly, draw power from your companions. Isphet, are you ready?"

She took a deep breath. "Yes."

"And you, Boaz? Tirzah? Yaqob?"

We looked at each other, sharing small smiles of support. "Yes, we are ready."

"Then begin, Isphet."

She was very calm, very sure. She shook her hair out, as I did mine, and locked eyes with each of us in turn. As she did, we touched power with the elemental energy about us—and, oh! it was so powerful!—and then touched each other, sharing power, supporting.

Isphet turned to the great pool, then cast out her arm.

The water trembled, then swirled, gathering speed until it roared about the pool like a great, angry animal.

Colors flared, blue, red, gold, green, and intermixed, caught by the raging waters until they were just one swirl of light.

I could feel the others, inside and about me, and we took comfort and strength from each other, and shared the strength among our fellows. Somehow, somewhere, I was aware of the Graces watching us, but they were inconsequential now.

There were only the four of us, now as one, and the swirling waters.

Isphet continued to direct, but I could feel Boaz's power underpinning all of us, and I think Isphet responded to some wish of Boaz's, for she did not take us immediately to the Vale.

Instead we saw Ashdod.

The land.

We saw as if from high in the sky, as if we were birds circling on a thermal, seeking a safe place to roost.

But there was no place to rest.

We wept, for Ashdod had been largely turned to rock.

Stone radiated out from Threshold like a cancerous web. It stretched almost to the borders of Ashdod, and in places fingers of stone probed into neighboring realms. The stone had spread over land, city, and palm alike, only the great serpentine of the Lhyl remaining free.

But the reed banks were stone, and the frogs silent.

Bands of stone-men shuffled to and fro, crumbling, moaning. Sometimes they shuffled with no apparent purpose, sometimes they marched bands of screaming, terrified people toward Threshold.

Nzame screamed—*Feed me!*

And we recoiled.

Lake Juit, I thought, and somehow that thought communicated itself to my three companions. The next instant we saw the lake, lapping gently, mournfully, at great stands of stone reed banks and marshes. Stone Juit birds lay dead on the banks and, in places, at the foot of the shallow lake.

I cried, and I felt the others cry with me.

The house, the beautiful, beautiful house where once I'd dreamed of a peaceful life with Boaz, lay sagging under a mantle of stone.

As our vision sharpened I saw a stone-man stumbling, shuffling, moaning along the stone path to the stone landing, waving his arms to and fro, his mouth hanging open in despair.

Memmon, as trapped by Nzame as every other life-form in Ashdod, doomed to shuffle between river and house, house and river, looking for visitors come to disturb his peace, looking for someone come to release him from his death.

Enough! Boaz cried, and we all agreed. Enough.

The Vale, Isphet said, and so we directed our power and our vision.

The waters before us swirled black, eating all color and light within the chamber.

Vision faded.

Cold seeped into my being, threatening to freeze the marrow in my bones. We traveled through a great . . .

Nothingness, Boaz said, and we agreed. This was a nothingness between worlds.

Be strong, Isphet called to each of us, *for if we falter here . . .*

We doubled our efforts, clinging to the power of the elements about us and to each other's power, sharing, reassuring.

Then the blackness changed. It was still cold, but there was a *something* here, rather than a nothing.

We are at the edge of the Vale, Boaz said. *Let us explore its edges first. Gain some understanding, before we enter.*

We thought that a good idea, and I wondered if we need enter at all.

We must, Tirzah. Isphet. *We must see.*

But first the edges. This was a tightly bound space, and I remembered what Isphet had said about the Vale when we'd queried her while still in Gesholme. It was a place of darkness and despair, and here, so close, I could understand that well. She'd said that it was a place deliberately sequestered from our world, as from all worlds.

Not anymore. Not now that Threshold had touched it.

Very gently, very, very carefully, we entered. It was a probe, a brief touch, nothing more, yet we reeled back in horror, retreating to the nothingness.

What we saw in the Vale was indescribable. It was all the bleakness and darkness that any could imagine, and then more. It was all the despair and misery that could be generated by living beings, and then magnified a million times.

But worst of all was that whatever was inside the Vale *thought.*

It lived, and it planned.

And now it had a fingerhold in Threshold. Nzame was terrible, but he was only a fraction of what the Vale contained, and what threatened to seep into our world.

And then into the Place Beyond.

It was the Soulenai, with us now, comforting, pleading.

Destroy it. Tear it apart. Boaz, help us, help us, help us, for the stone now laps at our borderlands. Listen to the frogs, learn what they have to tell you, listen, listen, listen . . .

HOW? Boaz screamed. *Tell me HOW!*

Before they could answer, there was another voice.

I see you.

The Soulenai fled, and we four milled in confusion, still somewhere within that nothingness, somewhere close to, but not quite within, the Vale.

I see you.

The waters screamed, and churned about the chamber.

I see you.

Turn your backs to him. That was Boaz, steady, calm now, bolstering Isphet's control. *Turn your backs. He sees, but he cannot—*

Wrong, stupid man. Wrong. I can touch, too. Feel?

Dread trailed through our souls. Icy, malevolent, toying with us.

To me, concentrate on me. Do not listen to him. He cannot harm us.

Wrong! I can—

Something seized my mind. Boaz. Grabbing, dragging, saving. He literally dragged us back from the nothingness, back from Nzame's touch, back into the chamber.

And yet . . . I could feel something racing after us . . . racing . . .

"Break it, Isphet!" Boaz screamed aloud as we blinked and reeled, our senses confused, our vision blurring, our hearts pounding.

I can tou—

"Break it!"

Isphet brought her hand down in a quick chopping motion, and the waters stilled.

All of us, even the Graces who had been watching in increasing horror, sank down to the crusty floor of the chamber.

"Thank you, Boaz," Yaqob said. "Thank you for bringing us back."

I put my hands to my face. I could not imagine the power—or the presence of mind—that Boaz had just demonstrated. If he hadn't acted when he did, Nzame would surely have followed us into this chamber, stepped into this chamber with us.

"That is the Vale," Solvadale eventually said, his color returning to normal. "And that is Nzame. He is one of the many entities that exists within the Vale. The one who seized the opportunity that Threshold was offering. Others, as you have seen, may yet follow once Nzame clears the path for them."

"Did you know," Boaz asked, raising his head, "that Nzame was going to see us . . . touch us?"

"We suspected it," Xhosm replied. "And we dreaded it, but this was a test for you. If you could survive this encounter, then you would have the potential to survive the ultimate battle with Nzame."

"Do you mean," I asked, "that you risked not only us, but *everyone* in this chamber and ultimately within the Abyss?"

"If you had failed," Solvadale said quietly, "and we had been killed, then it would only have been a death that was coming for us anyway. But"—he shrugged—"you have done well. As well as we had hoped. Now, is everyone going to continue to sit on this floor?"

We returned to the Water Hall.

"Boaz," Caerfom asked, "what were the Magi thinking of to so tap into the Vale?"

Boaz sighed and rubbed his face. "Threshold is a bridge of sorts. At one end it was supposed to touch Infinity, but the Magi believed it needed added power to do that. So the other end of the bridge was designed to touch the Vale. We did *not* know what the Vale truly was. We thought it a well of power, the power of Creation."

"It is what was set *aside* during Creation," Solvadale said. "It is what those supreme beings who directed Creation saw was miserable and bleak and so dammed up into the place that is the Vale. Now, the Magi have opened a door into it."

"We just thought it a well," Boaz repeated quietly. "A repository. Unfeeling, insensitive power. We did not realize that it *thought.* Or that it hungered for escape."

THIRTY-EIGHT

We sat, he and I, on a cool stone shelf beneath an overhang of rock. At our feet lapped the waters of the river. Above us the walls of the Abyss soared into the evening sky. The people of the Abyss were relaxing from their day's chores, sharing meals with friends, neighbors, lovers. I wondered if they shared laughter or not.

Not, I thought, or very little, for the mood of the Abyss was subdued. Stone crept inexorably toward us. Scouts and sentries reported that much of the Lagamaal Plains between the Lhyl and the Abyss Hills was now swallowed by Nzame's stone. If not this week, then the next, or perhaps six weeks from now, Nzame would snatch at this idyllic life. Here lay food.

Here *we* lay.

"Every time we touch the power as a group, Nzame knows," Boaz said quietly. "Lake Juit, now here."

"What do we do, Boaz?"

"Do? Do? Oh, Tirzah, don't you know? I am supposed to combine the power of the One with the *cursed* Song of the Frogs and save us all."

"Boaz, shush now, you will understand eventually—" I began.

"'Eventually' is what neither you nor I nor any one of those stumbling stone-men have. Oh, gods, Tirzah. Did you see him? Memmon? Shuffling up and down that path? Was he looking for me to save—"

"Stop it, Boaz! It is enough to have Zabrze wander corridors day and night fretting about his inactivity without you doing it as well!"

Zabrze had heard very little for weeks. Stone everywhere, expanding east and west, north and south, and stone-men, shuffling, shuffling, shuffling, but as yet nothing from those men he'd sent to neighboring realms. Had they got through? Or were they even now shuffling, shuffling . . . moaning?

I regretted the sharpness of my tone, and I slipped my arms about Boaz and held him tight.

We sat in silence, watching as a frog crawled from the river. Fetizza's frogs now numbered in their thousands, and populated the river the entire length of the Abyss. They had grown slightly in size, but they retained their beautiful amber hue. As if, almost, they *were* the frogs from the goblet come to life.

Three days had gone by since our experience in the Chamber of Dreaming. The four of us had met on several occasions to discuss what to do, but Isphet and Yaqob had as few answers as Boaz and I.

The key was the Song of the Frogs. But where was the key to use the key?

Fetizza appeared as if out of nowhere, making us jump, and bounded to the edge of the water. She was massive now, the size of a small dog, and uglier than imaginable. Warts wobbled over her mud-brown skin, splotches rusted apace by the day, yet her mouth grew wider and grinned more happily than ever.

And her eyes remained beautiful, and she blinked them slowly at us as she settled her bulk comfortably on a rock close by the river.

She yawned, and I expected to see yet another amber frog crawl to her lip and drop to freedom, but none appeared, and Fetizza closed her mouth with a snap.

Up and down the Abyss amber frogs crawled out of the river. As one they cleared their throats.

With a huge sound that was half belch, half croak, Fetizza began the chorus. She almost toppled from her rock with the force of it, and had to grip tight with her toes, but she recovered, and as her much tinier companions began their glorious peal she opened her mouth and croaked away happily.

"Are you sure," Boaz whispered in my ear, "that with your aptitude for languages you never learned frog croak at some point?"

"We had very few frogs in Viland, beloved, and those we did have were too cold to croak. Now whale song, *that* I can teach you."

We listened to the frogs' evening chorus for some time. It

had a beauty all its own. The croaking and muttering of a single frog was often an unlovely sound, but when frogs gathered into their hundreds and thousands, and sang to the moon or the sun, then their croaking attained something . . . magical.

But what?

I relaxed, half dreaming in Boaz's arms.

The frogs' chorus altered slightly, but I didn't pay it much attention until I felt Boaz tense.

"Boaz?"

"Shush, Tirzah. Listen."

There was excitement in his voice, and I sat up; carefully, not wanting to make a sound.

He was staring at the river, but his eyes were unfocused, and I realized he was concentrating intensely.

The frogs were still choraling, but there was a difference. They sang slower than normal, and they sang in distinct parts. A group of some thirty, five paces south from us, sang a throaty bass, while more, closer to Fetizza, sang in a faster tempo, and with sweeter voices. And so on, up and down the Abyss. Taken together it still sounded very much like the usual frogs' chorus . . . but if one listened closely . . .

Boaz reached out for my hand, and I took it. He was trembling with anticipation.

"Tirzah . . . Tirzah . . ."

He stopped, and though I wanted to take his shoulders and shake it out of him, I knew he was still concentrating, still trying to grasp the final meaning.

"Oh, gods," he whispered, and he paled and then shuddered. "Oh, gods."

"Boaz? *Boaz*?"

There was a movement to my right. Yaqob and Isphet. They would have heard the difference in the frogs' chorus, and they may even have felt a little of Boaz's excitement. Since that day in the Chamber of Dreaming we had found ourselves sharing thoughts and touches of emotion from time to time.

I shook my head at them, warning them to remain silent, and they sank down on the rock, their eyes on Boaz.

He had let my hand go now, and was leaning forward. His eyes darted up and down the Abyss, seeking out individual groups of frogs. Every so often he would mutter, "Yes . . . yes . . ."

And then, stunningly, in one single instant the frogs stopped. Every one of them in that Abyss shut its throat . . . and stared back at Boaz.

"Yes, yes," he breathed. "I think I understand. One more time. Please, one more time."

The frogs, again as one, opened their mouths in chorus.

Yaqob shifted irritably, and Isphet laid a hand on his arm. "Wait," she mouthed, then locked eyes with me.

Do you understand it, Tirzah?

I shook my head. *I can hear the difference, as can you and Yaqob. But I do not understand.*

It is slower, that is the difference.

Yes, and far more deliberate. Listen, they speed up now, and it sounds like normal.

Yes. Yes, I hear it.

We sat it through, alternatively watching the frogs and Boaz, and when it was finished, and the frogs had slipped beneath the waters and Fetizza had gone to sleep, I leaned forward. "Well?"

Boaz hesitated. "You are not going to like this," he said, "but . . ."

"But?" Yaqob asked. "But *what*?"

"But the Song of the Frogs is a mathematical formula."

"What?" the three of us cried as one.

"The Song of the Frogs is a mathematical formula. No, wait, it makes sense. Music has ever been closely allied with mathematics. All musical harmonies can be expressed as mathematical formulas. *Shetzah!* Why didn't I understand earlier that the reverse is true as well?"

Boaz took a deep breath, then forged on, impatient in his excitement. "Listen to me. You have heard Tirzah tell the tale of the Song of the Frogs from the Book of the Soulenai."

Yaqob and Isphet nodded, curbing their own impatience.

"Well, as thanks for weeping the tears that created the Lhyl River, the frogs gave the Soulenai a gift. A song. A path. A path to the Place Beyond. The Soulenai understood it, used it, and they were transported there."

"Yes, but . . ." I began, but Boaz waved me into silence.

"And isn't that exactly what the Magi have been doing at Threshold, except they built a building, a formula within itself, as a path to Infinity? Threshold is a mathematical formula expressed in physical form to provide a path into Infinity. The Song of the Frogs is a mathematical formula expressed in music to provide a path into the Place Beyond."

"That's . . . wonderful!" I cried. "Do you mean that if we learn the formula, then we can travel to and fro between this world and the Place Beyond?"

"Is that true, Boaz?" Yaqob said. "*Can* we?"

"No."

"But you said—"

"What I said"—and his voice was tight with strain—"was that the Song of the Frogs is a mathematical formula that will provide a pathway to the Place Beyond. Create an opening between two dimensions, if you will. But there is a catch, as there was always a catch with the Threshold formula—although none of the Magi minded about that."

"And the catch is . . . ?" Isphet asked quietly.

"It's a one-way trip," Boaz said. "You use it once, and once only, and you are transported into Infinity, or the Place Beyond, depending on which formula you use. But once there, you stay there. That is why the Soulenai have never come back."

We were silent, contemplating this.

"Can you teach us this Song?" Yaqob asked. "Can you show us how it works?"

"I can't see why not. Listen . . ." and Boaz expounded the mathematical properties of the Song of the Frogs in exquisite detail.

None of us understood a word he said.

"Boaz, can you explain it in simple terms? None of us have had any training in the mathematics. And what you say . . ."

Boaz frowned. "That *was* the simple explanation. But I will try to put it a different way."

All we learned was that only someone with a mathematical background could understand this cursed Song.

Boaz finished, and looked inquiringly at us.

We all shook our heads.

"It is impossible," I ventured, and Boaz snapped in frustration.

"It is *simple*! Have you no grasp of even the—"

"No, Boaz, we have not," Isphet said with the utmost dignity. Then she smiled, trying to relax us all. "No wonder Avaldamon wanted you Magus-trained. There was no other way to train a Cantomancer in the way of the Song of the Frogs, and if the Song is as critical to the destruction of Nzame as is intimated by the Soulenai, well . . ."

"Boaz," I eventually asked, my voice very quiet. "Do you have any idea *how* to use the Song of the Frogs to destroy Nzame?"

He hesitated, and that hesitation gave the lie to his answer. "No. No, I have no idea at all."

We were married, he and I, together with Isphet and Zabrze, two nights later.

Eldonor had been arranging a ceremony for weeks. He had wanted the best for the four of us, and the best is what he gave us.

All the people of the Abyss attended, and that created no problems of space, as we were married at the water's edge, with people lining the balconies of the Steps and frogs leaping and splashing in the shallows at our feet.

Among those watching were the five thousand who had followed Isphet across the barren Lagamaal, trusting her to lead them to a better life than they'd enjoyed thus far. I had been worried how they'd be assimilated into the Abyss, but there had been no problems at all. Most were skilled craftworkers or willing laborers, others experienced soldiers, and no community resents having such an infusion into its ranks. There was food enough for all, for the river was bountiful and the grain fields above accommodating, and there was no lack of space to put the extra people.

And most, if not all, of the five thousand had slipped back into the ancient ways with ease. There had been only one official and allowable religion in Ashdod, that of the One, and none from Gesholme with intimate acquaintance with Threshold could wait to discard it.

New marriages were rife among the five thousand, but Eldonor and the people of the Abyss wanted that of Zabrze and Isphet, and Boaz and me, celebrated with a little more aplomb than many others had been.

Lamps glinted up and down the steps, and scented candles floated in the river, making Boaz and me exchange secret smiles. It was a shame, I thought, that the river was not quite as private as that vaulted pool had been.

Yaqob stood quietly to one side. I thought he might not come, for surely this would be painful for him. But he did, and Boaz and I thanked him silently for that.

Our marriage was celebrated by Eldonor. The Graces played no part in such ceremonies, although they had come to witness. Traditionally, it was the father who conducted a marriage ceremony, and Eldonor was the only father available to all four of us. He led the vows that we repeated, and he took our hands and joined them, and we were married, and that felt very right.

There was music and song from the masses above, and a large congratulatory croak from Fetizza. As I watched Boaz observing the frog, I wondered at the sense of loss that once again swamped me.

Who would I lose Boaz to? Nzame? Or the Place Beyond?

We had barely managed to consummate our marriage, barely managed to catch our breath, when Zabrze—*again!*—burst into our chamber.

"Stone-men," he gasped. "Approaching the Abyss Hills."

And then he was gone.

THIRTY-NINE

I scrambled out of bed only a breath behind Boaz.

"Shetzah!" he cried as he saw me fumbling for my robe.

"Stay here, Tirzah!"

"No. I did not study the arts of cantomancy to lie in bed and worry about my husband. No. I am coming."

"Then you will stay behind the soldiers, where it is safest."

"I will be where I am most needed, Boaz. Gods! Is it dawn already?"

Boaz managed a grin as he slipped his sandals on. "You've kept me up all night, wife. I should be cross."

I returned his smile. "Come on. Zabrze is undoubtedly halfway to the top of the cliffs by now."

Not quite. Zabrze had paused to rally the units of his soldiers who'd fled Gesholme with him.

We found them crowding the stairwells before us, swords in hands, faces creased in concentration. Boaz, just ahead of me, slowed down.

"I wish you had stayed behind, Tirzah."

"None of us could, Boaz," came a voice, and Yaqob appeared out of the gloom, joined a moment later by Isphet.

"A poor way to spend your wedding night, Isphet," he said, and she managed a wry grin.

The climb to the top of the Abyss was taxing, made more so by the worry about what might await us once we got there.

I glanced behind me to Isphet. "What does . . . Zabrze know?" I managed between gasps of breath.

"Not much. Scouts . . . returned late last . . . night. They'd seen . . . stone-men . . . approaching . . . across the . . . Lagamaal."

"Many?"

"Not an army, but enough."

"Nzame."

"Yes."

I grabbed at the balustrade, thinking that the months we'd spent in the Abyss had made a weakling of me, and then there was blessedly cold, free air, and Boaz reaching and helping me, and then Isphet through the door at the top of the stairwell.

I stood taking great gulping breaths.

"Over there." Boaz pointed.

Zabrze was twenty or thirty paces away, snapping commands to his soldiers. He was dressed for battle, wearing only a brief hip wrap, sword belt, sandals, and a band about his head holding his braids away from his eyes.

There was nothing left of the man who had held such gentle conversation with me, who looked at Isphet with such love. This was the commander.

I was vaguely surprised to see Kiamet there as well, and looking as efficient and almost as commanding as Zabrze. I realized that Kiamet, for all his unassuming manner, held important rank within Zabrze's force.

Zabrze talked swiftly with several of the sentries who'd been posted throughout the Abyss Hills, then he shouted a command. The units wheeled away, running down the gully toward the first of the canyons at a smart trot.

"Come on," Yaqob muttered, and we were off after the soldiers, lifting robes and wishing, for my part at least, that I'd thought to wear something more sensible.

The sun had risen by now, but shadows still lay long through the gully. We had to leap and twist to avoid rocks, and more than once I heard someone curse as they failed to lift a toe high enough.

When we'd first arrived here, it had taken us a day to walk into the hills to reach the Abyss, but fear and the downhill slope now lent us speed, and by midmorning we reached a spot from where we could view the lower slopes and the plain stretching west.

Zabrze hurried the four of us behind a low rocky outcrop, then waved a hand out over the plain.

Still distant, but clearly visible as they were caught by the full force of the sun, was a contingent of stone-men shuffling across the final stretch of plain. There were some forty or forty-five of them, regularly ordered in ranks of five.

They were led by a horror that none of us had seen before, or even imagined.

It was clearly man-shaped, but its entire, utterly naked body was composed of that black, glassy substance with which Threshold had fused its inner walls. I could vaguely see the rocks it had just passed shadow through its body. The stone-men shuffled, their gait limited and stiff, but this blackened, fused man walked lithely and easily through the rocks, twisting his head this way and that. His eyes were as black as the rest of him, and I wondered if he saw, or just sensed.

Yaqob, immediately to my right, gasped and pointed. "Tirzah? See his nose!"

The horror angled his head to the right, and I saw a familiar bulbous outline.

"Kofte!"

Boaz froze. "*Shetzah!* What has Nzame *done* to him?"

Zabrze had heard our whispering and now scrambled over. Yaqob pointed out the black, glassy man. "It's Magus Kofte. From Threshold."

"Boaz?" Zabrze asked. "Explain."

"I cannot, Zabrze. This blackness, this substance, is something we'd never seen before. Threshold transformed its inner walls with this melted glass and stone. I do not know what to call it. But it is very hard. Unbreakable."

"Would Nzame have done this to all the Magi?"

Boaz shrugged. "Maybe. I cannot tell. Perhaps the favored few are thus transformed."

"Whatever the case," Zabrze said, "they are getting closer. It's not a large force."

"It must have been close when Nzame sensed our presence in the Chamber of Dreaming," I said, and Zabrze nodded.

"No doubt he has others on the move. Kiamet?" Zabrze moved off, and talked quietly with Kiamet and two other of his soldiers.

I was struck by the change in Zabrze. Since we'd arrived at the Abyss he had been at a loss, unsure of what he should do next. Zabrze was a man who hated inactivity, especially when Ashdod was gripped by such darkness, but there had been little he could do save make sure his people had settled in and wait for news.

Now he had a target for his frustrations. This was a Zabrze I'd not seen before, not even during the panic of the evacuation of Gesholme or the trip down the Lhyl. He had slipped easily into the role of commander, his movements economical, his decisions quick yet considered.

Each of his men had one eye on the approaching stonemen, one eye on their commander.

Zabrze signaled a group of some forty soldiers and they angled off to the south, moving swiftly, using the rocks as cover. Another group moved north, then Zabrze shifted the larger number of his command farther down the slopes. We slipped quietly behind, as careful as the soldiers not to be seen, and knotting our robes so that our legs were relatively free.

"I wish I had a sword," Boaz whispered.

"You idiot!" I whispered back, keeping my voice low only with strenuous effort—and even then a nearby soldier glanced warningly at me. "What do you think you're going to do—"

"What am I going to do crouched behind a rock?" Boaz hissed, then scrambled forward to Zabrze's side, Yaqob a step behind him.

Isphet restrained me from following them. "Wait, Tirzah. Wait and see. Zabrze isn't going to let Boaz or Yaqob rush into action. Both would be more hindrance than help."

The two groups of soldiers were now inching into position, hoping to attack the stone-men in a pincer movement.

What had once been Kofte stopped dead, catching a movement to his left. The stone-men halted behind him, although they kept rocking from to side to side, their moans reaching us on the northwesterly breeze.

Kofte opened his arms wide, tilted his head back, and wailed.

It was one of the most dreadful sounds I had ever heard; we all stiffened, and Isphet clapped her hands to her ears. Before me Boaz spoke frantically to Zabrze.

The two groups of soldiers attacked. They rushed the stone-men from both sides, each man running in a half crouch, sword in one hand, the other extended for balance.

Kofte wailed again, and waved his arms about in great cartwheels.

Then every one of the stone-men did the same. They opened their stone mouths and issued forth great wails, even more heartrending than their moans, and waved their arms about.

At another wail from Kofte, the stone-men broke ranks and divided into two groups, lumbering toward the attacking soldiers.

The stone-men's movements were ponderous, but effective. The soldiers attacked, but their swords splintered on impact with the stone bodies. As did the soldiers' heads. The stone-men did nothing save wail and wave their arms about, but that was enough to shatter the heads of a dozen soldiers, their blood and brains splattering across the stone bodies nearest them.

Zabrze leaped to his feet and screamed a retreat, then turned and waved his men among the rocks back into the first of the canyons.

Isphet and I scrambled back with them, and found ourselves huddled with Boaz, Yaqob, Zabrze, and three of his senior men in a small defile.

Another commander, who'd led the southern group against the stone-men, joined us.

"Eighteen men lost, Chad-Zabrze," he said, wiping the sweat from his forehead. "And the stone-men continue into the first of the slopes. I'm sorry we did not succeed. We—"

"You could do nothing. Not against such sorcery," Zabrze said, and waved the man to sit down. "Boaz?"

Boaz looked at Yaqob, Isphet, and myself, then shook his head tiredly. "I—we—need to study one close, Zabrze. None of us can do anything from this distance, and with no information."

There was a shout from the mouth of the canyon. Kofte had appeared, his blackness seeming to absorb all the heat from the sun, and behind him lumbered the stone-men. They were back in orderly ranks, none the worse for their adventure.

Zabrze swore. "We can do nothing save—"

"We can push them over," Kiamet suggested softly.

Every head spun in his direction.

"What?" Zabrze said.

"We can push them over," Kiamet repeated. "Look at those stone-men, Chad-Zabrze. They lumber and they shuffle. They do not like this rocky terrain. Their feet scarcely clear the ground. I would imagine that if one were pushed over, he would just lie there and moan and wail and wave his limbs about . . . and be no danger unless we came within grasping distance."

"We'd have to get close enough to push," Zabrze said carefully, "and I have already lost eighteen."

"We could roll rocks down the walls of the canyon,"
Yaqob said.

"And stretch trip ropes across the narrow passage," Boaz
added.

"And if men could get close enough to loop rope over their
waving arms," I said, "or even their necks, then you could just
pull them down."

"I thought you lot were supposed to be Cantomancers,"
Zabrze said, "yet here you are remembering childish games
to defeat our enemy."

But a grin took the sting out of his words, and he turned
aside to pass orders to his commanders.

"Make sure you leave at least one alive," Boaz said hurriedly as the commanders moved off, "for I need to study
them."

"Leave one *alive*, brother? I would appreciate knowing
how to *kill* one first."

Then he was off.

Runners left for the Abyss and rope, and as the sun passed
its noon crest, Zabrze eventually withdrew us all toward the
final gorge before the great chasm.

He waited impatiently for the rope, then he set men to
work even as shouts warned us of the stone-men's imminent
arrival.

Kofte was careful leading his force into the gorge, twisting
his head from side to side and up and down. He reminded me
of the puppet dolls I'd seen perform in Viland's marketplaces
on fair days, only those had not had the air of such malevolence that Kofte now wore. Nor had their porcelain hands
clenched into such fists of rage.

The stone-men were very close now, and I could see that
whatever features they had once worn as living men had been
flattened and blurred by the transformation to stone. Their
bodies were thick, their limbs stumpy, the joints at knees and
elbows so stiff they were almost unworkable. No wonder they
could hardly lift the blocks that had once been feet.

Zabrze let Kofte lead the stone-men well into the gorge. He
waited, tense, crouched behind a rock, then gave a hand signal
and a rope leaped into the air from the dust amid the stone-

men's shuffling feet. Men at both sides of the canyon pulled it taut as it reached shin height, and an entire rank of stone-men went down, their flailing arms catching those to either side, their crashing bodies subsequently pulling down several more before them.

Kofte shrieked and twisted about, his own arms flailing as he saw eight or nine of his command helpless on the ground.

Kiamet had been right. The stone-men could not rise again, their weight and their rigidity keeping them down. They moaned anew, and waved their arms about, but it did them no good.

Kofte rallied those of his stone-men still upright. As he shrieked, so they moved out of rank and shuffled in all directions, arms flailing in such great arcs that I thought if they'd been lighter they may well have launched themselves skyward.

Zabrze signaled again, and groups of some nine or ten men moved carefully forward. Their useless swords were sheathed at their sides, but they were armed with lengths of stout rope.

Each group stalked a stone-man, waiting until he had his back turned, then the soldiers threw loops of rope over stone arms or necks, and pulled the creature to the ground.

Then, once the stone-man had crashed down, the group loosened the rope and set off after another.

"I must help!" I heard Yaqob mutter beside me, and then he was off, darting between rocks to join in the fray.

"No!" I cried, and would have rushed after him but for Isphet who wrapped tight arms about me.

And then I realized Boaz had gone.

I looked frantically about. I heard Kofte shriek, and I whipped my head around.

"No!" I moaned.

Boaz was approaching Kofte, slowly, half crouched, with not even a sword in his hand.

"No," I moaned again, and at that moment Isphet shrieked. *"Yaqob!"*

I looked, and then screamed myself.

Yaqob, foolhardy Yaqob, had thought to topple a stone-man by himself. He had succeeded in that the stone-man he'd

selected *had* toppled over . . . but he had fallen on Yaqob, and
now Yaqob was all but invisible save for a red stain spreading
out from beneath the stone-man—and I did not think that
blood belonged to Nzame's creature.

FORTY

Isphet's arms loosened and I tore myself free—then hesitated, wanting to rush to both men at once.

"To Yaqob, you fool!" Isphet hissed. "Boaz still stands
and can look after himself."

My hesitation gone, I scrambled across the gorge, Isphet at
my side. Soldiers and stone-men still wove about between the
rocks, and we had to twist away as one stone-man shuffled toward us.

For an instant I had a close look at his face, and such was
the despair I saw there I cried out and would have halted had
not Isphet pulled me away.

"This way, fool girl!" she cried, and dragged me between
two groups of struggling stone-men and soldiers.

I stubbed my toe badly on a rock and grunted with the pain,
but Isphet's grip merely tightened more, and she hauled me
hobbling to where the stone-man atop Yaqob.

At first I thought he was completely crushed. There was
nothing save the red stain pooling beside the stone-man—still
moaning and waving his arms impotently in the air.

Isphet ducked around to the other side of the stone-man.
"Tirzah! *Quick!*"

I dropped beside her, the grasping stone fingers narrowly
missing my hair.

Yaqob, ashen but still conscious, lay crushed from the
thighs down by the stone weight atop him.

"Get out of here," he grated. "There's no point in you—"

"Shut up," Isphet said, and rested her hand on his chest.

"His heart races, but still beats strong," she said to me. "The stone-man's weight has stopped fatal bleeding."

"What are we going to do?" I whispered, taking Yaqob's hand between my own.

"Wait. Wait until some of those soldiers are free to help us."

Isphet lifted Yaqob's head so that it rested in her lap, and she stroked his hair and murmured to him, trying to soothe away his pain with her voice.

"If only . . ." I muttered, and then I saw a soldier lying dead a few paces away.

"Tirzah!" Isphet cried as I leaped to my feet, and Yaqob's eyes fluttered open in alarm, but I did not go far. I snatched the soldier's sword and sank back down by Yaqob's side again.

"Isphet, come on, we can use this to do something for Yaqob."

"What?"

I thought frantically. None of us had ever used our powers to heal, yet Boaz had managed to use his power to create life. But Boaz was stronger than any of us, and he'd had the Goblet of the Frogs to help him.

I rubbed my hand up and down the flat of the blade, feeling its agitated whispering. It mourned the soldier it had belonged to, for they had been companions many a long year, and the sword wished it had been able to avenge his death.

"Never mind," I whispered back. "You may help, in another way, this man who lies before us now."

As I spoke I looked for Boaz again. He was squatting some paces away from Kofte—they almost appeared to be talking—but Zabrze had sent several soldiers to guard him, and so I turned back to Yaqob.

He was resting quietly, letting Isphet's hands soothe him. She was staring at me. *What?*

I watched Yaqob's face. His eyes were closed, but the tightness of the muscles underneath his skin betrayed some of the pain he must be feeling. I remembered the pain that Boaz had caused me, the agony he had sent coursing through my body. I would have given anything then for someone to have taken my hand and absorbed that pain.

"Sword," I whispered so that only it could hear. "Sword,

you are a creation that thrives on pain. Will you accept this man's pain so that he may concentrate the greater on living?"

The sword's life force was strong, so strong I could see its glow about the blade. It would be easy to manipulate. I knew pain so intimately myself that I was sure I could create the enchantment that would allow the sword to absorb Yaqob's agony.

The sword agreed to my request almost instantly. Elements did not feel pain in the same manner that breathing creatures did, and this added energy would not harm it in any way.

"Yaqob," I said softly, "place your hand here, about the blade. Good."

I closed my eyes, and concentrated, reaching for the life force within the blade and using it to create an enchantment that bridged between it and Yaqob.

Yaqob drew in a stunned breath. "Tirzah . . . *Tirzah!*"

There was no pain in his voice, and I opened my eyes in relief.

His own had filled with tears, and his free hand grabbed at mine. "Tirzah. Thank you . . . thank you."

I smiled, and leaned down and kissed him. "We still have to get you out."

"Easy enough," Kiamet said behind me, and I turned. He had several men with him, and they cast ropes about the stone-man's arms. "Get ready to pull, my friends."

I sent a hasty message to the blade, using its now vastly increased life energy to also cauterize Yaqob's severed arteries and veins.

"Hold tight to that blade," I said to Yaqob, and I held hard to his other hand.

Kiamet and the men hauled, effort stringing the veins in their necks and forearms.

The stone-man wailed, and I wondered if somewhere within his new form he felt pain of his own, then he was rolling off, and Isphet and I pulled Yaqob away.

His legs were almost completely crushed. Bone splintered through muscle that was itself torn and shredded.

"Gods!" Kiamet cried, then he waved his men forward, and without further ado they rolled Yaqob into a blanket.

Isphet and I rose, intending to go with him, but Solvadale and Caerfom appeared behind Kiamet.

"We'll take him," Solvadale murmured. "You have done well, Tirzah. Very well, but we will take him from here."

I nodded, numbed by the horror of Yaqob's injuries, then I leaned down and kissed him again. "Keep that sword by your side, Yaqob. It likes you, and will do its best for you."

He tried a grin, and I was grateful he could not see the full extent of his injuries. "I thank you, Tirzah. Pain for pain, eh?"

"You have done nothing to deserve this, Yaqob!" I said. "Now go, and pay heed to Solvadale and Caerfom."

He kissed my hand, then let it drop as the soldiers bore him away, Solvadale and Caerfom in close attendance.

"That *was* impressive," Isphet said, "but now—"

"Now, Boaz."

Kiamet pointed with his sword, and I relaxed as I saw Boaz. He and Kofte had shifted, moving to the shade beneath a rocky overhang. Kofte was almost impossible to see in the dimness, but Boaz was clearer. He was standing now, only two paces from Kofte, and again I had the distinct impression they were talking, although their lips did not move.

I glanced about. All but two of the stone-men were now writhing helplessly on the ground, and the two left standing were hopelessly outnumbered by the soldiers closing in on them.

There was a sudden movement, and Zabrze jumped down from a ledge to stand beside us. His eyes took in the blood on the ground, and that smeared over Isphet and myself.

"Yaqob," Isphet hurried to explain. "Tirzah and I are fine."

Zabrze let out his breath. "Good." There was a loud thud, followed a heartbeat later by another. "Then we have only that blackness to deal with," he said.

We approached warily, none of us sure what it was that Boaz was doing.

"Boaz?" I asked quietly, stopping two paces behind him, Zabrze and Isphet at my side. Behind us were ranged a dozen soldiers. Kofte was trapped, but he looked dangerous.

"He is reporting back to his master," Boaz replied.

"Nzame sees us?" Zabrze asked sharply.

"Yes. Through Kofte . . . or what was once Kofte. Zabrze,

signal your soldiers to keep him ringed underneath this over-hang. I want to speak with you well away from him."

We moved some distance away, and stood with our backs to Kofte.

"Yaqob?" Boaz asked first.

"He will live," Isphet said. "But he is badly injured. Boaz, what has been done to Kofte?"

"He has given himself so completely to the One—or what he *thinks* is the One—that he has literally been re-created in the image of the One. Or Nzame."

"Boaz," I asked. "What is the exact relationship between Nzame and the One? I know you said that Nzame had appropriated the concept of the One to himself, but was not actually the One."

"I was not entirely sure myself until today," Boaz said. "But I think that through Threshold Nzame has absorbed the power of the One to complement the vast power he has brought across from the Vale. Kofte, as I imagine many Magi would have done, has given himself—literally body and soul—to Nzame, and Nzame has refashioned Kofte in his own image."

"Nzame looks like *that*?" Zabrze said.

"Not quite," Boaz said. "I think that black stony glassiness is as close a physical representation Nzame can get to what the Vale contains. That . . . thing . . . over there is not really Kofte at all, but an extension of Nzame."

"Yet you were talking to it," I said.

"No," Boaz said, too quickly and too sharply. "No, I was merely studying it."

"Can you destroy it, brother?" Zabrze asked.

"I think so, Zabrze, it is strong, but I do not think it is too dangerous. It is more an instrument than a weapon. Can several of your men wrestle it to the ground? I need to be able to touch it."

Zabrze signaled to some men close by, then turned back to us. "Yes. Now?"

"Now. I do not want to linger about this."

"Be careful, Boaz," I said.

"I have too much to live for, Tirzah. Of course I will be careful. Now, stay back. There is nothing any of you can do."

Five of Zabrze's men, Kiamet among them, surrounded

Kofte. He wailed, then shrieked and moaned, waving his arms about, clenching and unclenching his fists.

A man feinted toward him, and Kofte swung that way. The instant he was off guard, several other men lunged and bore him to the ground.

"Quick!" Kiamet shouted as more men hurried to hold Kofte down. "He is stronger than he looks!"

Boaz stood above Kofte's head, then he abruptly leaned down and placed his hand over the black face.

I shivered, remembering when he'd done that to me.

Power rippled across Boaz's face—the power of the One—and it took all my courage to keep my eyes on him. It was too easy to forget that Boaz could still use the power of the One as well as his Elemental arts.

Kofte screamed, and my eyes dropped. The creature jerked violently under the hands of those who restrained him, then again, and again once more.

And then his form blurred.

Boaz shouted to the soldiers, and everyone scrambled from the creature.

Kofte was literally melting away. His face ran and smeared. His hand, as he lifted it, dripped and then fell completely off, running into a small puddle by his side.

Within minutes his entire body had dissolved into a thick liquid, and Boaz ordered that it be dispersed among the rocks. "It will evaporate eventually," he said. "But better scattered about where it cannot reconstitute itself."

"What did you do, Boaz?" I asked.

"Nzame had used large amounts of the power of the One to maintain a link with Kofte. I broke that link, and once that was gone, so was the force that animated what was left of Kofte."

He looked about. Stone forms littered the gorge. "Now, to see what we can do about these animated rocks. I had thought that once the link with Nzame was gone these stone-men might dissolve too, but Nzame has used some other sorcery in their crafting."

Boaz chose a stone-man who was so jammed in a rocky cleft that he could hardly move his arms. He squatted down, and placed a hand directly on the stone-man's chest. He frowned, concentrated, then pulled his hand away, shocked.

"Boaz?" I was beside him almost immediately. "Boaz?"

He took a deep breath, collecting himself, then held my hand. "Isphet, come to the other side. Please. There is no harm."

As Isphet squatted down, Boaz put my hand on the stoneman's chest, and indicated Isphet should do the same. "Feel," he said.

"But stone contains no life—" I began, then wrenched my hand away as quickly as Boaz had pulled his back. An instant later Isphet reacted in the same way.

"What is it?" Zabrze asked.

"Stone should contain no life force at all, Zabrze," Boaz said.

"None of us have felt it within stone before," Isphet added. "Metal, gems, yes, but stone . . . no. Stone is dead. Or should be."

I merely sank down to the ground, staring at the stoneman. He had a burning well of life within him. The life of a man. *There was still a man in there!* No wonder the despair that issued from their mouths.

"Now I know how I changed that stone lock back to hair," Boaz said quietly. "I used the life force within it to effect the change."

Everything, even the breeze, seemed to still about me. "Do you mean that . . . that . . ."

Boaz took my hand, his eyes pleading. "Tirzah. I'm sorry . . . I didn't know then . . . I had no idea . . ."

"Boaz, what did you do with my father's stone body?"

"I had it broken into a thousand pieces, along with the other ten men, and thrown into the Lhyl."

I bowed my head, fighting back the tears. Had my father somehow still been alive within that stone? *Had all those men been salvageable?*

"Tirzah . . ."

I squeezed his hand. "You did not know, Boaz. Please. There is nothing we can do now. And Druse has been farewelled into the Place Beyond."

Boaz was distraught. "But if I had not broken them—"

"No, Boaz. It is done. Finished. But these we *can* save." I lifted my head and tried to smile. "Zabrze will have his people back, after all."

Boaz composed himself, but I knew he would need time to come to terms with what he'd done. Time to forgive himself.

How Nzame must have laughed, watching from the Vale.

"Boaz," I said gently. "Show Isphet and me what to do. We must help."

He nodded, and placed his hand back on the stone-man's chest. He concentrated awhile, then spoke softly, telling us how to use the life force to resurrect and transform.

He leaned on his hand more heavily, and the stone transformed. It marbled first, traceries of veins spreading from the central point of Boaz's hand, then the stone darkened to flesh and muscle. The man ceased his arm waving and instead lay still, and a moan issued from his lips—save this was a moan of surprise, not of despair.

And this was no man.

Isphet and I leaned back in shock as first the breasts, then the gently rounded abdomen of a woman emerged. Limbs lengthened and became smooth and sleek.

Boaz lifted his hand, and we saw her face. She was no more than eighteen or nineteen, and of attractive features. A slave, no doubt, if she had come from Gesholme, but who knew how far Nzame's transformations had wandered.

Her eyes fluttered open, and then she gasped and burst into tears.

"Someone give me a robe, or a cloak," Isphet snapped, and a soldier handed her a blanket.

"Where am I?" the girl stuttered, confused by her surroundings and the strange faces about her. "Who are you?"

It took Boaz, Isphet, and me the rest of the day to move about the stone-men. We transformed them all, exhausting ourselves in the process, but heartened by the reawakening of those who had been so abused. Most were men, but there were eight or nine women among them. All were confused, frightened, and troubled by vague memories that made them tremble and weep.

I thought they would suffer nightmares for months to come.

FORTY-ONE

I t was dark by the time all the men and women had been taken to quarters within the Abyss, and I thought they would need tender care over the next months if they were to resume full and contented lives.

Just as we approached the stairwell and Boaz laid his hand on the door, there came an urgent shout from behind us.

One of the sentries hurried up to us. "Three men," he gasped.

"Stone-men?" Zabrze asked.

"No, Mighty One. Men as you or I, but I do not know them."

"Where?"

"They are not far behind me, Mighty One."

"You go ahead," Zabrze said to us, but we all shook our heads. Strange men meant news.

The three men, escorted by several more sentries and four men from the unit Zabrze had stationed to watch over the lower hills, arrived and bowed low to him.

All three were travel-stained and weary; two of them wore insignia on their armbands that I had not seen previously.

"Ataphet," Zabrze said to one man. "What news?"

"Mighty One," Ataphet said. "I was the only one of my group to get through. I delivered my message, and—"

"And?" Zabrze had moved forward a step. "And?"

"And," one of the other two men said, "we come as personal emissaries from Prince Iraldur." He introduced himself and his companion, but their names flew over my head. Iraldur of Darsis!

"*And?*" I think Zabrze barely restrained himself from clutching at the man's tunic.

"My Prince sends personal messages of goodwill and friendship to you and your esteemed wife . . ."

I glanced at Isphet. Zabrze's esteemed wife was not the same one Iraldur had once known.

". . . and"—the man hurried on as Zabrze gestured in irritation—"my Prince asks me to inform you that he, too, has argument with this Threshold and its appetite—"

"Why?"

"Mighty One, our western borderlands have been raided over past months by men of rock that neither swords nor pikes can halt. Scores of men and women have been marched into land that has been turned to stone itself."

"Oh, dear gods," Zabrze murmured, and passed a hand over his eyes. "I was afraid of this."

"Mighty One, my Prince begs me to inform you that he will support you in whatever way you deem necessary to halt this abomination, but that he knows not what to do. He waits just inside Darsis's border with Ashdod, an army at his back, and he waits for word from you."

"I thank you, my good man. This is news I have long waited to hear."

"Mighty One." The man stepped forward, his face anxious. "My companions and I have journeyed long and hard to reach you here. Three nights ago we were woken by a great trampling of feet, and a moaning that tore into our souls."

My heart pounded, and Boaz clutched at my hand.

"Mighty One, to the northeast of here marches a great army composed of walking rocks."

"It marches south . . . south to *us*?"

"No, Mighty One. It marches northeast. North to meet Iraldur of Darsis."

His moaning woke me, and it terrified me, for it was the moaning of the stone-men.

"Boaz!" I grabbed his shoulder and shook him. *"Boaz!"*

He jerked into wakefulness, his eyes wide and terrified. "Tirzah."

"Of what did you dream, Boaz, to make such moan?"

"Nothing, Tirzah. It was nothing. Go back to sleep."

"No, I will not believe that. I know you too well now not to spot a deception. Boaz, you moaned as if you were a stone-man yourself."

He was silent, and then decided to tell me the truth. "I dreamed of Nzame. It was almost as if he were here with me . . . whispering into my ear . . . laughing at me."

"And of what did he speak?"

"Tirzah—"

"No, tell me."

He sighed. "He told me to take you and flee to Viland. He said that his appetite would never stretch that far. He said our cause was hopeless."

Boaz rolled over to face me. "Tirzah, perhaps he made some sense. Perhaps if you *did* return to—"

"No! I am needed here. Ten thousand stone-men wait to be transformed, and as yet only you, I, and Isphet can help."

The Graces had done their best, and their best was very good, but Yaqob would remain abed for weeks if not months, and even then would walk poorly for the rest of his life. I had wondered, drifting into sleep earlier, if his injuries were not entirely accidental, and if the Soulenai had decided it were better if one of us, at least, remained in the relative safety of the Abyss.

"No," I said more softly. "I must come with you."

Zabrze had given his soldiers a day in which to prepare, and then we would begin our march north. The stone-men shuffled but slowly, and if we pushed the pace we should be able to reach Iraldur before them.

Nevertheless, Zabrze had sent runners north this very night, not only sending word of our own imminent arrival, but advice on how these stone-men could be combated.

I stroked Boaz's arm. "You talked with Nzame through Kofte, didn't you?"

"Yes," he admitted. "There was nothing of Kofte left, save that dreadful nose. I touched briefly with Nzame. I wanted to know . . . I needed . . ."

"To know what you can do to defeat him, Boaz?" My voice was hard-edged. "And did you find out?"

"I found out what I needed, Tirzah. I will not risk that again.

Not if I find a hundred of those black, glassy men before me."

"Boaz, *can* you defeat Nzame?"

He laughed, and gathered me into his arms so that I could not see his face. "Of course I can, beloved. I have no wish to leave you."

But his laughter was forced, and his body tense, and I did not believe him.

Neither of us slept again that night.

"Yaqob? Are you awake?"

"Yes, Tirzah. Come in. You must be almost ready to go."

"Yesterday Zabrze was shouting at everyone. Today he is silent and tense. We leave in an hour."

I sat down by Yaqob's bed. The sword lay close to him, and I thought he would have need of it for weeks to come.

His legs were now splinted and covered with bandages, but I would never forget their terrible aspect as the stone-man was rolled away.

His color was good, and I'd heard that he had eaten well over the past day.

"I wish I was coming with you, Tirzah."

"I am glad you are not, Yaqob."

We were silent, looking at each other, thinking of the love we'd shared, and of all the things that could have been and yet never would be.

"And those that were stone? I have heard so little of them."

"They recover, but they will need a great deal of time to recover completely. They sit and think for hours on end with slight frowns on their faces, as if there is something they should remember, but cannot."

"They do not recall their time as stone?"

"Only in dreams. I think Nzame sometimes still calls to them in their dreams."

He sighed and looked at the ceiling. "My legs itch damnably, Tirzah."

"Then they are healing. Should I ask the sword . . . ?"

"No. No, you have done enough—and for that I thank you."

We sat in silence for some minutes. Eventually I stirred. "Was that Kiath I spotted leaving as I approached, Yaqob?"

He hesitated. "Yes."

"She would be good for you."

"Don't you *dare* dictate to me, Tirzah! Not after what you have done! Kiath shall not provide a salve for your conscience."

I hung my head and studied my hands. There was nothing I could say to that.

"Be careful, Tirzah. And come back and see me one day."

I blinked back my tears. I leaned forward to kiss him, then thought better of it. He held out a hand, and I took it.

"Thus we began, thus we end," he said softly.

I smiled for him now as I had then, but the tears ruined my face, and I snatched my hand from his and fled.

"How was he?" Boaz asked. "He seemed well enough when I said my farewells to him earlier."

Ah, I thought, but he cannot score your heart with such guilt as he can mine. "He recovers well. We shall not have to fear for him."

Boaz looked at me, then brushed a betraying tear from my cheek. "He has had his adventure, Tirzah. We still have a way to go."

"Yes. Are we packed?"

I looked at the packs awaiting us on the bed. We would travel light, for we still had the camels and mules who had given us such good service from the Lhyl across the Lagamaal. They had fed and watered to excess during their leisurely months in the fields above the Abyss, and it would do them good to work off some of their fat in the journey north.

"Are you sure you want to take the goblet and book, Tirzah?"

I had insisted that Holdat pack them. Would I come back? I didn't know. Even in happy times, the Abyss was a long way from anywhere else. So the goblet and book traveled with me.

"Yes. I am sure."

"Listen . . . Zabrze has caused the trumpets to sound. Come on, Tirzah, there are still a few farewells yet to be said."

We shouldered our packs and walked out into the hallway.

There was Isphet, her arms wrapped about her father. It must be doubly hard on Eldonor to lose her so soon after having found her.

We touched his shoulder briefly in farewell, but he only nodded and turned back to his daughter, and we left them in peace, climbing through the stairwell to the top of the cliffs.

Everyone else who was to accompany Zabrze was already above, waiting either here or farther down the gorge. There were the imperial soldiers who'd backed Zabrze in his fight against Threshold—some five hundred and forty—and another thousand composed of men from Gesholme and the Abyss. Among that thousand were not only those who could fight, but many of those strongest in the Elemental arts, such as Zeldon and Orteas. They may not be able to wield the same power as Boaz, Isphet, or myself, but they would still be useful, and they were friends, and I was glad they would come with us.

We heard the distant braying of a mule; they and the camels were waiting for us farther into the hills, carrying not only supplies but all the rope the Abyss could provide.

The Graces were there, Solvadale at their head, and they embraced Boaz and myself, then Isphet as she emerged from the stairwell. There were no words said.

Kiath was there also, holding Zhabroah, now a chortling happy boy some months old. Zabrze would not risk him on this mission. He could well be his only surviving child, and it would be pointless stupidity for Zabrze to insist that his son come with him. But Zabrze was a doting father, and he smiled and pinched the boy's cheek, and charged Kiath with his care.

Zabrze turned and stood at the lip of the canyon. I held my breath, thinking it an unnecessary bravery, but the crowds lining the balconies of the Steps loved it, and I heard a great roar as Zabrze waved them farewell.

The Abyss may never have been an integral part of Ashdod before, but if Zabrze should win, then I thought it would not remain so isolated in the future.

Far below the frogs sang, even though it was well after dawn.

"Fetizza?" I asked Boaz.

"I do not know," he said. "I looked for her this morning, but could not find her. She will choose her own way, Tirzah."

"Yes." I was overcome with the sadness of loss again, and was glad when Zabrze gave the command to move off.

FORTY-TWO

We did not march west to the Lagamaal Plains, but instead swung directly north, traveling parallel with the Abyss until it was swallowed by the rock and cliffs. The way was difficult, but even so it was a shorter route than traveling first to the plains and then north.

And we were less likely to meet stone-men this way. Our soldiers alone could not hope to manage Nzame's ten thousand.

"I hope Iraldur has brought a goodly force," Zabrze muttered as we made camp the first night. "Otherwise we shall be crushed."

We traveled through the hills for two days, then moved northeast into rolling grasslands, easy on foot and eye. The vast majority of us were walking, although Zabrze and several of the officers rode fine gray horses, gifts from the people of the Abyss. Despite the foot pace, we advanced quickly. This was a military march, and Zabrze kept us moving from just after dawn until dark had fallen.

"How long do you estimate before we reach Iraldur?" I asked Zabrze one evening.

"We march directly north for another week, then swing northwest. We should reach him in two weeks."

"Why would Nzame send his army to meet Iraldur rather than us?" Boaz said. "He knew where we were."

"Iraldur is the more immediate threat," Zabrze replied. "And would provide the easier feeding. How many months is it since we escaped Threshold? Four? Five?"

"And Nzame's appetite must be increasing by the day," I said quietly. "I wonder what incomposite number he is up to now?"

Boaz ran a hand through his hair. It was growing again, and I thought it was time I trimmed it back. Every time it grew past his neck it reminded me too much of the Magus.

"His power increases with each life he takes," he said.

Zabrze looked at his brother carefully. "Can you best him, Boaz?"

"Yes. I think so."

"How?"

I watched my husband carefully. Boaz would never talk to me of how he intended to defeat Nzame. Would he tell Zabrze?

"It is too complicated," Boaz said vaguely. "It involves mathematical formulas that would leave you blinking in confusion."

I looked away, not able to bear the lie in his eyes. Why wouldn't Boaz tell us what he intended to do? Was it because he expected to die in the process?

"Then tell me how I can help you," Zabrze said.

"Get me to Threshold," Boaz answered, looking Zabrze straight in the eye. "Get me *inside* Threshold."

"You're going to the Infinity Chamber?" I asked. Bloodied writing swirled once more before my eyes. *The Infinity Chamber?*

"Yes, Tirzah. It is the only place."

"And will you walk *out* of the Infinity Chamber, Boaz, once you are done?"

"Of course, beloved," he said with an easy smile, and for that night I let myself believe him.

After a week, Zabrze ordered the column to swing northwest. There the grassland gave way to shifting soil that made marching difficult.

After another day's march the soil gave way to stone.

Flat, bare stone.

We stood in the late afternoon sun, shading our eyes as we stared. Wind whipped off the stone, hot and unforgiving, twisting our robes around our legs, and catching at the cloths about our heads.

"Nzame has wrapped my realm in tombstone," Zabrze said.

It was both awe-inspiring and terrifying. I'd seen the stone land in the vision in the Chamber of Dreaming, but even that barely prepared me for the sight before me now.

The overwhelming impression was that the land was dead. Utterly dead. There was not a bird in the sky, nor so much as an insect crawling over the stone. The land had also been completely flattened. Even the barest of plains has undulations and dips in its surface. Not so this landscape. Small drifts of sand skimmed across its surface, as if searching for a place to rest.

I stepped to the dividing line between living land and dead and bent down. Trembling, I laid a hand on the stone.

Nothing. No life.

I glanced at Boaz. His hand was also flat on the stone. "There is no life," he said. "None." He sounded puzzled.

"Well?" Zabrze said, looking between Isphet, Boaz, and me. "Can you transform this land as you transformed the stone-men?"

Boaz stood up. "No. The stone-men are still alive, deep within their rock. Nzame did not kill that spark of life because he wanted the stone to move, to act out his will. But the land he has killed completely. I'm sorry, Zabrze. I don't know what I can do about this."

Zabrze looked at me, then Isphet, but we both shook our heads. He stared, his face hardening, then he wheeled his horse about and waved the column forward . . . onto the stone.

Once we were on the stone plain we found that it was not as entirely featureless as it had first appeared. There were odd cracks and fissures in its surface . . . and every four or five hundred paces there was a miniature Threshold.

Stone pyramids reared up, sometimes only the height of a finger, sometimes half the height of a man. But in the exact center of every face of every pyramid was an eye. Not carved, not chiseled, but black and glassy. Moving. Watching.

None of us, not even Boaz, could bear to go near them. Whenever one of the forward scouts found one they waved our column to the left or right so that we passed at least twenty paces away from the abomination. Zabrze had to be careful that in all this meandering we kept directly north, and I think he kept closer watch on the sun, and then on the first of the evening stars, than he did on the stone about him.

We camped out of sight of any of the miniature Thresholds. It was a cold and silent camp that night. No one felt like talking, and we rolled ourselves into our blankets early, shifting uncomfortably about on the stone.

I lay awake for hours before I slipped into sleep.

I dreamed I walked in grassy pastures filled with gold, red, and blue flowers, bright sky, warmth on my face, breathing in the fragrance of the pine resin from the forests bordering the pastures. It reminded me of Viland during its brief glimpse of summer.

I walked slowly, knowing it was a dream, but welcoming the escape from the harshness about me.

There was a movement behind me, and I turned. I was not afraid.

A handsome man stood there. He was dark of feature and eye, a southerner then, trapped in my dream of Viland.

"This is a green and lovely land," he remarked, casting his gaze about him.

"Yes. Yes, it is. This is my homeland, Viland."

"Where you were born? But how lucky you are! Surely you must ache to return to a land as lovely as this?"

I smiled at his enthusiasm. "No. It is beautiful for only one month every year. Other months gales sweep down from the north, and ice and snow bind us into our homes. I prefer the southern lands where the sun shines most days of the year."

"And where your lover is."

I blushed. "Yes."

"But the southern lands lie under the grip of stone, Tirzah." The man lowered his eyes, sorrowing. "They are no place to stay."

"I have hope."

He raised his eyes, and I recoiled. They were the glassy black eyes of the stone pyramids.

I tried to back away, but my feet were rooted to the ground.

I was too terrified to look down to see why. *I didn't want to know why my feet would not move!*

"Ashdod is a bad place. Tirzah. A very bad place." He rolled the "r" in the "very," and his voice was low like thunder. And like thunder I felt it more than heard it. "Soon all the southern lands will be stone."

"No."

"Yes. I shall eat them all."

"Please . . . please, let me go. Please . . . go away!"

"Yes to the first, no to the latter. I do not want to eat *you*, dear Tirzah. Such a pretty girl. I could have taken you in Threshold, but I did not. Too pretty to waste."

"Please . . ."

"Go away, Tirzah. Flee. Keep going north. Take your friends with you. I do not want to harm you. Go."

"Please, let me go!"

"Oh, I intend to, Tirzah, but hear me out. Go north, sweet girl, and do not look back. That would be . . . unfortunate. But I will not touch Viland. Take your lover and Isphet and Zabrze and flee north. Listen to me, Tirzah. Do as I ask and you shall live. Is that not what you wish?"

"Let me go!" I tried with all the power I had to escape, but he held me tight, and I could not move.

"If you do not go, Tirzah, then I will kill Boaz, and I will kill Isphet, and I will kill every one of those you cherish, and I will do it very, very slowly. *Do you understand me?*"

"Yes! Yes! I understand you!"

"Tell Boaz to go away."

"Yes!"

"Tell him he will not succeed."

"Yes!"

"Then go . . ."

A hand grabbed at my shoulder, and I screamed.

"*Tirzah!* What's wrong? It's a dream, Tirzah. A dream. Shush, now. Shush. I have you now."

Boaz wrapped me in his arms as I sobbed. He continued to soothe me, murmur to me, and I heard Isphet speak quietly to him, and then move away.

"Was it Nzame?" he asked eventually, his mouth close to my ear so no one else could hear.

"Yes. He . . ."

"Shush. He cannot hurt you in dream—"

"He turned my feet to stone!"

"And are they stone now, Tirzah?"

I wriggled them, almost believing they *would* be stone, but they were warm and they moved, and I felt Boaz smile as he rocked me.

"He said he would kill you, Boaz."

"He is afraid."

"So am I."

There was a long silence, then I raised my face so I could see Boaz's in the faint moonlight. "Boaz, answer me true. *Will* you succeed against Nzame?"

He took his time in answering. "It is why he is afraid. He knows I have a good chance."

"And *will* you walk out of the Infinity Chamber, Boaz, and back to me?"

He was silent, and I wept anew.

We drifted back to sleep eventually, but it was a light, uncomfortable sleep. Each of us feared Nzame's intrusion, and each of us feared the future.

Just before dawn a shout roused us. It was one of the sentries, and I heard Zabrze run off even as the shout died down. Boaz and I scrambled up, pulling on our robes.

Soldiers, swords drawn, ropes wrapped about their waists, were patrolling the perimeters of the camp, and one of them held us back.

"Wait until we know it's safe."

We peered forward. There was movement perhaps twenty paces away; Zabrze, I thought, and several soldiers. They were bending down to something at . . . their knees?

Then we heard laughter. Forced laughter to be sure, but laughter nevertheless.

There was a scuffle of movement, and they walked back toward us.

"What?" Boaz said. Then, *"Shetzah!"*

At Zabrze's feet bounded a thin, gray dog, pathetically grateful to have found something else alive in this sea of stone.

Boaz glanced at me, apprehensive, then he bent down and clicked his fingers.

The dog bounded over, whimpering and trying to lick Boaz's face.

Boaz wouldn't let it. He seized the dog's head and stared into its eyes, then he sighed in relief and looked up at me.

"It *is* a dog," he said, and the dog whimpered again and set to licking his face as thoroughly as it could.

"How could it have survived?" Zabrze asked, walking over to examine the dog. It was a half-grown bitch, probably a hunting dog, and had soft russet spots amid her gray coat.

"I don't know," Boaz said. "Perhaps she just wandered into the stone from the east."

"Would *you* just wander into this wickedness?" Zabrze asked. "Anything outside would sniff at its edges, then run in the opposite direction, tail between legs."

"Well." Isphet had joined us, and she could not keep a smile from her face at the antics of the dog. "At least we know that some things can survive. Nzame does not eat all in his path, it seems."

She met Zabrze's eyes.

Setkoth, I thought. Zabrze must worry constantly about his children there. Yet to ask that somehow they survived was, surely, to ask too much. Would we find them stone and salvageable? Or eaten and existing in memory only?

The dog whimpered, and darted behind Boaz's legs.

"I don't think she likes the look of your face—" Boaz began, grinning at Zabrze, then there was a thump.

Then another.

"Stone-men!" Zabrze shouted, and the camp burst into activity.

Zabrze had planned for this eventuality—stone-men would surely wander Nzame's stone land—and soldiers quickly sorted themselves into groups of five, unwrapping rope from waists, their faces grim.

Others moved to the camels and mules, soothing with voice and hands, and taking firm hold of their tethers. They carried our only supplies of water and food, and to lose them here would be unthinkable.

"Come on," Boaz said, and took Isphet and me by the hands. "It's safer farther back into camp."

The stone-men were only forty strong, and led by yet another Magus who was now nothing but the black glassy substance. Zabrze had almost fifteen hundred men, all armed with ropes. By dawn the perimeter of the camp was littered with the impotent bodies of stone-men, and not one soldier.

The Magus was held down by ten strong men and enough rope to moor five ships. Boaz disposed of him immediately—he did not even attempt to use him to communicate with Nzame—then the three of us turned to the stone-men.

This was exhausting work, and I would not let myself think of how we would cope with more than forty or fifty. Each stone-man took concentration and both physical and emotional effort, but it was reward enough to see the stone marble into flesh, and the chest heave with breath rather than moaning, and the eyes flutter open, surprised, yet confused and frightened.

Zabrze detailed some fifteen soldiers to feed and clothe them.

"What will we do with them?" I asked.

"We'll have to march them with us," Zabrze answered. "I cannot leave them, and I do not want to spare the men to take them east."

I looked over to the men and women. They sat in a tight, huddled group, slightly disoriented, fearful without knowing why. Many cried softly, others looked about, watching for the danger they knew was there but could not identify. Most were well featured, their faces and hands unlined, and I realized they must be townspeople. Not slaves from Gesholme.

"What am I going to do," Zabrze said very quietly by my side, "with a land full of people so damaged by their experience?"

He was not talking of their physical ordeal but their emotional and psychological trauma.

"It will take them time," I said, "but they will laugh again one day, Zabrze. Have no fear."

My words did nothing to reassure him, and he gave the order to break camp.

Isphet and I spent most of the day walking with the sad group, while Boaz strode at the front of the column, the dog leaping about his legs.

Whoever I talked to among this group said much the same thing. They did not know what had happened to them. They had been engaged in their usual chores and daily activities, and then . . . nothing. The stone had swept through their existence so swiftly they had not even been aware of the danger.

They said that they felt as if they'd been trapped in some dreadful, drugged sleep. Many said they felt as if they would slip back into that sleep if they closed their eyes even for an instant. All were nervous, all swept anxious eyes across the stone landscape that still held them trapped, none listened to our reassurances.

They were a sad, hopeless people and they passed so much of their sadness and hopelessness onto Isphet and myself that we were forced to leave them and walk ahead with Boaz.

That night I dreamed again.

This time Nzame dragged me into the Infinity Chamber.

"See the blood," his voice whispered about me, for he did not bother to take form. "See the blood."

It ran in rivulets down the golden walls. As I watched it slowed, coagulated, and formed words with its clots and strings.

Boaz will die here, Tirzah, they read, *here Boaz will die.*

"Take him to Viland, Tirzah," Nzame whispered to me. "You do not want to lose him, do you?"

Take him far, far away. Or lose him.

"Tirzah."

Again Boaz's hand and voice woke me. I had not screamed, but still he knew. "Do not listen to him, Tirzah. He will do anything, tell any lie, to make us turn aside. Do not listen to him. Do not believe him."

I did not cry this time, but still I lay sleepless until it was time to rise.

We marched silent through a desolate landscape. The sun beat down, baking the stone that in turn burned through the soles of our sandals. The representations of Threshold grew more bizarre. Some looked as if they had been exposed to so much heat their stark lines had melted, others looked so ancient their peaks had crumbled and their sides had begun to cave in upon themselves.

Yet always an eye stared out from each face, following our progress.

In the late morning the dog began to bark at something in the cleft of a rock. Her tail wagged so enthusiastically her entire rear half waggled.

Boaz and I shared a curious glance, then walked over to have a look. Zabrze rode up beside us, and waved in several more guards.

"Be careful," he said as we approached the now wildly excited dog.

Boaz pulled her back by the scruff of her neck, then peered into the crack. *"Kus!"* he whispered, totally shocked . . . but not scared.

Fetizza sat crouched in the cleft, squeezed so much by the rock to either side of her I thought she was in danger of exploding.

Boaz motioned to one of the soldiers to take the dog, then he lifted Fetizza out of the rock cleft.

The instant she was out she expanded to almost the size of the small dog. She gave a relieved croak, then relaxed in Boaz's arms, happily blinking at us.

I looked at Boaz, Boaz looked at Zabrze, and Zabrze just opened and closed his mouth.

"How?" he finally managed.

Boaz shook his head, then something in the cleft caught my eye.

"Look!" I cried.

Pure, crystal water was seeping forth. It filled the crack, then ran over. It pooled until we were forced to stand back, then it found another small crack, and flowed into that.

Fetizza croaked again, utterly self-satisfied.

The water burbled out over the stone until it found successive cracks, filled them, then flowed farther, seeking, exploring.

We all stepped back, watching it.

Now the water formed a narrow stream winding through the stone landscape.

"It's heading toward that stone pyramid!" Isphet said.

Everyone now stood riveted by the sight.

The pyramid watched, too. The eyes in the two faces that could see the water stared until the pyramid literally went cross-eyed.

I grinned. I could not help it. I had the feeling that far, far away Nzame was raging helplessly at the sight of this slim stream of water trickling toward his self-image.

The dog barked excitedly, and Fetizza croaked.

The water hit the pyramid. For an instant it foamed against the stone face, then the side of the pyramid split with a loud crack, and then shattered, and the entire pyramid collapsed and disappeared beneath the spreading stream.

The water continued to spread, seeping through cracks and fissures in the rock. We stood for an hour or more, watching. About twenty paces wide, the stream spread into the distance, back the way we'd come. A shallow, shining sheet of water.

We felt more cheerful than we had for many days. Even the Released, as Isphet had named those people who we'd freed from their stone prison, smiled and talked as we went.

It had been the sight of the cross-eyed pyramid, I think, collapsing beneath the gentle stream, that had done such wonders.

Boaz wrapped Fetizza in a damp cloth and carried her in his arms until we made camp.

Then he put her down, and she immediately nestled into another cleft in the stone surface.

Almost instantly water seeped up about her, and trickled away until, in time, it would join with the stream she'd created that morning. On its way I had no doubt it would encounter the twenty-four miniature pyramids we'd passed since Fetizza had reappeared.

We all bathed in the water before we ate, and it refreshed and renewed us. I saw that the Released smiled and laughed, and I even saw a few splash water over their neighbors.

I shared a relieved look with Isphet. Fetizza's water would do what no words on our part could.

There were no dreams that night, and when we woke, it was to the excited shout of one of the sentries.

Behind our camps stretched a massive sheet of water—Fetizza had been busy. Yet it was not so much the water that had so caught the sentry's eye but the thin, jagged sheets of rock that speared up through it.

The stone underneath the water had splintered and shattered. Through the shallow pools of water, and between the sheets of rock that had been cast aside, we could see new earth.

"The tears of the Soulenai," Boaz said quietly, "renewing the land."

FORTY-THREE

No more stone-men attacked us; Nzame must have realized the futility of sending small groups against our force. We marched across the stone landscape for five more days, tense but not as despondent as we had been. Behind us stretched sheets of water soaking into the newly wakened earth. The strips uncovered by the water were not yet extensive, but they gave us hope, and every night as we watched Fetizza settle into yet another crack we smiled as the water seeped up about her.

Fetizza seemed totally unfussed by the attention everyone gave her, and hissed and flattened only when the bitch approached. Not that the dog did that very often; she'd already found out that Fetizza could nip fiercely when provoked, and once the frog had almost drowned her in an ankle-deep puddle of water.

The Released continued to improve. We all bathed nightly,

and each evening the Released splashed about I could almost see a few more of their fears sliding away with the water.

I wished that the water could have done as much for my fears as it did for theirs. Nzame had not approached me in my sleep again, but I thought he was just biding his time.

Boaz was very quiet. He slept as undisturbed as I, but he was increasingly wrapped in inner thoughts.

On the sixth day after Fetizza had reappeared, we met Iraldur of Darsis.

There was a flurry of movement at the head of the column, and I lifted my eyes.

"Boaz, look! There are men ahead."

Zabrze rode forward to meet a war chariot pulled by two black steeds accompanied by a group of six horsemen. Even from this distance I could see the glint of chest plates beneath silken scarves, and the wicked curve of free scimitars. The man driving the chariot was more heavily armed than any of his soldiers.

As Zabrze hailed them, the man in the chariot waved at his horsemen, who pulled their mounts back and sheathed their weapons. Then he leaned over to take Zabrze's hand.

"Iraldur," Boaz said. "Come on, Tirzah."

Iraldur was about Zabrze's age, a fierce-looking man with narrowed eyes and an easy familiarity with his weapons and war chariot. He was also patently furious.

"A great army of stone-men shuffles two days' march to the west, Zabrze. You have harbored this pestilence within your realm, *fed* it, and yet now you ask for my help in disposing of it?"

"And I thank you for your assistance," Zabrze said mildly. "For here you are."

"The only reason I am here, Zabrze, is because this wickedness is nibbling at *my* people and land as well! Do you realize that now we stand on what was once fertile Darsis land? Grain fields have produced only stone this season, Zabrze, and for that I have you to thank!"

"I am not responsible—"

"You are *Chad*, Zabrze, for I hear Nezzar has finally tipped completely into madness, and as Chad you are responsible for every piece of excrement every one of your subjects produces. And this particular piece of shit"—he spat on the ground—"is most definitely *your* responsibility!"

Iraldur spotted us. "Ah! *Magus* Boaz! Have you come to explain what the Magi have set loose on my country? Have you come to explain to weeping mothers why their husbands are stone and their children are taken to feed the appetite of this—"

Then Iraldur spotted Fetizza in Boaz's arms and his mouth fell open.

"Much of what has been destroyed can be renewed, Iraldur," Boaz said, and set Fetizza on the ground. She found a suitable crack and squeezed in happily, emitting a loud sound that I hoped was a sigh of satisfaction.

"On behalf of the Magi," Boaz continued as Iraldur dragged his eyes away from the frog, "*I* must accept responsibility for what has happened. The Magi's greed for Infinity has loosed wickedness, but with your help, and that of Zabrze, I hope to put it right. Get me to Threshold, Iraldur, and I will win back for you your land and your people."

Just as Iraldur was about to reply his eye caught the gleam of water as it oozed up about Fetizza, and the frog croaked and grinned at him.

Iraldur led us to his camp, an hour's march away. He had set up camp on the stone, he explained, because he was afraid of what might happen if he camped just outside of it and Nzame decided to expand his influence.

"We would all be turned to stone in the winking of an eye," he said as he waved us inside an extravagantly draped tent. "And I am not yet ready for such a living death."

Isphet and I accompanied our husbands inside. Iraldur had been surprised to find that Boaz had taken a wife—I think that actually endeared Boaz a little more to him—but was stunned and saddened to find that Neuf was dead.

"I think not to insult you, my Lady Isphet," he said, "but I had known Neuf since my boyhood, and she was a friend."

Isphet inclined her head graciously. No doubt she would encounter more such surprise in the future.

Iraldur waited until we were comfortably settled, and then turned back to Zabrze. "Tell me."

Zabrze looked about us, then back to Iraldur. "There are four within this tent with stories to tell, Iraldur, and it is best for you to hear them all. You said this stone-man army is two days to the west?"

Iraldur nodded.

"Then you have this evening to spare to listen. No, wait. How great a force do you have here?"

"Six thousand men. As many horses."

"Then we shall dispose of these stone-men easily enough, and I think you shall be surprised to see what we do with them. Patience. These tales are important."

Iraldur stared at Zabrze, then he nodded curtly. "Very well." He waved at a servant, and we were served chilled fruit juice spiced with something that momentarily made my head spin, then gave everything in the tent a sharper edge.

"Boaz?" Zabrze asked quietly. "Will you begin?"

Iraldur sat and listened without comment as first Boaz, then Isphet, me, and lastly Zabrze, told our tales. The Prince waved the servant forward every so often, replenishing our glasses, and only interrupted to clarify a point or, when I spoke, to ask if he could see the Goblet of the Frogs and the Book of the Soulenai.

I sent word to Holdat, and he entered just as Zabrze finished his tale, and handed me the book and goblet. I passed them to Iraldur.

"It is a remarkable tale you tell," he said, and he looked at me, then Isphet. "Slaves become Cantomancers and then the wives of Princes and Chads."

Isphet held out her wrists. "Then chain us again, Iraldur, if you think we deserve it."

"I do not criticize, Isphet," Iraldur said. "Over the years I have heard many philosophers argue that slaves are the only ones within a society who exist in a true state of nobility. Today, perhaps, I have seen the truth of that theory."

Isphet's mouth twisted bitterly. "I doubt these philosophers have ever been slaves themselves, Iraldur. I have never yet met the slave who has reveled in the nobility of his or her existence."

"Win me back my people," Iraldur said very softly, "and I will oil and kiss your feet myself."

"*Will* you help us, Iraldur?" Zabrze asked. "We have two days before this cursed stone army reaches us. I cannot deal with it on my own. *Will you help us?*"

"Yes." Iraldur closed the Book of the Soulenai. "Yes, I will."

I thought to sleep well that night, but I was wrong.

Nzame came to me in the form of the handsome black-eyed man, standing again in the summer fields of Viland.

"Stone-men are but a fraction of the power at my disposal, foolish girl. Ten thousand I send to meet you, but I can as easily generate ten thousand more, and then ten thousand more to follow them. Can you deal with that many? Will you spend your life laying hands on that many? *Can you survive that great a challenge?*"

I thought that if I ignored him, if I turned away, he would tire of the game.

But my legs were stone to my thighs, and I knew I would age and die before Nzame grew tired of the game.

"I know what Boaz intends to do, Tirzah. Do you? Do you?"

I could not help myself. I looked up.

"He thinks, Tirzah, to wrap me in his power and drag me through to Infinity. *His* power? Ha!"

Nzame's laughter rang about me, then he stopped as suddenly as he had started.

"But even if he should succeed, Tirzah. Even *if* he should succeed. There we would be, trapped together in Infinity. Imagine. Your lover and me, locked in our own Infinity. It would not be your sweet embrace he would feel, but mine. For eternity, Tirzah. No escape. *My* embrace."

"No!"

"*Yes!* Tirzah, think. If he comes to me either he will succeed, or he won't. Which would be the preferable outcome, Tirzah? Would you prefer Boaz to fail . . . and die? Or would you prefer him to succeed . . . and spend Infinity in my embrace?"

I began to sob, twisting my body about, wishing I was free to run through the fields away from these taunts.

"*Is* he a good lover, Tirzah? Shall I *enjoy* Infinity in his embrace?"

Then suddenly my legs *were* free, and I had my wish. I turned and ran as hard as I could, barefoot through the soft grass and flowers.

Nzame's laughter rang after me. "Which would you prefer, sweet Tirzah? Which? I shall make sure that it happens. What is it you wish for your lover? Death? Or . . . ?"

FORTY-FOUR

We did not get the two days to prepare, because somehow Nzame infused his stone-men with more speed, and they attacked at dusk of the next day.

We had an hour's warning, for Nzame could not conceal their approach completely. There was an instant's awkward hesitation after the scouts had delivered their dreadful news, while Zabrze and Iraldur stared at each other, wondering which should take command. Zabrze, whose fight it truly was? Or Iraldur, who commanded the vast majority of men?

It was Iraldur who settled the matter. "Tell me how to use my men, but hurry up about it!" he snapped, and Zabrze commanded.

Isphet, Boaz, and I were relegated to Iraldur's gaudy tent, with a unit of men to guard us. Boaz fumed, but Zabrze would let him nowhere near the action.

"You are too important to waste under a tumbling body of stone," he said. "Already we've lost Yaqob when we could well use him. You will stay here. Kiamet! Make sure that they do!"

I felt sick with apprehension as I stood at the tent flap, watching him mount and ride away. Ten thousand stone-men. Ten thousand!

I let the flap fall and set myself to wrapping, then rewrapping the goblet and book, trying to keep myself calm.

"Lady," Holdat said softly by my side. "You shall break them with your fiddling. Here, I will take them."

"Be careful!" But he had already gone.

Fetizza no one worried about. At the first shout she had wedged herself into an impossibly small crack in the ground—even if a stone-man should tumble directly over her she would be protected.

The dog was more trouble. Whining and anxious, feeling the tension about her, she wound between people's legs and was eventually banished from the tent when she tripped Isphet over.

Boaz paced back and forth. "Damn!" he muttered as we heard a unit of mounted men clatter by, and he was out the tent flap before I could say or do anything.

"Tirzah!" Isphet shouted after me, but she was also too late, and I rushed outside into chaos.

Iraldur and his men already had a good idea of what it would take to defeat the stone-men, but they had been caught before their final preparations were completed. Now they rushed about, feverishly finding anything that might be used to trip thick, shuffling stone legs. Rope, leather reins, even girths from saddles. Many of the thousands of horses in camp were loose; others had been appropriated, but most men preferred to fight this battle on foot. No horse was going to remain calm in the face of a stone-man, and a mounted soldier would be too vulnerable to those flailing arms.

Twenty thousand flailing arms.

I had lost Boaz in the confusion, and I realized I'd wandered far from the tent myself. What was I doing? I was a fool.

Suddenly I realized that the stone ground was shaking beneath my feet.

The movement of all those about me, I tried to tell myself. But no human army or equine stampede could make the earth shudder as it did now.

Thump. Thump. Thump.

So close? So close? I trembled, then tried to reassure myself that twenty thousand stone legs could make a thump that might be felt a league away.

"My Lady!" Kiamet screamed behind me, then he seized me in strong arms and hauled me away.

Thump. Thump. Thump.

"What . . . ?" I began, struggling to find my breath as I recovered from the shock of Kiamet's assault. "What's . . . ?"

"Stone-men!" he gasped, and dragged me farther into the darkness. "Everywhere!"

And, oh, gods, yes, they were! I screamed as a stone figure lurched out of the gloom, its arms windmilling, its face twisted in desperate moaning. It struck Kiamet on the shoulder and we both fell, rolling away as a stone foot crashed not a hand's breadth away from my face.

Despite his injury Kiamet hauled me to my feet and we ran, ducking and weaving through bodies, flesh and stone, two-legged and four.

There was nowhere to hide. Nowhere to shelter. Nothing but flatness to aid the stone-men. Boaz! Isphet!

Kiamet's remaining good arm tightened around me again, and he pulled me to the left, and then we twisted to the right. A shape loomed before me, and we ducked and rolled, then rose and fled.

I was sobbing with terror, sure I was going to die. Stone-men *were* everywhere! Soldiers were among them, and many a stone-man tumbled to the ground . . . but there were thousands of them. So many . . . so many.

"They broke ranks before Zabrze could attack," Kiamet explained, his eyes searching through the darkness for the next threat. "They ran amok . . . in every direction."

"Oh, gods, Kiamet! What can we do?"

"Nothing, save survive," and we were off again, twisting, avoiding one stone arm only by a deep breath, another only through luck as my leg twisted and I dragged Kiamet down with me.

"What about Boaz? Isphet? There's no one . . ."

Thud, and we rolled away again and scrambled to our feet.

"Nothing I can do. I can save one of you and one only. And even that one . . ."

My leg was screaming, and I wondered if I'd broken it. I could hardly bear any weight on it, and I think Kiamet was virtually carrying me now.

We stopped, searching for escape, but there seemed to be none. There were more stone-men than soldiers, more traps than avenues of escape.

Then absolute horror reared before us.

Chad-Nezzar. Blackened and peeling skin ran from his face and body, but I knew who it was instantly. He had a scimitar, and he heaved it aloft with both hands. He opened his mouth and . . . and from it issued forth Nzame's voice.

Which would you prefer, Tirzah? Death? Or Infinity in my embrace?

I screamed until I thought I would rupture my throat.

Kiamet hit me. Not strongly, but enough to stop my cries.

Which would you prefer, Tirzah? Death? Or Infinity in my embrace? Chad-Nezzar can deal whichever you choose. His body is mine now. Do you like it? Would you prefer that—

A blade whistled through the air behind the grotesque puppet and sliced its head from its shoulders.

Iraldur, blood seeping from a wound to his head and more from an injury to his shoulder. "Get her out of here, you fool!" he yelled to Kiamet. "Or I shall take your head as well!"

Kiamet took him at his word and dragged me away . . . but it was away into more confusion.

I was so terrified now I could neither cry nor scream, just cling to Kiamet. I was sure I was going to die, sure we were all going to die. There was nothing but flailing arms, nothing but to curl up and wait for—

Tirzah! Tirzah!

Now I did find the breath to sob. Oh, no! Not him! Not him *again*!

Tirzah! Tirzah!

"Tirzah!" Kiamet panted in my ear. "Look, curse you, *look*!"

I raised my head. Then blinked, sure I was hallucinating in my terror.

Avaldamon stood some thirty paces away, beckoning urgently. I blinked again. Yes, Avaldamon. Wraithlike to be sure, but undoubtedly Avaldamon.

Kiamet hauled me toward the specter, and neither of us thought to duck or weave as we raced through the berserk arms of the stone-men.

Luck—perhaps something else—saved us, and we reached the spot where Avaldamon had been.

Had been. Now he was gone.

"Avaldamon!" I sobbed, then looked down. Fetizza sat huddled in a small cleft in the rock. She looked very, very angry.

Water was welling up about her.

I sank to my knees, then to my hands. What advantage would water give—

"Good girl," Kiamet said softly, and sank down beside me, reaching out to stroke Fetizza on the head. "Good girl."

I was soaking. I had never seen the water rise this fast before. It spread in a great pool about us, and Fetizza's huge black eyes had lost none of their anger.

A stone-man lurched in our direction.

I cringed, knowing we were dead.

He slipped in the water. For an instant a look of almost comical surprise spread across the stone face, replacing the despair, then he was down, crashing with such a thud that it shook the stone about us.

The water was now *cascading* from the cleft.

There was another thud, then another, then several at once.

Fetizza burped.

Water pumped out of every crack about us. I had to hook my fingers into a fissure in the rock to prevent myself from being carried away.

The sound of stone bodies hitting stone ground was now almost deafening, yet still I could hear shouts of triumph rise above the crashing.

Fetizza croaked contentedly, and wriggled about in her rocky fissure.

Kiamet and I wandered for hours, searching for Boaz. Isphet we'd found fairly quickly. She had stayed with the tent, relatively safe from the stone-men. Only three had come her way, and they'd got so tangled in the tent ropes they'd fallen over and protected her from further incursions.

She'd not touched them until the danger was past.

Now we searched through a landscape littered with moans and impotently waving arms. Every one of the stone-men left on his feet when Fetizza had set the waters free had been felled by the slippery water. They had accidentally killed or maimed several dozen of our men in the process.

And scores of other men had been killed in the confused terror beforehand. The ten thousand running amok had created the havoc Nzame wished. Gods knew what would have happened if Fetizza hadn't acted.

"Boaz?" I called softly into the night. "Boaz?"

Kiamet limped beside me. He was badly injured, and should have gone to the tents for treatment, but he insisted on staying with me.

"Boaz? Boaz?"

A figure loomed before me and I cried out, reaching out my arms.

But it was Zabrze, not Boaz, and while I was happy to see him alive, he was not my Boaz.

"Isphet?" he asked. *"Isphet?"*

"She's at the tent where you left her. Zabrze—"

But he was gone, running through the night.

I turned, and stared into the face of Iraldur.

"Still alive, I see," he grunted. "And we've won through, but at a cost I'd not expected."

Then *he* was gone, and I was crying, for I was sure I would not see Boaz again.

"Come on, my Lady," Kiamet muttered, "there's no good to be done wandering about here during the night. There's plenty you can fix in the morning. But for now—"

"For now I'll take her, Kiamet. Get yourself over to Iraldur's physicians' tents, for you need fixing yourself."

"Boaz!"

His arms wrapped about me, as tight as ever I could have wanted them, and we were crying and rocking together in the night, alone save for ten thousand stone-men lying on their backs and waving sadly to the uncaring moon above.

FORTY-FIVE

The scene in the morning was almost unbelievable—and contained its own terrors. The water Fetizza had called forth had worked its magic overnight, and now edges of rock speared into the sky revealing new earth, and further tumbling helpless stone-men into piles of rocky wreckage.

"How," Isphet said softly by my side, "are we going to cope?"

I linked my arm through hers, needing her support as much as she needed my comfort. Soldiers were wandering the field of battle, looking for any fallen comrades they may have missed in the darkness. They stepped carefully around the occasional stone hand that snatched reflexively at them.

Zabrze had told us this morning that one hundred and eighty of his men, and three hundred and four of Iraldur's, had been killed. Half the horses had fled and were now presumably wandering the stone plains, too terrified to come back while the stone-men were still alive.

Boaz was already working in the stone landscape. He leaned down by one stone-man, then stood again as stone marbled into flesh. He did not wait to see whether the stone revealed man or woman, but moved on to the next.

"Come on," I said. "He cannot do it all by himself."

But neither could three. We worked through that day, then the next, and then halfway through the day after that, until Zabrze laid his hand on Boaz's shoulder and said, "Enough."

We had released perhaps six hundred in that time, and the effort had exhausted us. Isphet and Boaz looked like automatons themselves, skin waxen and gray, eyes sunken, and I'm sure I could not have looked much better.

"But what can we do?" I asked. "We cannot leave them here—"

"Yes, we can," Zabrze said, and helped Boaz to his feet.

"We have won this field," Zabrze continued, "but Nzame still rages within Threshold. I don't want any of us trapped here, least of all you three. Perhaps that's what Nzame wanted, to have you ensnared by your compassion for the souls these stone-men contain."

"But—" Isphet said tiredly.

"They can lie here and moan until we have dealt with Nzame. I am sorry, Isphet, but they will remember nothing of it afterward, and even if you *could* release these ten thousand over the next few days without killing yourself in the process I have no means of feeding or caring for them. They are best left here."

Zabrze turned toward the west. "We head for Setkoth."

I looked at Isphet. Were Zabrze's children still in Setkoth? Had they been eaten? Or were they among this forest of stone still waving sadly at us?

We moved out the next day. Iraldur and several thousand of his men accompanied us; others remained behind to shepherd the Released toward shelter and land that could feed them.

Most of the horses had been recaptured in the days following the battle, and so many men had been killed or stayed behind that Iraldur had horses to spare.

Neither Zabrze nor Iraldur thought we would have much need of an army where we were going. Small groups of stone-men might still be wandering about, but they would be easily dealt with.

I shifted uncomfortably on my mare. I had never ridden before, and I clung to the pommel of the saddle, wishing I had the grace of even the oldest and stoutest of Iraldur's soldiers.

Boaz rode with the skill and grace born of long hours spent in the saddle as a child. Fetizza rode with him, slung about his back in a moistened blanket, and though they should have been a ridiculous sight, somehow the frog and the man radiated only dignity and assurance.

Setkoth lay directly to the east, and Zabrze led us hard and fast toward it. I crawled from the saddle each evening—generally either Kiamet or Boaz had to help me—and sank silently to the hard stony ground. Holdat, who had assigned

himself as general cook and servant to our group, would brew
a reviving tea, then pass around steamed grain and meat, with
a piece of fruit each to sweeten our palates afterward.

Once she had been freed from her blanket, Fetizza would
worry at Holdat until he threw some grain and meat her way,
then she would hop off to the nearest crack in the stone, eye it
carefully, then somehow, impossibly, squeeze herself into it.

As soon as Fetizza had chosen her crack for the night, the
entire camp would rearrange itself so that we lay to the north
and east of her. No one wanted to wake up in the midst of a
cold river.

Behind us stretched reawakening land, before us and to our
flanks stretched the stone, relieved only by the representations of Threshold. The eyes still watched, and sometimes I
thought they winked.

Nzame did not bother me on this ride to Setkoth. Perhaps
because I was so exhausted and unresponsive each night—
both from the effects of the day's ride and the lingering ex-
haustion of our attempts to reawaken so many stone-men. So
as soon as I closed my eyes I slipped into a deep sleep, awakening only when Boaz laid a hand on my shoulder and told
me I had to rise.

Yet if I slept well, Boaz often had dark shadows under his
eyes, and I wondered if Nzame disturbed his sleep now instead. But I did not ask. Boaz would only tell me that he slept
well, and that he would prevail against the demon when he
confronted him in the Infinity Chamber.

I did not like to have Boaz lie to me, so I did not probe.

We rode for twelve days until we reached the Lhyl River. It
wound its peaceful way through the barren landscape, surrounded by reed banks of stone.

"Why can't Nzame alter the water?" I asked Boaz as we
reined in beside it late one afternoon.

"Probably because it is descended from the tears of the
Soulenai," he answered. "It has too much magic."

Fetizza wriggled behind him, and he twisted about and
lowered her to the ground.

She bounded through the stone reeds and leaped into the
water with a huge splash.

"Look!" I cried. Wherever droplets of water had splashed, stone had turned to green.

I grinned at Boaz. "I think nothing can compete with the magic of Fetizza, and she was all your creation, beloved."

He smiled back. "*Our* creation, for she was born of your goblet."

We camped by the river that night. Setkoth was a day's ride away, and we all made a determined effort to be cheerful for this night. Who knew what horrors Setkoth would contain.

We bathed and splashed—even the horses were pleased to see such an expanse of water, and they rolled about in its edges.

And wherever water splashed, so green spread. By the time the evening meal was cooked, the riverbanks on either side of the Lhyl were green and fragrant for a hundred paces above and below the camp.

Holdat waved us to the campfire, but instead of handing out plates of food, he held a bucket and tipped its contents before Isphet, Boaz, and myself.

Hundreds of tiny stone frogs.

"I spent the evening wandering the banks, looking for these," he said. "Fetizza's efforts have produced the reeds. Now we need the song to serenade us to sleep."

Iraldur, who had sat down with Zabrze, stared as the three of us, laughing, transformed the frogs one by one. They were far easier to transform than people. Not only were they smaller than a stone-man, but their life force was much stronger.

"Will you have to do that to every creature within Ashdod?" Iraldur asked.

Isphet and I sighed, and left it for Boaz to answer.

"I hope not, Iraldur. I surely hope not. Once Nzame is gone, then I pray the land and all its creatures will return to life."

I dropped my eyes and let the last frog bound away into the dusk. For me, at least, the evening had lost its cheer.

Setkoth was a stone grave.

I remembered a city that was awash with color and almost indecent with vibrant life. It had spread along both sides of the river, glistening in the sun, banners and washing fluttering in the breeze, streets crowded with the businesses of trade and crime, brown faces and arms leaning from windows and balconies, bright eyes laughing at the passage of life.

Now all was stone. The buildings, the streets, the life, the hopes.

Tears ran down Zabrze's face. I had never seen him so openly emotional; not even Neuf's death had touched him so deeply. This had been his city, his home. Now it was a tomb.

And we trailed silently through that damned city like mourners come to acknowledge the dead.

We could see no one, flesh or stone. No dogs, no mules, no people.

The city was empty.

"If they were alive," Boaz said, "they would have fled. Everything, everyone."

"Where?" Zabrze asked, his voice harsh. *"Where?"*

"They would have followed the river, Zabrze. North perhaps, thinking to get to En-Do^r. They were our major trading partner."

"We had a few hundred come through to Darsis," Iraldur called from his chariot. "But as Boaz said, most would have chosen to follow the river north."

If they hadn't been herded south to feed Nzame. No one said that aloud, but I knew everyone thought it.

The dog ran ahead of us, nosing about the stone. She paused in a dark doorway, peered intently, then continued her run along the street.

We came to the main city square. Stalls were still set up about its edges, stone awnings drooping over stone produce, stone baskets littering the pavement.

"It looks as though the stone swept right through here, taking everything but the people," Iraldur said. "Look, those baskets have been dropped as they turned to stone—"

"And the people?" Zabrze asked. "Where are they?"

Iraldur stared at him, then jumped from his chariot and began shouting orders to his men, dividing them into search parties and fanning them out through the city.

"Zabrze?" Boaz asked softly. "Were your children at home?"

Zabrze jerked his head in a nod, then swung his horse into a northern avenue.

Boaz followed, Isphet and I, and a dozen soldiers, close behind. A moment later Iraldur seized a horse from one of his men and came after us.

Zabrze led us to a walled house that had once been very beautiful. It had relied on space and elegance to impart graciousness, and there were few outward signs that this was the residence of the heir to the throne.

The gates stood open, the courtyard empty. Gardens stretched behind the house—all stone, lifeless. The dog trotted inside, tail pricked curiously.

Zabrze followed, slowly and heavily. Isphet was at his shoulder, her eyes on her husband rather than the house before her.

Iraldur gestured for the soldiers to encircle the house, then he joined Boaz and myself as we walked inside. It was cool, stone working even more effectively than brick to keep the sun at bay.

Boaz took my hand and we walked slowly into the first of the reception rooms. It was empty, and so we walked into the next room, larger and more impressive than the other, and there encountered horror such as I could never have imagined.

Zabrze was standing in the center of the room, staring. Isphet had sunk to her knees, her hands to her mouth.

Before them ranged seven statues—except they were not statues at all, but people made stone.

Children made stone.

They stood in a perfect line, arranged as if to receive whoever came a-visiting. One hand of each was raised, as if to clasp that of the visitor. Their faces, even roughened and thickened by the process of entombment, had been forced into smiles of welcome—except such despair radiated out from these frozen smiles that most visitors would have run rather than stayed.

And there was something else. Something different about these stone-children. They had been so carefully, so artfully arranged.

As if Nzame had known Zabrze would eventually come back to find them.

Boaz looked at me, then moved to Zabrze's side. "Zabrze. There is hope. Let me touch them . . . and Tirzah. Isphet, you stay here."

Zabrze did not respond. He could not drag his stare away from his children.

Boaz and I moved to the first of the statues. It was of a small boy, only seven or eight, and Boaz laid a hand on his shoulder. He looked up. "Tirzah . . ."

I laid a hand on the other shoulder. There was a force, an energy, within this statue, but it was different from what we'd felt in any other stone-man.

My eyes met Boaz's. "We must try."

He nodded, although I think he was as scared as I.

I closed my eyes, took a deep breath, and concentrated, feeling for the force within the stone, feeling Boaz beside me.

We searched, but very carefully. We could feel something there, but it was strange. Then, just as we tentatively touched it, whatever it was snapped awake. It snatched at us.

It was going to trap us!

Boaz reacted first. As he had in the Chamber of Dreaming, he grabbed me with his power and hauled me back . . . back from something so dark and so malevolent it writhed . . . *seethed toward me with the evil of the demon awakened!*

My eyes flew open and I tore my hand away, trembling almost uncontrollably. Another heartbeat and it would have caught me. Trapped me into a similar horror to that which had trapped the poor boy.

Boaz and I had escaped—barely—but it was too late for Zabrze's son. The stone darkened and marbled . . . with death rather than life. Streaks of decay rippled over the boy's shoulders and arms, and then muscles and tissue formed and ripened into flesh that looked like it had been ten days dead and left in the sun to rot.

Boaz stepped about the horror and pulled me back five or six paces. Zabrze gave a great cry, and would have moved forward had not Isphet and Iraldur stopped him.

The stone continued to transform. The process was almost complete. A corpse stood before us, its arm extended, what was left of its face twisted into its macabre grin.

Bone poked through in spots, and the flesh had rotted and

slid off a portion of its skull, leaving a bare and pathetic patch to glint in the light.

"*Orphrat!*" Zabrze screamed, and twisted in Isphet's and Iraldur's hands.

What had been Orphrat spoke—and although the voice was not his, nor the words, we could all hear the soul of the little boy crying out behind it, screaming for help.

"Zabrze. You came. How nice. I—we—have been waiting. Do you like what I have done with your children, Zabrze? But, Zabrze, do not fear. I have left one in reasonable condition . . . but which one? Which?"

The horror twisted about and stared at Boaz and myself.

"Ah. The Cantomancers. Stopped off for a visit on their way into . . . Infinity." It cackled with laughter. "Or would they prefer to die? Your choice, beloveds, your choice."

I turned away, screwing my eyes shut, clamping hands over my ears, but still Nzame continued to speak, continued to *use* that boy in a way that desecrated his soul.

"Are you willing to try to release the one that *is* still alive? You felt what was in this boy, and you managed to escape only just in time. I wait in five of the others; ready for you now. Stronger. Only one is free of me. Only one just stone and soul. Choose. But make the wrong choice and I will seize you. Pick the wrong one to release and you will spend eternity with me. Choose. Or walk out of the house alive but knowing that you leave one child alive and despairing."

It stopped, and then there was the sickening sound of lumps of flesh falling to the ground.

I opened my eyes, unable not to witness this. Orphrat disintegrated until only bones stood there, one skeletal arm still obscenely extended.

And then even the bones crashed to the ground.

Zabrze screamed.

"Get him out of here!" Boaz shouted, but Zabrze hit out at Isphet and Iraldur as they tried to drag him away.

"*NO! NO! These are my children! I cannot leave them!*"

"Oh, gods," Boaz said.

"He might have been lying," Isphet said quietly. "They might all be dead. They might be nothing but a trap."

"Or they might all be *alive*!" cried Zabrze.

Silence.

"No," I said finally. "I think he was telling the truth. I think that only one of those statues still contains a living soul."

"So why can't you touch them and find which one it is?" Zabrze asked. "Why?"

"He has infused these statues with such malevolence—with pieces of his own spirit—that Tirzah and I only barely escaped. I think our touch awoke him in the stone. He knows we're here now. He's waiting. Five of these statues will trap us. One we can save. But which? Which?"

I flinched at the unconscious repetition of Nzame's taunt. Which?

"There is no point standing here debating the matter," Iraldur said. "We do not need to make up our minds at this very instant."

He tugged at Zabrze's arm, and this time Zabrze did not object. "Isphet, take Zabrze into another room. I'll send in some soldiers to remove what is left of Orphrat. Boaz, Tirzah, wait here for me."

When Iraldur returned his manner was brusque, but I could see he'd not been unaffected by what had happened in this room. He must have known these children.

"Well?" he said. "If you cannot discover the solution to this deadly puzzle I will order my men to block up the windows and doors into this house and entomb these children right here."

"No!" Boaz said. "You can't—"

"I cursed well can," Iraldur snapped, "if you can't tell the difference."

I stared at the row of statues. One was alive. Could he or she hear us? See us as we stood debating?

"You are too important," I said to Boaz. "You cannot be risked here."

"And I will not risk you," he said tightly. "There is nothing we can do, Tirzah. Nothing. Iraldur, you may as well order your men—"

There was a low growl, and we jumped. I whipped about, expecting one of the statues to talk, to taunt us again with Nzame's voice. But it was only the dog, sniffing about the feet of the nearest statue.

She growled, and bared her teeth at it. She backed away a step, stiff-legged, the hair raised in a stiff ridge down her spine.

"Get that cur away from my children!" Zabrze, back in the doorway, Isphet anxious beside him.

"Zabrze," she said gently. "Come away. There's nothing we can—"

The dog sniffed the next statue and snarled and snapped at it.

"Get that cur away from—"

"No!" I shouted as Iraldur stepped toward the dog. "No, let her be. Zabrze, I want to see her reaction. Please . . . please."

He stared at me, but kept silent, and we looked back to the dog.

She reached the third statue, sniffing tentatively about its feet. She sniffed again, more confidently, gave a brief wag of her tail, then trotted on to the next in line. This she growled at almost immediately, as she did at the remaining two.

We all stared at the third statue. My heart was hammering in my chest.

"Are we going to trust a dog?" Boaz asked quietly.

"Or is it yet another trap?" Iraldur said. "Why did *that* dog survive in the stone land when no other did? I say we entomb the children as they stand. Zabrze, it is the only sensible thing to do. Isphet has a womb to replace what you've lost."

That was entirely the wrong thing to say.

"Then you can entomb me with them!" Zabrze screamed. "For it was I who left them here to die!"

"I will—" Boaz began.

"No," I broke in. "Isphet and I will. Isphet? Will you do this with me?"

She nodded, spoke quietly to Zabrze who looked as horrified at risking Isphet as he did at leaving his children, then joined me.

I called the dog over and led her gently to the third statue.

Again she sniffed it, her tail wagging slightly, curiously, then stared at me as if asking what the fuss was about. I let her go and she trotted away.

"Isphet?" I said, and was horrified to hear my voice tremble. Boaz was staring at us, stiff, frightened. We knew that if the statue was a trap then neither Isphet nor I would have the strength to pull back.

Isphet took my hand, and squeezed it gently. "If I'd known you were going to prove so much trouble I'd have slammed that door in Ta'uz's face the night he led you to me."

"If I'd known you were going to prove so bad-tempered I'd have braved the guards' spears to run from you."

We both tried to smile, but neither of us managed it.

Then we placed our hands side by side on the statue's shoulder.

I think everyone in the room shifted forward slightly as if they were going to pull us back.

We increased the pressure of our hands, feeling the other's presence, taking strength and courage from it, seeking out the energy within the statue.

We found it instantly, and both of us flinched and recoiled.

Behind us, Boaz cried out and made as if to move forward. Iraldur, sensible to the last, grabbed him and held him back.

All this I saw as if through a curtain of pain. The pain and misery of the girl trapped within the stone.

Help me! Help me! Help me!

Isphet was crying, sobbing, and I think I was too. We reached out with all the strength we had, and pulled that girl through the monstrous veil of sorcery that had trapped her.

The transformation was instantaneous. Suddenly there was flesh, not stone beneath our hands—and it was good flesh, firm and cool. She collapsed into our arms with a pitiful wail, and I—

Screamed as the remaining statues exploded about us. The girl, Isphet, and I were thrown to the floor, bleeding from dozens of tiny cuts from the shards of stone that flew through the air.

I lost consciousness for a moment, then felt hands drag me to my feet. Coughing and spluttering, I choked on the thick dust that had filled the room.

The dog was howling, and I could hear others coughing and retching. They dragged me through the room, through the choking cloud of dust, then eventually out of the house into the blessedly hot, clear sunlight.

I was still coughing, although not so badly, and someone threw water into my face.

It shocked me enough that I opened my eyes. Boaz had his arms about me, his own face gray with dust, his eyes wide and reddened.

Beside us Zabrze had his arms about the girl and Isphet.

Everyone, I realized, was crying.

Her name was Layla, and she was eighteen, the eldest daughter of Zabrze and Neuf.

The story she told would keep many of us awake through a multitude of nights.

That evening we sat in Setkoth's main square, a small fire flickering before us, the dog cuddled in Layla's lap, Layla herself cuddled in her father's arms. Zabrze could not let her go; Isphet and I had tried to take her aside to wash the dust from her face and limbs, but Zabrze had been so insistent that streaks of dust still ran down her cheeks and matted her hair.

The house Zabrze had ordered destroyed. Now it was rubble lying over the rubble of his children's bodies.

"We'd heard of the problems at Threshold," Layla said softly. "We'd heard that Consecration Day had run amok. And we'd feared. But we did not know what to do. We waited for Father and Mother to come home . . ."

Zabrze winced and closed his eyes.

". . . but the servants said that we had nothing to worry about. That we were the sons and daughters of Prince Zabrze and that no one would dare touch us. They told us it was better to stay home, stay inside; better that than fleeing north with the thousands who'd taken to the river transports."

She paused, her eyes lowered, her hand stroking the dog. She was very pretty underneath all that dust and the horror of the memory.

"So we did. One day the stone came. It . . . it *crackled* through the city. I was on the roof balcony with Orphrat and Joelen, and we could see it spread in a gigantic arc from the south. It rippled toward us, a sea of stone, and we were terrified, but we could not move.

"And then everything turned to stone about us. We were left

with flesh and breath, but the balustrade beneath our hands and the tiles beneath our feet turned to stone. The birds in the sky dropped and shattered. Even the air seemed heavier.

"But the worst thing was the silence. Setkoth had been alive with noise, then there was nothing. The silence of death."

She paused, and I saw Zabrze's arms tighten. All the love he'd harbored for the other six was now focused on Layla. I hoped he would eventually be able to let her go.

"We fled inside. No one knew what to do. Many of the servants—most people still in Setkoth, I think—had been left alive, but they were panicked. Who can blame them? They fled—"

"I will *flay* the skin from their—"

"Zabrze," Isphet said gently. "There is no guilt or blame here, only fear and the spreading stone. Hush, now."

He glared at her, but he quietened down.

"Imran and I . . ."

Imran had been Zabrze's eldest son.

". . . took the others into the reception room where . . ."

Her voice faltered, but she took a deep breath and continued. "Where you found us. We waited. We didn't know what to do. Oh, Father! We should have fled with the others! We should—"

"Hush," Zabrze said, and stroked Layla's hair and kissed her cheek. "Isphet is right. There is no blame in this nightmare. None at all."

She trembled, then gathered her courage again. "We sat for hours, not knowing what to do. No one was left. We thought you'd—"

She broke off, but we all knew what she'd been going to say. We thought you'd come. There they had sat. Seven frightened, beautiful children, waiting for their mother and father.

"There were steps outside. We did not know whether to run and hide, or to stay where we were. But we were the children of Zabrze and Neuf"—and she straightened her back—"and so we chose to stay and receive whatever came."

Zabrze hid his face in her hair; I had tears running down my cheeks.

"It was . . . men of stone. Oh, Father! They moaned, and waved their arms, and we all screamed and tried to run, but it was too late, too late. There was nowhere to go, nowhere to hide."

She stopped, swallowed, and collected herself. "Then Chad-Nezzar came in. At first I was relieved. Help *was* here! But it was not really Chad-Nezzar at all. He was blackened and twisted, and he said many blackened and twisted things. He said that we were to die and yet not die. He said we were to serve Nzame, and he would be all the father and mother and lover we would ever need."

She was stumbling, rushing her words now.

"He ran toward us, his arms cartwheeling about, screaming, and we screamed, and then pain such as I could never imagine overwhelmed me. I felt as if I was on fire, and— strangely—I could feel the pain of my brothers and sisters as well and it was all too much, but I could not let go. I wanted to die but I could not. And then I felt this . . . this *thing,* this *demon* tear into the souls of my brothers and sisters and warp them and rip them and *change* them until they lived only for death, lived only to deal death, and oh, *gods!* I could not escape them, I was trapped with them, and every minute seemed a lifetime, and a thousand, thousand lifetimes I passed with the twisted dead souls of my brothers and sisters until you . . . you . . ."

She broke down, and Zabrze held her and rocked her and told her how much he loved her.

I realized why Nzame had left her alive, and had left the dog alive to reveal her. He had wanted Zabrze to know of the suffering of his children. The full horror. It was not enough that they should just die.

We sat in a silent circle, watching, witnessing, sorrowing with and for them, until Layla and Zabrze sat up and wiped their eyes.

Then Holdat served us the evening meal, and that touch of normality did us all more good than a single word or look of compassion, and I thought that Holdat was wasted as a cook.

Despite all she'd been through, all the despair she'd suffered, Layla retained a sweetness that was humbling in its purity.

After we had eaten she kissed and thanked Isphet and myself, and smiled and kissed Isphet again when Zabrze told her that she was his wife. She cried for Neuf, but she had experienced a good deal of death over the past months, and I think she thought that Neuf's death in the Lagamaal Plains was a gentle passing compared to the many others Layla had shared.

FORTY-SIX

Fetizza ran amok as we slept. She must have done, for when I awoke it was to find the square and surrounding streets puddled with water, and spears of rock jutting toward the sun. Houses had reverted to their mud-brick, tiles to their ceramic glory, and reed . . . well, to reed.

Frogs choraled from the river.

"Threshold," Boaz said to Zabrze.

"Tomorrow," Zabrze said. "We'll go down tomorrow."

I think he wanted to spend a day of peace with Layla. Just one day, before we confronted the full horror of Nzame.

So we spent the day about Setkoth. As we'd thought, and as Layla had confirmed, many if not most of its people had fled north to En-Dor.

Others had not been so lucky. Layla said she was aware, locked in her stone, that the stone-men had shuffled through Setkoth day and night for weeks, searching for live flesh to drive down to Nzame.

"I would hear screaming, and the thud of stone feet," she said to me. "And I would hear . . . feel, I don't know . . . hear Nzame screaming for food. He had to be fed every day."

She was quiet for a minute or two, and I tightened my hold on her arm. She was a lovely girl, in character as much as feature, and I was not much older than her. I wished I could have come through my trials with as much grace as Layla had.

"I lay awake for a long time last night," she said, and she

smiled at me, blinking in the sun. "I listened for the frogs. I never realized before now how beautifully they sang."

I studied her carefully.

"And when Holdat served my supper last night, I swear that the ladle he used whispered to me."

"Layla . . . Layla, you must speak with your stepmother soon. I think she has a great many things to teach you."

"Yes." Layla squeezed my arm. "You and she both, I think."

"You have been much altered by your experience," I remarked.

"I have been illumed," she said. "Isphet is going to be very good for this realm and this people."

After that, there was not much left to say.

One more day. One more day and it would all be over. One way or another. Boaz was so introspective he would hardly speak, but the manner in which he made love to me that night did all the talking that was necessary.

Sweet, loving, bitter, sad. Good-bye. I could *feel* it.

I walked the summer meadows of Viland again, locked in dream. Cool grass brushed my ankles, fragrant flowers teased my senses.

I wandered, alone, afraid, trapped. Waiting.

He *slithered* across the meadow toward me, snakelike yet man-formed.

Go away. Go back. I will kill him!

"I can say nothing to deter him."

Fool! You have not even tried! Take him away, Tirzah! Flee to Viland before I decide to vent my wrath on you!

"You tried that, with Zabrze's children, and failed."

That was nothing but a diversion . . . did you like what I'd done to those children? Did you appreciate it?

"You could not touch Layla's sweetness, Nzame. Her purity remained untouched by your stain."

He hissed. *Go back! Go Back!*

"Why? Do you fear us? Is Boaz going to destroy you?"

I told you before, bitch. There are only two options for him. He fails and dies, or succeeds in dragging me through to Infinity where he will spend eternity locked in my embrace.

And in that instant realization hit me. I understood why the Song of the Frogs was so important. Why the Soulenai had insisted Boaz be able to use it. My mouth dropped slowly open.

Tell him to go back! There are no other options! Tell him—

I was so stunned at my own discovery I paid Nzame no attention. My mistake.

He seized me by the hair and dragged my head back. I tried to scream, but nothing came out.

Tirzah, listen to me well. He intends to meld with me, use the power of the One within Threshold to meld with me and drag me through into Infinity.

But, sweet Tirzah, there is a trap he does not yet know about. Shall I tell you? Yes, yes I shall. Tirzah, you and he are so closely bound in power and in love that should he meld with me there is a chance that for an instant he will give me an opportunity for escape.

He paused. I was sobbing with terror by this stage. How could I have been so foolish as to relax about this demon?

Where, Tirzah? Where? Into your womb, Tirzah. I think I shall grow me new strength in your womb. For a single instant when Boaz merges with me his bond with you will provide me with a bridge . . . a bridge to that tiny, fragile, vulnerable body you harbor in your womb. What shall you do, Tirzah, when you wander bereft as Boaz lingers in Infinity and I grow in your womb? What shall you do? What shall you do? What shall—

I screamed and screamed, rocking up with such force I hit my skull on the head of the bed.

Boaz grabbed me. "Tirzah? *Tirzah?*"

I couldn't reply. I covered my face with my hands and sobbed.

"He *lies,* Tirzah. Whatever he said, it was a lie."

"Boaz—"

"Don't believe him."

"Boaz, would you come back with me to Viland if I asked you? Would you—"

"Tirzah!" He forced my hands from my face so he could stare into my eyes. "Tirzah," he said more gently. "If I leave

Nzame to grow in Threshold nowhere will be safe. I must go in tomorrow. I must."

"Will you come back, Boaz?"

He was silent, dropping his eyes.

"I know what you will do. I believe what Nzame told me, for it makes sense. You will use your power as a Magus to drag him all the way through into Infinity."

"I will not be trapped, Tirzah."

"No," I said bitterly, "you will not be trapped in Infinity, Boaz, but you *will* be trapped in the Place Beyond."

I knew what the Song of the Frogs meant. Boaz would use the power of the One to drag Nzame through to Infinity, then use his arts as a Cantomancer and the power of the Song of the Frogs to escape from Infinity to the Place Beyond. But there he would remain. There was no pathway from the Place Beyond back to here.

"Sometimes," Boaz said, "we have to take what we are given. Tirzah, I am so very, very sorry. But it is the only way."

I lowered my head and wept. "I want a husband alive and trapped in my arms, not dead and at peace with his father!"

"Tirzah—"

"Boaz, I'm pregnant."

"You *can't* be!"

"The damage you did was not permanent. I healed, slowly, but I healed." I tried to smile. "This baby we conceived while we were training in the Abyss. Boaz"—tears threatened, and I took a moment to blink them away—"Nzame said that if you melded with him, our shared love and power would create a bridge between you and me, and Nzame said he would take refuge in the baby. He said . . . he said he would grow within my womb while you . . . while you . . ."

"Why didn't you tell me earlier?"

"It took me over two months to believe it myself, and then I thought you would insist I remain behind in the Abyss. And then . . . well, there was so much happening about us . . ."

"Tirzah, I don't know if he's right or not. I just don't know. But to be safe, it would be better if you—"

"No!"

"Tirzah, *listen* to me. If he *is* right . . . do you want to grow

Nzame within you? Give him physical form? Rid yourself of the child, Tirzah. You must."

"It is all I will have left of you," I whispered. "All. Don't make me do this. Please . . ."

"Oh, gods, beloved. Do you think I *want* you to discard this child?" He slid his hand down over my belly, feeling for the life within me, cradling it gently. "A child is the greatest gift you could give me, but I cannot risk you like this. Nor could I submit a child of mine to the horror that enveloped Zabrze's children."

"Boaz . . . don't make me . . . please . . ."

He said nothing, but folded me in his arms.

"Please . . ."

FORTY-SEVEN

We were silent in the morning. What do you say to someone you love and will lose that day? There are no good-byes possible.

Everyone was still and silent, as if our mood had spread throughout Setkoth. Zabrze had found several riverboats, and Boaz and I boarded the first of them with Zabrze, Isphet, Iraldur, and a unit of soldiers. Other soldiers boarded the boats behind us.

But I did not think soldiers could help us very much this day.

Layla stayed behind, as did Kiamet and Holdat. I left the Book of the Soulenai and the Goblet of the Frogs with them. What need would I ever have of them again? What comfort could they give but bitter reminders of the man I had lost?

The oars dipped and bit into the river, the frogs chorused, and I think I hated the entire world at that moment. Isphet came to talk to me but I threw off her hand, and walked to the prow. I had four or five hours left. Four or five.

Boaz joined me and we stood silently, looking forward.

"Do you know," he said softly, "that I loved you from the moment you carved those frogs in the glass in Setkoth?"

I remained silent, bitter. The breeze whipped hair about my eyes, and I twisted it back behind my ears with sharp, jerky movements.

"We sat there, opposite sides of the table, the glass connecting us, seeding love. I wonder what it thought, beloved, at the touch of both our hands?"

I bit my lip, determined not to look at him.

He sighed. "Tirzah, I wish it could have been different for you and me. I wish we had met as water-carrier and laundress, and then nothing would have stepped between us."

A stray Juit bird rested among the reeds, and I wondered what it was doing here. Had Fetizza's influence spread so far that the lake was free? Or did the Juit bird sit here, waiting for Fetizza's magic to release the lake and marshes?

"We could have danced through the spring festivals on the banks of the river and spent a drunken night amid the reeds."

I smiled despite myself, then bit it back.

"I would have begged your father for your hand, and he would have sat back and pretended to think about it. But he would have agreed, for water-carriers are ever the good catch for young laundresses."

Damn him. *Damn* him!

"And we would have married under the summer solstice, and you would have grumbled at the number of children I gave you to trip your feet to and from the wash trough."

He took a deep shaky breath. "But all of that was denied us, Tirzah. We were Magus and slave, and so I spent months maltreating you, and caused you more pain than any person should have to bear."

"Boaz—"

"And now I shall cause you further pain. Tirzah, can you forgive me for all I have done and will do to you?"

"*Stop it!* Boaz, you and I would have made a worse water-carrier and laundress than we did Magus and slave. I don't want to talk. Please. All we will do is sadden these last few hours."

"I think nothing can sadden them any more than they will

be, Tirzah," he said, but he held me in silence for a long time and we watched the river slide by.

The stone was thick and callused the closer we slid to Threshold, and I thought that Lake Juit must still be entombed. Was Memmon still wandering demented the path between river and house? I shuddered, and Boaz's arms tightened.

"And what I regret most of all is what I must ask you to do to our child. Tirzah, I do not want to pass into the Place Beyond knowing that Nzame grows safe and secure in your womb. I could not bear that. Please, I beg you, I don't want to leave you with Nzame."

"I will do as you ask, Boaz. I promise."

"Thank you," he whispered. "Now I know that our sacrifice will be worth it."

Stone-men wandered the banks, moaning. Not many, and the soldiers could deal with them.

Before us reared Threshold, looking cruelly beautiful, alive, vibrant, growing.

Waiting.

Its shadow winked.

Gesholme had crumbled to piles of stone rubble about it; Nzame wanted nothing to spoil the view of the river. The pyramid did not look very different from the one we had fled from; the golden capstone glinted in the sun, the plates of blue-green glass shone, and the dark mouth still yawned.

"Brother . . ."

Zabrze stood behind us, uncertainty welling in his eyes. "Brother, are you sure you can succeed?"

"Yes, of course I am," Boaz said, and managed a confident smile. "From this afternoon you shall have your realm back, Chad-Zabrze." He clapped Zabrze on his shoulder, then strode past him toward the landing.

"Tirzah?" Zabrze asked. "Will you stay here?"

"No," I said. "I am going to see this through." And I likewise pushed past him.

Zabrze knows, too, I thought. Somehow he knows.

Isphet caught me up. "Tirzah?" Her fingers were sharp about my elbow. *What is Boaz going to do?*

Boaz was down on the landing now, watching impassively

as a group of ten soldiers disabled the three stone-men who wove our way. He looked so beautiful, clad in a simple white robe with his hair combed back. Tonight, if all went well, he would rest with the Soulenai.

If all went well.

"He is going to trap Nzame into Infinity," I said. "And then he will use the Song of the Frogs to escape to the Place Beyond."

"But that will mean—" Isphet stopped as she saw the look on my face.

"Yes, Isphet, I know exactly what it will mean."

She stared at me, then nodded. Isphet was not going to waste time on useless platitudes, and for that I was grateful.

"Then let us see this through, Tirzah. Let us share the witnessing."

I took a deep breath, inclined my head, and we walked off the boat arm in arm.

The Magi were planted about Threshold. Hundreds of their black forms greeted us as we walked down the avenue, waving to and fro, moaning Nzame's name, their feet merged to the ankles with the black glassy rock that had spread out from Threshold's skirts. They looked like a garden, neatly planted, and I supposed in a manner they were.

No stone-men bothered us once we'd passed the wharf.

Nothing bothered us save Nzame's throbbing presence.

As we drew closer to Threshold we saw that it was not entirely as before. The pyramid had grown in size. It was almost twice the height and circumference it had once been. And behind the plate glass writhed eyes, thousands of them, and hands and faces pressed against the glass for an instant and then dissolved away into nothingness.

All the souls of those Nzame had eaten. Trapped forever in the glass of Threshold.

We stopped some twenty paces from the ramp that led to its mouth.

I felt sick and faint. I could not believe that Boaz was going to walk up that ramp and into Threshold.

Boaz looked at Zabrze, and nodded, then he turned to me. He wrapped his arms about me and pulled me close. I clung to him as tightly as I could, wanting to scream at him not to go, not to go in. *Oh, gods, don't leave me like this, don't go, don't go . . .*

"I have lived my life in the thrall and service of this beast," he said very quietly. "It is fitting that I end my life, and its life, in this manner."

He tipped my head back. I could hardly see his face through the blur of my tears. "Oh, Tirzah, please don't cry. We will meet again, you and I, in the Place Beyond. There we will spend eternity. Please, Tirzah, please smile for me."

I tried, gods know how I tried, but I could not do it. I buried my face in his chest and sobbed anew, loathing myself that I could not smile for him.

Hands gripped my shoulders and pulled me back.

Zabrze.

"Good-bye, Tirzah," Boaz whispered, and kissed me softly, then he was gone.

Nzame raged. We could hear him, we could feel him, and somehow we could also feel Boaz walking through the corridors, walking up and up, walking forward into the Infinity Chamber.

I don't know how he survived that far. Perhaps he managed to use his powers as either Magus or Cantomancer to fend off Nzame, but eventually he walked into the bleak, dreadful Infinity Chamber.

Fool! Doomed fool! Go back! Go back!

The faces and hands pressing against the walls of Threshold became even more frantic, the shapes of their noses, foreheads, and chins bulging through, their hands beating, pressing, seeking escape, escape . . .

Nzame screamed, wordlessly now, and I let Zabrze hold me tight.

The faces and hands disappeared, and were replaced with bloodied writing wriggling across the entire outer walls.

Within, Boaz had activated the Infinity Chamber.

Energy buzzed up through the soles of my sandals, and each of the Magi planted down the avenue and about Threshold tipped back his head and screamed.

Light flashed deep within the pyramid, and then the entire structure illuminated as if it contained a sun.

I cried out, as did every person around me, and Zabrze wrenched me about, trying to shield my eyes with his hand.

Tirzah!

Something screamed. I don't know what it was, what . . . who was it?

Tirzah!

And then nothing.

Nothing.

The light had faded. The writing had disappeared. The faces and hands trapped within the glass had gone.

Threshold glinted peacefully in the sun.

Innocently.

Nzame had gone.

As had all of the Magi. They had melted into pools of black mess, and even these were rapidly evaporating in the afternoon sun.

There was a resounding crack, and a fissure split from the river to the southeast corner of Threshold. And then another, running from the river to the southwest corner.

And then the entire land about us was cracking and rupturing.

"Boaz!" I screamed, and wrenching myself from Zabrze's grasp, ran inside Threshold.

It was black, everything was black. Nzame had fused everything into black.

Black and slippery. I fell over a dozen times as I ran up the main corridor toward the Infinity Chamber, once hitting my face so badly my nose began to bleed, but I scrambled up, dashing the blood away from my face, running, running, running.

I felt nothing from the pyramid. Nothing.

I ran about the final few bends, vaguely hearing someone far behind me, but unable to distinguish the steps over my own hoarse breathing.

Light trickled around a bend. Bright light. The Infinity Chamber.

I rounded the bend and stood, staring. Light almost as strong as a sun blazed from the door leading into the chamber.

And I could hear something.

The glass. The golden, caged glass was chattering to itself.

I walked forward slowly, very unsure, blinking against the light. I reached the door and extended a hand inside.

Nothing. Just the bemused chattering of the glass.

I hesitated no longer. I had nothing to lose. The light faded—or changed, I'm not sure what—the instant I stepped inside. It was still bright, but now I could see without effort.

I turned around slowly. The chamber was utterly empty.

And the glass glistened cheerily.

Isphet burst in, her chest heaving. "Well?"

I didn't reply, but moved to one of the walls and laid my hand on the glass. Whatever had caused it to scream once—Nzame's influence stretching from the Vale—had now gone. The bridge to the Vale had been broken.

I took a deep breath, listening to the glass. It was happy now, reveling in its beauty.

I felt Isphet lay her hands beside mine.

"Talk to us," she whispered, and the glass did.

There had been a great battle. A man had entered, and had wrestled with Nzame. There had been much pain, and many shouts.

Then the man had opened the bridge into Infinity.

"And then?" I whispered. "And then?"

Then the man and Nzame had vanished. Gone.

"Did Boaz drag Nzame into Infinity?" I whispered, my hands pressed so hard against the glass its edges cut into my palms and fingers. *"Did he drag Nzame into Infinity?"*

The glass supposed so. Both had gone now, hadn't they? They couldn't feel Nzame at all.

"Was . . . was there a bridge created anywhere else?" I asked. "To anyone else?"

The glass was confused. What did I mean?

Isphet turned her eyes from the glass to me.

"Was there a chance that Nzame went . . . elsewhere . . . other than Infinity?"

The glass didn't care. He was gone. That was all that mattered. He was gone. It chattered happily to itself, losing interest in my questioning.

"Tirzah," Isphet said. "Come on now. It is over. He is gone. Come away, now."

And so saying, so whispering, she dragged me out of Threshold.

FORTY-EIGHT

He's gone. They've both gone," Isphet said to Zabrze. "It's over."

Is it? *Is it?* My hand slipped to my belly.

Zabrze turned aside for a moment; he had lost a brother as I had lost a husband. "Setkoth?" he said finally.

"Yes," Isphet said. "Setkoth. We need to get Tirzah . . . we *all* need to get away from here."

"I'll have the soldiers organized into work gangs," Zabrze said, "and pull this thing—"

"No!" I wrenched out of Isphet's hands. "No," I repeated more quietly. "Zabrze, please, leave it for the time being. Boaz might come back. Threshold should remain intact, just in case."

It was a poor argument, I knew, but I did not want to see the Infinity Chamber destroyed. Not yet. Just in case.

"Tirzah. I cannot leave it as it is. It's complete, and too dangerous. I'll order the capstone removed, but not destroyed. And the entrance to be blocked up. If need be, these measures can be reversed. But I will *not* leave it intact for something *else* to seep into it!"

I nodded. He was right.

"Tirzah." Isphet hugged me close. "When we get back to Setkoth, we'll look into the Place Beyond. That may comfort you."

Yes, and perhaps Boaz's shade could tell me . . . give me

some indication . . . I felt queasy, and wondered if I had not escaped pregnancy sickness after all.

Nzame had gone—somewhere—but had he gone far enough and completely enough for his enchantments over land and people to dissipate? Stone cracked and shattered; stone-men revived to wander and blunder as aimlessly as they had when entombed. As Isphet and I stood on the deck of the riverboat watching the banks slip by, we realized that we would both have to spend time ministering to the land and people. Life had revived, but it was saddened and lost.

I would not be allowed much time to grieve.

"Perhaps we can send word to Yaqob," Isphet said. "We will need help."

"Perhaps."

"And those ten thousand stone-men, released, must be wandering the plains between Setkoth and the Darsis border, completely bewildered and without food or clothing. Something must be done about them. Soon. The soldiers left with them will not cope."

"Yes."

"Iraldur can do something on his way home."

"Yes."

"Tirzah, Ashdod needs you, its people need you. Don't slip into a useless morass of self-pity."

I rounded on her, furious. "Do I not even get an hour alone to grieve, Isphet? Must I shrug my shoulders and say, 'Well, what's done is done'?"

"Tirzah—"

"All you can do is stand there and tell me to roll up my sleeves, for work awaits! Do it yourself, Isphet! Call Yaqob if you wish, but *I* want nothing to do with it!"

And I strode away into one of the cabins, slamming the door behind me.

Once there I stood in the center of the cool room, staring about uselessly. My face crumpled, and I began to cry, sinking down to the floor, wrapping my arms about myself and rocking to and fro.

Boaz was gone. He had become so much a part of my life,

so much my complete life, that it was difficult to realize I'd loved him only a year. And then I'd lost him.

Anger replaced grief. *Curse him!* To leave me like this! To so steal my life and then leave me!

And to tell me to kill the child as well. I should do it. I knew the risks. But the threat to the child had just been one more of Nzame's lies . . . hadn't it? And Nzame had truly gone, for otherwise the land would not regenerate so spontaneously . . . would it?

The child would be easy to scathe away now. It had scarcely taken hold, its life still tenuous. A herbal, a night of discomfort and cramps, and then it would be gone.

But it was all I had left of Boaz.

And surely it hadn't been infested by Nzame. I had felt nothing. And I *would* have felt something . . . wouldn't I?

Curse Boaz for leaving me and, in leaving me, telling me to rid my body of his child. That had been the Magus talking. He hadn't wanted the child because even after so many months of repressing that side of himself he was still revolted by the idea of a child, of subdividing the One.

Yes. That was it. Boaz just didn't like children. Didn't want to subdivide.

He knew Nzame had been lying, but Nzame's threat had been a good reason to frighten me into ridding myself of his child.

Yes. Well, curse him! I wasn't going to do it! Had he not hurt me enough already? Anyway, there were still some weeks before the ridding would become dangerous. I could wait. Make sure.

I took a deep breath and wiped my eyes. Isphet and I could talk to the Soulenai—talk to Boaz's shade. Boaz could tell me that all was well, that Nzame was trapped in Infinity. The baby was safe. He would be glad I hadn't aborted it.

I smiled, thinking. I was repeating the pattern of Boaz's father and *his* Tirzah. The father dead, the young wife pregnant. Continuing Avaldamon's magical line.

I stood up and brushed myself down. Boaz had been wrong. Everything would be all right.

Zabrze was Chad, Nzame was defeated, but life *would* need help before it reverted to normal. I apologized to Isphet, she hugged me and cried too, and we did what we could.

We did not contact the Soulenai or the Place Beyond for several weeks, because Isphet and I thought Boaz would have a difficult journey from Infinity and it would take time. So we waited. I told Isphet about the baby, and she cried and laughed and patted my cheek and rushed to tell Zabrze.

I did not tell her about Nzame's threat, and she did not think to connect the question I'd asked the glass in the Infinity Chamber with my pregnancy.

The stone had retreated across Ashdod, but left disorder and sometimes destruction in its path. Iraldur agreed to leave five thousand of his men in Ashdod to help. People trickled back into the country from wherever they'd fled, only slowly, but they were coming home. Within days Zabrze had organized work parties to begin the reclamation of the land from the chaos.

People were more difficult. Many had died, no one really knew how many, but Threshold had claimed the lives of thousands in one way or another. Other lives, principally those who had been released from their entombment in stone, would never be the same again. Iraldur's men herded back to Setkoth great crowds of disoriented and emotionally bruised people.

Isphet, Layla, and I spent most of our time with these people, talking, explaining, trying to give hope. Of us all, Layla had the most success. She could remember her own experience, and explain to them why they felt so confused and restless. Most had nightmares that frightened and threatened them without giving a form to that fear. Layla would take their hands and soothe them, often without words.

Isphet was practical, and sometimes that was what they needed. I wandered uselessly for a day or two, not knowing what comfort to give, until I remembered the Book of the Soulenai.

Hold me, soothe me, touch me, love me.

I read to them what tales I thought would help, and even though many of the tales held little direct relevance to their experience, the people would sit about, as close to my knees as they could get, and listen with peaceful eyes and gentle smiles. They liked to hear of the Soulenai, and Holdat told me one day that many of those I'd read to spent their evenings down by the reed banks of the Lhyl, listening to the Song of the Frogs.

Hold me, soothe me, touch me, love me.

Zabrze had, as was his right, appropriated the royal palace in Setkoth, and Isphet and I moved in. Isphet as his wife and now Chad'zina, I as a royal in my own right, both of us as Cantomancers.

Setkoth accepted us with few raised eyebrows and almost no comment. Everyone had lost family or friends; Chad-Zabrze's loss had been worse than many others, and no one blamed him for taking a new wife. Isphet's background as a slave was known . . . but stranger things had gripped this land recently than a slave marrying royalty.

And as for our arts as Cantomancers, well, they were accepted too. There were no Magi left, and the Way of the One had disappeared with them. Elementals moved about openly now. A number had traveled with us from the Abyss, and more were traveling to Setkoth; one group was bringing Zhabroah back to his father. Old ways quickly resurfaced; Elemental magic had been banned, not exterminated.

Amid all this activity my mind returned to Boaz constantly. I worried about the child—perhaps I *should* have rid my womb of it when Boaz died. My sleep was disturbed by nameless dreams—sometimes I thought I heard desperate voices calling my name, thought I saw hands reaching out to me, pleading, but I assumed it was only the effect of watching the faces and hands press against the glass of Threshold that dreadful day.

But mostly I thought of Boaz. I missed him dreadfully. I missed not living my day for him; I missed not planning my every move about his; I missed the arguments, the tensions, the love. Above all, I missed him as a friend, for he had been my only true confidant, and I had been his.

It was cruel that it should have ended like this.

Three weeks after we'd arrived in Setkoth, Isphet came to my room. She brought Layla with her.

"Tonight," she said, and my shoulders slumped in relief. I had thought this moment would never come. I'd considered trying myself, but I wanted Isphet's support.

Now I'd have Layla as well. I knew Isphet had been instructing her in the Elemental arts, and tonight would be her first experience of contact with the Soulenai and the Place Beyond.

There was a circular bathing pool deep in the palace. I'd avoided using it because it reminded me too vividly of the vaulted pool Boaz and I had shared at Threshold, but Isphet said it would suit our needs well.

I ran my fingers through my hair, nervous, excited. I would see Boaz again! A shade only, but it would be his spirit, his essence, and even that would console me.

A movement, and it was Isphet and Layla; Isphet cool and calm, Layla as excited as I, if for different reasons. Both kissed me, and Isphet stroked my cheek with the back of her hand.

"Soon," she whispered, "but now you must be strong for Layla. This is her first time, and she has not the ability of you or Boaz. Be strong for her, support her."

Isphet's power no longer needed the help of the metaled powders. She made sure that Layla and I stood calm and focused by her side, then she cast out her arm.

The water swirled.

Excitement threatened to overwhelm me, but I calmed myself and concentrated, feeling Layla's nervousness and reaching out to her with my own power.

Isphet's hand arced again, and the vivid colors swirled within the water.

"Watch the colors, Layla. *Feel* them. Listen to them . . . listen . . . can you feel us listening as well? Can you feel me? Can you feel Tirzah?"

"Yes," Layla whispered.

Feel. Listen. Submit.

It was so sweet to submit to the Soulenai. *Oh . . .* I closed my eyes, feeling their power ripple through me, explore, touch, soothe.

I exhaled, then took another great breath. Beside me Layla hesitated, then submitted, and I shared her wonder at her first intimate contact with the Soulenai.

They surged through me, excited, almost frenetic, and I thought that it was because it had been so long . . . so long . . .

I opened my eyes and let the swirling colors carry me deeper into the embrace of the Soulenai, feeling Isphet and Layla race beside me, feeling the Soulenai . . . feeling . . . reveling in their presence and their touch.

Tirzah! Tirzah!

Yes, I am here.

Tirzah! Tirzah! What is wrong?

I have been sad, but now—

No! No! Something is wrong. Where is Boaz? Where is—

I shrieked, and instantly felt Isphet wrap me in her power, maintaining my contact with the Soulenai.

Where is Boaz? Did he not understand the Song of the Frogs? He should be here! He should—

I cried out again, and now Isphet physically touched me as she spoke to the Soulenai. *He understood. But . . . do you not know what happened?*

He disappeared.

And Nzame? I cried out to them. *And Nzame? Where has he gone? WHERE?*

They both disappeared. Vanished. We could not follow them where they went.

Into Infinity?

Possibly. We would not be able to follow them there.

I calmed myself using all the courage I had. *It must be a long and difficult journey from Infinity into the Place Beyond.*

Perhaps. We hope that is what it is. Maybe Boaz and Nzame still battle through Infinity and he has not yet had a chance to sing the Song of the Frogs.

And maybe Boaz was dead and Nzame . . .

Isphet extended her power, and we glimpsed into the Place Beyond. All we saw was agitation, hands reaching, faces pleading . . .

"I'm sorry, Isphet," I said aloud. "But I do not think I can stand any more of this."

She farewelled the Soulenai and broke the contact.

"Tirzah. The Soulenai were right. Time means nothing in the Place Beyond, or in Infinity. Boaz may still be in Infinity, not knowing that the Soulenai cry out for him."

I lowered my eyes.

"Layla," Isphet said softly, "this is all we will do tonight. Go back to your father, tell him what has happened."

"Yes." Layla kissed my cheek.

"Come," Isphet said, and led me back to my apartment.

"Tirzah, be strong. There is nothing either of us can do but wait. We will try again in a week."

I nodded.

She stared at me, then held me close. "I will stay with you," she said, "for it is not a night for you to be alone."

But Boaz was alone, somewhere, whether in death or Infinity.

We tried, again in a week. Nothing but the Soulenai, asking, pleading—*Where is Boaz?*

Save for the growing mound of my belly, I grew thin and pale, losing interest in life. I lay for hours, clutching the Goblet of the Frogs to my breast.

Hold me, touch me, soothe me, love me.

But it didn't, and I cried.

Isphet left it a month before we tried yet again. A month. Surely a month would do it.

Zeldon and Orteas joined us this time, adding their strength. Isphet was concerned for me, and she wanted more support than Layla alone could give her.

We stood about the pool, Zeldon's arm around me, the love and support of all about me.

The colors swirled.

Tirzah! Tirzah! LOOK!

And, oh, by all the gods, there he was! I cried out, and extended my arms, but he did not see me, and turned his back and walked away, his head down. He was very indistinct, fading into the background glow.

"Boaz! Boaz!"

Tirzah, Tirzah. It has been a long and hard journey for him. The Song of the Frogs almost was not strong enough. It almost failed. Even now Boaz needs to take the final step.

And Nzame? Nzame? I did not really want to know. It was

too late to scathe the babe away now. This child would have to be carried to term. Whatever it was.

Ah, Tirzah, he will not talk to us—he avoids us. He will not let us accept him. We do not know what happened. But he is worried. Worried. He frets.

Frets?

Frets for you, Tirzah. He worries about the baby. There is something about the baby . . . something wrong . . .

Sickness gripped me, and I would have fallen had it not been for Zeldon's strong arm.

. . . something about the baby . . .

. . . something wrong . . .

FORTY-NINE

Isphet took me to my apartment again, closed the door firmly, and sat me down.

"In the Infinity Chamber you asked the glass if there was a chance that a bridge was created to anywhere or *anyone* else . . . if there was a chance Nzame had gone somewhere other than Infinity. Tirzah, *look at me!* Did you fear that Nzame had escaped into the child you carry within you?"

I thought about lying, but I nodded.

"Tell me." Her hands tightened about mine.

I did. I told her everything—the dream, Nzame's threats, Boaz's concerns, and his wish that I miscarry the baby.

"You stupid, *stupid* girl!" Isphet hissed. "Why didn't you do it!"

"Why did Raguel carry her child to term!" I cried. "I *couldn't* kill it, Isphet. Can you possibly understand that? I *couldn't*!" I tore my hands from Isphet's and rested them protectively on my belly.

"Well, it is far too late now." She sat and looked at me, her eyes unreadable. "We will just have to wait for the birth."

"You will not murder this child, Isphet," I said as calmly as I could.

"I will tear its head from its body the moment I even suspect it is Nzame, Tirzah. Has Boaz's sacrifice been for nothing? Have all the deaths, all the sufferings, been for nothing? Do you sit there protecting *Nzame*?"

"Don't you think I don't worry about that every minute of the day and night, Isphet? But what if the child is *not* Nzame? It is all I have left of Boaz. All. I don't want to kill the last chance I have for some happiness."

Three days later we tried again. We had to know. We had to speak with Boaz.

At first he did not appear. The Soulenai were there, agitated again.

We cannot understand it . . . we do not know . . . he cries and frets about the baby, and calls your name, Tirzah. He pleads, calls, cries. He disturbs the peace of the Place Beyond.

Avaldamon was among the Soulenai, but Boaz was beyond him, too.

He turns away and will not look at me, Tirzah. He refuses to be accepted among us. What is wrong? He is with us and yet not with us. He cries about the baby. What is wrong, Tirzah? What?

And then Boaz was there—yet so insubstantial. He held out his hand, pleading, crying.

I screamed his name, but he appeared not to hear me. He was there, but not there, and unable to be touched by our arts.

Tirzah, his mouth formed. *Tirzah? Are you there? Are you there? Can you see me?*

He sobbed, brokenhearted, and I could see his mouth form the word "baby."

I was beside myself, Zeldon again holding me lest I should attempt to cast myself into the Place Beyond.

Tirzah? Tirzah? Oh, Tirzah, I need you. I need you.

I cried out, and fainted.

Isphet would not try again. It was too much. I was sick, almost demented, and she confined me to my bed.

"You will rest here until the baby comes, Tirzah. And in this you will obey me."

Older, healthier, and Chad'zina—I could not argue with her. I lay in my bed, a prisoner, trapped by the baby in my womb. I lay, my hand on my belly, feeling the baby, wondering what it was that moved about inside me.

What about the baby, Boaz? *What is it you want to tell me?*

Kiamet took up guard by my door as he had watched over Boaz and myself in Threshold, and Holdat brought delicacies that he thought might tempt me. He fed me fruit wines from the Goblet of the Frogs, and left the Book of the Soulenai within easy reach. He often sat with me in the evenings, and if I refused to read from the book, he would sit silently with it in his lap, his tanned hands gently stroking it.

Layla came often, with the dog by her side, and Kiath had arrived from the Abyss with Zhabroah. She and Layla sat and played with the baby before me, laughing and saying that soon I would have a baby of my own to play with.

I tried to smile, but too often I saw Isphet's eyes in the dimness by the door, watching, waiting.

I knew she would take this baby from me as soon as it was born. Smother it, drown it, but kill it surely.

. . . *something about the baby . . . he cries and he frets . . . something about the baby . . . something wrong . . . we cannot tell what . . .*

Zabrze came many evenings. Isphet had obviously not told him her fears, for he too laughed at my growing roundness, and put his hand on my belly to feel the baby move.

"So I used to feel Boaz move within my mother's belly, Tirzah. I swear this baby kicks more than he, or any of my children did. It is a feisty babe!"

Ashdod was recovering well. Crops were sprouting forth from land once covered in stone, and the soil proving more fertile than it had in generations.

"And the people have been altered by their experience, too, Tirzah," Zabrze said one evening, Zhabroah crawling about the floor at his feet. "Zeldon and Orteas now lead congregations of Elementals within Setkoth, and the Elemental arts are flowering . . . encouraged by my fine wife." He smiled at

Isphet, and she returned it. I wished she would smile at me with such unfeigned affection.

"Isphet takes many under her care—and sends others to the Abyss to train with the Graces and Yaqob."

Yaqob had stayed within the Abyss. His legs had healed, but he did not walk well, and he was loath to move from the peace of the chasm.

Zhabroah began to fret, and Zabrze bent down and picked him up. "I'll take him back to his nurse, Isphet. You stay here for a while yet. But do not linger overlong." Zabrze gave Isphet a wink, bent down to kiss my cheek, then left.

"I spoke to the Soulenai again today," Isphet said as soon as the door was closed.

"And?"

"And much of the same. Boaz still wanders among the Soulenai in the Place Beyond . . . yet not with them. They cannot understand it. He does not talk to them, yet they can hear him fret and cry. 'The baby,' he cries, 'the baby!' He calls your name, too, and holds out a hand, as if to seek you."

Tirzah? Tirzah? Are you there? Can you see me? The baby, oh! The baby!

I lowered my face into my hands and wept.

"The child must die," Isphet said. "You know that. It is the only way Boaz will find peace."

She sat and watched me weep, but did not move to comfort me. After a while she stood, laid a hand on my brow, and left.

"Lady Tirzah? Lady Tirzah?"

I jerked my head up. Holdat rose out of a dark corner. Gods, Isphet and I had forgotten he was here.

"There, there," he said, and sat on the bed and held me as I wept. My sobbing increased, and I burrowed my face into the comfort of his shoulder. It was the first time that I'd allowed myself to fully grieve, for Boaz, and for the baby.

He let me weep, softly stroking my hair, whispering nonsense that I clung to and that did, indeed, soothe me.

"Lady Tirzah," he said eventually, "I heard what the Chad'zina said. I am sorry, for I do not mean to pry."

I sniffed and sat up.

"Why did she say the baby must die?" he asked.

Holdat had been delighted when I'd first told him of the child, and I could imagine his hurt now.

"Holdat," I said, and sighed. Would he understand the truth if I told him? But anything less than the truth, after what he had done for Boaz and me over the months, and after what he'd just heard, would be an insult.

So I told him.

"Oh, Lady Tirzah," he said as I drifted to a close. "Is there no way you can tell if the child has been harmed or not?"

"Isphet and I have done our best, but we cannot see behind the protective barriers of the womb."

"Well then, there is only one thing that we *can* do."

He went back to his dark corner, then returned with the Book of the Soulenai.

"Oh, Holdat, do you think I have not considered that? I have read it constantly these past months, and it has told me nothing."

"Nevertheless," he said, and sat down on the edge of the bed. "Look one time for me."

I took the book, balancing it awkwardly on my shrinking lap, and flipped through it. All the tales were as they should be. There was nothing that could aid my plight.

I sighed again, but just as I was closing the heavy leather cover, the contents page caught my eye.

"What is it?" Holdat asked.

"Uh, the tales are all familiar and unhelpful, but the contents page is different. Look."

"Lady, you know that I cannot read."

"Oh, sorry. Listen . . ."

1. Once about Lake Juit
2. Lake Juit and the Sun
3. The Day the King came to Lake Juit
4. How Lake Juit was formed
5. Lake Juit Boating Procedures explained
6. Picnic at Lake Juit
7. Walks and Paths about Lake Juit
8. How the Soulenai passed by Lake Juit
9. Dawn on Lake Juit
10. Through the Mists of Lake Juit

"And so on," I said. "There are another fifteen titles, all simply 'Lake Juit.' "

"And do the tales within match the titles on the contents page?"

"No, they do not. All that is different is that one page. Ah, this tells me nothing!"

"Lady, you know what it tells you." He put the book back in its box, then he walked to the door and bowed. "I shall pack and be ready in the morning," he said, then he was gone.

That night I dreamed.

I dreamed I was walking through the summer meadows of Viland, and I was very afraid.

The grass brushed cool and damp about my ankles, and the fragrance of flowers teased at my senses.

Tirzah! Tirzah!

I moaned, and ran, but I was encumbered even in this dream, and the child dragged at my belly and my robes tangled about my legs.

Tirzah! Tirzah!

I was running through a great wasteland where heat throbbed and snatched at my breath and life. I cried, slowing. Would I never escape?

Tirzah! Tirzah!

I stumbled on, sobs rasping in my throat, and I ran across a land all of stone where pyramids watched my passing with great black glassy eyes that followed, followed, followed . . .

Tirzah! Tirzah!

I couldn't get away. The voice would not let me go.

Tirzah! Tirzah!

"Boaz!" I sobbed. "Boaz!"

Tirzah? Are you there? Help me, Tirzah, help me!
Boaz!

The stone cooled and softened beneath my feet, and I saw I

was running through earth newly turned and fresh with burgeoning life.

I thought I saw him, a hint, a shadow only, and I ran harder.

Tirzah? Can you hear me? Help me! Please, please help me!

"Oh, gods, Boaz! How? How?"

River reeds tangled about me and I fell, tumbling over and over, through water, beneath water. I fought my way to the surface, screaming as I exhaled. "Boaz? *Where are you?*"

Red and pink flames roared about me—birds, millions of them, lifting into the dawn air.

Juit birds.

Tirzah . . . Tirzah . . . the baby, Tirzah. The baby? How is the baby?

I woke, surprised to find myself in my bed and not tangled in reeds.

I lay still for a very long time, my hand on my belly, a small smile on my face, peace in my heart.

Boaz had not been warning about the baby at all. *He had been asking after it!*

"Isphet?"

"Hmm?" She had come in to wish me a good morning.

"Isphet, I'm hungry. Will you tell Holdat to bring a large breakfast this morning?"

She looked at me.

"And then, Isphet, we are going to pack. I think I would like to give birth at Lake Juit. Please, indulge me in this."

FIFTY

She was instantly suspicious.

"Please, Isphet. I am sick of Setkoth, and the peace of the lake is what I need for my final months. Please."

"I will come with you," she said carefully.

"That would be nice, Isphet. Do you think Layla might like to come too? And Zabrze? It would provide peace for all of us after the confusions and sadnesses of the past few months. Besides, Lake Juit is where Boaz was born. Please, Isphet. I want to go. I would feel close to him there."

She gave in.

We embarked three days later, me, Isphet, Layla and dog, Kiamet and Holdat, and several units of soldiers.

"But I'll be down for the birth," Zabrze said. "I'll not miss the arrival of my first niece or nephew."

Isphet had the grace to look uncomfortable. I felt sorry for her. In her position I hoped I would have the strength to do the same thing. But Isphet did not understand, and if I told her of my dream then she would think it only a phantasm of a woman determined to protect her child.

Zabrze stepped back and looked at the soldiers. "They'll provide protection," he said, and threw a puzzled look at Isphet. "No one has been down to the Juit estate since . . . since Nzame disappeared."

"All will be well," I said. "Memmon has sent report that the land blooms as never before."

Memmon had woken from his entombment with everyone else when Boaz had dragged Nzame into Infinity. I wondered if the experience had improved his temper at all.

"Good-bye, Zabrze. Do not linger overlong here in Setkoth."

The journey was uneventful. We passed Threshold that first day. The capstone had gone, and I noticed that Zabrze had ordered the entire pyramid covered with reed matting.

The Infinity Chamber must be dark and lifeless.

I turned back to the river. I did not know why I had to go to Lake Juit, but I trusted the Book of the Soulenai.

My sleep had been uneventful and dreamless, and my days peaceful. I ate well now, disturbed by how weak I'd grown in those months fretting about both Boaz and our child. The baby moved about in my womb, and I leaned back in my chair and enjoyed the warmth of the sun.

Isphet ordered a leisurely trip, and she was pleased that I so enjoyed it. The river air was sweet, and the frogs sang well into the day and still further into the night.

Ten days after leaving we arrived at Lake Juit. Kiamet helped me to my feet, and I stood and gazed, entranced. It was far more beautiful than I remembered, the lake spreading for leagues in every direction, the marshes and reeds stretching even farther.

A voice broke my reverie. Memmon, standing on the landing, the house rising serene and graceful behind him.

By his feet sat Fetizza, croaking cheerfully.

I gasped, then laughed. No one had seen the frog for months. She had disappeared with Boaz's departure, and I had thought that perhaps her existence was somehow tied to his.

But here she was, now looking irritably at the dog barking by Layla's side, and her presence was surely nothing but a good omen.

Isphet kept close but companionable watch on me. We spent our days wandering the riverbanks, or sitting in the shade of the verandahs, sipping iced fruit wine and gossiping.

"Do you remember . . . ?" one of us would ask, and we would mention a moment, or a friend, or a day in the hot workshop that had somehow been memorable.

Isphet thought she was helping me grieve, helping me let go of the past.

I was simply passing time, waiting, watching for something that I did not yet recognize. And so I would talk softly and smile, and take another sip from the Goblet of the Frogs.

Kiamet and Holdat were constant companions as well, always at hand to offer sweetmeats, or iced wine, or conversation. Layla spent many evenings with me, asking about Viland, and listening to me read from the Book of the Soulenai.

The weeks passed. The sun rose and set over Lake Juit and the marshes . . .

. . . *it was the marshes, I knew that now, something about the marshes* . . .

. . . and the mist formed, thickened, and then dissipated with each dawn and dusk.

My belly swelled.

The soldiers patrolled and stood about my window at night. Memmon grumbled about the accounts.

And Isphet relaxed.

She confided that she was with child herself, and I smiled, and said that she'd be hard put to beat Neuf's total at her age.

Isphet blushed, and changed the subject. I knew she was embarrassed, not at my comment, but at the fact that she should be bearing a child that presented no threat.

Neither of us talked about my approaching confinement.

Three weeks before the baby was due, Zabrze arrived in a riverboat garlanded with silks and banners.

Ashdod must truly be recovering, I thought as I struggled from my chair.

Zabrze had brought Zhabroah with him, and Layla rushed to take her brother. We would all be here, I thought, for whatever it is we await.

Zabrze brushed my cheek with his lips, and laughed, then seized Isphet and kissed her with more abandon. "I have missed you, wife," he said.

I looked away, but only to give them privacy rather than through any grief that Isphet should have a husband left to touch her so.

But Isphet noticed, and drew back from Zabrze's embrace, and called us together for an afternoon of conversation on the verandah.

Memmon grumbled about the extra guests, but I noticed he talked to the household keys that hung at his belt as he walked away to the kitchens.

I turned my head and smiled.

Zabrze told of the new trading partnership he had forged with Darsis and En-Dor. "They are pleased that Threshold no longer consumes all our wealth, and that we shall have some coin to pay for their exports. I think"—and he grinned—"that Ashdod's exports for the foreseeable future shall be nothing but rock. Darsis and En-Dor can build from our misery."

Then the conversation turned to the Juit estate, and Memmon arrived to stand stiff and tall and give account of the produce and the new crop of foals and calves that the previous month had brought.

"Good," Zabrze said, and waved him away. "Life is very good."

He looked toward the marshes. "And if I could think how to turn those reed-choked swamps into profit I would. Currently they are good for nothing but getting lost in."

I opened my mouth to object, then saw the grin on Zabrze's face. I smiled myself and . . .

. . . and remembered what Zabrze had said that day we'd approached Lake Juit after fleeing Threshold.

It is too easy to get lost in there. Many fishermen have gone in and never come back. Fallen over the edge of the world, I think. Or trapped with the gods in some Elysian paradise.

I remembered the day Isphet had led the rite to contact the Soulenai on Lake Juit. I remembered how close they'd felt. How vital. How vigorous. *Different.*

Close.

I shuddered.

"The sun has gone, Tirzah, and you are cool." Isphet leaned forward. "Come, we shall go inside."

River reeds tangled about me and I fell, tumbling over and over, through water, beneath water. I fought my way to the surface, screaming as I exhaled. "Boaz? Where are you?"

I blinked. Something roared, and I thought it was the blood beating through my head. I blinked again, and saw that millions of Juit birds had launched into the yellow and orange sunset, millions and millions of them, pink and red, screeching.

"I wonder what has disturbed them?" Zabrze said.

Tirzah? Can you hear me? Help me! Please, please help me!

"Tirzah?"

I blinked again, then smiled, radiant. "Yes, Zabrze. I think I shall come inside."

I lay in the bed, unable to sleep. The baby had shifted during the afternoon and now lay awkward and uncomfortable. My back ached, and I hoped I had the strength for what I must do.

Tirzah? Can you hear me? Help me! Please, please help me!

As the night deepened, I closed my eyes, touched the power of the Goblet of the Frogs in my hand, and worked my cantomancy.

I waited two more hours, then rose, wincing as the ache flared across my back. I crossed to the door, and opened it quietly.

I'd whispered to Holdat as I'd made my way to bed, and I hoped he would not let me down.

I should have trusted. Here he was, moving swiftly and silently to my side. He nodded at the question in my eyes, put a finger to my lips, then led me slowly through the house.

Everything was quiet, still.

The front door stood ajar, and thick marsh mist seeped through. It touched the outline of everything in the room, giving all a ghostly aspect.

The door abruptly swung open, and I tensed, but it was Kiamet, and he grinned and waved me through.

The house, as everything within two hundred paces of the river, was shrouded in the mist. Guards stood posted at every window and entranceway . . .

. . . *watch for the Lady Tirzah, watch lest she try to escape and bear her child in secret* . . .

. . . but Isphet had severely underestimated the Lady Tirzah, and now, no doubt, lay as heavily in enchanted sleep as these guards nodded over their spears.

Kiamet waved me forward again, impatient. Holdat took my arm and we walked down the path to the landing where Kiamet had moored a small punt.

"My Lady," he whispered. "Let Holdat or myself come with you. You are in no condition—"

I kissed his mouth softly, stopping his words. "Dear Kiamet. Thank you, I am ever in your debt. But this I must do alone. Come now, help me into this boat."

The flat-bottomed punt wobbled alarmingly as I settled my weight into it. I shook my hair out, then took the pole Kiamet handed me, and smiled at the two of them one last time.

"Good-bye, my friends. Watch for me as the sun burns the mist from the river."

I dug the pole into the soft riverbed and pushed, and Kiamet gave the punt a shove from the landing.

And so I drifted into the mist.

I did not know exactly where I should go. Kiamet had placed a small lamp in the far end of the punt, and it glowed in the mist, encasing the boat in a soft puddle of light. As soon as I saw the first of the reeds on the western bank I poled in that direction.

I slid in among the reeds without a murmur, and they parted before the flat prow of the punt. It was silent in here. A different world . . . and that was what I was counting on. The marshes. A borderland; somewhere in here this world touched that of the Place Beyond.

And there Boaz would be waiting for me.

I think I understood what had happened now. Boaz had learned while in Infinity. He had learned how to manipulate the Song so that he was transported to the edges of the Place Beyond, but not propelled directly into it. Thus the feeling that he was there but not there. With, but not with the Soulenai. Refusing to be accepted among them. Not talking to them.

Agitated, disturbing the peace of the Place Beyond, crying out to me, to the bond between us, to find him and bring him home.

Wondering about the baby.

"Boaz?" I whispered into the mist. "Where are you?"

There was nothing but the soft swish as reeds parted gently before the prow of the punt and the bobbing light.

I poled for hours, until the small of my back screamed in agony and my hands blistered on the rough wood of the rod. A breeze arose, shifting the mist but not dislodging it, and lifting my hair. It tangled with the pole, and I paused to take breath and lift my hair away and over my shoulder.

The baby shifted, and the ache in my back flared into something more urgent, more primeval.

"Boaz? Boaz?"

There was nothing.

The pain coursed through me again, and I sobbed, then muttered to myself and took grasp of the pole again. Somewhere Boaz waited . . . waited . . . and this child demanded to be born. Here, where Isphet was far, far away.

I bit down the pain, and pushed the punt through the reeds. The lamp was duller now, or was the night less dark?

I cried, for I understood that I had to find him by dawn, or lose him forever.

A frog croaked to one side, but I ignored it. Just another unwelcome reminder of how close sunrise was.

The mist thickened so much I could hardly breathe. I paused, one hand to the mound of my belly, the other on the pole. I pushed weakly, unable to use both hands now.

Another frog croaked, and then the punt rocked so violently I lost my grasp on the pole and dropped it into the water.

I cried out and lunged for it, but I was too awkward, and the punt rocking too much for me to find it. It had gone, and I was stranded.

Both hands on my belly now, I looked up.

Fetizza had climbed onto the prow of the punt; it was her weight that had rocked the vessel so alarmingly.

She stared at me with great liquid dark eyes, then slowly blinked.

Another frog, much tinier than Fetizza, leaped into the punt.

I flinched as yet another frog jumped in, over my shoulder this time.

Then I cried out as hundreds of tiny frogs rained into the punt. Some landed on my head and tangled in my hair, and I raised my hands and tried to free them, flinching again and again as frogs hit me and then bounced into the punt.

A great contraction banded my body, and I groaned, and gripped the side of the punt.

Every one of the frogs in the punt was staring at me. Motionless. Waiting.

Fetizza opened her huge mouth . . . and sang. The other frogs in the punt joined in, as did the millions of their brethren clinging to the reeds of the marsh.

The punt slid forward.

I could do nothing but sit and gasp, blinking at the droplets of moisture that adhered to my eyelashes and ran down through tendrils of my hair. My robe was soaked, clinging to my ungainly body.

The frogs' chorus surrounded me, and I lifted my hands to the sky.

"Boaz!"

Tirzah! Tirzah! Please . . . hurry!

"Boaz!"

My hands dropped to the sides of the punt, and then amazingly I saw the pole floating by. I seized it and pushed down with all my will.

Tirzah! Tirzah! Hurry!

The frogs roared, and I thought I saw Fetizza rear up on her hind legs and scream.

"Tirzah! Tirzah! Hurry!"

"Boaz!" I shouted, *"Boaz!"* I pushed down with the pole, grunting with the effort, and then again. And, oh, gods, again. I could see nothing but the thick reeds and the clinging mist . . . then there was a gap, a space of clear water tinged with the redness of dawn light and . . .

. . . the punt wobbled and tipped, and the frogs jumped up and down in a frenzy, then sideways into the water. Fetizza bounced about excitedly, and the punt lurched from side to side. I clung on frantically, but it was too late, the punt was rocking wildly, and the pain in my body was too great, I couldn't fight everything at once.

I fell into the water with a huge splash, tumbling deeper and deeper until I felt my hands and face press into the soft mud. I fought to the surface, fighting not to open my mouth and gasp at the pain that rocketed through me, fighting, fighting, fighting . . .

Strong hands grasped me and my head broke the surface. I heaved in great gulps of air, trying to call out his name, trying to clear the mud from my eyes, then he pushed me beneath the water again, impatient hands clearing mud from my face, and then, then I was free and splashing and spluttering through the water trying to find him again and . . .

. . . and millions of screaming Juit birds launched themselves into the air, their shrill cries and the throb of their wings filling the sky and my soul. The mist had cleared, and the world was shifting pink and red against a dawn sky, and I blinked, and blinked, searching frantically, and then there he was, his hands reaching out for me.

I clung tight with arms and legs, and we sank below the water again, and when we finally broke the surface he grabbed hold of the side of the punt and laughed.

"Why try to drown me, Tirzah, when you have only just found me?"

One hand on the punt, the other arm about me, Boaz leaned over to kiss my mouth, but I was sobbing too freely, and he could only hold me close and kiss my forehead and cheek and eyes and nose.

Thank you, thank you, thank you.

I don't know who said this, Boaz, me, or the frogs, or perhaps all of us.

I calmed down eventually, and seized his face between my hands and stared at him.

"Boaz."

He finally managed to kiss me, and then, as if for the first time, realized the mound of my belly.

"Tirzah! The baby! Oh, thank the *gods,* you kept the baby!"

"It's not—?"

"No, no!" He grabbed me tight. "Nzame wallows lost in Infinity. The baby is safe. I thought you would . . . oh, gods, Tirzah, thank you for not listening to me . . . *Tirzah!*"

I had gasped with pain, and it was worse than ever. "Boaz, this baby demands to be born."

"What!"

"Here, now . . . *ah!*"

"I don't know anything about delivering a baby!"

"Then you're about to add to your store of knowledge, Boaz. *Get me into that punt! NOW!*"

He heaved me over the side of the punt and I rolled into it, hoping all the frogs had escaped. I squeezed my eyes shut as another contraction racked me, then opened them to see Fetizza staring curiously from the far end.

Boaz climbed into the punt, almost falling out again as it rocked to and fro.

"Tirzah, I don't know how—"

"Boaz," I ground out between my teeth, "if you can survive Infinity you can survive the birth of your child. You are going to deliver this child, and you are—oh . . . *gods!*—going to do it—*now!*"

Boaz shot one frantic look at Fetizza—

"Boaz!"

—then bent down to me. "Tell me what to do, curse it, tell me what to do!"

He did magnificently, as did I. For a first birth the child issued forth with blessed brevity, rushing its way into a dawn that rang with the cries of the Juit birds and sparkled with the curious eyes of the frogs. We were very close to the Place Beyond, and through my pain and the sweat that ran into my eyes I saw the Soulenai standing about the punt, their mouths and eyes opened in astonishment.

A baby! A baby! A baby!

I think it had been a very long time since any of them had seen, let alone participated in, a birth.

Boaz lifted the baby, as astounded as the Soulenai, stared at her, then stared at me.

The expression on his face was the sweetest thing I have ever seen.

I struggled up onto an elbow. "Tie the cord with a strip from my robe, Boaz. There, yes, and there too. Now bite."

He paled, opened his mouth to object, then bit down on the cord.

He placed the baby very gently into my arms, leaning down to kiss me.

"A daughter, Tirzah."

"Yes." She gazed at me with deep blue eyes.

"Boaz, will you name her?"

He looked at me, his hair plastered to his forehead with sweat and worry, more lines about his eyes and mouth than I remembered, and so dear I thought I would embarrass myself before all the spectral Soulenai and burst into tears again.

He smiled, very slow, very tender. "I shall give her your name." He paused. "Ysgrave."

I drew a deep breath. Ysgrave. The name he had taken from me the day we met.

Ysgrave, the Soulenai whispered. *Ysgrave.*

Ysgrave, and an insubstantial hand drifted over my shoulder and touched the girl's forehead in blessing.

Avaldamon. He kissed my cheek, and I was surprised to find his touch warm, and then he lifted his hand to Boaz.

Boaz. You have surprised us. We did not realize the Song of the Frogs could be so manipulated. We could not understand why you refused to join us, why you refused to talk to us. I think we needlessly worried Tirzah.

"I wish I could have told both you and Tirzah what was happening," Boaz said. "But I was trapped in these borderlands, lost, and I could only call to Tirzah, call to her to fetch me."

"Fetizza sang," I said, and smiled fondly at the frog. "When I was too exhausted, the frogs brought me to you."

Avaldamon drifted away. *We cannot stay here. The sun crests the reeds. We cannot stay . . . but come back! Come back! Come back!*

Boaz lay down beside me and we rested awhile, sometimes talking, sometimes touching, but mostly just lying, sharing life and love.

Eventually I roused, and asked Boaz to help me wash myself and our daughter, and then I told him to make himself truly useful and pole us back to the river and the Juit house.

FIFTY-ONE

Holdat and Kiamet, stunned but with tears of joy in their eyes, stood back and let Boaz and me step onto the verandah of the house. Boaz paused, showing them our daughter.

The guards, awakened from their magical sleep, eyed me curiously.

What should they do now?

Before they could make up their minds, I stepped inside.

I know I must have looked dreadful. My robe was tattered and stained, and still wet. My hair hung lank to my hips and probably had water weed tangled through it.

And I was very obviously no longer pregnant.

Isphet stepped forward, her face strained and deeply upset. "Tirzah, what have you done?" she whispered. "Tirzah, please, don't torture yourself like this. You can't hide the baby forever. Give it up now."

Behind her, Zabrze and Layla frowned, puzzled at her words.

"I have no intention of hiding my daughter, Isphet. She is far too beautiful."

And Boaz walked through the door with our daughter cradled in his arms.

I think I shall treasure the look on Isphet's face forever.

"Her name is Ysgrave," Boaz said very softly, his eyes on Isphet, "and she is not what you think. Nzame is gone. This baby will harm no one."

Isphet put her hands to her face and burst into tears, and then Zabrze stepped past her and embraced his brother.

I slept that day through, Boaz beside me, our daughter between us, then in the evening we all sat on the verandah and watched the Juit birds return in a disordered, bright, bloodied cloud to roost in the reed banks. The baby suckled at my breast, and everything was very well in this world.

"Explain," Isphet said softly, and Boaz did.

"Nzame had taken advantage of the bridge the Magi— we—had created from the Vale to step into Threshold. He was peculiarly tied to the power of the One and Threshold, although had he been allowed to stay and grow he would have eventually freed himself from Threshold's restraints."

I thought of the dreams Nzame had used to touch Boaz and me, and perhaps many others. If he had this ability while tied to Threshold then I dreaded to think what he could have accomplished free.

"He was tied by the One, and he could be trapped by its power. What I did was use the One to seize him, bind him, merge with him, and then activate the Infinity Chamber so that I could drag him through into Infinity."

Boaz paused. He had used few words for what must have been a hideous battle, but the pallor of his face and the faint tremor in his fingers betrayed the horror of the memory.

"Infinity." He stopped, and his eyes were very far from us. "What was it like, brother?"

Boaz roused himself. "It was nothingness, yet it was everything. We have developed language to suit the world and the reality in which we live. It cannot hope to explain what I found there."

"You were there for weeks," I said. "We thought you lost."

"Weeks? I suppose I was." He smiled at me. "Else you have used your skills at cantomancy to grow that girl very quickly. Yes, well. Weeks. I did not realize it was that long. Time has no meaning, no dimension in Infinity. I explored, examined. I wish . . ."

He did not have to finish. If it had not been for me, Boaz would never have come back. But what he had discovered had changed him; I could see his newfound knowledge eddying about the shadows of his eyes.

"While in Infinity I realized that the Song of the Frogs—the formula that can transport a person into the Place Beyond—had subtle nuances that I might be able to manipulate so that I journeyed only as far as the borders of the Place Beyond, no farther. The borderlands are dangerous, though, and I did not know if I would be forever trapped there, or if I could eventually escape. But I thought it worth the risk. I wanted to come home."

My eyes filled with tears at that simple statement.

"And so I sang the Song, and as I transported—almost into the Place Beyond—I had to use all my strength and skill to halt at its borders. The Soulenai did not know what was wrong, they wanted me to come through . . . but I thought . . . I thought that I still had a chance to come home."

He paused and took a deep breath. "But I could not move, not of my own volition. The Song had done its work and dissipated. I will never be able to use it again. I could not even move completely through into the Place Beyond had I wanted to. Trapped, trapped in the borderlands."

Boaz lifted my hand. "Trapped, waiting for you to save me. The bond between us has been forged by pain and fear, and cemented by love, trust, and power. It drew us together when we were separated by vast distances of space and dimension."

He paused. "But that bond also contains something else, something I cannot quite explain."

"The frogs," I said.

"Yes, the frogs. I don't think any of us yet appreciate the power and the mystery of the frogs. Tirzah and I share a bond, not only with each other, but with the frogs."

"And in the end it was the frogs that enabled me to reach you." I explained to the others how the frogs had sung when I'd been lost and too exhausted to go on. "I was so close to Boaz, but could not get to him. The frogs completed my journey."

We were silent for a very long time. Ysgrave slept warm and safe by my breast, and Boaz's hand rested on my shoulder. Isphet and Zabrze sat as close as Boaz and I, and the dog was curled at Layla's feet. Across the table Kiamet and Holdat were sharing a jug of wine, listening and watching.

The Juit birds had settled for the night, and the frogs choraled among the reeds.

"Zabrze," Boaz said, "you do not need me in Setkoth. Tirzah and I will stay here for some time. Rest. Think. Study. Listen to what the frogs tell us. Explore the marsh."

"Don't get lost," Zabrze said sharply. "I—none of us— want to lose either of you again."

"No," Boaz said, and his hand tightened a little on my shoulder, "I don't think that we will."

"And Infinity?" Zabrze asked. "Will you ever go back there?"

"No. Whatever else you do in Setkoth, Zabrze, you must discourage any resurrection of interest in the Infinity formula. Nzame is not destroyed, merely trapped in Infinity. Who knows what he will learn there over the ages. I want no more bridges built into Infinity, because the moment one is completed, I fear Nzame will rush straight back across it. Darker than ever before."

"Then I shall burn the libraries of the Magi," Zabrze said. "Remove every trace of them."

"Good."

Zabrze leaned forward. "Boaz. Tell me what to do with Threshold."

"Remove the plate glass from the outside. Melt it down and sell it as bead necklets—the En-Dorians will love them. Strip the Infinity Chamber of the golden glass, and melt it. Bury it. Do the same with the capstone. Then block up every shaft and entranceway so that *no one* can ever find their way inside again."

"You do not want to pull the entire structure down?"

"No. It has taken eight generations to build, and would take two or three to pull down. More would die in the process, and I do not think I could stand that. No. Fill the shafts and corridors with stone and block up all the entrances. Then leave the sand to drift over the stone and the memories. Leave Threshold for future millennia to puzzle over—but leave them no trace of its secret."

Look for

NAMELESS DAY

by SARA DOUGLASS

Now available!

From Tom Doherty Associates

Turn the page for a preview

PROLOGUE

The Friday within the Octave of All Saints
To the Nameless Day
In the twenty-first year of the reign of Edward III
(7th November to Tuesday 23rd December 1348)

St. Angelo's Friary, Rome

"**B**rother Wynkyn? Brother Wynkyn? Sweet Jesu, Brother, you're not going to leave us *now*?"

Brother Wynkyn de Worde slapped shut the weighty manuscript book before him and turned to face Prior Bertrand. "I have no choice, Bertrand. I must leave."

Bertrand took a deep breath. *Sweet Saviour, how could he possibly dissuade Brother Wynkyn?*

"My friend," he said, earning himself a sarcastic glance from Wynkyn. "Brother Wynkyn . . . the pestilence rages across Christendom. If you leave the safety of Saint Angelo's—"

"What safety? Of the seventeen brothers who prayed here five weeks ago, now there is only you and me and two others left. Besides, if I choose to hide within these 'safe' walls, a far worse pestilence will ravage Christendom than that which currently rages. I must go. Get out of my way."

"Brother, the roads are choked with the dying and the brigands who pick their pockets and pluck the rings from their fingers." Prior Bertrand moderated his voice, trying to reason with the old man. Brother Wynkyn had ever been difficult. Bertrand knew that Wynkyn had even shouted down the Holy Father once, and Bertrand realized there was no circumstance in which he could hope for respect from someone who was powerful enough to cow a pop. "How can you possibly overcome all the difficulties and the dangers roaming the roads between here and Nuremberg? Stay, I beg you."

"I would condemn the earth to a slow descent into insanity if I stayed here." Wynkyn lowered the book—he needed both arms to lift it—and several loose pages of closely-written script into a flat-lidded oaken casket bound with brass. It was only just large enough to take the book and the pages. Once he had shut the casket, Wynkyn locked it with a key that hung from a chain on his belt.

Bertrand watched wordlessly for some minutes, and then tried again. "And if you die on the road?"

Wynkyn shot his prior an angry glance. "I will *not* die on the road! God and the angels protect me and my purpose."

"As they have protected all the other innocent souls who have died in the past weeks and months? Wynkyn, *nothing* protects mankind against the evil of this pestilence!"

Wynkyn carefully checked the casket to ensure its security. He turned his back to Bertrand.

"Rome is dying," Bertrand said, his voice now soft. "Corpses lie six deep in the streets, and the black, bubbling pestilence seeks new victims on every breath of wind. God has shown us the face of wrath for our sins, and the angels have fled. If you leave the friary now, you will surely die."

Still Wynkyn did not answer.

"Brother," Bertrand said, desperation now filling his voice. "Why must you leave? What is of such importance that you must risk almost certain death?"

Wynkyn turned about and locked eyes with the prior. "Because if I don't leave, then it is almost certain death for Christendom," he said. "Either get out of my way, Bertrand, or aid me to carry this casket to my mule."

Bertrand's eyes filled with tears. He made a hopeless gesture with his hand, but Wynkyn's gaze did not waver.

"Well?" Wynkyn said.

Bertrand took a deep, sobbing breath, and then grasped a handle of the casket. "I wish peace walk with you, Wynkyn."

"Peace has never walked with me," Wynkyn said as he grabbed the other handle. "And it never will."

Wynkyn de Worde had undertaken the journey between Rome and Nuremberg over one hundred times in the past fifty or so years, but never had he done so before with such a heavy heart. He had been twenty-three in 1296, when the then pop, the great Boniface VIII, had sent him north for the first time.

Twenty-three and entrusted with a secret so horrifying that it, and the nightmarish responsibility it carried with it, would have killed most other men. But Wynkyn was a special man, strong and dedicated, sure of the right of God, and with a faith so unshakeable that Boniface understood why the angels had selected him as the man fit to oversee those yearly rituals whereby evil was thrust back into the Cleft—the gateway into Hell.

"Reveal this secret to any other man," Boniface had told the young Dominican, "and you can be sure that the angels themselves will ensure your death."

Already privy to the ghastly secret, Wynkyn knew truth when he heard it.

Boniface had leaned back in his chair, satisfied. Since the beginnings of the office of the pope in the Dark Ages, its incumbents kept the secret of the Cleft, entrusting it only to the single priest the angels had said was strong enough to endure. As this priest approached the end of his life, the angels gave the pop the name of a new priest, young and strong, and this young priest would accompany the older priest on the man's final few journeys to the Cleft. From the older, dying priest, the younger one learned the incantations that he would need . . . and he also learned the true meaning of courage, for without it he would not endure.

These priests, the Select, spent their lives teetering on the edge of hell.

In 1298, Boniface informed Wynkyn de Worde that he was the angels' choice as the new Select. Then, having learned from his predecessor, Wynkyn performed his duty willingly and without mishap for five years. He thought his life would take the same path as the scores of priests who had preceded him . . . but he, like the angels, had underestimated the power and cunning of pure evil

Who could have thought the papacy could fail so badly?
Wynkyn had not anticipated it; the angels certainly had not.
In 1303, the great and revered Pop Boniface VIII died, and
Wynkyn had no way of knowing that the forces of darkness
and disorder would seize this opportunity to throw the papacy
into chaos. In the subsequent papal election, a man called
Clement V took the papal throne. Outwardly pious, it quickly
became apparent to Wynkyn, as to everyone else, that
Clement was the puppet of the French king, Philip IV. The
new pope moved the papacy to the French-controlled town of
Avignon, allowing Philip to dictate the papacy's activities and
edicts. There, successive popes lived in luxury and corrup-
tion, mouthing the orders of French kings instead of the will
of God.

When a new pope was enthroned, either rthe first among
the archangels, St. Michael, or the current Select, revealed to
him the secret of the Cleft—but neither St. Michael nor
Wynkyn had approached Clement. How could they allow the
fearful secrets of the angels to fall into the hands of the French
Monarchy? *Sweet Jesu*, Wynkyn had thought as he spent sleepless nights wondering what to do. *A French king could seize
control of the world had he this knowledge in hand. He could
command an army so vile that even the angels of God would
quail before it.*

So both Wynkyn and the angels kept the secret against the
day that the popes rediscovered God and moved themselves
and the papacy back to Rome. After all, surely it could not be
long—could it?

But the seductiveness of evil was stronger than Wynkyn
and the angels had anticipated. When Clement V died, the
pope who succeeded him had also preferred the French
monarch's bribes and the sweet air of Avignon to the word of
God and the best interests of His Church on earth. And so
also the pope after that one . . .

Every year Wynkyn traveled north to the Cleft in time for
the summer and winter solstices, and then traveled back to
Rome to await his next journey; he could not bear to live his
entire life at the Cleft, although he knew some of his prede-
cessors, stronger men than he, had done so.

He received income enough from what Boniface had left at

his disposal to continue his work, and the prior and brothers of his friary, St. Angelo's, were too in awe of him to inquire closely into his movements and activities.

Brother Wynkyn de Worde also had the angels to assist his work. As they should, for their lusts had necessitated the Cleft.

But now here Wynkyn was, an ancient man in his mid-seventies, and it seemed that the popes would never return to Rome. God's wrath had boiled over, showering Europe with a pestilence such as it had never previously endured. Wynkyn had always traveled north with a heavy heart—his mission could engender no less in any man—but this night, as he carefully led his mule through the dead and dying littering the streets of Rome, he felt his soul shudder under the weight of his despair.

He was deeply afraid, not only for what he knew he would find awaiting him at the Cleft, but because he *did* fear he might die . . . and then who would follow him? Who would there be to tend the Cleft?

"I should have told," he muttered. But who was there to tell? Who to confide in? The popes were dissolute and corrupt, and there was no one else. No one.

Who else was there?

God and the angels had relied on the papacy, and now the popes had betrayed God Himself for a chest full of gold coin from the French king.

Damn the angels! If it wasn't for their sins in the first place . . .

It took Wynkyn almost seven weeks to reach Nuremberg; for that he even reached the city at all he thanked God's benevolence.

Every town, every hamlet, every cottage he'd passed had been in the grip of the black pestilence. Hands reached out from windows, doorways, and gutters, begging the passing friar for succor, for prayers, or, at least, for the last rites, but Wynkyn had ignored them.

They were all sinners, for why else had God's wrath struck them? Wynkyn was consumed by his need to get north as fast as he could.

Far worse than the outstretched hands of the dying were

the grasping hands of the bandits and outlaws who thronged the roadways and passes. But Wynkyn was sly—God's good gift—and whenever the bandits saw that Wynkyn clasped a cloth to his mouth, and heard the desperate racking of his cough, they backed away, making the sign of the cross.

Yet even Wynkyn could not remain immune to the grasping fingers of the pestilence forever. Not at his age.

On Ember Saturday, Wynkyn de Worde had approached a small village two days from Nuremberg. By the roadside lay a huddle of men and women, dying from the plague. One of them, a woman—God's curse to earth!—had risen to her feet and stumbled towards the friar riding by, but as she leaned on his mule's shoulder, begging for aid, Wynkyn kicked her roughly away.

It was too late. Unbeknown to the friar, as he extended his hand to ward her off, the deadly kiss of the pestilence sprang from her mouth to his hand during the virulence of her pleas. He planted his foot in the hateful woman's chest, and when he raised his hand to his face to make the sign of the cross, the pestilence leaped unseen from his hand to his mouth.

The deed was done and there was nothing the angels could do but moan.

Look for

SINNER

by SARA DOUGLASS

Available September 2004
From Tom Doherty Associates